ORDEAL AT DONNER PASS

The skeletal man dipped his pointed chin. "Maybe it is God's will that most of the Donner party are going to die up in those mountains, Captain Sutter."

"No!" Sutter cried, his voice reaching up from the very depths of his soul. "Please, tell me what happened to all those provisions and the five pack mules I already sent over with my Indians?"

"We ate everything, sir, even your mules."

"And the Indians, too." A short, sun-blistered woman giggled, her eyes merry with lunacy. "We ate them along with Mr. Dolan and Mr. Fosdick and—"

"Shut up!" the man shrieked.

The woman blinked and looked away to sob brokenly. "Mr. Sutter—I must have forgot. We didn't eat your Indians, not *really*. Honest!"

Sutter reeled and Morgan heard his captain cry, "My poor Indians. Dear God, they've *eaten* Lewis and Salvadore!"

Rivers West
Ask your bookseller for the books you have missed.

Book 1 — THE YELLOWSTONE by Winfred Blevins
Book 2 — THE SMOKY HILL by Don Coldsmith
Book 3 — THE COLORADO by Gary McCarthy
Book 4 — THE POWDER RIVER by Winfred Blevins
Book 5 — THE RUSSIAN RIVER by Gary McCarthy
Book 6 — THE ARKANSAS RIVER by Jory Sherman

≈ **RIVERS WEST: BOOK 7** ≈

The American River

Gary McCarthy

BANTAM BOOKS
NEW YORK · TORONTO · LONDON · SYDNEY · AUCKLAND

THE AMERICAN RIVER

A Bantam Domain Book / February 1992

ISBN 0-553-29532-2

Published simultaneously in the United States and Canada

PRINTED IN THE UNITED STATES OF AMERICA

OPM   0 9 8 7 6 5 4 3 2 1

For Virginia,
wife, front-line editor and best friend

"Without the discovery of gold, I would now be the richest man on the shores of the Pacific."

JOHN AUGUSTUS SUTTER, 1874

≈   PROLOGUE   ≈

Monterey, California, July 4, 1839

Young Morgan Beck waited impatiently in the small rowboat on sheltered, pristine Monterey Bay. There were two ships anchored in the deep blue harbor besides their eighty-eight-ton brig, *Clementine*. One was a Mexican sloop with a hull heavily encrusted with barnacles, the other an American whaling vessel that reeked of blood and oil. The Mexican ship appeared abandoned except for a large dog whose incessant barking carried loudly across the flat surface of the water.

Morgan frowned and shielded his gray eyes from the sunlight as he gazed across the glistening bay. From a distance of half a mile, he could plainly see the impressive customs house, the presidio and its chapel, and many adobe homes with their colorful red tile roofs.

The beach itself was as white as the foam on the sea, and the town was ringed by steep mountains covered with oak and Monterey pine. Clinging majestically to the rugged seaside cliffs were ancient, twisted cypress, and there were several small fishing boats in the water. Morgan's father, Eli, had told him that Monterey was handsome, but Morgan hadn't been prepared for the rugged beauty now before him.

A limp Mexican flag hung over the presidio and another over the governor's headquarters. He doubted if Governor Juan Bautista Alvarado even remembered the fine horse and silver inlaid saddle Morgan's father had once presented to him. The governor received such gifts as a matter of course, an expected cost of doing business in his California province.

Morgan's hands worked the oars, holding the boat very still as the sun warmed his broad back. He was nineteen years old, slightly over six feet tall, and fair of skin. Wisps of blond hair trailed out from under his seaman's cap, and his hands were large and long-fingered. He listened to the strident cries of seagulls quarreling over the *Clementine* even as Captain Sutter gave last-minute instructions to the crew and his Sandwich Island followers.

Tilting his face into the sun, Morgan shouted, "Captain Sutter, the tide is going out! We need to pull for shore right now!"

"Coming, coming!" Sutter called, a moment before appearing to climb down the *Clementine*'s stiff rope ladder.

"Hold her steady, now," Sutter ordered, carefully placing his foot into the craft and almost losing his balance because he was clutching a leather case wrapped in oilskin.

Morgan waited until Sutter was seated and composed. "Ready, Captain?"

"Yes, yes," came the absent reply. Then, "By the way, isn't this what Americans celebrate as Independence Day?"

"It is."

Sutter smiled and his blue eyes locked on the distant presidio and adobe mission. "Then I'd say that this happy coincidence bodes well for us. I trust that this will also prove to be *my* day of independence."

Morgan slipped the oars deep into the water. He leaned forward the pulled hard, enjoying the feel of his own power and the way the boat surged away from the brig. Facing the *Clementine*, he looked up as he heard the beautiful Manuiki call out to Captain Sutter, who, dressed in a fine Swiss military uniform, removed his campaign hat, twisted about, and waved with the innocent exuberance of a fresh-faced schoolboy.

Morgan had never met anyone even remotely like

John Augustus Sutter. In personality, appearance, and taste, Sutter was the exact opposite of Morgan's father, Eli, a former mountain man turned California trader, who was tough, cynical, and suspicious of all Mexicans except his Mexican wife, Estella, whom Morgan also adored.

Eli had not much warmed to Captain Sutter, who was, in the old trapper's opinion, just "too damn excitable and talkative."

Morgan smiled remembering his father's assessment, because it was largely true. Sutter could talk for hours and hours. The amazing thing, though, was that people would listen and then most likely find themselves nodding in agreement. Morgan had offered to help for free in return for the captain's expected future business. Even Eli had fallen under Sutter's spell, something that Morgan wouldn't have believed had he not seen it with his own eyes.

"You row strongly," observed the captain.

"Thank you."

"And I have it on good authority," Sutter said with a wink, "that you are an expert marksman, hunter, and trapper."

"There are better, even in Alta California," Morgan said, "my father being the best of them all."

"I can believe that from the stories I heard him tell."

"He's lived more in one lifetime than most men would in ten. He broke the trail into Blackfoot country. He's fought and killed more Indians than we'll ever see, Mr. Sutter."

"Well, I don't know about that."

"It's true, sir. Pa was with William Ashley and Jim Bridger the very first time they broke new trails through the Rocky Mountains."

"Is that right?" Sutter brushed the tips of his mustache with his thumb.

"That's right. It was in the summer of '22. A couple of years later, Pa and Bridger were the very first white men ever to see the Great Salt Lake."

"Was that the same year he killed a grizzly with a knife and a Ute spear?"

Morgan frowned and kept his oars working. "I think so. He told you about that, huh?"

"He sure did. It's a shame to realize that a man of your father's talents is forced to eke out a living hauling hides and working for Mexicans who treat him second rate."

Morgan's face stiffened. "That'll change. He's feeling poorly right now, but he'll get stronger soon. He just needs a warmer climate."

"Like the one I'm going to tame." Sutter leaned forward intently. "You should talk to him for me. I could use him, too, Mr. Beck, providing he's going to be strong enough to work."

"He will be," Morgan insisted. "I can promise you that. Just give him a few months in warm weather and Pa will be a new man."

"Why is he so set against joining up with me?"

Morgan shifted his callused hands on the oars and glanced over his shoulder. He was still several hundred yards away from the beach.

"Mr. Beck, did you hear me?"

"Yes, sir, I did. And I don't rightly know why Pa is so against what you plan to do. He just . . . just gets set in his ways, and I guess he didn't want to leave my stepmother."

"I understand." Sutter inhaled deeply and stretched his legs. "But I'll tell you something: He needs to change his mind about my inland colony. I can offer him—and you—more opportunity than you'll ever see in Yerba Buena. *I'll* be in charge, not the Mexicans."

"Yes, sir."

Sutter relaxed. "Anyway," he said, "I'm just glad to have you along with me right now. I could have used your father's influence with the governor, but I'm sure that you'll be very helpful with the introductions. I've got a feeling you're a young man with a very bright future."

Morgan felt his cheeks warm, even as he realized that he was being flattered by a master. Annoyed at being such an easy victim, he pulled even harder at the oars and felt the boat surge ahead.

One last time, Manuiki, the young Kanaka woman, called melodiously, "Bye-bye, Captain Sutter!"

Sutter chose to studiously ignore her, but Morgan was enjoying the show too much to make a similar effort. Besides, Manuiki was too pretty for any man to ignore. Her long black hair shimmered lustrously, and her bare arms and shoulders were the color of ripe wheat. Morgan could not help but grin at Sutter's obvious embarrassment at the fact that Manuiki's voice could be heard probably to Monterey.

Morgan finally said, "She just wants you to call out a good-bye one last time, Captain. I don't think she'll be still until you reply."

"Oh, hell," Sutter grumbled, turning around and favoring Manuiki with an offhanded wave in the hope of silencing her. "Good-bye!"

It worked. Manuiki, at last satisfied that she had not been ignored, disappeared. Sutter expelled a deep breath and turned around before saying, "Mr. Beck, in what little time we have, tell me about Governor Alvarado."

Morgan did not alter his stroke. "I'm afraid that I don't know that much. My father has dealt with him much more than I."

"But your father is not a very communicative man, and I must know whatever I can about the governor."

When Morgan frowned, Sutter grew impatient. "Begin by telling me his age."

"I would guess he is about your age—mid-thirties. Perhaps he is a little older."

"Temperament?"

"Serious and formal."

"Even imperious?"

"What it is," Morgan said, not sure that he knew exactly what imperious meant, "is that Governor Alvarado *expects* things."

"Then I take it you are not..." Sutter appeared to grope for the correct word, "not greatly warmed by him."

"No. Nor is my father. You see, Captain, as Americans, we have always had to court official favor in order to remain in California and conduct business."

"But I thought your stepmother was related to the Alvarado family."

"She is, distantly. But even so, it is not easy. My father can be a little outspoken and it grates hard on him to offer the governor a gift each time he arrives in Yerba Buena."

Sutter's eyebrows arched. "And that is how business is done in Alta California, is it?"

"My father said it was no different when the Spaniards were in charge. Even the padres expected gifts."

"I am told Governor Alvarado was once a revolutionary, that he seized his office at the point of a gun."

"True. Less than three years ago, Alvarado and a small rebel band attacked the former governor's residence. They fired only one cannonball and were rewarded with victory." Morgan shook his head in a gesture of contempt. "Not a drop of blood was shed. The previous governor had no stomach for fighting."

"I wonder," Sutter mused aloud, "if Governor Alvarado, faced with a similar revolution, would give up just as readily."

"Whatever else may be said of Alvarado, he is not a coward. He would fight to the death rather than be humiliated."

"You think so?"

"I do, and so does my father. One of the men who helped Alvarado was also a mountain man. He said Alvarado was prepared to die before a defeat."

Sutter leaned back, removed his campaign hat, and turned his face up to the sun, causing Morgan to think that he had never seen a man who looked more confident or calculating. The captain's calm attitude was surprising, really, considering this visit was so vital to his ambitious plans.

"If I am granted enough California land," the captain mused, his Swiss accent lending an air of culture to his voice, "I will build an empire—a Swiss colony, which I will call New Helvetia. I will send away to Europe for good families and I will give them land and help them build houses, a church, and a school."

Sutter's head dipped, his chin resting on his chest. "You see, Mr. Beck, I come to build, not to plunder and run like a pirate or a common thief. And so I wish very much to help the governor by taming the great inland valley called the Sacramento."

Morgan had heard all this before but still had his doubts. "Captain, it might not be possible, even with the best of intentions. You see, to the governor's way of thinking, and to all the other Mexican officials, we are foreigners, people never to be trusted, not even if we marry into their families."

Sutter chuckled. "My young friend, you are far too pessimistic. It is because you have lived in California as a second-class citizen—first to the Spaniards, then to these Mexicans. But nothing stays the same. And as for what difficulties I now face, there is something you must understand."

"I'm listening," Morgan said, irritated by the man's condescending attitude, an attitude exactly like that of Governor Alvarado himself.

"You see," Sutter began, "when two men both stand to profit from an arrangement, then there is nothing to overcome except misunderstanding and suspicion. Agreed?"

Morgan kept rowing.

"And these letters of introduction," Sutter said, tapping his leather case with a forefinger, "they should end all suspicion concerning my character. That means I must only dispel all possible sources of misunderstanding between Governor Alvarado and myself."

The captain made it sound too easy; Morgan was sure that this entire affair was doomed from the start. Eli thought so, too.

"Mr. Beck," Sutter said, interrupting his thoughts, "you wear the look of a skeptic. Do you think I have come so far—all the way from Switzerland—to fail now?"

"I . . . I don't know. But even if you are successful in this appeal for land, it is doubtful that it would do you any good. As my father explained, it is very dangerous inland and filled with hostile Indians. No offense, Captain, but you are not a seasoned woodsman."

"No offense taken. But do me credit for examining the difficulties I face. After all, your father showed me that old Blackfoot arrow wound in his side. I have also noted the prominent terrible scar across the back of your right hand. Indians?"

"Yes. My father and I were jumped as we were trapping beaver along the shores of Suisun Bay. We are lucky to be alive. There have been others who have gone inland and never returned."

Sutter's eyebrows knitted. "I'm sure that is true," he conceded, "but I *know* Indians. I learned of them while trading in Santa Fe, and I learned even more about them when I accompanied the Hudson's Bay Company trappers all the way west to Fort Vancouver. Furthermore, I observed Alaskan Indians in Sitka and found them no more intimidating than the Russians, who use them exactly as I intend to do—firmly but with kindness. And of course, there are my Kanaka. They are Indians, too. And though they seem happy, I am told they can be very fierce in war—even the women."

Morgan suppressed a smile. He had noticed that Sutter got along very, very well with his hired Kanaka, especially with the lovely Manuiki, whose large brown eyes never seemed to stop laughing at them both.

Sutter unwrapped his leather case from its oilskin and studied a sheaf of papers. Morgan took the opportunity to study the man. Sutter was handsome and exuded immense and unwavering confidence. His hair was fashionably long and he wore sideburns and a mustache which lent him a military aspect exclusive of his uniform. Some said that the captain bore a remarkable resemblance to the South American liberator Simón Bolívar, but Morgan had no way of knowing if this was true.

It was obvious that the captain was very intelligent and possessed a superior education. He spoke French, German, and English fluently and knew more than a few words of Russian and Spanish. Sutter had been an officer of the Swiss Guard in the French service and had revealed himself to be an able student and admirer of Napoléon; that also seemed to impress people.

Sutter's head snapped up. "Mr. Beck, assuming I receive a big land grant rather than being compelled to take it by force, you must help me satisfy the Mexican government's official demands, no matter how petty or troublesome they become. Do this, and I promise I will see that you are generously rewarded."

"With money?"

Sutter chuckled but shook his head. "No, with something far more valuable—land."

"Free land is worth nothing except to the Indians. I'll take the money."

"Don't make foolish statements like that. Always remember that good land, the kind I intend to settle, is worth far more than gold. A man can lose his soul to money, but the land will always give him sustenance. It asks but little and gives abundantly. All that it requires is honest effort and, once it is plowed, planted with seed, and tended with care, it will repay its keeper a thousandfold."

"But Captain, I have no desire whatsoever to be a farmer."

Sutter's eyes flashed with annoyance. "Then what would you become?"

Morgan shrugged. "I don't know. I do a little hunting and some beaver trapping. I help my father in his shipping business, and we build and sell boats like this one. I am happy."

"Happy?" Sutter clucked his tongue with pity. "Happiness is doing something with your life of lasting importance. It is finding a quest worthy of your abilities and pursuing it to its completion." Sutter's voice thickened with passion. "You *must*, Mr. Beck, learn to strive for more than the simple day-to-day pleasures. You must believe that you have greatness in you and seek a noble destiny!"

Morgan tore his eyes from Sutter's excited expression and tried to concentrate on his rowing. The man's zeal made him uneasy because he had no real vision of

which to boast. His pleasures were quite simple. He
enjoyed pretty women and good books. He loved hunting and riding a good horse. The sound of the ocean
was his music. In truth, Morgan had to admit his
favorite pleasures seemed childish compared to Sutter's
lofty dreams.

But no matter, he reasoned, because the captain was
blind to reality; he was a hopeless fanatic. And, as Eli
had prophesied, those who flew so high were bound to
fall very low indeed. Eli, while offering his son's services, had privately believed that Governor Alvarado, a
shrewd man, would see right through Sutter and toss
him out on his high-and-mighty ear.

"Mr. Beck?"

Morgan glanced up from his shoes, where he had
fixed his attention. He was surprised to see that the
captain looked quite upset. "Sir?"

"I . . . I wish to apologize," he said with obvious difficulty. "I had no right to pontificate. You see, I occasion-
ally fall victim to my own visions and dreams. Dreams
that—within the next hour—might very well crash down
around my feet, making me look a total fool."

This confession was so unexpected and uncharacteristic
of Sutter that Morgan suddenly discovered that, like his
father, he really wanted the Swiss to succeed. "I hope
not, Captain. I mean that."

"Thank you!" Sutter brightened. "And I'll try to keep
myself in check from now on. But . . ." Sutter groped for
the right words, "but you must understand that dreams
freely spoken with passion cause jealousy. Men with
dreams almost always stand alone, subject to ridicule. I
would advise you to remember that, even though I
cannot."

"Yes, sir," Morgan said, feeling awkward. "Captain,
we are nearing the surf. You'd better protect those
papers and hang on tight."

A sadness, or perhaps a disappointment, passed quickly across Sutter's eyes. "Yes, Mr. Beck, of course."

Sutter quickly rewrapped his papers and case in the
oilskin as the surf rumbled in their ears.

"Mr. Beck, I have no wish to insult you, but please

don't allow this craft to capsize. It would not do to have Captain Sutter present himself dripping wet like a dog to the governor of California."

"No, sir," Morgan said, bringing the rowboat expertly through the gentle surf and beaching it on the sand.

Morgan jumped into the shallow water and hesitated, wondering why the captain did not do the same.

"My boots," Sutter explained without budging. "They are polished."

"Oh. I forgot."

Morgan pulled the little boat up higher and Sutter hopped onto the white beach, where he revealed a trace of nervousness by smoothing his coat and picking at a speck of imaginary lint.

The captain's eyes lifted to the persidio and he said, "It would be far more impressive if we had arrived in a fine carriage. But there's no help for that, so come along. You can make the introductions and then leave the rest to me."

"Yes, Captain."

Without further hesitation, Sutter marched forward, arms free-swinging, head up and back straight as a martinet. In contrast, Morgan plodded through the sand feeling like a draft horse. His wet boots caked thickly with sand, making them very heavy. And even though he was taller than the captain and had much longer legs, Morgan had to work to keep up with Sutter. Why, he wondered, was this man in such an all-fired hurry to have Governor Alvarado humiliate him and then coldly dash his dreams?

Morgan wished he knew how to prepare Sutter for Alvarado's customarily abrasive manners. But sometimes, he supposed, a man had to learn the hard way.

"Come along, Mr. Beck, don't hang back! And let me remind you once again that we are men about to change the course of Western history!"

"Yes, Captain," Morgan called, hurrying after the man but not believing a word of it.

Two hours later, Morgan stretched his long legs across the brown tile floor outside the governor's office and wished he were somewhere—anywhere—else. He and the captain had been kept waiting for nearly three hours, and Morgan sensed that Sutter's patience finally was wearing thin.

But suddenly the door opened and one of the governor's aides beckoned them forward with a slight bow and a perfunctory smile.

They were ushered into a very large office, dim but with enough light to see that the large French desk was occupied by the governor. The man was dressed in his own military uniform festooned with even more gold braid and medals than Sutter wore.

"Governor Alvarado," Morgan said, removing his cap and bowing slightly, "you are most gracious to see us on such short notice. Allow me to introduce my good friend, Captain John Augustus Sutter."

At the sound of his name, Sutter marched right up to the governor's desk. When he came to a halt, his heels clicked smartly together and gave a crisp salute, which he held until Alvarado, clearly taken by surprise, popped up from his desk and hastily returned the salute.

Sutter's right hand arced gracefully down to his creased trousers. "What a supreme pleasure, Your Excellency! You do me great honor by receiving me without an appointment. And sir, I must tell you that I have journeyed across half the world for this very moment."

Alvarado blinked. Morgan was sure that the Mexican was momentarily off balance, and that probably was a good sign.

"Captain Sutter, exactly what does bring you to me?"

"Fate?" Sutter smiled quizzically. "Dare I suggest even destiny?" He paused dramatically. "Who can say for certain? I am sure of only one thing—that this meeting one day will be recorded in the history books."

"Who *are* you?" Alvarado exclaimed with exasperation, his eyes darting to Morgan and then back to Sutter.

Morgan ground his teeth, searching for. . . for what? An explanation? An apology? Something to salvage the damage.

"I am," Sutter persisted with a bright, undaunted smile, "a friend of kings, nobles, and men of immense influence. May I present my letters of introduction? I believe they will attest to my character."

"Señor Beck, do you and your father recommend this man as one of good character?"

"Yes, Your Excellency. He is to be trusted and has something important to say. His letters of introduction speak for themselves."

The governor's eyes locked with those of Sutter.

"Then come, come, let me see them," Alvarado demanded, snapping his fingers with impatience.

Morgan thought his captain was going to salute, but instead Sutter swept off his hat with a flourish and placed it on a chair before opening the oilskin packet. He then removed the crucial letters of introduction. Morgan knew them to be from officials of the powerful Hudson's Bay Company as well as Russians from Sitka and the important British and American consuls Sutter had met in the Sandwich Islands. Even Eli had been impressed.

"Sit . . ." Alvarado's gaze touched the first letter of introduction, which Morgan recognized as one from the British consul, "down, Captain Sutter."

Alvarado's voice softened dramatically as he quickly thumbed through the other letters.

Morgan risked a glance at Sutter, and the captain brazenly winked. The man's cool demeanor and unbridled confidence caused Morgan to stand a little straighter.

When at last Alvarado had digested the letters to his satisfaction, he stacked them neatly on the outside corner of his desk.

"Brandy?" he asked with a warm smile.

"Yes, we will," Sutter said. "And thank you."

Morgan saw that somehow they had passed a test, and he relaxed.

"So," Alvarado said as he poured the brandy, "you speak well, but you have yet to tell me anything. What brings you to Monterey?"

"I come to offer you my services. I want to conquer your inland wilderness. I want to civilize your Miwok Indians and reap for Mexico the wealth of the Sacramento River country."

Alvarado had been about to propose a toast, but he paused and said, "I am sure you promise more than you can deliver—as did the earlier well-intentioned but naive padres."

"I am here as a businessman, not a missionary. I have, on the brig *Clementine* waiting in your harbor, cannon, supplies enough to outfit a post for one year, seed, and tools, enough to reap an abundant harvest."

Alvarado blinked, and Sutter pushed on. "I also have determination and experience enough to win your confidence and trust."

"Then to trust," Alvarado said after studying Sutter intently, "and to men of vision and destiny."

As they drank, Morgan had the distinct impression that something very strong but indefinable passed between the two military officers, something which he would never be able to share or even understand. Morgan knew only that, during the next few hours, he became just an observer.

At the end of that time, Alvarado and Sutter were still poring over a map, speaking of Indians and arms, cannon and corn. Once, Alvarado scooped up the captain's sheaved letters of introduction and said, "No one before has ever come with so many!"

Sutter merely laughed, and then Alvarado laughed, too, and before their meeting was over the pair were talking about dinner.

The governor looked up from the map of California spread out across his desk and seemed to notice Morgan for the first time since their introductions. "Ah, Señor Beck, what about you? Will you join us tonight?"

"No, thank you."

When the governor's eyebrows arched in question, Morgan quickly added, "My father asked me to give his regards to an old friend."

Alvarado did not bother to pretend disappointment. And neither did Sutter.

Morgan had the rest of the afternoon and evening to himself. He debated rowing back to the *Clementine* but decided to remain in town instead. Monterey was a larger pueblo than Yerba Buena, and it deserved to be explored. All the houses were of adobe, and many were whitewashed so that their red tile roofs stood out in sharp contrast. Morgan noted that the citizens of Monterey, unlike those of Yerba Buena, appeared to expend a great deal of effort cultivating bright flowers, none of which he could name but all of which he appreciated. Several of the homes, like the Casa Amesti, were two-storied with wide upper balconies. Others surrounded courtyards, and from one he heard the strum of a guitar accompanied by laughter.

Thirty minutes of strolling through the town, visiting the plaza, the ruined mission, and some of the village's finest casas was more than enough. When his father's old friend was not at home, Morgan wandered back down to the waterfront, where cheerful Mexican fishermen squatted in the sand, working on their boats and nets while talking and sipping what Morgan supposed to be the potent aguardiente.

"How is the fishing today?" Morgan asked a small group of grinning fishermen.

"It is very slow," a robust Mexican without any front teeth lamented. "We catch only two or three."

"Maybe tomorrow, then."

The men shrugged as if it did not greatly matter. Another asked, "Señor, you want some fish and tortilla? Maybe a little something to wash it down?"

"*Gracias.*" Morgan was pleased by this invitation, even though he knew it would prove costly. A place in the sand was made for him, and fish was cut, then skewered on a roasting stick.

Morgan pushed the fish out over the low fire, while the man next to him singed a big corn tortilla. When the fish began to drip and sizzle, Morgan accepted the tortilla and wrapped it around the fish. He gobbled it down and smacked his lips to indicate his pleasure.

"*Gracias!*"

One of them handed him a jug, and Morgan upended

it. The liquor seared his throat, made his eyes water,
and caused his new friends to laugh.

"Ahhh!" Morgan exclaimed, making a show by clutching
his throat. "Very strong!"

They all nodded in rapid agreement, smiles all around.
More food and drink was pressed at Morgan, but all too
soon the jug was empty and the fishermen stared at him
with hope in their soft brown eyes. Morgan did not
disappoint his compadres, and when he drew out money it was accepted and exchanged for two fresh jugs
within a very few minutes.

The party had begun. The fishermen were very
happy with Morgan, and as he ate and drank he also
started to feel very happy with himself.

It was late evening when Morgan excused himself
from the circle of drunken, singing fishermen and,
swaying precariously, eventually found the Casa Alvarado,
a long, low adobe with a red brick front porch. When
Morgan knocked on the door, he had to wait a long time
for an answer.

At last, a pretty girl in a simple cotton dress opened
the door. When she smelled Morgan, she wrinkled her
nose and took an involuntary step backward.

"Señor?"

He removed his sailor's cap and crumpled it up in his
big hands.

"Señorita," he said, making a slight bow, "please be
good enough to tell Captain Sutter that Señor Morgan
Beck is here as instructed."

But the girl just stared at him. She was tall, with a
heart-shaped face and unusually large brown eyes that
swam into and out of his own.

"Did you hear me, Señorita?"

"Yes, but I don't think you should come inside. It
would not be wise."

His indignation flared. "What is that supposed to
mean?"

She planted her feet solidly in the doorway and
folded her arms across her bosom. "You are drunk,
Señor. You would disgrace not only yourself but also
your captain."

Morgan intended to argue, to shout and maybe even cuss, but instead he just stared dumbly at the girl.

"Who are you? What is your name?"

"Rosalinda. But please, Señor Beck, it is best that you do not come in now."

He did manage to clench his fists at his sides, but when she looked down at them so innocently, he felt like a fool. "You're probably right," he whispered, reaching up with the intention of removing his sailor's cap, only to discover that it was gone. "Then please be good enough to tell Captain Sutter that I will be waiting for him down the street."

"Down the street, Señor?"

"Yes," he repeated, turning around so that he could point down the street, almost losing his balance. "Under that big tree. Yes. I will wait right there."

The girl stepped back inside, and Morgan thought he was being dismissed except that she reappeared a moment later with a pitcher of water and a towel.

"Señor, drink first, then wash a little. You should not be left waiting in the street."

Morgan grinned. He closed one eye because he was seeing double and said, "You think I'm drunk and unpresentable, don't you, Señorita?"

"Si."

Morgan imagined he saw a hint of amusement tugging at the corners of her lovely mouth, but he could not be sure. Drawing himself to his full height, he said, "Well, you're right."

When she did not reply, Morgan drank from the pitcher, slopping water down his chin and shirtfront. When he'd had his fill, he dipped the towel into the pitcher, then scrubbed his face and shook his head.

"Thank you, Señorita."

She curtsied and took the pitcher and towel he extended. "The tree?"

"Yes, the tree. Whenever the captain is ready."

The pretty girl rolled her eyes, then closed the door behind her. While Morgan watched in confusion, she placed the pitcher on the ground, then shyly took his arm and turned him around as if he were blind or feebleminded.

"Come along, Señor Beck."

"I can get there myself."

"But not so good, eh?"

The way she smiled when she said it disarmed him completely. Besides, she smelled of roses, in sharp contrast to his reeking of fish and aguardiente.

He took a few more steps and was dismayed to discover that the effects of the aguardiente were getting stronger with each passing moment, causing his poor head to spin.

"I want to thank you for your kindness, Señorita, and I beg you to forgive my poor manners. I do not usually act like such a lout."

She frowned. "You drink far too much."

"Yes," he admitted, "and I ate too much fish and tortillas on the beach."

They were finally nearing the big cypress tree. Morgan's stomach was rioting all the way up to his mouth. Sweat was popping out across his forehead and he felt weak.

"*Adiós, Señorita Rosalinda,*" he said with a groan. "Go now!"

She took one look at his pale face and nodded, then turned and ran back toward Casa Alvarado. Morgan staggered forward, grabbed the trunk of the tree to steady himself, then began to retch violently.

What a fool he was! Thank God for that girl having the good sense to turn him away from the door. If he had gotten sick inside with the governor and the captain . . .

Morgan bowed his head, overcome with nausea. Even as his legs buckled, he knew that he was fortunate, because this was small payment compared to the embarrassment he had almost caused himself, the captain, and his father.

Thank God for the pretty Señorita!

"Mr. Beck, there is a time for drinking and a time for business." That was the only thing Sutter had said to him that night as Morgan weakly rowed back to the

Clementine. "And you don't seem to be able to distinguish between them."

"What business did I have?" Morgan groaned.

"The business of learning. You could have occupied yourself with observing instead of partaking gluttonously of fish and whatever they were drinking."

The next day, still shaky and pale and vowing never to drink strong spirits again in his life, Morgan rowed Sutter back to meet again with the governor. They talked little that morning, but everything was forgiven or forgotten late in the afternoon when Alvarado himself walked them to the beach.

"My dear friend," Alvarado said, clasping Sutter's hand warmly, "I will see you in one year, at which time, if you are successful, you shall have both Mexican citizenship and the title to the land."

Sutter drew himself up to his full height. "I will be successful, and I will see you in one year to the day, Governor."

"Godspeed, then," Alvarado said, clamping his hand on the captain's shoulder as if they were comrades-in-arms.

The governor turned to Morgan. "Captain Sutter assures me that you are going to help him found his colony. Is that correct?"

Morgan was so surprised that he could not speak.

Captain Sutter did it for him. "The young man has the follies commensurate with his age, but he is strong and brave. He has learned the way of the wilderness, and I'm sure that he will prove invaluable in my service."

"Good!" Alvarado said, gripping Morgan's hand and shaking it firmly. "Tell your father that I appreciate the help he has offered to Captain Sutter."

It was all that Morgan could do to nod his head, and then the captain was climbing into the stinking little rowboat with as much ceremony as if he were boarding a command vessel.

Morgan pushed out waist-deep into the surf, then hopped in and, with the sunset pouring liquid gold across Monterey Bay, he angrily demanded, "What the devil else did you tell that man?"

"Oh, many things."

"Well, I didn't promise to be a part of them, and neither did my father!"

Sutter shrugged innocently and turned his face toward the brilliant sunset. He looked positively beatific, as if he had himself seen and charmed the ghost of Father Junípero Serra, whose bones were resting onshore.

"So it begins," John Augustus Sutter whispered, closing his eyes and pursing his lips. "So now it *really* begins!"

Morgan wanted to get angry but found it impossible. Sutter had tricked him, his father, and the governor. Morgan drove the bow of the boat at a slight angle into the crashing surf, causing a wave to thoroughly drench Sutter. The captain barked his displeasure and used a silk handkerchief to mop his face.

Morgan grinned at his small but satisfying revenge. Maybe he would stick with the captain awhile and watch to learn how history is made—or not made. At worst, it would be mildly interesting; at best, profitable beyond his wildest dreams.

≈ 1 ≈

The fog had not lifted completely even by early afternoon, and the great San Francisco Bay was blanketed by a dark lid of clouds that threatened rain. Yerba Buena seemed to cringe against the deep chill. Three American ships could be seen at anchor waiting to fill their bellies with hides, still the currency of Alta California. Farther out in the bay, a few fog-shrouded islands huddled like surly guards.

Morgan Beck could see a stand of trees marking a failing rancho that once had been mission land covered with herds of grazing sheep and cattle. Beside him, Eli sat on his rickety little dock with a fishing pole. He had just finished coughing so loudly that he now sat pale and visibly shaken. Morgan tried not to look worried, but he knew that his father's consumption was getting much worse.

Eli was, like Morgan, tall and broad-shouldered, with deeply set, piercing eyes. His chin seemed much sharper, though, because he was missing most of his teeth. Like Morgan, he had big, competent hands. The former mountain man was wrapped in a colorful Ute blanket that had not faded over the years and that always brought him memories of the high country and bright, clear days. He still wore moccasins and fringed buckskins with leggings, too, sending all the way to Taos for them each spring.

"Fish ain't bitin' today," the old man breathed, a

21

rattle in his lungs. "Ain't like fishing in the high mountain rivers. I don't even like saltwater fish."

"Then why do it?" Morgan asked.

"Dunno. Mama Estella likes 'em."

Morgan glanced over his shoulder toward their small, cluttered boatyard, the storage sheds, and the rickety, clapboard cabin. He could smell tortillas cooking, and that caused his stomach to seize up a little in memory of his Monterey drunk. Mama Estella was cooking him going-away food. She had accepted his decision to accompany Sutter inland, but Eli still had not.

Morgan turned back to his father. Eli looked old, tired, and gray, just like this huge harbor.

"You think a lot about the mountains, don't you."

It wasn't a question, and Eli nodded, for this was something that they talked a good deal about.

"I'm always cold here," Eli confessed. "The fog seeps into the marrow of my bones."

"Then you should leave."

"What about her?" Eli asked, jerking his thumb back toward their shack.

"She'd go wherever you went," Morgan said. "And we could make a living somewhere else where the climate is warm and dry."

Eli snickered. "Somewhere like up the Sacramento?"

Morgan was stung by his father's cynicism. He blustered, "Well, why not? Captain Sutter said he'd give me land if I helped him. Good land, too!"

"And what'd we do with it, son? You don't know a damn bit more about farmin' than I do."

Morgan had foreseen the question, and he had a ready answer. "We could trap the Sierra rivers. They're bound to be full of beaver. We could do that, sir."

"I'm a little long in the tooth for fightin' Indians and buckin' a pack of pelts up and down the mountains."

"Then I could do that part," Morgan said quickly. "Mama Estella could stay near the fort where she'd be safe. Other people would come and she'd have friends."

Eli laid his fishing pole down beside him. "You make it sound so easy. You been hangin' around that Swiss captain too damn much."

"It wouldn't be *that* hard!"

Eli chewed slowly. "Beaver won't last, even if we could. Then what?"

"We could raise sheep, horses, and cattle. I'm good with livestock. You know that."

Eli looked into Morgan's eyes. "It sounds like you just about got things all figured out. Trouble is, you're counting on Captain Sutter to do what he says he'll do."

"If he fails, maybe we could do it ourselves," Morgan said, realizing even as he spoke how impossible it would be to tame the inland wilderness.

Eli did not mock him. Instead, he laid his wrinkled, liver-spotted hand on his son's shoulder. "I wish you wouldn't be thinkin' about goin' with Sutter. It's a fool's journey, boy. No good will come of it. We got a livin' right here."

"But you're not doing well. The climate is bad for you, and this life isn't to your liking. You're not happy."

Eli barked a laugh without humor. "What the hell has being happy got to do with livin'?"

Morgan sighed. His father wasn't going to change his mind, but something kept prodding Morgan to try anyway. "It's just that I *promised* Captain Sutter that I'd go along with him. He'll be sailing by today and expecting me, Pa. I can't rightly go back on my word."

"I ain't asking you to do that," Eli said, "but so far, you haven't even gotten paid."

"But I will be!"

"When?" Eli nailed him with his hard eyes.

"I . . . I can't rightly say. The captain is real short on money."

Eli snorted. "And long on talk. Well, talk don't fill our larder. Buildin' boats and haulin' hides out to those Boston ships in the harbor does."

"I know that," Morgan said, "but we work too hard for too little. All day rowing back and forth with a pile of stinking hides for damn little money. You coughing and spitting in the cold and fog, and me bending my back so it feels like my spine is about to splinter." Morgan shook his head. "That's no good for us, sir. We'll never

have enough to buy lumber and build a sailing vessel
that would really bring us a profit."

"And Captain Sutter is going to change all that?" Eli
asked bluntly.

"I think so. At least, I think it's worth a try to find
out. The captain promised me land. He really needs me
to hunt game and parlay with the Indians. Needs me
bad enough to promise me some money, too."

"Ha! Where's he going to get his money? In the
rivers? Is he going to find hisself a river of gold?"

Morgan blushed with humiliation. "No sir. Captain
Sutter believes his gold is to be found in the soil. He
means to get the Indians to work the earth, same as
they did for the missionaries."

Eli snorted in derision. "Son, use your damned head!
Them Indians went wild about an hour after the Mexicans
threw out the Spanish missionaries. They took to the
hills and went wild as the deer."

Eli's voice lifted. "And ask yourself this—if you was a
free Indian, livin' off what you could hunt, grub, or fish,
would you put a yoke around your neck and labor like a
beast in some white man's fields?"

"No, sir," Morgan said after a long pause, "I guess I
would not."

"Well, neither will they. And even though I'll admit
that Sutter sweet-talked me just like he's doin' everyone else, I see the truth of it now. The man is *all* talk."

"Maybe so," Morgan admitted, "but he'll be sailing
up this bay on more than talk. He's got two good sailing
ships loaded with provisions, Kanaka Indians, and even
some white men willing to believe."

"There has never been a shortage of fools in this
world," Eli drawled. "And I don't care about the rest of
them—it's your hide I'm worried about."

"I'll be fine."

"Better be 'cause after I'm gone someone has to take
care of your mother in her old age. Besides, to me it's
the same as if I was loanin' that Swiss songbird a good
ox or mule that I was worried I might not see again."

"I understand. But you know what?"

Eli didn't respond, so Morgan continued. "I don't

think the Captain has much money, maybe not even enough to pay for the loss of a good mule or ox."

"Then how the hell is he gettin' sailing ships and supplies?"

"Sutter has good credit. He just gets things by asking for them on credit."

"Humph!" Eli snorted. "Same as he got you from me, I suppose."

"He's a talker," Morgan conceded, "we both knew that from the start. But Pa, we need to try something better than what we've been doing so far. Your health isn't improving."

"We're eatin', ain't we?"

"Yes, but we deserve more than to spend the rest of our lives licking some Mexican official's boots and paying Governor Alvarado a tribute from our hard-earned profits."

Eli clamped his mouth shut hard so that the tip of his hooked nose was almost touching his pointed chin. Morgan knew he'd hit a nerve—being beholden to the Mexicans was eating away at his father, killing him faster than the consumption.

"I got to do this, Pa, because I believe that Captain Sutter just might make things better for us."

"The man is all talk. Nothing will come of this. Nothing good."

"General Vallejo thinks differently."

Eli frowned. "He went to see Vallejo?"

"That's right. And Captain Sutter also talked the general into giving him supplies on credit."

General Vallejo was Alvarado's uncle, a rich, highly respected man. On hearing this, Eli shook his head almost mournfully. "So old Vallejo went for it, too."

"He did. I was there. And he also struck some kind of deal with the Russians at Fort Ross."

"Damnation! That Sutter could talk a grizzly bear into servin' cookies and cream!"

"Pa, I'm determined to give Captain Sutter enough time either to succeed or to fail. And if he begins to fail but is too stubborn to quit, then I'll make a boat and row it home."

"You forgettin' the Indians? 'Member what they did to us the last time we had our little run-in?"

"I remember. I'll be careful."

"Mama Estella is going to be pretty unhappy with me if I let you go with that fool."

"I'll speak with her right now," Morgan promised. "I'll tell her that if Sutter is successful, it will mean money in our pockets. And land. Enough good land to start over. It'll mean a better life. You'll feel good again where it's dry and warm. You can see the high mountains every morning when the sun breaks over their peaks. Just like before."

Eli smiled softly, and the hardness drained from his thin, wolfish face. "Ain't ever going to be like before. Not for me."

"It'll be *better*," Morgan said with emphasis. "You just wait and see."

Eli dipped his pointy chin. "You're starting to sound like him already."

"Who? Sutter?"

"Yep."

Morgan barked a laugh. "I'll never have his way with words. It's a gift."

"Or a curse."

"Yeah," Morgan said, climbing to his feet and heading up the hill to their little cabin.

She was expecting him, baking corn and beans, then wrapping them in tortillas and packing everything in linen in spite of Morgan's insistence that Sutter was well provisioned. He did not have the heart to argue with her about the food. You could not really argue with Mama Estella. She would just listen, nod her double chins, and then do what she wanted to do anyway.

Mama Estella was plain and heavyset. Morgan's real mother had died in St. Louis when he was four. Six years later, Eli had arrived in California and soon after had met Señora Estella Escobar Alvarado Contreras at the plaza in Monterey. She was already a widow, her husband having died after getting drunk one night and falling off the deck of a sailing ship. The señora, scarred by a pox when she was a child, had never expected to remarry, and when Eli showed interest it had seemed like an answered prayer.

But her second prayer—for many children—had not been answered, and so she had devoted herself to Eli and Morgan during the ensuing years, even to the point of spoiling them during the feast days of the Church.

Morgan stepped over to her side and encircled her thick waist with his arms. "I won't be gone so long. I will probably be back within a month. Maybe even sooner."

She turned to look at him. "You might get killed. It almost happened before."

"When it was just Pa and me," he reminded her. "This time there will be many men. Maybe thirty or more. And we have a cannon. Don't worry. We will be strong enough against the Miwok or any other tribe."

But she shook her head. Mama Estella could not hide worry. Her round, innocent face was as open to read as her Bible. "I do not know this for sure."

"I will be fine."

"Your father does not like this man. Can he be trusted?"

Morgan could not lie. "I believe so. Especially as long as I am valuable to him as a hunter, pathfinder, and interpreter with the Indians. Captain Sutter could someday become very rich and powerful. He intends to build a colony."

"He should build it closer to people."

"I know. Everyone is telling him that. But he doesn't listen. I don't think he wants to be under Governor Alvarado's thumb. I think he is too proud and independent to take orders."

"Proud men die young."

"I am proud—of *you*, Mama." Morgan kissed her cheek.

She managed a tired smile. "You must take care of yourself, and I will pray the rosary for you every day. You should also pray for yourself."

"I will," he said, knowing that he would not.

"Here. Eat and take the rest before I eat them all or give them to your poor father."

Morgan sat down, his back to the door. He liked to watch his mother work in her cramped, smoky little kitchen. When she was happy, and that was most of the time, Mama Estella would hum a little song or refrain, or even sing in a sweet, deep voice.

But today, as the Beck family waited for the captain's chartered schooners to take him up the wild, largely unexplored Sacramento, there would be no singing, and no humming, either.

A short while later, Morgan heard the sound of a rifle echoing across the water. He came to his feet and hurried outside to scan the vast expanse of the bay.

"It's Sutter!"

"Take your food and make sure you keep your powder dry," she ordered, not even bothering to turn away from her brick stove.

Morgan nodded, the elation draining away because his mother did not share his hopes and Eli was no longer down on the dock fishing. Morgan supposed the old man had just walked up into the hills rather than face Sutter with his big show, all resting on bluster and promises.

"Mama," he shouted back through the doorway, "I'm certain that something good is going to come of this for us. I got a feeling growing deep in my bones."

His mother reached for firewood and fed her stove. With a sigh of resignation, Morgan scooped up the linen-wrapped package of food she'd prepared, grabbed his old Hawken rifle, and strode off to the shore.

More than two weeks later, a thoroughly exasperated Sutter was pacing up and down the deck of the chartered twenty-ton schooner *Isabella*. An English bulldog that he had picked up in the Sandwich Islands dozed fitfully in the shade of the mast. Behind their schooner came the smaller vessel, the *Nicholas*, pulling a little four-oared craft which Sutter preferred to use in very shallow water or when exploring river tributaries.

Morgan knew better than to get in Sutter's way when

he was agitated. They had already spent too much time searching for a perfect building site. Tensions were high. At night, fearful of an Indian attack, Sutter ordered his boats to be secured closely together onshore. Even though they had not seen an Indian, they had been devoured by swarms of mosquitoes until they were all cross, with swollen hands and faces.

After a difficult and anxious journey far up the Sacramento, the sailors on board the *Isabella* finally had refused to go on and had threatened mutiny. With great exasperation, Sutter had been forced to turn back, and now, as he ordered his vessels to sail up the American River, Sutter was visibly excited. For the last several nights, after camp had been made and guards posted, Morgan had accompanied the captain as he surveyed the land and examined the richness of the soil.

"It is very, very good, this delta earth," Sutter kept pronouncing. "It is dark and rich, eh, Mr. Beck?"

And, as Sutter also pointed out, the countryside bordered by the American and Sacramento rivers was flat and ideally suited for cultivation. Timber necessary to construct a fort was abundant in the form of sycamore, elm, and cottonwood. Even the two rivers themselves seemed perfect for navigation, having deep middle channels and sandy bottoms with no large rocks likely to rip into a vessel's vulnerable hull. And the prevailing wind was from the west, which would make it very easy to navigate up the current and then drop the sails and return to the ocean with the fruits of the abundant harvests that Sutter expected to sell at the Mexican presidios and at Russia's Fort Ross just up the coast.

"This is it," Sutter could be heard repeating with mounting passion in his voice. "I can feel it in my bones. We are almost there!"

"I don't know," said a half-Sandwich Islander named Kanaka Bill. "We've seen bunches of Indian feathers tied to bushes all along these shores. And plenty of burned campfires. I tell you, the Miwok are watching us and just waiting to spring a surprise party."

But Sutter would hear none of this threatening talk.

"Nonsense! They have nothing but stones and spears to throw, along with a few crude bows and arrows. We have rifles and cannon! We have nothing at all to fear."

But no sooner had he said this than more than a hundred warriors appeared in a cove nearby, shouting and pumping their weapons up and down. They looked angry, with faces painted red, yellow, and black.

"I say we open fire!" a sailor called, his face pinched and pale with fear. "Captain, they mean to take our scalps if they can get aboard."

"No!" Sutter cried. "I will shoot the first man who fires a rifle at those Indians."

Then, before anyone realized what was happening, Sutter strode to the Jacob's ladder and descended into a dinghy.

"Captain!" Morgan shouted. "What the hell are you doing?"

Sutter didn't look up as he untied the little boat and gripped a pair of oars. "Keep a sharp eye out, Mr. Beck! If they kill me, this expedition is over and you must return these vessels to their owners."

"But—"

Morgan had never seen the captain row before, and Sutter did an extremely bad job, flailing away with his oars at the river's strong current until he managed to reach the shore, where his boat was immediately surrounded by Indians.

"He's a dead man for sure," a sailor whispered.

Morgan thought so, too. The Kanaka began to wail, and poor Manuiki fell sobbing to her knees.

"Amigos! Amigos!" they heard Sutter cry as he jumped out of the dinghy and raised his open hand in a sign of peace.

Morgan lifted his rifle, knowing it was useless against so many, and just as he was about to take aim, an old Indian wearing a faded red blanket stepped forward and croaked, *"Amigos, sí!"*

His words rendered the other Indians silent.

"What the hell is going on?" a sailor swore.

"Shut up!" Morgan ordered. "Look!"

Sutter's voice could not be heard clearly, but it was

plain he was speaking in his halting, labored Spanish and that the Indian understood and was also conversant in Spanish.

"What the—" Kanaka Bill started to say.

Morgan supplied the answer. "He's got to be a former mission Indian!"

Sutter was making elaborate gestures toward the schooners, and the old Indian was soon joined by several other elder tribesmen, and they all began to nod their heads with understanding.

Well, goddamn, Morgan thought in utter amazement, the captain is even going to get *them* to help.

Sutter turned and cupped his hands to his mouth. "Mr. Beck, there's some beads and trinkets in my locker. Bring them to me at once!"

Morgan turned from the rail and Kanaka Bill grumbled, "How does he propose you do that?"

"Swim," Morgan said. "How else?"

In no time at all, Morgan was standing dripping wet beside the captain and helping Sutter with his Spanish so that the former mission Indians clearly understood his message.

"Mr. Beck, emphasize very strongly that we mean these good people no harm. We are not Spanish and will not force them to work. Tell them that we do not come to make war or carry off slaves. We come only to live here as their friends."

Morgan translated, and things would have gone very smoothly indeed if the mission Indians had not all tried to translate to the others at the same time. Even so, it was clear that Sutter's message was being correctly interpreted, because the Indians began to smile through their thick war paint and they were very pleased with Sutter's gifts.

"Then this is where we will build?" Morgan asked in English.

Sutter gazed up toward a low rise of land that would be safe from floods and command an excellent view of both the Sacramento and American rivers.

"No, up there." he said, pointing his finger. "That is the place. Order the men to start unloading the supplies."

"What about these people?" Morgan asked in English so that they could not understand.

"We will first unload one of the small cannon. They will see it and understand. Also, tell them that they should go away."

Morgan hesitated. "I'm not sure that would be the best thing to do, sir. We've just gotten into their good graces. It'd be a shame to ruin things now."

The captain frowned. "Then tell them to camp somewhere else and that we will have them as guests for a feast when we have established our fort."

Morgan nodded and reverted to Spanish. The older Indians nodded and ordered the others to return to their village. The Indians obeyed and vanished into the heavy woods that bordered the riverbank.

For the rest of the day Sutter's men worked feverishly in the hot sun unloading the tons of supplies. The work went slowly, for besides the dinghy they had only a couple of little rowboats, and it was long past dark when the last of the supplies were finally deposited on the riverbank.

"Post guards all around," Sutter ordered, visibly staggering with weariness.

"Sir? What about our schooners?" a seaman asked.

"Tomorrow morning they return to Yerba Buena for more supplies."

For the men returning to the coast, this was more than welcome news. They might even have celebrated a little except for the grim expressions on the faces of Sutter's colonizers who would be left behind, their last tether to civilization severed.

Sutter, noticing the contrast between those who would sail off to the safety of Yerba Buena and those who would remain in this wild country, said, "Tonight, I want a bonfire as high as the trees, and it must burn until dawn. We will open a casket of rum and celebrate this great event."

This raised everyone's spirits a little, and when the cannon were positioned and ready for action and the bonfire roared high, they all felt much safer. The cask of rum was too small for so many, but the toasts Sutter made were eloquent, and Morgan wished that his father could have been a part of this happy occasion.

That night the mosquitoes were as merciless as always. The moon shone brightly and the Sacramento Valley air was hot and muggy. Morgan thought again about his father and how haggard and drawn Eli had appeared on the dock. It made him resolve to do everything he could to ensure Sutter's success. He dipped into his pack and munched on Mama Estella's tortillas, and that made him think of Monterey and Rosalinda.

Who was she? Simply a maidservant for the governor and his wife? Perhaps even Alvarado's mistress? No, Alvarado would be more circumspect than that. Then perhaps just a maid. Still, she seemed too...what? Refined? Confident and sure of herself to be a maid?

Morgan didn't know. All that he was sure of was that Rosalinda had saved him from a great embarrassment and that she was stuck in his mind, like a burr in a saddle blanket. She was beautiful, like Manuiki, only very different. Rosalinda was wise and a little mysterious—Manuiki was like a woman-child who smoldered and fired a man's blood when he looked into her bold eyes. Yes, the two women were very different indeed.

Several times during the long night Morgan alternated with the others at guard and at tending the huge bonfire.

Come daybreak, everyone was red-eyed and on edge, but the Indians did not reappear.

"They'll be watching us right now, though," Kanaka Bill warned. "You can be sure of that much, Captain."

"Then we'll give them a little something to think about when the *Isabella* and *Nicholas* depart for the bay," Sutter replied with just the trace of a smile.

The crews returning to Yerba Buena made their preparations to sail in record time, and there was some snickering among those who would remain with the captain.

"Stand by to give our Indian friends a show!" Sutter commanded when the two crews were on board and had thrown off their lines.

Sutter's "show" was a nine-gun salute fired at some nearby trees. At the first cannon shot, thousand of birds erupted from the tules along the riverbanks, and from the surrounding hills wolves and coyotes howled and yipped.

The hair on Sutter's bulldog stood on end, causing the captain to laugh. "Fire again!" he bellowed.

The second cannon rocked back on its foundation, belching smoke and fire. More birds shot skyward and circled wildly overhead. Indians who had been hiding in the thickets watching the camp suddenly lost their nerve and bolted and ran for their lives.

"Again!"

Over and over Sutter's cannon boomed, and when at last the firing ended, a heavy stillness descended on the banks of the Sacramento and the American.

"I guess," Sutter said, "that will serve as a warning to these people that I mean business."

Morgan saw three Indians in a tule canoe paddle furiously down the river, outracing the schooners. He could hear the ridiculing laughter of the ship's crew. Overhead, he heard the cry of wild geese that the cannon had flushed from the tules alongshore; the birds circled for altitude, then beat their way east toward the majestic Sierra Nevada Mountains.

"All right, there are supplies to hump up that hill and a fort to build!" the captain shouted. "Let's get to work!"

Morgan, unwilling to release his Hawken rifle, reached for a heavy box.

"No, no!" Sutter snapped, grabbing his rifle and pulling it away. "You saw the effect of my cannon. The Indians are afraid of us—like children. We have nothing to fear from them, Mr. Beck! Leave your rifle here or you will be worthless today."

Morgan hesitated, then carefully leaned his rifle against the trunk of a cottonwood tree before lifting a box and starting up the hill. In a thousand more trips, they might even have everything in place by sundown and be ready to start chopping down trees and building Sutter's wilderness fort in the morning. As far as Morgan was concerned, that part of the job could not begin a moment too soon.

Later that afternoon, when most of the supplies had been carried up the hill, Sutter ordered their tents to be set up, and he put his Kanaka to work making their traditional grass houses, *hale pili*. The Kanaka were much happier in these accommodations and were expert at using reeds and tules as thatch.

"Mr. Beck?"

"Yes, sir."

"I want you to take that Indian boy I brought and go hunting. It will be your job to keep us well provisioned with meat—not just elk and deer, but also geese, ducks, and whatever else you can bag."

"Yes, sir."

"And, of course, I don't have to tell you to be careful. We were fortunate that there were a few mission Indians to greet us yesterday. You might not be so lucky while out hunting."

Morgan nodded. He understood the dangers completely.

"Listen," Sutter said, clapping him on the shoulder, "as soon as we begin to get some organization and defenses erected up here, I'll make it a point to join you in visiting all the Indian villages. We *must* have their help."

"If they took a mind to it," Morgan said, "they could attack all at once and overrun us easily. It won't take them long to lose their fear of your cannon."

"I know that. But by then I think we'll have a stockade. Good hunting, Mr. Beck! Oh, and one other thing."

"Sir?"

"As you move around, take notes of the country. And especially look for beaver."

"Beaver?"

"Yes. Until we can harvest crops, fur is going to be our main source of income." Sutter frowned at the look of confusion in Morgan's eyes. "Is something wrong?"

"Well, no, sir. It's just that I didn't realize that I was going to be your trapper."

"Well, why not? You told me that your father had taught you how to set traps. I have some ordered. They'll be here when the *Isabella* returns. I'm really counting on you to help me get through the first few years until my orchards and fields, along with the livestock I'm getting, are fully productive."

"Yes, sir."

"I know that you won't let me down, Mr. Beck. I could see that you were a young man of character the moment I set eyes upon you. No wonder your father did not relish the idea of letting you go."

"Thank you."

"Think nothing of it," Sutter replied, dismissing him as he turned to shout orders to the other men.

Morgan's thoughts were whirling as he went to get the Indian boy. Nothing before had been said about being a full-time trapper. He'd supposed the captain had needed him as an interpreter and a builder. Morgan was good with his hands—Eli had taught him to be a fine carpenter—but that line of work had never brought him much satisfaction. Hunting and exploring this wild country was a task much more suited to his liking, but it would also be far more dangerous.

≈ 2 ≈

In the busy weeks that followed, Morgan discovered why his father had been a mountain man and a trapper for so many years. True, the Sierra foothills and valleys were not nearly as spectacular as the Rockies where Eli had hunted and trapped, but this was still wild, largely uncharted country.

Then the thing that Morgan had been dreading happened. On one of his hunts a dozen or so squat, powerful-looking Indians suddenly appeared in a meadow just in front of him. They stared; Morgan stared. The Indians wore only breechclouts made of strips of leather and carried bows and arrows. Two of them were distinguished by the fact that they wore the heads and antlers of deer and held short round sticks instead of bows and arrows.

Morgan wanted to run but knew that would be a terrible mistake, because these hunters were very accurate with their arrows at anything under fifty yards. Furthermore, if he was to survive as Sutter's hunter and trapper, Morgan knew he had to become friends with these people.

He turned to tell his Indian companion to freeze, but it was too late. The boy was already diving headlong into the woods and racing off in the direction of the fort.

Not knowing what else to do, Morgan raised his left hand and mimicked Sutter.

"*Amigo*," he called. "*Mi Amigo!*"

There was a long, heart-pounding silence before one

of the older Indians raised his own hand and repeated, "*Amigo.*"

Morgan nearly sank to his knees with relief until the mission Indian made it clear that he was to follow them. He wasn't pleased, but he mustered up a grin and nodded in agreement.

Falling in with them, Morgan was led across the meadow, then into the pine forest, where they followed a game trail several miles to a stream that Morgan guessed might be a tributary of the American River. The stream was a chain of beaver ponds, and Morgan vowed to return with his traps—if he survived.

After a few miles, the Indians left the stream and stopped at the edge of a huge field ripe with golden wild oats and dotted with massive California oaks, their ancient branches twisted into amazing shapes. One of the Indians suddenly grunted, and everyone dropped to his knees. Morgan did the same.

He followed their eyes toward a handsome buck and two does that had just entered the field of oats and were grazing warily. The hunters separated to creep through the oats and flank their quarry, and the two men wearing deer heads slipped back into the forest and took positions in the thickets so that only their antlers were visible. The deer, perhaps sensing danger, jerked up their heads and stiffened, causing the disguised hunters to begin rubbing their round wooden sticks together.

Morgan suddenly realized the Indians were intent on making the deer think they were safe, because the rubbing sounded very much like a buck sharpening his antlers against the rough bark of a tree. The ruse worked, and the deer resumed their grazing.

Now the drama unfolded very quickly as the hunters hurried through the tall grain. When they were in position, an unspoken signal passed between them and they jumped up, unleashing a swarm of arrows.

One doe dropped instantly, two arrows through her heart and lungs. The buck was the main target, and he ran only twenty or thirty feet before he staggered and collapsed, his neck and forequarters pincushioned. The second doe leapt into the air, an arrow in her shoulder, and raced straight at Morgan, who instinctively raised his .50-caliber Hawken and fired.

Over the roar of his rifle and through a puff of billowing smoke, Morgan saw a rose blossom in the center of the animal's chest just as it cartwheeled and lay quivering in death. But the Indians did not look at the doe—they stared at him and at the big Hawken rifle, and they did not stop staring until the echo of his rifle shot fled into the Sierra foothills.

Morgan shifted uncomfortably. He wasn't sure whether or not he'd made a terrible mistake, and he dropped to one knee and quickly reloaded, concentrating on the act instead of the Indians.

When he finished, he saw the Indians were dressing out the buck and the doe they'd killed. Seeing no harm in dressing out his own doe, Morgan drew his Green River knife and quickly completed the task. Then he picked up the animal and dropped it on his broad shoulders before waiting to see what would happen next.

"Come, amigo," the mission Indian said, looking at him with new respect.

Morgan followed them on up the stream, noting how his rifle shot had sent all the beaver into hiding. No matter. If he survived this experience and made friends with these people, he would return many times until all the beaver were trapped and pelted.

It was almost an hour before they came within sight of an Indian village of perhaps a hundred men, women, and children.

Morgan paused to take in the unfamiliar scene. Funny—until this very moment, he had not even thought of Indians as a people, with their own homes, families, and society.

These were Miwok Indians and they lived in small, dome-shaped houses, several of which were in various stages of construction, no doubt in preparation for winter. Morgan thought it rather ingenious the way these Indians dug a shallow circular pit and then bent slender poles and tied them over the center of the pit with vines. Next, willows were woven tightly through the poles so that the house looked like a big upside down wicker basket except for the smoke hole in its center. Morgan saw bare-breasted women weaving tule mats to place over the willow supports before everything was finished off with a covering of wet clay.

A band of happy women and children entered camp from the east, carrying large woven reed baskets filled with acorns. Morgan had heard that the acorn was the staple diet of these people, and he had once attempted to eat one but found it too bitter. He wondered if these people tasted things differently than white people or if somehow they had discovered a way to make the acorn palatable.

A young Indian woman paused and unexpectedly gave Morgan a radiant smile. Surprised, he smiled back, and the woman blushed.

"Come!" the old man ordered in Spanish as he led Morgan through the village to the entrance of a very large and thickly thatched lodge.

They entered the lodge with Morgan still carrying his doe draped across his shoulders. It was dim inside and the air was heavy with smoke. At one end of the lodge, Morgan saw a gathering of men sitting cross-legged around a fire. They stared at him, but nothing moved except an old, arthritic dog that came over to sniff and then lick at the congealing blood on the doe's legs.

"There, sit," the mission Indian ordered, pointing to a place behind the circle of elders. Morgan eased the doe to the ground, and when the dog began to worry it, one of the elders threw a wooden bowl and hit the dog in the head. It yelped, ducked its tail between its legs, and crabbed out the door.

Morgan started to move closer to the circle of elders, but a powerful young Indian with close-cropped hair and a bent nose growled in anger and, waving his hands threateningly, indicated that Morgan was to give him the Hawken.

Morgan hesitated, then realized he had no choice but to hand the rifle over. It wasn't enough. The Indian sneered and pointed to Morgan's Green River knife.

"Uh-uh," Morgan said in Spanish, shaking his head.

"This stays with me. You're all carrying knives, so I've no advantage."

The young Indian flushed with anger. *"Knife!"* he barked.

"No," Morgan repeated. The knife had been a special gift from his father and was his most prized possession. It had finished off a raging grizzly bear up in the Yellowstone country and more than one Blackfoot warrior.

Morgan placed his hand on the bone handle of the knife. "I keep," he told all the Indians.

The young Miwok warrior snarled and grabbed for the knife. Morgan latched onto the Indian's wrist, pulled it across his body and gave the warrior a hip throw exactly as Eli had taught him. The warrior crashed to the hard dirt floor, grunting as the air was knocked from his lungs. Morgan tore his Hawken from the Indian's grasp. The Indian reached for his knife, but one of the others shouted, *"No, Tiok!"*

There was more said, but Morgan didn't understand because it was in the tribal tongue. All he knew was that the young warrior's face was twisted with hatred as he staggered out of the lodge.

Morgan picked up his rifle and was careful to keep its barrel pointed to the ground. As he turned back to the elders he was shaking in his boots but trying his level best to appear calm. Eli had always told him that friendly Indians were supposed to offer strangers a peace pipe, but these Indians showed no indication that would be the case.

"Mi amigo," he said, raising his bloodstained hand.

The tribal elders continued to stare, so Morgan opened his pack and held up Sutter's strings of cheap trade beads and several colorful handkerchiefs that he carried for just such an emergency. The Indians were reserved in taking the gifts, but as soon as they did, Morgan could tell that they were very pleased because each in his turn bowed politely and repeated, *"Gracias, Señor."*

Thank God for the Spanish padres!

Morgan had one of Sutter's good trade knives in his pack, but he decided to keep it hidden until he knew which of these tribal elders was the chief.

"I come in peace," he began in Spanish. "I come as your friend on behalf of Captain John Sutter, who is building a settlement between the two big rivers to the south."

Morgan elaborated about Sutter, making him sound like the second coming of Christ except to emphasize that the captain would not hesitate to use his cannon against his enemies.

"We want to be your friends," he told them slowly, waiting as his words were translated to the few who spoke only Miwok. "Captain Sutter will pay you for the help of your young braves."

One of the oldest climbed to his feet. "I am Chief Anashe. How much will the captain pay?"

It was such an obvious question that Morgan inwardly cursed himself for not having a ready answer. But the truth of it was that Sutter did not like to talk about money—especially his own, which was in such short supply. Morgan knew that the captain had promised to pay each of his Kanaka an arranged sum if they would remain with him for three years before returning to the Sandwich Islands. However, he doubted that the captain would be willing to pay these Indians anywhere near what he would pay the skilled Kanaka.

"I don't know," he admitted. "You would have to ask Captain Sutter—but he is a very generous man."

"We will go tomorrow," the chief said, his eyes shifting to the carcass of the doe. "We will feast plenty now."

That night they did feast. Morgan was given a place of honor beside Chief Anashe. The Indians dressed themselves in feathers and brightly colored quill headbands, shell necklaces, and deerskin aprons. Some of the men wore beautiful feather capes and vermilion quills, while the young women decorated their hair with strips of soft buckskin and pretty beads made of pink and gold manesite. Their skirts were decorated with seeds patterned in intricate designs of many colors.

Chief Anashe explained that his people had songs for all occasions. They had songs for their ancestors, songs for good fishing, and songs for good spirits and a good harvest of acorns.

"This is the acorn dance," Anashe said, and then fell silent so that Morgan could watch and listen to the music.

To Morgan's way of thinking, the music was damned awful. Several of the Miwok used sticks split down the center to slap in their palms with a cracking sound, while other Indians played wooden flutes. Others compounded the racket by blowing into whistles of bone or shaking rattles made of hollow gourds filled with shells and stones.

What was enjoyable, if it could have been heard over the flutes, rattles, and sticks, was the way everyone sang, even Chief Anashe. And the acorn dance was a very entertaining pantomime. Around and around the campfire, young women danced with their woven baskets, pretending all the while to search for oak trees. When the imaginary oak trees were discovered, the young women squealed with pleasure, dropped their baskets, and then pretended to climb the trees and shake their branches. Watching their lush breasts jiggle and glisten with perspiration, Morgan felt his cheeks warm. He glanced sideways at the chief, hoping no one noticed how the bare-chested women excited him.

Now children rushed into the dance, pretending to gather the fallen acorns and throw them into the baskets. The women mimed climbing down, and everyone made the movements of carrying the baskets back to the village, bending as if the baskets were very heavy. All of the Miwok seated around the dance circle thought this acting very funny, and Morgan found it impossible not to join their laughter.

When the acorn harvesters finally reached the imaginary village, older women stepped into the dance, acting out how they ground the acorns with mortar and pestle, then poured boiling water over the acorn meal, which Morgan supposed might rob it of its bitter taste. The music stopped to a signal that the song was ended, and a shy little girl of about ten brought the chief and Morgan a plate of venison and a whitish paste.

"What is this?" Morgan asked, indicating the paste.

Chief Anashe looked at him as if he were daft. "Eat,"

he said with a grunt, using his fingers to scoop up the paste, then lapping it up with obvious enjoyment.

Morgan did the same and decided it was acorn meal—with none of the bitterness he would have expected. In fact, it was delicious. When he smiled in approval, the little girl clapped her hands together happily and danced off to rejoin her parents.

"Good," Morgan said in Spanish, presenting the chief with the trade knife.

Chief Anashe was very pleased with the knife. He neatly sliced away a piece of venison and popped it into his mouth. "Very good, my friend!"

The music started again, along with a new dance. Morgan used his Green River knife to cut his own venison. In doing so, he could not help but think that Eli would have approved of the way he was conducting himself and that he had courageously refused to hand over his knife to Tiok, who was even now glaring at him across the campfire, his eyes hotter than the campfire's coals.

"The padres said that Christ the Jesus gave us fire, or maybe it was his God the Father, I forget," Anashe said, chewing with gusto. "But we know different."

Morgan looked up with a question in his eyes.

"Yes. Do you want to know how we got fire?"

Morgan nodded, his mouth full of venison.

Chief Anashe raised his hand, and the rattles, whistles, and flutes fell silent. The acorn dancers came to gather around, and their bodies steamed as they leaned forward in anticipation.

"A long time ago," Anashe began, "maybe even before Jesus the Christ, our people had no fire. Only Kareya, who helped your God make the world and all things, had fire."

The chief paused to reflect. "For reasons the People cannot understand, Kareya gave fire only to two old women who would not give it to the People."

"Two old women?"

The chief nodded solemnly. "But our good friend, Coyote, said he would help us steal the fire. So he went to the lodge of the old women and asked if he could come inside to get warm. They did not want to do this at first, but he began to howl, so they let him in through their back door. Coyote began to warm himself. Then one of the People rushed to the front door. When the old women tried to chase him away, Coyote grabbed a burning stick and ran out the back door."

Anashe gazed thoughtfully at the fire, the reflection of dancing flames in his dark eyes. No one in the village said a word, and they were patient because they knew the story.

"What happened then?" Morgan finally asked.

"The old women saw that they had been tricked. They chased Coyote, who ran and ran until he grew tired and gave the burning stick to Mountain Lion, who ran even faster."

Morgan wanted to make sure he understood. "With the two old women still in chase?"

"Yes," said Anashe. "They were very strong and fast old women—great runners."

"Oh." Morgan had forgotten his food, though he was still very hungry. He could not help but smile and lean forward a little.

"And so when even Mountain Lion grew tired," the chief continued, "he gave the fire to other animals, but they also tired. The old women almost caught each of them until the burning stick was at last given to Frog."

The chief used his new trade knife to dig meat out from between his teeth. He looked at Morgan and said, "But as you know, Frog cannot run."

"So they caught Frog?"

"No. Frog swallowed the burning stick and jumped into a river, holding his breath in order to keep the fire alive. The old women were very angry. They also jumped into the water and grabbed Frog's tail, pulling it off."

"So," Morgan said, "that is why frogs have no tails today."

Anashe dipped his chin in agreement. "Frog swam underwater until he could hold his breath no longer. Then he came to the surface and spat fire onto a floating log. The fire stayed in the wood, and that is why the People always get fire when they rub two sticks together."

The Miwok all began to clap their hands and make

music to show their approval of this ancient story, and
Morgan grinned and wolfed down more meat.

"It is a better story than the padres could tell, eh?"
the chief asked.

"Yes, much better."

Anashe was pleased. Wiping grease from his face with
the back of his forearm, he belched and stood up, then
waved his new knife toward the fire and began to dance.

Morgan was offered some more acorn meal, and he
did not decline. He could hardly wait to return with
these good people to Sutter and then, later, tell his
father of this adventure. Maybe it wasn't equal to killing
a grizzly bear with a knife, but the story of the fire,
Coyote, Frog, and the fast old ladies was one that he
would never forget.

Early the next morning, Chief Anashe and four of the
elders joined Morgan in returning to Sutter's fort. It
was a long hike under a hot sun, but the Miwok leaders
seemed tireless in spite of their ages. Morgan could not
help but compare them to his own father and feel a
sense of sadness.

Damn the consumption and the cold, foggy weather
of Yerba Buena! Soon, soon, the fort would be strong
enough to protect his mother and then Eli would see
the wisdom of this dry, sunny climate.

When they came within view of the fort, Chief
Anashe and his friends were astonished. Morgan himself was impressed that so much had been accomplished
in the few weeks since they had landed.

Fields had been cleared and prepared for spring
planting of crops and orchards, and there were cattle
and horses being tended by several Mexican vaqueros.
But the eyes of everyone were pulled to Sutter's first
permanent structure, a long one-story adobe building
which contained a blacksmith shop, a kitchen, and
Sutter's own office and sleeping quarters. The roof was
made of tules thatched by the Kanaka, whose skill
elicited considerable admiration among the Miwok Indians.

"Well, well!" Captain Sutter said in a loud voice

when he saw them. "What a wonderful surprise! Mr. Beck, who are these fine gentlemen?"

Morgan made the introductions, starting first with Chief Anashe. "They have a big village just about fifteen miles to the east of us on a fork of the American River."

"I see. I see. Do they speak Spanish?"

"Most do. I did not ask them in which of the Spanish missions they might have learned it."

"That's not important."

Sutter, ignoring the other Indians, beamed at the chief. "Chief Anashe, I see that Mr. Beck has presented you with one of my trade knives. Very good steel, that." He had been practicing his Spanish since his arrival, and it was already considerably improved.

Anashe nodded very formally.

"Mr. Beck, why don't we escort the chief into my office and get right down to business?"

"What about something to eat first? We've been walking since early morning."

"Are they hungry?"

"We all are," Morgan said.

"Very well, we'll eat first and then get down to business."

It was late afternoon before everyone had eaten his fill. After bringing Chief Anashe to his office, Sutter reposed himself in a leather chair that he had bought in Monterey, while Morgan and the chief sat on a rough wooden bench.

"I need your men," Sutter announced without the courtesy of small talk. "I need as many strong workers as you can provide, and in return I will pay you with many gifts." He reached into his desk and pulled out his trade goods, holding the samples up one at a time. "Good steel knives, red handkerchiefs, beads, mirrors, and many other things of great value."

Morgan looked sideways at the chief. The old man was nodding his head, and it was clear that he wanted the gifts, which he stared at with longing. For some reason, this depressed Morgan. The gifts were not worth more than a day's labor, not even the knives,

which were of decidedly inferior quality to the one he
had given the chief.

"Tell him that he will receive two of each of these
gifts if he can provide twenty-five warriors for one
month."

"Twenty-five!" Morgan lowered his voice. "But Captain, altogether that stuff isn't worth—"

"Tell him, Mr. Beck!"

Morgan blinked. Sutter had never before spoken to
him in that tone of voice. It hurt.

"Yes, sir." Morgan translated, and to his credit Anashe
held up all the fingers on one of his little hands.

"He wants five of each."

"Yes, yes," Sutter snipped, "all right, then, I will
give him three. *Tres*, Chief Anashe. *Tres*."

Anashe grunted impassively. "*Quatro*."

"No, too much. *Tres*."

Anashe shrugged his bare shoulders and climbed to
his feet, indicating that there was nothing further to
discuss.

"Where is he going?"

"I guess he rejected your terms, Captain," Morgan
said, trying hard to disguise his pleasure at this show of
Anashe's independence.

"All right! All right. *Quatro!*"

Anashe was at the door. He turned around and
grinned, and then he said, "*Gracias, Señor Sutter.*"

Morgan and Sutter watched the chief as he walked
out the door. The little old warrior paused for a moment
to admire once more the Kanaka's fine job of roof
thatching before he continued on to rejoin his people.
There was a quick discussion among the Miwok before
they turned and waved good-bye.

"Is that it?" Sutter demanded. "They're just leaving?"

"Looks like."

"Go after them. Stay with them and make sure that
those twenty-five workers are brought to me at once."

"Yes, sir," Morgan said. "But I doubt that we will be
back for a few days."

"Just be back soon," the captain said. "There's a lot of
work we can still do before the winter rains. We've got

a mountain of firewood to be cut and more fields to be cleared. We need to build pens, sheds, and more shelters for the men as well as the livestock."

Morgan had his doubts about whether the Indians were going to be very productive. Those able to do a full day's work would be too young to remember the skills taught by the old Spanish padres. These Indians were hunters, fishermen, and gatherers of food.

"They will need constant and close supervision," the captain was saying as he hurried along beside Morgan. "I know that they'll barely earn their keep at first, but I consider that an investment."

Morgan stopped, because a question was very much on his mind. "What if the younger Indians refuse to come?"

"They won't," Sutter said. "They must do whatever their chief commands."

"Is that right?"

"It is. A chief cannot force them into battle, but he can order them to do whatever work he chooses. I told you before, Mr. Beck. I *know* Indians."

"I don't remember my father telling me that things worked among the Indian peoples that way."

"Your father, with all due respect," Sutter said patiently, "is not quite the final authority on Indians. Besides, I don't believe the customs of the Rocky Mountain Ute Indians necessarily reflect the customs and ways of these California Digger Indians."

"Digger Indians, sir?"

"Just a term used to describe them, because they sometimes dig for their food. Grubs, roots, things like that. These are not the proud Plains Indians racing after buffalo on mustang ponies. They are grubbers and diggers."

"Maybe so," Morgan said defensively, "but they tell damn good stories and they know how to hunt deer."

"Just run along and bring them back. Tomorrow or the next day, if possible. I need men to help build a road up from the American River. I'm expecting a boatload of fresh supplies from our new neighbors. We

must began to think in terms of commerce, Mr. Beck.
Speaking of which, where are your beaver pelts?"

"I left them where I dropped them, and our little
Indian friend ran away."

"You left them?" Sutter was aghast. The traps were
very expensive and had been shipped all the way from
Philadelphia.

"I'll find them without any difficulty," Morgan said.

"See that you do."

"I need someone to replace the boy."

Sutter frowned. "I suppose you do. Anyone in
particular?"

"Yes, Pablo Gutierrez."

Sutter was not pleased. Gutierrez was one of his best
men, a muleteer who had been with him since his visit
to Santa Fe.

"Why?" Sutter asked, anxiously watching as the Miwok
disappeared in the distance.

"I trust Pablo to back me in a pinch," Morgan said
bluntly. "And he's the only one I trust."

"Outside of myself, of course."

"Of course," Morgan said, quickly realizing his mistake.

"Dare you wait until he can be found and provisioned?"
Sutter asked.

"Don't worry," Morgan assured the captain. "I can
follow Indian tracks, but even that won't be necessary.
I know where they live."

Sutter nodded and hurried off to find Pablo Gutierrez.
Morgan smiled. He and the young Mexican had hit it
off right from the start. Pablo was bright, resourceful,
and had ventured out several times with Morgan in
search of food. It was then that he'd proven himself an
excellent shot and had admitted to being a horseman of
some skill.

Yes, Morgan thought, *Pablo will do just fine.*

≈ 3 ≈

They dropped the last pack of beaver pelts into the rowboat, and Morgan straightened, his gaze rising. Distant thunder growled, and moments earlier a timid sunrise had revealed a sky dark with the threat of rain. Along the American River, the water-loving cottonwood trees shivered, their naked branches uplifted in sharp profile against a lid of rain clouds.

Pablo was big for a Mexican, and tough, but the strain of carrying hundred-pound packs of beaver pelts down from Sutter's New Helvetia had him winded.

"She sits pretty low in the water, Señor Beck."

"I know," Morgan replied, stepping into the boat and placing the oars in their locks. "Give me a push."

Pablo hesitated. "But not so low that I could not come along to help."

"You don't want to help," Morgan said with amusement. "All you want to do is find a pretty Señorita in Yerba Buena."

"*Eee-iii*," Pablo yipped as he clasped his hands behind him and did a little Mexican jig. "Eez true!"

Morgan laughed. In the months that he and Pablo had trapped and hunted together, they had become very close friends. Despite his lack of experience, Pablo was a good man to break trail with. The Mexican was always cheerful and quick to lend a hand or a smile, no matter how miserable the circumstances. Morgan had gotten Sutter to buy Pablo a Hawken just like his own.

"You watch out for yourself, eh, Señor?" Pablo said,

his smile dissolving with worry. "Those furs, they are worth plenty."

"I know that," Morgan said, unfolding an oilskin to cover the pelts so that they would not tempt anyone. "I'll be back soon after the first of the year."

"Feliz Navidad," Pablo said, bending to push the rowboat off the shore.

"Same to you," Morgan called as the heavily laden rowboat drifted sluggishly into the current. The American River was very low this winter, but Morgan did not have to worry, because his boat was flat-bottomed and, even carrying hundreds of pounds of beaver pelts and his own considerable weight, it drafted less than a foot.

Locking the oars that he had carved himself, and turning the boat that he had built of pine felled by Sutter's Indian workers, Morgan dipped and pulled hard. He felt the boat edge into the strong current. Morgan knew that he had a good hundred-mile run down to Yerba Buena, but it was only about ninety miles to home. Later, when he had navigated the boat through the treacherous confluence of the Sacramento and American rivers, Morgan rowed out into the main channel, traveling much faster than a man could walk.

Glancing up at the sun, which was just peeking over the snow-capped Sierra Nevada Mountains, Morgan said aloud, "If all goes well, I'll be home for supper."

But an hour later his hands were beginning to sting. More recently accustomed to the Hawken than to an oar, his palms would blister unless he used his scarf to wrap the oars. By noon a rising westerly wind from the Pacific was stirring whitecaps on the river and blowing cold spray. Thoroughly miserable, Morgan kept rowing, his hands locked on strips of wet scarf. When lightning split the sky and ignited a tree just a few hundred yards downriver, Morgan knew that it was foolish to keep rowing, but he was too eager to see his mother and father to quit. Soon a hard, freezing rain began to pelt his face, and he tugged his cap down low over his eyes.

"You ain't going to stop me!" he yelled up at the pouring rain. "No, sir! I've already spent too damn many nights in a cold, wet camp!"

Shivering, singing old mountain man songs taught to him by Eli, Morgan reminded himself over and over that this was easy compared to the hardships Eli had endured on rivers like the Yellowstone, the Green, and the Snake. Up in that northern country, instead of this rain, snow or sleet would be blowing hard in his face and tears would freeze to his cheeks. Morgan knew this because Eli had told him of a time when he and a mountain man named Seth Travis had rafted four hundred pounds of prime beaver pelts out of the wild Yellowstone country after their canoe had been destroyed by Indians.

All day long Morgan rowed with stoic determination, and the rain kept falling so hard that he did not quite realize that sundown was upon him until he blindly drove the bow of his rowboat into a half-submerged log. For one heart-stopping moment, Morgan felt the log roll underneath as the rowboat canted hard to starboard. He threw his weight to the port side and barely averted being swamped. The boat tore free, but a jet of water spurted up between the decking planks like blood from a ruptured artery.

Morgan tore the sodden strips of scarf from his oar handles and pinched them into the cracks with the blade of his knife, then rowed hard for shore. Crashing through a tangle of thickets, Morgan shielded his eyes and saw that he'd plowed into a high, steep bank that dropped into the water.

He cussed and backed the boat off, then pulled hard with one oar and raced downriver again, knowing that he was in danger of hitting another submerged log and capsizing. Dear God, if he did that and lost the pelts, Captain Sutter would go crazy; these pelts were going to wipe out some long-overdue debts.

Morgan dropped an oar and shielded his eyes, searching for a good landing. When he at last found one, he rowed furiously, bringing the boat hard onto the shore. Morgan grabbed his Hawken and pack, lifted them high overhead, and jumped onto the beach. He tossed his rifle and gear up onto the bank and strained until the boat was completely out of the river then tied it to a tree. He removed Sutter's pelts and lugged them up to high ground. Then he covered them with the oilskin and lashed the cargo down tight.

Lightning speared an oak less than fifty yards away, and Morgan spun around, covering his eyes and seeing flashes of red and yellow. Thinking himself blinded by the flash, he felt panic seize him. He dropped to one knee and held on to the bow of his boat, blinking a mixture of tears and rainwater until he could see again.

God, he was miserable! Even in the pouring rain he could smell lightning-seared wood; cannonading thunder made the sand underfoot undulate like a snake. Morgan rolled the boat over himself, his Hawken, and his few belongings. The rain stopped beating at his eyes. The cutting wind and river spray no longer stung his cheeks. He sighed. He was freezing but was on high enough ground to be safe unless the river flooded its banks completely, and even then he would have at least a few minutes' warning, enough to climb and save the pelts, if not this leaky boat.

"Sleep," he told himself as his hand groped for his rifle, found it, and clutched the cold steel barrel. "There is nothing to do now but try to sleep."

Sleep, however, proved elusive. The storm intensified in the night, and the rowboat actually began to rock. Morgan feared it might be tossed into the air, so he locked his arms under the seat board and held on tightly.

All night long he could feel water rivering down from higher ground, and when dawn finally peeked under the rowboat, Morgan was shaking violently as if he had the ague. When he tried to push the boat off him, he found it to be a surprisingly difficult task.

But it had stopped raining, and Morgan could see cracks of blue in the otherwise dark sky. He fumbled in his pockets and found some jerked venison and a couple of dried apples. Having no appetite but knowing that he must eat, he chewed slowly, gazing out at the dark, rough water while attempting to recognize a landmark along the shoreline.

Where the hell was he? Had the headwind blowing

up from the west slowed him so that he was still on San
Pablo Bay? Visibility had been so poor all yesterday
afternoon that it was certainly possible. Morgan could
not tell. He was on a bay, that much was plain, but
whether it was San Pablo or San Francisco, he could
not be certain.

When he finished eating, Morgan felt sick, and while
he dragged the boat down to the water he threw up
violently. Collapsing to his knees, he waited, shudder-
ing and retching dryly until he could stand and go back
for the furs and his own things.

For the first time in his life, the water appeared
mean and threatening. Morgan dragged the furs down
to the boat and loaded a pack on board before he
remembered the leak. Angry at himself for his forgetful-
ness, he unloaded the heavy pack and spent a half hour
caulking between the decking planks with pitch carried
for just such emergencies. Thank God for Eli drumming
that lesson into him from his earliest years.

It seemed to take Morgan forever to reload the furs
and row onto the bay. Without a river's current, he had
to work for every mile. Staying close to the safety of the
north shore, he fought off recurring bouts of nausea and
tried to lose himself in a rowing rhythm that had, over
the years, become second nature.

Morgan lost track of time and space. He just rowed.
The sky never really opened up, and the sun never
dried his clothes or warmed his flesh.

"Morgan!" a voice called. "Morgan!"

He shook himself from a dull reverie and looked up
to see his father standing on their dock. Morgan stopped
rowing. His teeth were chattering like dice and his
hands were ice talons. He tried to raise his hand and
wave, but the talons refused to release the oars. Numbly,
Morgan pulled for their dock.

The bad weather did not clear for two weeks, and
Morgan's fever departed with it, leaving him weak and
anxious about Eli.

"If you are so worried about your father," Mama
Estella said, watching him stare out the window toward

the harbor, "then you should go down and wait on the dock. He will be back today, or in a few days at most."

"I shouldn't have let him take Sutter's furs off to market all by himself," Morgan lamented. "There are too many men who would try to rob, even kill him for the money they'll bring."

"You were not strong enough to go," she said. "Your father wanted to do this. He will be all right. He has many friends in Yerba Buena. They will not let him come to harm."

Morgan could have said that his father had many enemies, too. Being outspoken and crusty, Eli had insulted pretty nearly everyone except a few merchants and Mexican officials who had the authority to close his business.

He sat down heavily on his bed and stared out at the bay. "Mama, I want you and Pa to come back with me to Sacramento next spring. By then we will have shelter for you and maybe even a cabin."

She was mending a canvas sail, and now she glanced up at him. "And what would we do in such a wild place?"

"It isn't wild anymore. It is civilized."

"Civilized. Is there a priest at this fort? Or even a chapel?"

"No, but—"

"Then it is *not* civilized," she said. "And besides, your father doesn't like Captain Sutter."

"He's a better man than we first gave him credit for. You should have seen his courage the day we landed and he was surrounded on the bank of the American River by all those Indians. It was one of the bravest things I've ever seen. I tell you, I wouldn't have done it, and I'm sure Pa wouldn't, either."

"It sounds stupid to me," she told him, not looking up from her work. "Stupidity is never to be admired."

"The captain is anything but stupid, Mama. He's a builder, and you should see his fort."

She was not impressed. "I have heard that he owes General Vallejo and everyone else much money. I have heard that your captain is always writing letters asking for things."

He had often seen the captain writing these letters, pleading night after night for goods, supplies, and stock—all on credit. The amazing thing was that the captain usually got what he asked for from his already impatient creditors.

"In the spring we will have a good crop. And come harvest time, the captain will pay everyone off in full. Why, the furs that I brought out alone will net us more than three thousand dollars! And the captain is giving me ten percent."

Now Mama Estella looked up. "And you do one hundred percent of the work! So why is this such a good thing? The beaver are there for anyone to trap."

Morgan had to admit that he had asked himself the same question a time or two. But he'd come to terms with the arrangement.

"It's fair because the captain's name helps me with the Indians. If I was just out there myself, or even with Pa, we might not be so lucky. Besides, Sutter is the man with the trade goods. He's the one the Indians respect. You should have seen the way they ran the first time we fired those cannon! I thought those Indians were going to die of fright. They took off like a covey of quail!"

Mama Estella did not find the image of terrified Indians scattering the least bit amusing. Looking at her stepson, she said, "I do not think that your father will go to Sacramento to work for a man he dislikes."

"But it isn't even like working for someone," Morgan argued. "I'm always free to come and go as I please. No one tells me what to do. As long as I provide the fort with fresh meat and trap the beaver, the captain is more than happy. And the share I'll get from this bunch of pelts is more money than Pa and I made all last summer. With Pa helping me, we could make twice as much, maybe even more."

Mama Estella put her mending down. "Don't you see that your father is too old and stiff to work cold rivers anymore? His lungs are bad."

Morgan was stung and shamed by his thoughtlessness. And yet, he knew that Eli's life would be longer and better in Sacramento. "You are right, Mama. And of course Pa can't do what he used to do with Jim Bridger and the other mountain men. But he could still get along pretty well if he could breath better. And I wouldn't expect him to go hiking over any mountains or set traps in freezing streams. Just having him along would be enough. He could show me things that I'd never learn otherwise." Morgan studied blisters just now healing on the palms of his hands. "And . . . and he'd feel better about himself, too. He wouldn't have to be kissin' up to Governor Alvarado and his friends anymore. Sutter wouldn't bother him none. He'd be a free man."

"So," she said, "there is no church. Are there any other women? Would I be the only one?"

"There are two Kanaka women, and we see Indian women at the fort more and more. The captain has even got some of them working."

She looked down at her mending very quickly. "I do not want to work for that man, either."

"But why? He's generous to his friends. He's even mentioned how he could use a good woman who could cook and clean. It would be easy for you."

Mama's head snapped up. "Did you tell him I would work for him?"

"No! But I thought maybe you could work a little, and perhaps being with other people would make you feel better than sitting around watching Pa cough his lungs out."

"I feel good here."

"But Pa doesn't. Can't you see that the best thing we could ever do for him would be to leave this foggy coast? Can't you see that he needs to live where it is dry?"

"So, you are a doctor now?"

"Of course not!" Morgan pushed himself to his feet. "But Pa did see a doctor once, and that's exactly what he told him—go where it's dry. That's why Pa came to

California, only he wasn't supposed to live by the ocean."

"I am tired of all this talk," she said. "Go wait on the dock for your father. If he does not come today, he will be here tomorrow or the next day."

Morgan went outside and hiked slowly down to their dock. He stared out at the bay, feeling the cold wind brush his slightly feverish face. He looked back left and right; there were no neighbors in sight. Someday there might be, but Morgan doubted this land would ever be worth much. The climate was too cold and damp to raise crops, and the soil was too rocky. Not enough sunshine. But inland . . . now, that was another story.

Eli did not return from Yerba Buena that day, or the next, or even the next. In fact, he was gone almost a week before he sailed his little boat up the bay and wearily climbed onto the dock.

"Where have you been so long?" Morgan asked, trying to hide his worry.

"Monterey."

"But—"

"I couldn't get a fair price for the fur here," Eli explained, furling the sail and securing his sailboat. "They were trying to scalp me, so I figured that I had damn little to lose by going to Monterey."

"How much did you get?"

Eli shoved his hands deep into his coat pockets and looked away. "Not as much as you expected. Two thousand."

"Is that all?" Morgan's heart sank. Not only would he get a hundred dollars less than expected, but Sutter would not be able to pay even his most pressing bills. "Pa, what happened?"

"The buyers didn't like the fur. They said it was too short. You shouldn't have mixed the shorter-furred summer pelts in with what you took after it got cold. The buyers discounted everything." Eli dropped a hand on Morgan's shoulder. "It was bad timing all the way around. The Russian American Company had just sailed in with a couple of thousand otter pelts, and next to them the beaver didn't look too prime. I did the best I could."

"Sure you did," Morgan said. "And our cut of two hundred dollars is still not too bad, is it?"

"Hell, no!" Eli grinned and removed a packet of bills from the inside of his shirt. "Here. Carrying all this money makes me nervous."

Morgan took the money. "I guess we ought to have a celebration, even if we did come up a little short, huh?"

"You're damn right. I—" Whatever Eli was about to say was lost as he exploded with a violent, wrenching cough.

Morgan had to look away. He couldn't stand to see the way his father's face went pale and his eyes bulged as he gasped for breath. But soon—next spring at the latest—he was going to get both of his parents away from this dismal, chill bay.

"Come on," he said, taking his father's arm, "let's get you up to the house and beside the fire."

Eli nodded. Shaking visibly, he said, "Maybe you were right about getting away from the coast. Maybe next spring Mama and I will come up to Sacramento to visit."

Morgan grinned. "You just wait and see what the captain and his Kanaka will have accomplished by spring. Fields will be planted and calves, lambs, and foals will be dancing in the sunshine. And the heat will bake your lungs dry, Pa. You'll feel as frisky as a colt in springtime yourself."

"We'll see," Eli said. "There's still Mama Estella to convince."

"If I have to cut the wood and build it myself, I'll have a chapel. Next summer the captain is returning to Monterey to get legal title to the lands around his fort. It'll be a year, and he'll be eligible for Mexican citizenship. And he'll ask the governor to give me a land grant, too."

"And you'll build your mama a chapel before you even build a cabin?" Eli asked, forcing a stricken grin.

"Yeah, if that's what it takes."

They both managed a chuckle.

"Sorry about the poor fur prices, son."

"It wasn't your fault. Let's get you warm. Hungry?"

"I could use a feed." Eli looked at his tall son's own pinched face. "You're looking a little wolfish yourself. Ain't the captain feeding you well enough?"

"He sets a pretty good table, but me and a fella named Pablo Gutierrez—we eat out in the woods mostly, or with the Indians."

"Then no wonder you're too lean," Eli said as they moved slowly the rest of the way up to their cabin.

Once they were inside, Mama Estella wasted no time in getting food on her stove and feeding her husband. Later that evening Eli surprised Mama Estella with the gift of a silver crucifix. It was beautiful, and Mama's eyes shone with admiration.

"Thank you," she whispered. "I have never had one such as this!"

Eli beamed. "I bought it in Monterey. I think it once belonged to some old padre. Maybe Padre Serra himself, who knows?"

Mama stroked it gently with a forefinger, then made the sign of the cross. "It is so heavy."

"Solid silver," Eli told her.

"But it must have cost so—"

"Just never you mind that," Eli said, cutting off her argument. "I haven't given you much, and you've never asked for anything. But when I saw this in a silversmith's window, I knew you were meant to have it."

Mama Estella threw her arms around her husband, and tears rolled down her cheeks. Looking over her shoulder, Eli winked at Morgan. "I got a little surprise for you, too."

"Sir?"

"Well," Eli confessed, "since I was in Monterey, I took it upon myself to pay court to the governor. He was not in his office but at home, and when I went there, I was greeted by a very pretty young señorita."

Morgan felt his heart jump.

Eli winked. "This gift is from Señorita Rosalinda Navarro. You must have made quite an impression on her the night you and Sutter visited the governor's casa."

Morgan tried to hide his embarrassment. He had never told his father and mother about getting drunk on the beach and almost humiliating his family. "I suppose I did."

"Here," Eli said, reaching into his pocket and drawing out a little packet wrapped in paper and tied with a red ribbon.

Morgan took the packet and stared at it, remembering Rosalinda with a mixture of shame and excitement. "Did she . . . did she say anything?"

"Not much. Only that she and her uncle, Don Mariano Vallejo, have invited you to visit them in Sonoma." Eli glanced at his wife. "I got the feeling that our boy is a little special to the señorita."

Mama Estella clutched her new crucifix tightly. "Maybe it is a sign from heaven of good things."

"I think I'll go for a walk," Morgan said, shoving the packet into his coat pocket.

"But you must eat while the food is hot!" Mama protested.

"Let the boy go. Can't you see he wants to open his present alone?" said Eli. "Probably a letter in there, too. He'll be back soon. Isn't that right, son?"

"Yes, sir."

Morgan hurried down to their rickety dock, not caring if his parents were watching as he tore open the packet. Inside, he found a letter and a beautifully carved ivory sea lion, perfect in every detail. It was drilled and affixed to a leather thong so that it could be worn around the neck.

Morgan tore open the accompanying letter, which read:

Dear Señor Morgan,
I hope that you are feeling better today. I am fine, too, and I thought that you might like this small gift which my uncle received from one of the

Aleut hunters at the Russian Fort Ross. I have several, one a mate to this.

Morgan felt his heart quicken as he read on. Sure enough, Rosalinda was inviting him to visit her at Vallejo's *palacio* in Sonoma during the Christmas holidays. Her last line read:

Your father tells me that you have taken ill. If you are too ill to come, I will try to come and visit you. God speed your recovery. Rosalinda Navarro

Morgan sighed and squeezed the sea lion, oblivious to his painful blisters. He reread the letter over and over until darkness fell across the bay. Rosalinda's sweet voice was music for his ears alone, and the memory of her face and the smell of roses made his senses reel.

Of course he would go visit her! He would never want her to see how poorly he lived here with his good parents. And he would use a part of his two hundred dollars to buy some nice clothes—clothes like Captain Sutter wore to impress officials.

Morgan folded the letter and slipped it into his shirt pocket. He rubbed the smooth bone seal like a good luck charm, and for the first time in his life he could actually visualize a future for himself with wealth and prominence, one in which he owned thousands of acres of good, rich Sacramento land and a big adobe casa with fields of wheat and corn around it and some pens of horses and cattle.

And a beautiful wife. One exactly like the lovely Señorita Rosalinda Navarro.

≈ 4 ≈

Morgan and Eli were working on a thirty-foot sailboat that had been contracted for delivery in Yerba Buena when a supply schooner appeared through the fog, moving up the bay. When the ship drew abreast of Eli's rickety dock, it furled its sails and dropped anchor.

"Now, what do you suppose they want?" Morgan asked.

"I don't know. Maybe they want to buy something."

Morgan recognized one of Sutter's men standing on the forecastle. "More likely they're bound for New Helvetia and have news for me."

A few minutes later a rowboat was lowered and a burly ex-seaman named Ben Dunn came rowing up to their dock.

"Morgan Beck!" he called as soon as the rowboat touched shore. "Captain Sutter wants me to bring you back to the fort."

Morgan set down his hammer and chisel. "I've already told Captain Sutter that I'll be coming back after Christmas."

The man hopped out of the rowboat and secured it to the piling. He nodded to Eli, then turned back to address Morgan. "Captain Sutter needs you back right now."

"Why?"

"He don't explain things, he just expects them," Dunn growled. "Now come along!"

Morgan bristled at the tone of Dunn's voice. "I'll come, but only if I've a mind to."

"You'll come, one way or the other," Dunn hissed. "I got my orders. I won't leave without you."

"He's carrying a gun," Eli warned as he reached for his knife. "It's stuck under his waistband. Maybe you'd better tell him to take it out and lay it on the dock."

"You heard him," Morgan said.

Dunn flushed with anger, but Eli's big hunting knife had all his attention. "You think I'd shoot you?"

"You'd do whatever it took," Morgan said, his hand going to his own knife. "So, nice and easy, put the gun on the dock."

Dunn had little choice. "Morgan, you can stay if you want, but I got orders to take back the fur money and give it to the captain. I was supposed to pick it up on deposit in Yerba Buena. It wasn't there."

"It's safe with me," Morgan said. "Tell the captain I'll deliver it personally."

Dunn's jaw muscles corded like rope across his cheeks. "I got my orders. The captain needs that money—now. He can't wait."

Eli waved his knife. "Let me show you how to gut a man."

"No!" Morgan stepped in front of his father. "The captain has a right to his money. But I'll deliver it to him myself."

"Dammit!" Eli swore. "You ain't fit yet."

"Yes, I am," Morgan said. "I'll get the money, say good-bye to Mama, and be right back."

Dunn looked ready to froth at the mouth. "What the hell am I supposed to do?"

"Get off my dock," Eli said, "before I whittle you down to a nubbin."

"You'd best do as my father says," Morgan advised.

Dunn started to reach for his pistol, but Morgan shook his head. "I'll bring it along. Now get out of here."

"You sonofabitches are crazy," Dunn swore. "You're two of a kind."

Morgan picked up the man's pistol and cocked it,

watching Dunn's eyes widen with fear. "I think you'd better get back into that boat and row like hell while you still can."

Dunn did not need further encouragement.

It took Morgan less than twenty minutes to pack his few belongings and dig up the tin he'd used to protect the buried money. When it was time to go, he handed Eli almost two hundred dollars.

"Buy Mama and yourself what you need and put the rest away somewhere safe," he instructed. "Come springtime, when I get my own land grant, I hope to have a lot more to go with it."

"You be careful," Eli said. "That big fella, he's got the eyes of a snake. You ask me, he had plans of his own for that money."

"It'll be safe enough on board, and I won't dare turn my back on him."

Morgan waved good-bye to his mother, and just as he was turning to go, Eli said, "If Sutter gives you any problem about the fur prices I got, you tell him exactly what happened in Monterey."

"I will," Morgan said as he picked up his rifle and started for their rowboat.

Morgan was not looking forward to his next meeting with Sutter, when he'd have to tell him the disappointing news. He was certain the captain would be extremely upset and would question him in great detail about the lower-than-expected prices. Morgan knew his answers would not be satisfactory, since he had not been the one to sell the beaver pelts. But prices did fluctuate wildly, for tallow, hides, furs, and most anything else that could be marketed out of California. He hoped the fur market would be much stronger next year.

When the schooner docked on the American River, Morgan saw a big crew of Miwok Indians grading a wagon road up to Sutter's adobe. The road was wider than most city streets, and if he knew Sutter, it would be paved with flat river stones so that it would not get sloppy with mud in the wintertime. It was just like the captain to have such an impressive entrance to New Helvetia.

Morgan smiled to see his good friend Pablo driving a pair of fine new oxen who were straining to pull boulders from the road. When the big Mexican saw him, Pablo dropped his lines and the oxen gratefully halted in their tracks. The Mexican, all smiles, hurried over to greet Morgan. "Hey," he called, "just like El Camino Real, eh, Señor Morgan?"

"Just like." Morgan chuckled at Pablo's joke, knowing full well that the old "King's Highway" was now little more than a footpath between the crumbling remains of the once prosperous California missions.

They shook hands, and Pablo said, "The captain wasn't expecting you so soon. Neither was I. What happened?"

"I'll explain later. I'll only be here a night or two, and then I'm going back downriver until after New Year's Day."

Morgan, his rifle in one fist and almost two thousand dollars in his coat pocket, continued up the road, greeting the younger Miwok Indians he recognized from Chief Anashe's village.

Sutter was surprised when Morgan entered his Spartan office and living quarters, and Morgan also was surprised to find Manuiki sitting on the captain's unmade bed. When she saw Morgan, she let out a squeal of delight and rushed to his side.

"Morgan," she purred, "it is so good to see you!"

"Yes," Sutter said, appearing a little ruffled, "we didn't expect you back until after the holidays."

"I came up for just a few days to give you the fur money. I'll be rowing back to spend Christmas with my family."

"You don't have to do that. That supply schooner you came up on will be returning day after tomorrow."

"Sounds good." The memory of his hard trip downriver was very fresh in his thoughts.

"Whiskey?"

Morgan was surprised by the offer. The captain had

never before offered him a drink, except for a little rum
and some poor wine.

"Thanks."

"Manuiki, would you pour us a couple of drinks,
please?"

The Kanaka girl nodded, her hand lingering on
Morgan's forearm before she turned and went to a small
table where the captain kept his liquor and crystal
glasses. Manuiki poured the drinks with practiced skill,
giving Sutter his first but favoring Morgan with such a
bold, secretive smile that he had to look away to keep a
blush from rising in his cheeks.

"Manuiki," Sutter said, "as soon as you make my
bed, why don't you run along and find some other
things to do? Mr. Beck and I have business to discuss."

Morgan thought he saw a flash of defiance in the girl's
eyes that he had never noticed before. It surprised him.
Manuiki, it would seem, had developed a recent streak
of independence. Morgan suspected it was due to the
captain's attentions.

"It is good to see you again, Mr. Beck," Manuiki said
as she began to make the bed. "We have missed you."

"Thanks," Morgan replied, feeling very uncomfortable under the captain's steady gaze.

"Hurry up and run along, now," Sutter ordered, an
edge to his voice.

Manuiki did not hurry but made the bed very slowly.
Then she tossed them both a smile and sauntered out
the door her hips swaying enticingly.

Sutter downed his whiskey and poured another. "That
girl is getting too damn sassy, but she's as bright as a
new coin. I'm teaching her to help me in the office."

"Yes, sir."

Sutter raised his drink in a toast. "To our mutually
profitable fur-trading enterprise—may it last and grow."

Morgan drank, and the whiskey was good. He placed
his glass down, and Sutter indicated that he should take
a seat.

"I brought the money personally," Morgan began,
then quickly explained why his father had taken the
furs to sell in Monterey.

"That was good of him," Sutter said, "and I'll find a way to repay him for his trouble. As for your health, you do look a little peaked. What you need is a few weeks of rest before you go out trapping and hunting. Pablo won't like that, but he's invaluable to me in the road-building."

"I'm sure he is," Morgan said, reaching into his pocket for the envelope of money. "Sir, I'm afraid that my father was not able to sell the beaver pelts for what we'd hoped."

Sutter's expression of anticipation dissolved. "What is *that* supposed to mean?"

Morgan gave Sutter the envelope. "We got two thousand dollars instead of our expected three. I took my commission, and there's eighteen hundred dollars in that envelope."

"Eighteen hundred!"

"Yes, sir."

Sutter went white around the eyes. "I need at least a thousand more! I've promised Señor Martinez most of it, and there are a number of accounts that I *must* settle in Yerba Buena. I can't do it with eighteen hundred dollars!"

Over in the corner of the room near a cast-iron stove, Sutter's bulldog lifted its head. Reassured that its master was safe, it went back to sleep.

"I'm sorry," Morgan said. "I was counting on a bigger commission myself."

The captain's fists clenched and he abruptly pushed himself out of his chair, then turned away, fighting to maintain his composure.

"This is very, very bad, Mr. Beck. This is . . . terrible."

Morgan considered pouring them both another drink. Instead, he said, "I think that we'll do much better in the spring, sir. Part of it is that the Russians are marketing too many sea otter pelts."

Sutter spun around, his face livid with anger. "And part of it is that the Hudson's Bay Company trappers are invading my territory and trapping beaver right under our noses!"

"Sir?"

"Pablo Gutierrez saw five of them last week when he went out to hunt elk. They were all Americans. Bold as brass, they came right here and admitted that they were trapping the Sierra rivers. *My* rivers, Mr. Beck!"

Morgan shifted uncomfortably in his hard wooden chair. "I don't see what we can do to stop them, sir."

"You're right. I can't." Sutter pounded his desk in frustration. "I've no authority—yet. I don't even have title to this land. But I will! Next summer I will have completed the residency requirement of one year, and *then* I'll have some authority."

"It'll be different then, sir. We'll both have land grants, and we'll protect what is ours."

"Yes, but the American trappers will keep coming. When I asked them if they were worried about getting caught by the Mexican authorities, do you know how they responded?"

Morgan shook his head, though he expected he knew the answer. If these Hudson's Bay trappers were anything like his father—

"They laughed! They thought I was joking! Why, they're more afraid of grizzly than they are of a Mexican soldier."

"Have you written to the governor telling him about these illegal Americans?"

"Certainly! But he'll do nothing." Sutter tossed down his whiskey. "I tell you, Mr. Beck, out here we are entirely dependent upon ourselves. The Mexican government—even if it wanted to—hasn't the capability of enforcing its own laws. That's why Governor Alvarado allowed me to settle this land. He couldn't do it himself."

"I understand." But Morgan didn't understand. "Captain, if they won't help, what can we do about the American trappers?"

"Right now? Nothing. But once I have the authority I need and fully expect to be given, then we shall see. Then we shall see!"

Morgan steered the conversation to other, more pleasant topics. "Just in the short time I've been gone, I can see that the Miwok have made a big difference."

"They have, they certainly have," Sutter said, "but

we must constantly watch over them or they will run away. And only the other night, my bulldog actually bit two of the traitorous wretches."

"What?"

"It's true."

Sutter walked over and petted the bulldog, whose stumpy little tail wiggled furiously. The beast weighed at least sixty pounds, and Morgan would not have enjoyed being in the grip of its powerful jaws.

"Yes," Sutter continued, "I was in these very quarters, visiting with a young Frenchman whom I had met at the Martinez rancho, when we both heard a terrible cry. We raced outside to find an Indian in the grip of my bulldog's jaws."

"What happened then?"

"We dragged the scoundrel inside, and before I could even question him, we heard yet another cry! So we ran back outside and there was a second Indian in the grip of this brave animal."

"They were plotting to harm you?"

"Yes, yes! I think the entire group was in on a murderous scheme to kill me and loot my settlement."

"What did you do to them?"

"I warned them that if anything like that ever happened again, I would punish them most severely—perhaps even hang them!"

"I don't understand this at all," Morgan said. "You've fed them, housed them, and treated them fairly."

"Of course I have. And when I asked why they would plot to kill me, they had no answer except that they wanted my possessions. Can you imagine?"

"Did you tell Chief Anashe?"

"I did, and he was very upset with his tribesmen. I told him that henceforth I would also be using other tribes. That will make things much safer for me. I'm also training a personal staff of soldiers. They will wear special uniforms and enjoy privileges none of the others receive. I've already chosen a half dozen."

Sutter poured them still another glass of whiskey. Red of face and very agitated, he began to pace back and forth between his desk and bed. "They will be my personal staff. They and my bulldog will be my protection against treachery from within my own settlement. They and a few chosen friends like yourself, Mr. Beck."

"Thank you, sir." Morgan remembered how sick he had gotten from the aguardiente he'd shared with the Mexican fishermen in Monterey and did not touch the refill. When Sutter noticed this, he excused Morgan. "You've had a long, hard journey. Eat now and rest."

Morgan headed for the door. "I'll be returning to my parents for Christmas on the schooner."

"Fine," Sutter said. "And by the way, who bought my furs from your father?"

"A Señor Garcia who buys and sells merchandise in Monterey."

"Thank you."

Morgan nodded and left Sutter's quarters just as the sun was going down. He saw the Kanaka march the Indians up the hill and feed them what looked like thin porridge in a long wooden trough. The sight of the Indians kneeling before a trough like pigs deeply revolted him.

Ben Dunn must have read his expression, because the big seaman swaggered over to plant his feet before Morgan.

"What's the matter?" he asked belligerently. "Did you expect that the captain would feed them on linen tablecloths with silver service?"

When Morgan found himself momentarily at a loss for words, Dunn mocked him with a coarse laugh. Morgan balled his fists and sledged Dunn in the face, breaking his lips and knocking him skidding across the dirt.

"You crazy sonofabitch!" Dunn bellowed, covering his ruined lips. "What's the matter with you!"

Morgan leaned his Hawken rifle up against the adobe. "You want another one?"

Dunn jumped up. He was not as tall as Morgan, but heavier, and he had the mentality of a two-fisted brawler as he lunged forward. Morgan stepped aside as Dunn plowed past, and then he drove his elbow backward into the man's kidneys.

Dunn grunted in pain and momentarily crumpled at the waist.

Morgan whirled around and pounded two wicked blows to the man's face, staggering him badly. Dunn covered up, then lunged forward with outstretched arms intended to crush his opponent. Despite Morgan's best effort, Dunn managed to lock him in a bear hug.

"Ahh!" Dunn shouted, jerking Morgan off his feet and driving his knuckles into Morgan's back in an attempt to crack his spine. "Ahhh!"

With a daggerlike pain radiating all the way to his fingertips, Morgan tripped the heavier man down. They rolled, and Dunn hammered him twice in the face. Morgan saw lights flash behind his eyes. Dunn reached for his knife, but Morgan smashed his nose to a pulp and grabbed his wrist. When Dunn, his face a mask of blood, tried to bite his hand, Morgan reared up and drove his knee into Dunn's groin.

Dunn bellowed like a wounded bull and began to writhe on the ground. Morgan staggered to his feet. One look at Dunn told him the fight was over.

"You ever even look wrong at me, I'll kill you."

Dunn was locked in the grips of such agony that it was doubtful he heard the warning.

"Mr. Beck!"

He turned to see the captain standing in the doorway with a glass of whiskey in his hand.

"Sir?"

"What in the hell is going on?"

Morgan picked up his Hawken. One eye was swelling shut, but with the other he gazed back at the Miwok, seeing their thin brown faces dripping with Sutter's porridge. Morgan turned a hard one-eyed gaze on the captain and said nothing.

"Mr. Beck, I asked you a question, and I demand an answer!"

"Just a little difference of opinion," Morgan was able to say. "It's settled now."

"*What* difference of opinion?"

"Better ask him," Morgan said, sure that his own explanation would not please the captain.

Sutter started to say something, then took another look at Dunn and changed his mind. He swung around and disappeared back inside.

The Kanaka and most of the white men had seen the fight. So had the lovely Manuiki, who rushed to Morgan's side a moment later, carrying a wet towel.

"I think you'd better help Dunn," Morgan said, feeling the captain's anger and jealousy just before he heard the yell.

"Manuiki, that's enough!" Sutter bellowed.

But Manuiki shook her head and applied a cold compress to Morgan's eyes and cheek. He gently pushed it away.

"Him," he said, motioning toward Dunn.

Hurt sprang into her eyes, and she turned, flung the wet towel at Dunn, and stomped off. Morgan looked at Sutter, and he wanted to say something to the captain, but the man wheeled about and slammed the door behind him.

Morgan picked up his Hawken rifle and said to Dunn, "If you ever come at me again, it'll be the last time."

Pablo Gutierrez fell in beside him, and they walked toward the American River.

"Are you all right, amigo?"

"Yeah," Morgan said, "but I think I'm in trouble with the captain."

"For whipping that man?"

"No."

"Then—"

Morgan's fingertips brushed his swollen cheek, still feeling Manuiki's cool, gentle touch.

"I'll tell you about it some other time, but until this supply schooner heads back down the American, I think I'd better sleep on deck."

Pablo didn't understand. And maybe, all things considered, it was just as well.

Morgan did not visit with Sutter again before the schooner left, and neither did he see Dunn or Manuiki, except from a distance when the Kanaka girl came down to the American River to wash Sutter's clothes. When he saw the beautiful girl kneeling beside the water, Morgan felt something wrench at his insides. For her own part, Manuiki stared at him for a long time before she went back to her work and then slowly— almost reluctantly, it seemed to Morgan—walked back up the rise to Sutter's adobe.

Morgan spent two days doing nothing but recovering his strength. His eye swelled completely shut and blackened. Pablo poked fun at the way his cheek ballooned out as if he had it stuffed with almonds.

"Like a one-eyed squirrel, eh?" Pablo said with a wink.

"I think," Morgan said, "that I will sell you to the Indians and have them roast you for their dogs."

Pablo didn't seem overly concerned by the threat, and when the schooner at last raised its anchor and prepared to sail back to Yerba Buena and he saw Manuiki again by the water, the Mexican finally understood.

"So," he said, "you are going to get yourself in big trouble with that one. Can't you find another pretty girl?"

Morgan couldn't even smile.

"Listen, amigo," Pablo said, turning Morgan aside so that he could not stare at the Kanaka woman, "you know and I know that she is the captain's woman. You do not want big trouble. Manuiki is much woman, but also much grief. *Comprende?*"

"Yeah."

"Then go," Pablo ordered. "Go see that one who kept you from making a big fool of yourself in Monterey. What was her name?"

"Rosalinda Navarro."

"Yes! Go see her."

Morgan nodded. "But it is not much better. She is related to both Don Vallejo and to the governor himself. I doubt that either man will be happy when I show Rosalinda my attentions."

Pablo rolled his eyes. He had a natural comic streak, and he could make Morgan chuckle even under the most taxing circumstances. "Why can't you find a nice, fat peasant or Indian girl?"

"Adios, my friend," Morgan said. "I hope that the captain will allow me to come back so that we can trap more beaver."

"You should not worry," Pablo said with complete confidence. "A little jealousy never hurt a man. Besides, you are very good at trapping beaver."

"You've learned enough to go off on your own," Morgan said.

"Never! We are amigos!"

"Yeah," Morgan said, clamping his big friend on the shoulder, "I'm sorry for even mentioning it. Forgive me."

Morgan disembarked on the northern shore of San Pablo Bay and from there was able to buy a ride on a creaky old Mexican two-wheeled *carreta* that carried him to Sonoma, where he would visit Rosalinda Navarro, niece of the famed and rich Mariano Guadalupe Vallejo.

At a very early age, Vallejo had assumed great military responsibilities from former Governor José Figueroa. It was Figueroa who had been, like the Spaniards before him, most concerned about the Russian influence at Fort Ross. The governor had appointed young Vallejo and given him the lofty title of Military Commander and Director of Colonization of the Northern Frontier.

Vallejo soon demonstrated his mettle in hard skirmishes against rebellious Indians, earning him the additional responsibility of halting the Russian influence while assisting in the secularization of Mission San Francisco Solano. The young general also was given the job of colonizing and protecting the small northern settlements of Petaluma, Santa Rosa, and Santa Ana y Farias.

Vallejo had handled all these important responsibilities well and had been richly rewarded in land and gifts. Like Captain Sutter, the general was a man with big designs. The plaza at Sonoma was huge, and the general had built his two-storied home on its northern perimeter. Other casas, mostly owned by Vallejo's relatives, were built around the plaza.

Sonoma boasted about thirty prosperous families. Morgan noted a blacksmith shop, a tannery, a butcher shop, and many other small businesses. Thousands of head of the general's cattle, sheep, and horses could be seen grazing the brown hills surrounding Sonoma.

The Mexican who owned the big wooden-wheeled *carreta* bragged that he was a distant cousin of the general's and added, "Don Mariano provides us with everything, Señor. And the general, he has even made the giant Suisun Indian chief, Sem-Yet-Ho, our friend. No longer do we fear attack from the Indians."

"What about the Russians to the north?" Morgan asked, noting a company of soldiers being drilled at the far end of the plaza.

The Mexican shrugged. "I don't think they will be in California much longer, Señor. I think they are hungry all the time."

Morgan scarcely had time to digest this bit of news before he saw Governor Alvarado, his wife, and the lovely Rosalinda for a moment before they disappeared into Vallejo's immense home and courtyard.

"Is there a tailor in this pueblo?"

"A tailor, Señor?"

"I need to buy some clothes suitable for visiting the general's *palacio*."

"Over there," the Mexican said, pointing to a little adobe.

Morgan went to see the tailor, who turned out to be courteous and expert. For seven dollars, Morgan bought a suit of new clothes that had been ordered by a young man who, unfortunately, had been killed when roping a grizzly. The grizzly was to have been placed in an arena and chained to a Spanish fighting bull, which would have provided the entertainment at the young man's wedding festivities.

"Let's hope that I have better luck than he did," Morgan said as the tailor lengthened the sleeves and the trousers. "What about a new pair of boots and a hat?"

The tailor showed him a fine hat, black with a flat brim and a colorful band with gold stitching that matched the suit.

"No boots, Señor."

"Then mine will have to do," Morgan said. "But first a shave, haircut, and a bath."

"Come," the tailor said. "By the time you are ready, I will have completed these alternations."

The tailor was as good as his word, and when Morgan emerged some time later, he thought himself equal to paying a visit to Señorita Rosalinda.

When he arrived at the Casa Vallejo, Morgan was greeted by a houseman who politely but firmly interrogated him as to the purpose of his visit. When the man was finally satisfied that Morgan really did know the governor and his niece, Morgan was admitted into the general's home and led down a red-tiled corridor past several huge and very impressive rooms.

Entering the courtyard, Morgan saw Governor Alvarado and about a dozen ladies and gentlemen. He was announced, and all eyes turned toward him. Rosalinda gave him a smile; the others gave him nothing but curious stares. Morgan shifted self-consciously, no longer feeling handsome or even presentable.

Rosalinda excused herself and came to his side. "Señor Morgan," she said warmly, "I hardly recognized you!"

"Do you like the suit?" The smell of her and roses filled his nostrils, and he felt almost giddy.

Her eyes said that she did.

He stammered, "It was made for Señor Ignacio Valdez. I understand he was killed by a grizzly just last week before he was supposed to get married."

"Yes," Rosalinda said quietly. "It was very sad. Come, I want you to meet my family and friends."

Morgan hesitated. "I was hoping that we might talk a few minutes alone together."

She was taller than he had remembered and even more beautiful. She arched her eyebrows. "It would be very poor manners not to make the introductions first."

Morgan dipped his chin, realizing that she was right. Besides, he might not be very important or even a gentleman, but he was the son of Eli Beck, and that meant something. "All right. I have heard a great deal about General Vallejo—all good. And, of course, my father and I have often had the pleasure of meeting the governor."

"Of course."

Rosalinda took his arm and led him across the courtyard. Conversation stopped. Morgan knew that his eye was still very dark from the terrible fight with Dunn, and in spite of his new clothes, a fresh shave, and a haircut, he was not from the same mold as these ladies and gentlemen, who represented some of the wealthiest and most prominent families in all of California.

As the introductions were made, Morgan did not even attempt to remember all the names, noting only General Vallejo himself, a portly man of medium height with bushy muttonchop whiskers who was said to be one of the richest men in California.

"And of course," Rosalinda finished, "you are well acquainted with Governor Alvarado."

Alvarado pinned Morgan with his cold, probing eyes. "What brings you here, Señor Beck?"

"I . . . I come to extend greetings from Captain Sutter." Morgan turned to the general. "He especially wishes to thank you for your generous terms and great patience."

Vallejo seemed amused. "Do all Americans plead so eloquently as your Swiss captain but repay so poorly?"

Morgan swallowed, feeling like a complete fool. Everyone was staring at him. Rosalinda seemed caught off guard, and Alvarado's aristocratic face was a hard, handsome mask.

"I am the captain's chief trapper," Morgan stammered. "I am pleased to tell you that this year's take of beaver pelts was very good."

"Yes," Governor Alvarado said, turning to General Vallejo. "Captain Sutter received three thousand dollars in Monterey for his furs. General, you should press hard for payment."

Morgan heard himself whisper, "Did you say *three* thousand?"

"Why, yes. It was paid to your own father. Is something wrong?"

"No, sir." Morgan felt sweat burst from his pores. He

suddenly wanted very much to bolt and run for fresh
air.

Rosalinda saved him when she took his arm and said,
"May I show you the general's fine paintings?"

"Yes," Morgan gasped. "Thank you."

He didn't remember the paintings, only dimly recalled
seeing huge oils in gilt-edged frames hanging from
walls. He heard unfamiliar names of European artists,
and when he did not respond to a question, Rosalinda
looked up into his stricken face.

"What is it?" she asked with deep concern. "Are you
going to be sick again? Is there something that I can do
to help?"

"No," he said, feeling a numbness spreading inside
him as he realized that his own father had lied and
cheated Captain Sutter of a thousand dollars. "I am
fine."

"But you don't look fine."

Morgan was desolate. "Would . . . could you go for a
walk with me?"

"It would not be considered proper to walk alone.
But perhaps after dark we could meet for a few minutes
outside in the plaza."

"Are you sure?"

She studied his face. "You will not get drunk on
aguardiente?"

"No, never again," he said quickly.

"Then I will meet you when the moon rises outside
my uncle's door."

"Thank you," he whispered. "Now I must go."

A protest formed in her eyes. "It would be bad
manners to go without saying good-bye."

"Please, I am not feeling well. Would you give my
apologies to your host and the others?"

She nodded.

Morgan hurried outside and walked blindly across
the plaza, then out into the country, not seeing the
vaqueros who stared at him curiously from the backs of
their horses.

He walked until the sun went down and the moon
began to rise. Then he turned around and walked back

to meet Rosalinda. One thing was sure, he would not tell her of this great shame that his father had put upon him.

Rosalinda took his arm and pulled a lace mantilla over her black hair and close around her face. "I have been thinking only of you," she said as they stood in shadow. "I have been thinking and remembering your face when my uncle said that the furs sold for three thousand dollars. It was those words that made you sick."

"Yes," he said in a choked voice.

Rosalinda was so alarmed that she moved around to study his battered face. Morgan did not realize he was crying until she stood on her toes and kissed his wet cheeks.

"What is wrong!"

Something broke inside Morgan, and he crushed her into his arms, not wanting her to see him weep. How could he ever confess to this beautiful young lady that his own father was a liar and a thief?

≈ 5 ≈

A cold drizzle was falling on the day that Morgan Beck arrived back at Sutter's New Helvetia. He had spent two weeks in Sonoma just to be near Rosalinda, despite the obvious disapproval of her family. Then, instead of returning to his parents' home, he'd traveled down to Monterey, where he'd visited the office of Señor Antonio Garcia, prominent Pacific Coast trader and buyer of furs and hides.

"They were good quality pelts, Señor Beck," the man had said. "I gave your father a fair price. Just over three thousand dollars. Did you bring more beaver?"

"No. Maybe this summer," he remembered telling the trader, his mind numb and in a fog. "Adios."

"Adios. Tell your father I pray for his health."

"*Gracias*," Morgan had said as he'd left the day before Christmas.

During the month of January, Morgan had worked on the cargo docks of Yerba Buena, helping to load two Boston ships with the stiff, stinking hides of ten thousand cattle. When the miserable job was finished, he'd earned almost seventy dollars, but the money seemed nothing when Morgan thought of the great debt to Captain Sutter that his father had placed upon him.

Still, seventy dollars was a start, so he'd caught a supply schooner back up through the San Francisco Bay. Morgan had turned his face south across the bay when the supply ship passed his father's dock.

Now, as he procrastinated in the rain outside Sutter's

adobe, Morgan felt a dread that seeped into the very marrow of his bones. Finally he removed his hat and knocked at the captain's door. Munuiki opened it, and when she recognized him, she smiled, but Morgan's expression quickly killed her joy.

"Is the captain in?"

Manuiki nodded.

"Please tell him I'd like to see him."

"Come out of the rain, Morgan," she said in that voice that he felt, rich and warm, right down deep in his belly.

When Morgan entered the room, Captain Sutter was seated at his desk, and at the sound of Morgan's voice he turned but did not rise.

"Mr. Beck, it is the fourth day of February. Where have you been for the last six weeks?" Sutter's tone was cool and detached, but his eyes were hot.

"In Sonoma, then to Monterey and back to Yerba Buena."

"Monterey? Why?"

Morgan shifted his feet nervously. "Captain, I have come to tell you something important. My father . . . lied."

Sutter displayed absolutely no reaction.

"Captain," Morgan said, thinking Sutter did not yet understand, "my father kept a thousand dollars."

"And you knew nothing of this?"

"No, sir, I swear it."

Sutter steepled his fingers and leaned back in his chair. He glanced at Manuiki for a moment, then returned his gaze to Morgan. "Did you get my money back from your father?"

"No, sir."

"Why not?"

"I kept trying to go back and ask him about it, but I can't."

Sutter reached into one of the pigeonholes of his rolltop desk. He thumbed through a stack of letters and found the one he wanted, removed it from its envelope, and unfolded it.

"This letter is from Señor Garcia. In it he thanks me for my 'Sacramento fur' and mentions that he was extremely pleased to pay your father three thousand and ten dollars."

"So you already knew."

"Yes."

"What are you going to do about it?"

"I want my money. I have debts to pay. More than you could imagine."

Morgan took a halting step forward. "Sir, of the thousand dollars you were cheated, ten percent, or a hundred, would have belonged to me."

"That's true."

"Then if you will allow me to work out the debt without taking action against my father—without even telling anyone—I will pay you the full thousand."

"But I would rather have the money now. So would my impatient creditors, who seem to take a perverse delight in hounding me."

"My father would never admit to the theft," Morgan blurted. "He would rather die. And besides, if you agree to forgive his debt, I swear that I'll work hard to repay the money. I'll stay out in the forest, returning only to deliver the furs. I believe I can trap enough beaver to repay my father's debt before summer."

Sutter was quiet for several moments. Then he said, "All right, then—a thousand dollars without your commission deduction."

"Agreed," Morgan said, feeling a vast sense of relief. "And I'm sorry if this has caused you hardship."

"I'm afraid it has," Sutter admitted. "I must now pay additional interest to my creditors, and I will most certainly lose face if I cannot explain this theft."

Morgan's heart jumped. "Please, Captain, my father has wronged you but—"

"And you," Sutter told him. "Your father has not only dishonored himself, but he's caused you pain and humiliation."

"He's sick," Morgan said, knowing how lame this excuse must sound. "And he's bitter and feels as if he's failed in life."

"That does not excuse dishonesty."

"No, it doesn't. But I beg you to promise that you'll

never tell anyone about this. It would kill my father."

Sutter finally dipped his chin in agreement. "Manuiki, my dear, why don't you pour us a drink? Mr. Beck and I have an agreement to seal."

Manuiki nodded and poured. Only this time, Morgan was grim and there was no joy in him as there had been before. He tossed his whiskey down with a shudder and replaced his sodden hat on his head to let Sutter know that their business was finished.

"You can find yourself a bunk in the new sleeping quarters I've built," Sutter told him. "But in the morning, I expect you to be gone."

"I want Pablo Gutierrez."

"No. I need him to work here. You go alone for a while. Maybe next winter I will allow Pablo to go out with you."

"What about the promise of land?"

Sutter looked him right in the eye. "Maybe someday we can talk about it again, Mr. Beck."

Morgan stuffed his rage. "Thank you, Captain."

"You're welcome. Good hunting, Mr. Beck."

Morgan paused by the door. "What would you have done if I hadn't confessed that my father was a thief?"

"I hadn't made that decision," Sutter told him. "But I'm glad that at least *you* are honest."

Morgan shot a glance at Manuiki, and then he hurried outside into the rain. Before Morgan had left Rosalinda in Sonora, General Vallejo himself had taken Morgan aside and obliquely suggested that he might be more welcome in the future if he were willing to keep them informed about Captain Sutter's progress on the American.

"I won't be an informer," Morgan had said, tempering his anger.

"Not an informer," Vallejo had argued, "but a true friend of the Californians. Besides, this Sutter fellow has dangerous ambitions."

"Then you should tell that to the governor."

"I have," the general had admitted. "But sometimes he does not listen, even to me. Anyway, maybe next time you come to visit, you will be asked to stay here at

my casa. All things are possible among friends, eh,
Señor Beck?"

Morgan had mumbled something about honor and
left. Now, thinking about how Captain Sutter had forced
him into the equivalent of servitude for the next several
years, he wondered if his loyalty had not been misplaced.

During the next few months, Morgan lived a solitary
existence as he trapped and hunted in the Sierra foothills. Every few weeks, when he could no longer stand
the solitude, he would return to spend a few days with
Chief Anashe and the Miwok. During the winter it
often rained, and there was sometimes a heavy, cold
blanket of fog in the lower valley, which the Indians
escaped by moving their camp a little higher into the
foothills.

As Morgan trapped the middle and north forks of the
American River, he often gazed up to see powerful
snowstorms battering the highest Sierra peaks. And
once, just for the pure novelty of it, Morgan and three
of his friends from the Maidu tribe, a branch of the
Valley Nisenen People, hiked up to the snow.

They came upon it first in a deep, shadowy canyon,
and Morgan found in the glistening ice crystals a feeling
of wonder and delight. Shouting at the top of his lungs,
he cast his dark mood away and threw himself into the
snowbank, then rolled over and over until he was
frosted like a birthday cake. His Maidu friends thought
him utterly insane, and when he scooped up a snowball
and pelted one of the startled warriors, it precipitated a
huge fight. In an instant the air was filled with snow-
balls erupting like flushed coveys of quail.

Morgan and Maidu ran and fought, wrestled and
tackled until at last they lay winded, billows of steamy
breath pumping quickly from mouth and nostrils. Lying
there beside his friends, Morgan thought he could hear
the distant, almost ethereal wanderings of their laughter in and out of the mountain corridors of stone. He
brushed snow from his numb face, and his fingertips
revealed that he was smiling. It was, he thought, good
to have friends, and he felt as one with these people.

Shivering, they finally gathered their belongings and hurried away from the cold, dark canyon of white and did not stop until they found a meadow where the sun warmed their faces. Using brown grass, pine needles, and then sticks, they built a fire. Morgan shot a deer, and they undressed, hanging their wet clothes on sticks around the fire, to dry while they prepared the venison.

Later, with bellies full, they found a tall rock and stood against a dying sun, naked and filled with wonder at the sight of sunset dropping a veil across the magnificent Sacramento Valley.

"Look," Morgan said, pointing to where two golden threads met to form a strand. "That is Captain Sutter's New Helvetia."

Noiti, a quiet young man Morgan's own age said in Spanish, "What does it mean, New Helvetia?"

"It means New Switzerland. It is a place on the other side of the world, where the sun goes now."

The Indians stared at him but did not ask any more questions. Noiti finally said, "Do know how the world was made, Morgan?"

"If this is to be a long story," he said, "can we first get into our dry clothes?"

Noiti grinned, and when they were seated fully dressed around their campfire, gnawing on charred bones and sucking warm marrow, the Indian began his story.

"A long time ago, before man was born, the earth was covered by water. Only Turtle watched the sun as he rested on a floating log."

Morgan thought of the Miwok story of fire and almost asked if Turtle's log had fire, but he resisted, knowing that Noiti would not appreciate his feeble attempt at humor.

"One day," Noiti continued, "Turtle saw the Great Spirit slide down from the heavens on a rope made of feathers. The feathers were of every color Turtle had ever seen, like a sunset. 'I am the maker of worlds,' the Great Spirit said. Turtle was very pleased, because he was tired of always floating on a log."

Noiti stared into the fire, and its flames seemed to

mesmerize him as he gazed straight back into the
ancient time of creation.

"The Great Spirit told Turtle that he would have to
go to the ocean floor and bring him up some soil. Turtle
agreed. He swam to the bottom of the ocean, and he
did not return for six winters."

That's a long time to hold your breath, Morgan
thought.

"But when at last Turtle returned to the spirit-world
maker, the mud from the bottom of the ocean had all
washed away except a little from under his claws. Turtle
was very sad, but the spirit was pleased. He took the
little speck of mud and rolled it around in heaven until
it became Earth. He could have rolled all the water
away, but he left some for the Turtle to swim in, and he
made these mountains to feed the rivers until the end
of time."

"That is a good story," Morgan said after a long
silence. "Shall I tell you the Miwok story of how fire
was created for the world?"

"No," Noiti said, and his friends agree. Noiti leaned
forward and stared across the flames. "My friend, I ask
you to tell us the story of how Captain Sutter will create
a good life for our people."

Morgan frowned. "I do not know that story."

But Noiti did not accept that answer. "Look into the
flames. See the future. Tell us. We are your friends.
Only a white man can know the heart of a white man.
Tell us of Sutter's heart."

Morgan was silent for a long, long time, but the
Indians did not mind. It was their way to think deeply
before speaking.

"Sutter's heart is good," Morgan said at last. "He
wishes the Indian happiness and better things. But... but
he is a man who will always do what is best for himself
first. He has a dream of a . . . a tribe of people."

"From this place called Switzerland?" one of the
Maidu asked.

"Yes, but also of other peoples. He wants to be a
great chief and rule the peoples and make life good for
all of them."

"But what will happen to the Indian when all the white peoples from across the world come here?"

"I . . . I don't know."

There was another very long silence, and then a man named Oita said, "If you were one of the People, would you help the captain and live in his huts?"

Morgan glanced up at the first evening stars. "I would rather be free and live each day as this one."

"Then why do you work for the captain and kill the beaver, then throw the meat into the willows? Why are you not free, Morgan Beck?"

"I will be," he heard himself say. "Someday soon, I will be again."

Morgan knew that his words did not make sense to his friends, and what sense he had made caused them to be uneasy and troubled about him, and about Captain Sutter. But he had told these people the truth, and in his heart, if he had been Indian, he would have been uneasy, too.

The beaver-trapping was slow during that winter, so Morgan perfected his skill at trapping fox and otter. He also shot four large timber wolves but gave their fur to Chief Anashe, who was extremely pleased by the gifts and offered him a young Miwok girl to warm his nights. With some difficulty, Morgan refused. Eli would have thought him crazy, but Morgan no longer cared what his father did or thought.

That spring, when Morgan returned to New Helvetia with a cache of prime fur, the cottonwood and sycamore trees along the rivers were just beginning to bud. Morgan was feeling better, but he was not in good spirits, and there had not been a day that he hadn't tried to understand why his father had cheated Sutter, lying all the while so expertly.

"Mr. Beck," Sutter called as Morgan approached the captain's adobe and outbuildings, "you couldn't have timed your return better. We've got Indian trouble. Prepare yourself for battle in thirty minutes!"

"What? But sir, I—"

"Later, later," Sutter shouted, hurrying away to make his preparations.

Morgan didn't know what to think, but fortunately
Pablo Gutierrez explained a few minutes later that the
Chucumnes Indians, whom Sutter had been using most
recently, had suddenly slipped out of the settlement,
and the rumor was that they intended to attack the
moment that the captain and his people let down their
guard.

"Here he comes," Pablo said.

Sutter was dressed in his Swiss military uniform,
complete with his saber and campaign hat.

"Attention!"

Morgan had never stood at attention in his life, but at
Sutter's command, the other five men especially chosen
for this expedition did at least a pretty fair imitation of
the military posture. Supposing he ought to do the
same, Morgan put his heels together and dropped his
hands at his sides, feeling ridiculous.

"Gentlemen," Sutter began, pacing back and forth
before them, "as you know, the Chucumnes suddenly
vanished from our settlement, and I have it on good
authority that they are preparing to attack."

Sutter paused for dramatic effect, but was too excited
to hold it for long. "Now," he rushed on, "I don't know
about you, but I am unwilling to wait for an attack. I
prefer to take the offensive. That being the case, we
will sally forth and take to the battlefield. We will
defeat the wretches and instill in their hearts a fear and
appreciation for my authority that will well serve New
Helvetia's illustrious future!"

"Sir," Morgan said, "I have always been treated with
respect and kindness by the Chucumnes. Exactly what
makes you think that they mean your settlement harm?"

"Why, they've all left my employ, haven't they?"
Sutter whirled around, his arm sweeping in full circle.
"Look about you, Mr. Beck. Do you see any Indians
working my fields or tending my herds?"

"No, sir, but—"

"One of my 'home guard' Indians overheard the
plot."

"Sir," Morgan objected, "I don't mean to disagree,
but—"

"Then don't, Mr. Beck!"

Sutter turned, shouldered his rifle, and with a slashing gesture of his arm, yelled, "Follow me, men!"

"Well, goddammit!" Morgan muttered, looking at Pablo with exasperation. "Amigo, what the hell kind of—"

"I am going, Señor," Pablo said. "You can come . . . or stay. But I work for this man, and so I will fight for him."

Morgan remained planted with indecision and watched Sutter lead the four off to the southeast. "Aw, hell," he growled, calling for the Indian boy who had once deserted him to come and take care of the furs.

Minutes later, he hurried to catch up with Pablo, Captain Sutter, and the rest. Morgan hoped he could simmer the captain's stew a little with a pinch of reason. The Chucumnes were not one of Morgan's favorite tribes, and they could be truculent and arrogant but they were hard workers and honest, if treated with fairness.

All day long the men marched until at dusk they came to the Cosumnes River. Far in the distance they could see a campfire on the riverbank.

Sutter gathered his men around. "They have no idea that we intend to initiate this fight," he said. "Our attack will be a complete surprise. We will strike just before dawn."

The men stared at the big Indian campfire. Morgan, who was by far the most knowledgeable about the California Indians, guessed that there would not be more than twenty or thirty Chucumnes in that camp or else they'd have built additional cooking fires.

"Mr. Beck," Sutter snapped, "may I have a word in private with you?"

"Sure." Morgan followed Sutter out of hearing of the others.

"I want no more dissension from your lips," Sutter said in a hard voice. "I am a captain of the Swiss Guard, a military officer. You, Mr. Beck, are merely a trapper and a trader. Furthermore, it is *my* settlement that is being threatened, while you have absolutely nothing at stake."

"My life is at stake if we attack that Indian camp," said Morgan. "And as for the Chucumnes, I think there's been an unfortunate misunderstanding that—"

"The only misunderstanding we have is the one that is between us," Sutter interrupted. "And if you refuse to cooperate and fight, then I will consider our agreement terminated and will take action against your father. Is that clearly understood?"

Morgan trembled with fury. Somehow he kept his hands balled at his sides and managed to nod his head.

"Very well, then return to rest with the others. We will advance upon their camp after midnight and open fire at dawn."

"Without warning?"

"No warning was to be given by them in their attack on my settlement!" Sutter exclaimed. "Do we have an understanding, Mr. Beck?"

"Yes, sir."

"Good!"

Sutter whirled and marched back to camp. A few minutes later Morgan followed him. Avoiding Pablo's questioning eyes, he spread his blankets out on the ground, tore a hunk of pemmican from his pack, and chewed it in angry silence. Finished, he rolled up in his blankets and counted the stars until he fell asleep.

He was awakened just after midnight by Pablo. With only the cold moon and starlight to guide them, the party headed upriver, Sutter in the lead. It took them two hours to sneak up the Cosumnes River to the Indian camp and another tense hour to maneuver into a position that satisfied their captain, a very loose semicircle around the sleeping Chucumnes so that there was no place to escape except into the river.

Despite the hour and the chill of the night, Morgan's palms were clammy with perspiration as he gripped his Hawken rifle. He glanced sideways and exchanged silent communication with Pablo. Morgan was upset with his friend for being so abrupt with him as they were marching out of New Helvetia, and he supposed he felt he'd been reprimanded by Pablo for his lack of loyalty. But Pablo didn't know about Eli and the devil's pact

Morgan had been forced into with the captain. Pablo might not have believed him if he'd tried to explain, anyhow.

Morgan heard Sutter make a soft clucking sound with his tongue and cheek. It was the signal to get ready to fight.

But nothing happened. In the sickly predawn light, Morgan watched Sutter's silhouette frozen in place like a rock. Dawn created a faint light in the eastern sky, low and timid against the eastern horizon. Huge oaks began to emerge with their great arms fingering the dying stars.

Sutter came to his feet and started forward.

"What the hell is he doing?" someone down the line hissed.

Sutter bellowed, in Spanish, "You are surrounded. Do not attempt to fight. Surrender."

"Jesus Christ!" Pablo Gutierrez swore, jumping to his feet and cursing as he ran forward.

Morgan saw a flash of musket fire from the camp. Sutter dropped and fired. Wraithlike shadows of Indians sprang from the earth, and Pablo fired his Hawken. Morgan watched a silhouetted figure crumple to the earth.

All was chaos for the next few minutes as sunrise burst over the Sierra Nevadas. Morgan fired, reloaded, and fired, over and over. He was unaware of arrows being launched in his direction, but as the light grew stronger he was amazed to see them jutting from the earth all around him.

Suddenly the whine of bowstrings fell silent and the Chucumnes began to cry out in surrender.

"Hold your fire!" Sutter shouted. "Hold your fire!"

Morgan, gunpowder making his eyes burn, stood up and reloaded. Then, falling in with the others, he trailed Sutter into the Indian camp. The Chucumnes were prostrate on the ground. Morgan counted four dead and two others dying. Several more were wounded and might not recover. Some wept; others held their leaking bullet wounds in dazed, stoic silence.

An Indian Morgan recognized begged for his life and

the lives of his tribesmen. Seeing this man grovel for
mercy like a beaten dog filled Morgan with pity and
revulsion. Vivid, unbidden memories of Eli's Indian
versus mountain man stories assailed him. He recalled
the tales his father had recounted to him since his
boyhood about Indian courage and their indomitable
will to fight to the death rather than endure the disgrace of defeat.

These really are Digger Indians, Morgan thought
with contempt. Certainly they bore no resemblance
to the fierce Cheyenne, Blackfoot, Ute, Arapahoe, or
Sioux—all tribes Eli Beck once had known and sometimes fought—nor to the Apache, Shoshone, Pawnee,
or Comanche.

"Mr. Beck!"

Morgan hurried forward to stand beside the captain,
whose face twitched with excitement and triumph.
Sutter began to tell the Indians that if they promised
never again to fight, their lives would be spared.

The Indian Morgan recognized slithered forward like
a whipped dog. Over and over he swore never again to
fight. To prove this, he reached back generations and
even made the sign of the cross.

"Bloody Christ!" Morgan swore out loud, turning his
back on the scene and stumbling away to stand facing
the river so that he could not hear the Indian's whining
voice or the wails of the Diggers that were dying.

Morgan did not spend much time at New Helvetia through the remainder of that spring. When he did return for supplies or to deliver pelts, he saw hundreds of Chucumnes, Miwok, and Maidu Indians working at the settlement. Vast acreage was planted in wheat and corn; adobe bricks by the thousands were being used to construct new buildings.

Sutter had even created his own coinage system whereby the Indians were paid daily. They could redeem their tin coins for trinkets or goods at his store. Sutter told Morgan that the Indians no longer worked strictly on the orders of their chiefs.

"I pay the workers directly now. I treat them fairly, but firmly," he boasted. "They are fed, clothed, and cared for when sick. If life weren't better than what these Indians had known in the wild, they wouldn't be here now."

Morgan could do no more than nod his head, although he could not understand how the young warriors could trade their fish nets and hunting bows for crude farming tools and slop served in a pig trough. But that, he knew, was their decision, not his own.

When summer arrived, Morgan's pelts were loaded onto a cargo ship bound for Yerba Buena, and this time Sutter himself accompanied them to market. Morgan wished the captain well and agreed to remain at the settlement to hunt and oversee the building of a tannery down near the river, where the smell of green hides could not reach the fort unless carried by the wind.

A hot summer day at New Helvetia found Morgan and Pablo sitting in the shade of the captain's adobe watching Indians complete a new barracks, a bakery, and a mill. Hundreds more Indians were busily constructing an eighteen-foot adobe wall thick enough to repel cannon fire.

"Instead of New Helvetia," Morgan observed, "this place will be known as Sutter's Fort when these stockade walls finally are up."

The Mexican nodded. They had both been present the day that Sutter and his Indians marked the boundaries of his new fort. The enclosed compound was to be three hundred twenty feet long and roughly one hundred fifty feet wide.

"Bigger by far than Bent's Fort or Fort Laramie," Sutter had proclaimed with pride.

Pablo turned to Morgan. "Amigo, when will you go to visit Señorita Rosalinda?"

"Why do you ask such a question?"

"You look sad."

Morgan frowned. "I've decided never to see her again."

"But why?"

He gazed out toward Sutter's immense fields of wheat and the corn that already was waist high. "I . . . I just think that she's too refined for me, Pablo."

"Ahh!" the Mexican snorted in protest. "That is not true!"

"It is true. What could I offer to compare with Casa Alvarado or Casa Vallejo?"

"But you are still very young."

"So are you, Pablo, but you'll never have any wealth, either."

Pablo accepted this evaluation without argument. "But it is different with me. I am not a man with great talent or ambition. I like to take my ease and find my simple pleasures."

Morgan chuckled. It was common knowledge that Pablo Gutierrez was spending his nights with a Miwok

Indian girl and that he would rather drink aguardiente and dance at the fiestas than work too hard.

"But you—" Pablo continued, "you are the one for whom Captain Sutter will soon receive a big land grant from Governor Alvarado."

"No," Morgan said with finality, "there will be no land grant for me. Like my father, I'm never going to have much more than what I wear, shoot, or steal."

Pablo raised his eyebrows in question. "But I thought . . ."

For the past hour Morgan had been acutely aware of Manuiki watching him from inside the adobe. Now the Kanaka woman appeared in the doorway, raised a glass of whiskey, and motioned him to come join her.

Morgan tried to look away. Pablo was asking him something, but he hadn't been listening. He was compelled to look back at Manuiki.

Pablo followed his eyes and chuckled. "So you want that one, eh?"

Morgan dipped his chin in assent. "She's on my social level."

"But she belongs to the captain!"

"She doesn't think so," Morgan said, coming to his feet and walking into the doorway.

Manuiki was sitting alone at Sutter's desk, and when he entered the room, she poured him a drink, raised it, and whispered, "To us, Morgan. To the slaves."

He hesitated for only a moment before he took his glass and raised it. "To the slaves."

They both tossed their whiskey down neat. Manuiki was not a drinker, and she coughed and tears sprang to her large brown eyes.

Morgan shuddered. He set his glass down and closed and then latched the door. "Even slaves ought to have a few pleasures in life. Don't you agree?"

Manuiki nodded, and her eyes were hot with desire as she rushed across the room and threw herself into Morgan's arms. When their lips met, he felt the island woman shiver with ecstasy.

"I don't much like the fact that the only bed in this room is the captain's," he said in a thick voice.

"I am used to it. The bed is hard, but I am soft."

Morgan untied the string that gathered Manuiki's dress at the neckline. The garment fell to her shoulders and then, with agonizing slowness, to the floor.

Morgan took a long moment to admire the island girl's body. It was beautiful, round and sleek and golden.

"Come lie with me, Morgan," she breathed, reaching for his belt and slowly pulling him toward Sutter's bed.

Morgan found her mouth with his own as she pulled him down beside her. When he roughly entered her, Manuiki gasped and enfolded him, then bit his ear and giggled like a little girl. Only she wasn't a girl, and when Morgan moved deep into her, Manuiki's passion swept him away like the high, hard winds of a tropical hurricane.

The next morning, the muffled boom of a ship's cannon echoed up and down the American River. As they had on the day Sutter first arrived and claimed this land, huge flocks of waterfowl erupted from the marshes and took wing. Ducks and geese circled high, voicing their displeasure.

"He's back!" Manuiki cried with alarm as she gripped Morgan tightly.

"Yes," he said, pushing up on his elbows and looking down at her. "At least he gave us one day."

Manuiki's eyes filled with tears. "I want to stay with you."

"I'm afraid that's no good," he told her gently. "I can't give you anything. You'd hate it in the forest without nice things around you. Trapping is hard, dirty work, and you'd soon be desperately unhappy and maybe even bitter. I couldn't stand to see you that way."

"But—"

He kissed her lips. "I'm not the one you need."

"But neither is the captain!"

Morgan came to his feet and began to dress. "Listen," he said, "if you treat Captain Sutter right, he'll probably marry you."

"No!" Manuiki cried. "He is *already* married."

Morgan blinked. "What?"

"He left a wife and five children in his Switzerland."

"That's . . . that's impossible."

"It is true! One night when he was drunk, the captain showed me letters from his wife. He even read some of them to me."

When Morgan's face reflected disbelief, Manuiki jumped out of bed naked and rushed to the captain's desk. She procured a hidden key and unlocked the desk, then rummaged until she found a packet of letters.

"Here. Read them if you don't believe me."

Morgan took the letters and stared at them, not wanting to pry into the captain's private life. He heard the cannon boom again even louder and told himself that he did not have time to waste.

"Read them, please!"

"Just one," he said, opening a letter postmarked from a town in Switzerland. The letter was written in a bold hand, and he did not have to read past the salutation: *My dearest husband.*

Morgan dropped the letter, and Manuiki scooped it up and returned it and the others to the drawer, which she locked.

"See, I told you! He will never marry me."

"Get dressed."

"But—"

"Get dressed, dammit!"

Manuiki began to cry. Morgan stifled the urge to leave her and said, "Listen, maybe he can't ever marry you. I don't know or even care about any of this. But the captain is crazy about you, Manuiki. So just . . . just be good to him, and he'll take care of you."

The island girl began to weep louder.

"Stop it!" Morgan demanded. "The captain has probably brought you back gifts. Do you want him to see you all red-eyed from crying? He'd know something was wrong."

"I asked him for gold earrings," she sniffled. "Big, pretty ones."

Morgan pulled on his boots. He eased the curtains aside and saw that everyone was rushing down to the

wharf where Sutter would disembark and cargo would
be unloaded from the supply schooner.

"Finish dressing, and we'll go down to greet him,"
Morgan said, walking over to stand beside the girl. "I'm
almost certain he remembered to bring you those gold
earrings."

She brightened at once. "Do you really think so?"

"Yes."

Manuiki jumped to her bare feet, padded gracefully
over to a mirror, grimaced at her reflection, then poured
cold water in a basin and splashed her face before
pinching color into her cheeks. A few seconds later she
furiously attacked her long, black hair with a pretty
abalone-shell brush that Sutter had given her for
Christmas.

"Wear that red dress with the white ruffled lace, the
one that the captain bought you the last time he went
away. He'll like that."

She spun around, her chin high and proud, like her
bare breasts. "Go to hell, Morgan!"

He was glad that she had regained her spirit. Weeping, she held no allure, but happy or angry, she fired
his blood. "Maybe I'll go down to the river alone."

Down on the American River, Sutter was jubilant,
shouting and waving his arms in triumph as the sweating sailors loaded and reloaded the cannon, firing across
the water into distant cottonwood trees.

Morgan watched Sutter descend the gangplank as
his followers and hundreds of Indians cheered, and
thought about the man's secret wife and five children. What kind of man could take up life in the
wilderness and build an empire with no thought of
his own family?

"My friends!" Sutter cried, motioning for silence. "I
am happy to tell you that Governor Alvarado has bestowed
upon me the honor of Mexican citizenship and I am
now officially Señor Juan Augusto Sutter! But to you, I
am *Captain* Sutter!"

It was meant as a joke, but no one laughed; they only
cheered.

Sutter's eyes picked out Morgan from the huge welcoming crowd. He nodded, lips stretched tightly under a bushy little mustache.

"Furthermore, I have been assured by Governor Alvarado himself that within the next few weeks I will be named Justice of the Peace and the official representative for the Sacramento District of Alta California!"

Again, cheers. Morgan alone showed no response. But he knew, more than any man present except for Sutter himself, that the captain soon would hold the power of life or death over every Indian and white in this vast Sacramento Valley.

It also occurred to Morgan that if the captain found out about him and Manuiki, the man would feel terribly betrayed. This thought was so depressing that Morgan was about to turn away when his father and his stepmother suddenly appeared on deck. Eli was coughing and bent, his face bloodless and old. Mama Estella and a sailor were supporting him, and Mama's eyes were anxiously searching the crowd. Morgan started to turn, and he supposed he would have left if Pablo Gutierrez had not seized his arm in a powerful grip.

"That must be your father and your mother!" Pablo exclaimed.

"Let go of my arm!"

"Morgan!"

He looked up to see his mother waving frantically, but Morgan's eyes went to his father and he was shocked by the man's appearance. Eli's once proud, even arrogant features were twisted with pain.

An involuntary sound escaped Morgan's lips, and he momentarily leaned on Pablo for support.

"Whatever he did," Pablo whispered, "it *must* be forgiven while there is still time! It is the only way to save your soul from hell!"

"Yes," Morgan heard himself reply.

Pablo released his arm, and Morgan bulled his way through the crowd. He hurried across the wharf past Sutter and rushed up the gangplank to take his father in his arms. With a cry of joy, Mama Estella hugged his neck.

"What happened to you?" Eli demanded, his eyes
sunk deep in his bony face. "Last Christmas we waited,
every day I waited on the dock—even in the fog. But
you never came. You promised and you never came!"

"I wanted to," Morgan said. "Now . . . now let me
help you up to the fort. Look! Look how the sun is
shining and the air is dry. Even by the river. It will be
good for you."

Eli said, "Maybe I was wrong about Captain Sutter."

Morgan traced his father's eyes up to the captain,
who, surrounded by hundreds of men, was marching
up the hill toward Manuiki, who stood in her red dress,
black hair gleaming.

Morgan turned away, struggling to hide his feelings.
"Father, let me help you."

But Eli had more to say. "The captain promised us
his hospitality as long as we needed it. He said Mama
could help with the cooking. And once I get stronger, I
could help, too. Do a little carpentry. Maybe even be in
charge of the pelts you trap. The captain said he
couldn't pay us wages, but we'd never have to want for
food or shelter."

"I'm glad."

Eli could not hide his growing excitement. "Son, I
tell you, Captain Sutter is a damned fine fella! He's as
good as his word, and you're lucky to be his friend. You
know what he did?"

"Tell me."

"He anchored right off my dock with that big schooner of his and had hisself rowed ashore. And do you
know what he brought?"

"No."

Eli beamed. "Show him, Mama."

His mother pulled back her hair to reveal a pair of
beautiful gold earrings. "They are much too beautiful
for me. When you marry someday, I will give them to
your new wife for our wedding present."

Morgan knew damn good and well that Sutter had
originally intended those earrings for Manuiki. "They're
beautiful," he said, trying to sound sincere.

"Hell, yes, they are! They're solid gold!" Eli exclaimed.

"Why, I tell you, son, if we hitch ourselves to the captain's wagon, we'll go far—real far. And he must think damned highly of you, or he'd never have brought us up here for free."

"This is true," Mama Estella said, her own excitement equal to Eli's. "And things will be much better for us all now. Only—"

Her eyes suddenly filled with tears. Because he'd been so shocked by Eli's appearance, Morgan had not really looked at his mother until now. "Mama, why have you lost so much weight!"

"*Por nada!* It is nothing. My heart sings now that I am here with the warm sun on my face and my son and my husband at my side. Life will be good for us now in this place."

"That's right," Morgan said, trying to force enthusiasm into his words. "It's what I've been trying to tell you all along."

Mama started to weep.

"What's wrong!" Morgan cried with alarm.

"Now, Mama," Eli begged, stroking her gray hair with his bony, twisted fingers, "it'd be better if you just don't even think about it."

"What!"

Eli's jaw jutted out. "How you did us wrong, dammit! You was supposed to come home for Christmas, and you didn't. Not a word, either. Mama and I nearly went crazy, and we was both sure you were dead until we heard different from Captain Sutter." Eli's voice shook with righteous fury. "You wonder why your mama looks so thin! Well, it's because she was too worried about you to eat!"

Morgan stepped back and ran his hand across his eyes. "I'm sorry," he whispered. "Forgive me."

Eli's pointed chin finally dipped in acceptance. "It's done and forgot."

Eli gazed up at the big adobe buildings, the unfinished stockade wall, and Sutter's fields of golden wheat. "Ain't it all somethin'!"

Morgan turned and looked up, too. From down on the American River, the settlement always appeared

much larger and more impressive. The walls towered.
"It is," he admitted.

"You started Mama's chapel yet, son?"

Morgan noted a twinkle in his father's eye.

"No, sir."

"Good. We'll build it together when I'm feeling
stronger. The captain says we should build us a cabin
outside his New Helvetia first."

Morgan heard a cheer, and he turned to see the
captain sweep Manuiki up in his arms and swing her
around in a full circle. She was laughing, and he
supposed that meant Sutter had kept some other fine
gift besides the gold earrings to present to her
tonight.

"Let's get you settled in," Morgan said. "We've got a
lot of catching up to do."

They talked late that night. Early the next morning,
Morgan was summoned from his sleep by Captain
Sutter. Morgan's first thought was that Manuiki, probably in a fit of remorse, had confessed to the captain that
she and Morgan had made love during his absence.

"Sit down," the captain ordered.

Morgan took a seat and waited.

"Whiskey?"

"No, thanks."

"Then me neither," Sutter said. "When are you
planning to go out trapping?"

"I should leave right away."

"Don't. I want you to help build your parents a
cabin—a good, solid one. Just use whatever lumber
you'll need and get a few of my carpenters to help."

Morgan was very pleased. "All right. Anything else?"

Sutter leaned back and laced his hands behind his
head. "I'm sure, when you saw your father and mother
at my side yesterday, you were somewhat shocked."

When Morgan said nothing, Sutter continued. "I can
understand that. After all, your father cheated me out
of a thousand dollars."

"But I am working it off."

"Yes. Of course. But still, I didn't need to bring the
man who stole from me into my home."

"Then why did you?"

"Because I had heard that your father and mother were literally starving. Mr. Beck is too weak to work, and you'd told me your dream of bringing him here for his health. I just decided that it would be the Christian thing to do."

"I see." Morgan stood up and glanced over at Manuiki, who was pretending not to listen. "So I suppose that I ought to thank you."

"It doesn't matter," Sutter said expansively. "But I hope that it might make you work a little harder on my behalf."

"I will. Did my mother tell you that she wanted a chapel?"

"She did. I explained that I would have no objection, but that there were other, more pressing needs." Sutter began to pace back and forth, suddenly growing agitated before he blurted, "Mr. Beck, Manuiki told me that she informed you I have a wife and children in Switzerland."

Morgan glanced at the girl, wondering what else she had told the captain.

"Is that true, Mr. Beck?" Sutter asked, coming to a halt to study Morgan with great intensity.

"Yes."

"And did you believe her?"

"I figured it was none of my business."

"That's true." Sutter returned to his chair. "Manuiki, my dear, would you mind going outside? I want to talk to Mr. Beck in private."

She hurried away, and when they were alone Sutter took a deep breath and expelled it slowly. He swallowed and began what Morgan quickly came to realize was a confession.

"Mr. Beck, the truth of the matter is that I did leave behind a wife and five children in Switzerland. I . . . I had had some financial difficulties and was in danger of being thrown into a debtor's prison. Everything I did went wrong. My dear wife and I both decided that it would be best if I fled to America."

"I understand."

"You do?" Sutter's jaw dropped. "You really do?"

"Of course. This is a wild and violent country. Just to get here you had to travel through hostile Indian lands. And you didn't know what you would face here. It would have been irresponsible to bring a family into that kind of danger."

"Of course it would have!" Sutter exclaimed. "That was my reasoning from the very beginning. I would found a settlement and tame the Indians, make it safe for civilized peoples, and *then* I'd send for my family."

Morgan nodded and believed the captain.

"However," Sutter added heavily, "I have not seen my wife in six years, and now as I am sure you have observed, I have fallen victim to the weakness of the flesh."

Morgan felt his cheeks warm. He wished Sutter would say no more, but now that the man had revealed his great secret, the captain couldn't stop talking.

"I know that you probably hold me in contempt for not being strong enough to resist that Kanaka girl, but someday you might also give in to loneliness... or desire."

Morgan wanted out of this room. He was the last person in the world qualified to judge Sutter's weakness for a girl like Manuiki.

"Sir, I—"

"Please," Sutter said, raising his hand. "If I don't finish now, I won't be able to later. And this all comes back to your father."

"Sir?"

"I didn't intend to stop and invite him to New Helvetia. My heart, as yours, was hardened against him. But then I realized that, just as I must forgive myself for my own weaknesses, I also have to forgive my enemies and those who have trespassed against me!"

Sutter was perched on the edge of his chair, expecting... something. For a crazed instant, Morgan was seized by an almost overpowering urge to make his own confession about making love to Manuiki. But the urge passed, and he managed to say, "I'm happy for you."

The captain's face dropped with disappointment. "Yes," he said, shaking his head after a moment. "Thank you."

Sutter poured himself a strong drink. He avoided Morgan's eyes and abruptly changed the subject. "I am worried about General Vallejo. He is writing letters to Alvarado and others, saying that our presence here is a danger to the authority of Mexico."

"But you're Mexico's official representative!"

"Exactly so. Anyway, it would not be seemly for me to confess to the general that I have heard these slanderous rumors. However, I recall that you are on somewhat better terms with Vallejo and his lovely niece, Rosalinda."

Morgan held his silence.

"Therefore," Sutter continued, "I want you to pay a visit to the general and assure him of my undying loyalty to Mexico."

Sutter winked. "Given the señorita's obvious charm and beauty, I'm sure that it would not be an unpleasant task."

"No, sir."

"Good, it's settled. After you help your parents build a cabin, you should trap to the north, then pay a visit to Sonoma and Casa Vallejo."

"Yes, sir."

A month later, Morgan prepared to journey up the Sacramento River with even more traps and a stronger determination to pay off his father's debts.

"I wish I could go with you this time," Eli said, sitting on an empty cask. "But I'm not strong enough right now. Maybe later, when the days cool down. It's mighty hard to do much in this heat."

"The Indians don't seem to mind," Morgan said, watching them laboring in the fields.

"Hell," Eli said with disgust, "them ain't *real* Indians—them is just Diggers."

"You sound like the captain."

"Maybe I do," Eli said, "but it's the gospel truth. You'd never catch real Indians grubbing around like beetles. Real Indians are hunters, with lances and

arrows, riding wild mustang ponies and fearing nothing
but God and grizzly."

"These people are Indians, too," Morgan said, recognizing Noiti covered with mud as he worked on his
hands and knees forming new adobe bricks. How, Morgan
wondered, could a once proud warrior like that allow
himself to be sucked into Sutter's web of avarice?

"You get well," Morgan said, grabbing his Hawken.

"I'm feelin' stronger every day."

Morgan said good-bye to Mama Estella and Eli and
to Pablo. As he passed the captain's adobe, he heard
Manuiki's laughter spliced with Sutter's distinctive laugh.
They both sounded happy. Morgan's last stop was the
blacksmith shop, where he picked up a new set of
beaver traps.

"What do you think of 'em?" the blacksmith asked,
setting his hammer down on his forge.

"They're good. Real good. But I lost more than that
this last winter. The captain said that you'd have those
replaced, along with some extras."

"No iron. The captain tells me he's writing letters
every day beggin' for the stuff. If I had more iron, I
could forge more plows and tools. Most of the Indians
are digging, planting, and weeding with nothing but
sharp sticks. I need iron for plows, shovels, picks, and
hoes. I need it to repair no less than five wagons, and I
need it for making axes, wedges, and saws so the
Indians can cut logs and make more lumber—and files
so they can do it with good sharp tools."

The blacksmith picked up his hammer. It was battered,
nicked, and misshapen like his old anvil.

"Beck, you ought to be grateful that I was able to
replace most of the beaver traps you lost, and you
should try and be more careful."

"I'll remember that," Morgan said as he picked up
the traps, shouldered his pack, and grabbed the Hawken.
"Yes, sir, I'll sure try and remember that."

The blacksmith followed him outside with a lecture.
"You got life easy! You just come and go like you please.
Nary a worry. No one breathing down your neck night
and day, checkin' on you every hour to make sure that

you don't sit down and relax in the hottest part of the day."

But Morgan kept walking and scarcely heard the man. He was thinking about Sutter's orders that he go north up the Sacramento River and see some new country, then double back and visit General Vallejo in Sonoma.

Could he even face Rosalinda? He knew that in another year he'd be rid of his father's shameful debt to Sutter. Maybe then he'd build his own fort and apply to the Mexican authorities in Monterey for a huge land grant of his own.

But long before that happened—if it ever happened—Morgan was sure that Rosalinda Navarro would have found herself a rich, handsome young Mexican aristocrat to marry and father her children.

Still, orders were orders, and if he saw Rosalinda, Morgan knew he could no more resist her than he had resisted Manuiki.

Morgan had been forced to build a tule canoe in order to ford the turbulent junction of the Sacramento and the smaller but swift and powerful Feather River. He would have felt much safer in a wooden rowboat, but without an ax to cut and shape the wood or even pitch to seal the seams, Morgan chose reeds. His canoe, like those of the inland tribes, was about eight feel long and weighed less that fifty pounds. Its bow and stern were high and pointed where he had tied the reeds together with strips of leather. It took him almost as long to whittle a crude paddle as it did to construct the entire canoe.

His crossing of the Feather River was harrowing. But once across, Morgan hid his canoe in the marsh grass and continued to follow the Sacramento north, up the warm, silent valley. Day after day he came upon old campfires, and a few appeared to be made by white men rather than the Maidu who claimed these northern Sierra foothills. He managed to trap a few beaver living in the lagoons and small inlets along the Sacramento, but the hunting was not good. Still he continued north, marveling at the size of this great river. He recalled hearing that this waterway originally had been called Rio de San Francisco by the Spanish explorers. Only much later had it become known as the Sacramento, meaning "Holy Sacrament."

Late one afternoon, Morgan shot a beaver through the skull and roasted its tail on willow sticks. But the tail was too greasy for his taste, so when bullfrogs started croaking out in the shallow lagoon, Morgan decided that roasted frog legs would be more to his liking.

He lashed his knife to a six-foot-long cottonwood branch and tested its heft as a spear. Removing his clothing, he waded out into the shallow water, searching for the very same frogs that only moments before had been croaking up a full-blown serenade.

"Come on, come on," he grumbled, edging forward in the tricky footing and swatting mosquitoes that found his pale body a most delicious target.

A big frog splashed and shot out from between his feet, propelling itself underwater with amazing speed. Morgan drove his spear at the frog, missed and tried again.

"Damn!" he cussed because the frog had disappeared in the murky water. He was just about to give up frogging when he heard a shout, then twisted around quickly to see a reed canoe much like his own.

Morgan stared at a big white man dressed in buckskins in the company of a very beautiful woman. The woman was staring at Morgan, and he squatted down into the water, feeling like seven kinds of a fool. With great longing, he eyed his pants and shirt up on the beach.

"Hello, there!" the man shouted.

"Hello," Morgan replied without much enthusiasm.

The pair were in their forties but strikingly handsome. The big man said something to the woman which made her giggle. Morgan blushed, sure that he was the object of their humor.

"Could you possibly get my clothes for me or else ask her to turn around, sir?"

"I'll close my eyes," the woman said with a Spanish accent.

Morgan rushed out of the water and jumped into his clothes without bothering to dry off first. He turned around to see the big man churn hard with the paddle to bring his canoe into the little lagoon.

"Greetings!" the stranger said in heavily accented English as he propelled his canoe up onto the bank so that his woman did not even have to get her feet wet. "Sorry about our bad timing."

"Think nothing of it," Morgan said, wondering at the man's accent but feeling his eyes drawn to the woman dressed in buckskins and beads. Her long hair was braided and tied with leather thongs, and her feet were encased in beaded moccasins.

"Who are you?" the man asked.

"My name is Morgan Beck. I'm a hunter and trapper for Captain John Augustus Sutter."

The man smiled graciously. "This is my wife, María. My name is Anton Rostov. I work for myself."

"You are Russian?"

"I am. María is Spanish. What are you?"

"American with Mexican citizenship. My father and mother now live at New Helvetia. It's going to be the finest settlement in this whole great valley. Captain Sutter has just been given a grant of over fifty thousand acres."

"I see." The man did not look very impressed. He turned and began to unload a bundle of beaver pelts.

"You'd better not let the captain see those," Morgan warned. "The Mexican government has appointed him as its official representative in this valley. He frowns on intruders trapping his beaver."

"*His* beaver?" the woman asked with a smile. "They are God's beaver and belong to no man except the one who traps them."

Morgan felt like a fool. Time and time again, Sutter had directed him to warn any trappers he might meet in Alta California and tell them to leave. "Well," he stammered, "mostly the captain is worried about American trappers from the Oregon country."

The Russian finished unloading and gestured toward Morgan's fire. "I have some fish we caught earlier. Would you like some?"

"No, thanks. Want some beaver tail?"

"Thank you, no," the woman said. "We eat too much of it already."

"I wanted some frog legs," he said. "That's . . . that's what I was doing out there when you showed up."

"So we guessed," the Russian said. "We didn't think you were prospecting for gold in the nude."

Morgan blushed and nibbled on the fat beaver tail. The Russian and his wife cooked their fish and ate it with their fingers. Somehow the woman managed to do it looking like a lady.

Later, just after sundown when the swallows were dipping over the lagoon after mosquitoes, the Russian revealed his past.

"In 1812," he began, "Governor Baranov sent Captain Alexander Kuskov, forty Russians, including myself, and about eighty Aleut hunters from Sitka to colonize Alta California. We chose what is now called Fort Ross."

"I've heard of it quite often, but I've never been there."

The Russian stared into the fire, and Morgan thought he recognized a trace of sadness or perhaps bitterness in the man's voice when he said, "Not much to see anymore, Mr. Beck. But once it was something. Now I think my country will sell it."

"After a quarter century of struggle? Why?"

"It is simple. No more otter, and the land is not so good for growing crops. It is much too cold and foggy along the coast."

"Yes, it would be."

"So if you work for this Captain Sutter, what are you doing up this river? The pelts are finer and the beaver more plentiful higher in the big mountains."

"That's true." Morgan did not have a good answer to this man's direct question. "But I wanted to see this river. I have never followed it this far north."

Anton Rostov and his wife smiled. That caused Morgan to chuckle at himself. He felt good and comfortable with this pair, though they were, to his way of thinking, certainly unusual and not a little mysterious.

"Mrs. Rostov, did you also come from Russia?"

"No," she said. "My father, Don Arguello, owned a great rancho below the bay of San Francisco. Later, I decided to become a nun. I worked at the little mission at San Rafael to help the sick mission Indians."

"A nun? Oh, I see."

She laughed. "I don't think you do, but it is a long story. Anyway, I fell in love with God first and then with my husband. He does not mind being second in my heart."

Morgan started to laugh, thinking this was a little joke, but then he clamped his mouth shut when he realized it wasn't a joke at all.

"Where are you going now, if I may ask?"

The Russian extracted a pipe and some strong tobacco from his coat pocket. He lit the tobacco with a firebrand, then said, "We are going to see our friend, General Mariano Vallejo. He gives us the best price for our pelts and is very kind to us. He also has excellent brandy and pipe tobacco."

"I know the general."

María looked at her husband. "Mr. Beck has furs. We could sell them all together, and the general would be pleased."

The Russian nodded. "Do you like that idea, Mr. Beck? Perhaps you are acquainted with the general's beautiful niece, Señorita Rosalinda Navarro?"

"I have had that honor."

"Excellent! Then you should come. We can be there in a week. Maybe trap some together, eh?"

Morgan found himself nodding. Something told him this big, friendly Russian was an expert woodsman like his own father, but also high-born and a gentleman, in spite of his current rough appearance.

"I'd like that very much, Mr. Rostov, Mrs. Rostov."

"Good!" María said, clapping her hands together with delight. "But if we are going to travel together, we must address each other informally, by our first names—like friends."

She was so happy and had such purity and innocence that Morgan felt a rush of affection for her. "I think so, too."

"How well do you know the family?" Rostov asked. "Have you stayed with them?"

"I have," Morgan admitted.

The Russian glanced at his wife. "Señorita Rosalinda, she is very beautiful, no?"

"Yes," he said, his eyes dropping to the flames. "Very beautiful."

Morgan glanced up and saw that their eyes were filled with amusement. *Hell,* he thought with exasperation, *they can read me like a child's first book.*

≈ 7 ≈

General Mariano Vallejo's farewell dinner for Morgan was superb. Roast duck, pork, wild rice smothered with mushrooms, and a zesty cinnamon-flavored apple sauce. There were fresh vegetables and fruits and Swiss chocolate and English toffee for dessert. The imported French champagne and wines were as sweet as nectar.

Everything, Morgan thought, was perfect, except that Señorita Rosalinda was missing.

"A small indisposition," Vallejo assured them. Then, turning to Morgan, he said, "The señorita asked me to extend her regrets that she cannot be here tonight. She wishes you a safe return to New Helvetia and understands that you cannot wait until she is well enough to receive you."

"I understand," Morgan said, knowing that the man was lying through his perfect white teeth.

Rosalinda would have to be nearly on her deathbed before she would miss his farewell dinner. Morgan had seen her in good health this very afternoon, and she had confided that her uncle had forbidden her to join this dinner party. And rather than create a scene, she had promised to see him later night when they could share a few minutes alone.

The general turned to Anton Rostov and María. "It will perhaps be of interest to you, my dear sir, to hear that the commander of Fort Ross, Captain Alexander Rotchev, has offered to sell me the Russian settlements—not only Fort Ross itself, but also the inland farms."

Rostov lit his pipe with slow deliberation.

"Well," Vallejo said with impatience, "what do you think?"

Rostov looked up. Through a cloud of smoke, he said, "General Vallejo, I think you should do what you want."

It was obvious to Morgan that Vallejo wanted and expected more from the Russian, because he was unwilling to drop the discussion.

"As you know, I have often been a guest at Fort Ross, and I've seen the farm at Bodega Bay. The Russians are asking thirty thousand dollars, part in cash, part in trade goods. Do you think this is a fair price?"

"I haven't even seen Fort Ross in years."

"Yes, I know that, but you helped build the fort. And besides, the problem I face is that neither Spain nor my own country has ever accepted the Russian presence in California. Therefore, I should be considered unpatriotic to buy from the Russians what we do not believe they own. Do you see the problem?"

"Of course."

"And so," Vallejo was saying, "I can only offer to buy the Russian American Company's livestock, cannon, tools, and buildings. And these things are not worth nearly the asking price. At most, I can offer only eight or nine thousand dollars."

"They will refuse that offer."

Vallejo frowned. "I think so, too. But what am I to do? I cannot pay them a value for land that my government says they do not legally possess."

Rostov smoked his pipe in silence. It seemed apparent that the matter did not concern him in the least.

"My friend," Vallejo said at last, "would you negotiate with the Russians on my behalf? I would pay you very—"

"Never!" Rostov's black eyes flashed. "Never!"

Vallejo blinked. He looked to Morgan and then to María Rostov but found no help.

"Anton," Vallejo said, turning back to the Russian, "please reconsider. I believe a Russian can best deal with Russians. And besides, I am offering you the priceless gift of retribution against the same Russian

American Company that once unfairly stripped you of your citizenship and officer's commission, simply because you married a Pomo Indian girl."

Rostov poured himself more wine and tossed it down. He appeared menacing as he regarded the general. Then he said, "You also know that the Russian American Company had no choice but to banish me from their fort. I freely chose to marry an Indian girl. I knew the consequences because company rules were plain. I have no bitterness toward the company, and I seek no retribution."

"But surely the Russian officials could have made some allowances for a man of your quality. Instead they drove you from the fort into the wilderness. You became an outcast!"

"Enough of this talk," Rostov growled.

Protest flared in the general's eyes, causing María Rostov to plead, "General Vallejo, my husband will not change his mind on this. Better to find someone else."

"There are no other Russians who would bargain against their country."

"And neither will this one," she said.

As if to emphasize his wife's words, Rostov surged to his feet, bumping the table so hard, his glass of wine spilled. He seemed not to notice.

"General," he said in a quiet voice that was somehow very loud, "you are our host and friend, but *never* broach this subject of Fort Ross to me again. Is that understood?"

Vallejo had no choice but to nod in grim silence.

But Anton Rostov was seething. "General, if we are to remain friends, you must understand that I am as Russian as you are Mexican. The fact that my country lost what should have been a new Russian empire on this continent—or that your country soon will lose that as well—has nothing to do with our loyalties. We are patriots to our motherlands until death."

After a moment Vallejo sighed heavily, then pushed himself out of his chair. "Agreed, my friend. I was insensitive not to have understood that honorable men must

be both patriots and prisoners of their motherlands."
Raising his glass, he said, "To Mexico!"

Everyone drank.

"To Russia!" Anton said with passion.

Again they drank, and now María stood and raised her
glass. "To my Spain—to her conquistadores and padres
who first colonized this land."

"And to The United States of America," Morgan
added when everyone turned to him. He hoisted his
own glass, paused, and then said what he believed: "To
America, the next to lay claim to this rich land!"

Vallejo slammed his glass down on the table with
such force that its stem shattered. Anton and María
exchanged worried glances and then excused themselves for the evening.

Morgan drank his bold toast as Vallejo fumed in
silence.

"I do not think," the general finally managed to say,
"that it would be wise for you to return to this house or
to this town, Señor."

"Why? Because I just told you what you already
know, that Mexico City hasn't the will to hold what it
took from Spain?"

"I believe Captain Sutter," Vallejo said, his words
clipped and sharp-edged, "is being financed by the
American government to foment rebellion and bring a
revolution against Mexico. I also believe that the
Americans—through Sutter's Fort—intend to seize all
of California."

Morgan almost laughed. "The captain is financed by
no one! We survive on hope, credit, and promises. And
I will tell you in truth, General Vallejo, my captain is
very loyal to Governor Alvarado."

"I'm afraid that I don't believe that. And anyway,
your captain must also be loyal to *Mexico!*"

"Why? Is Mexico doing anything to help the Californios?
My own father was bled almost to death by your
corrupt officials."

Vallejo clenched his fists. "Your father had the extreme good fortune to marry well. He could have been
one of us, but he was a stubborn fool. He never joined

the Catholic Church or pledged his allegiance to Mexico City."

It took all of Morgan's resolve not to lash out at Vallejo. Perhaps what stopped him was knowing that, deep in his heart, most of what Vallejo said about his father was true. They were the same words that Mama had whispered with despair because her proud American husband would not bend his back or his will to the Mexican officials.

"And what," Vallejo asked, "will you choose to do, Mr. Beck?"

"I will never pledge my allegiance to Mexico," Morgan vowed.

"Then, like your father, you will be nothing," Vallejo said with contempt, "and that is why I forbid you to see Rosalinda again."

It was the one threat that Morgan had feared and that Vallejo was smart enough to use. All Morgan could think of to say was, "Rosalinda is not your prisoner, General. She is strong-willed and will do what she most desires."

"Do you love her?"

The question was totally unexpected, and he was momentarily confused. "Why, yes!"

Vallejo's expression softened. "Of course you do. Anyone could see that in your eyes. But . . . but if you love her, you must also see that the señorita is much too delicate a lady to live with a man like you. You are too different. You have nothing in common."

Vallejo paused, then said, "You haven't a shred of breeding or culture. She is far above your station, Señor. I am sorry. I mean you no unkindness. But what I say is most obviously true, and if you really love her, you will agree."

Morgan reeled backward. He blinked and then blurted, "You're wrong, General!"

"Am I? Please be honest, Señor Beck! There is no chance of happiness between two so different."

"Isn't there? What about my mother and father? *Your* cousin, General. She is happy!"

Vallejo's lip curled with contempt. "How happy can a

lady be who lives in a shack without beauty or books?
Without art or treasures? And if it were not for me—"
Vallejo caught himself and sighed. "Señor Beck, Rosalinda
should never have to live in a cabin. It is not in
accordance with her nature. I beg you to do what is
best for her and not think only of yourself."

Morgan was touched by this man's concern for his
niece and, however misguided, there was no doubting
his sincerity. "General, I'll have a rancho of my own on
the Sacramento River someday. It might not be as big
or as rich as yours or Sutter's, but it will not shame
your family or put your niece to hardship."

"Phhh!" Vallejo grunted, his cheeks blowing out with
derision. "You will have nothing, because like your
father, you are too proud and stubborn to bow to
Mexico."

Stung deeply, Morgan turned to leave before he
struck his host and not only disgraced himself but
demonstrated that he was indeed unworthy of standing
in the company of gentlemen.

"Wait!"

Morgan halted, then turned.

Vallejo seemed to deflate, and there was no hint of
arrogance or victory in his voice when he said, "You are
my guest, and I have treated you badly."

"Forget it."

"You must understand that I have a responsibility to
ensure that Rosalinda will marry well and find happiness."

"I said, never mind!"

"I have been too frank with you, but honest. Now be
honest with me—why is your captain building those
stockade walls?"

"Because the walls will offer him protection against
surprise Indian attacks."

Vallejo raised his eyebrows in question. "I have been
told that your captain has gained the complete trust of
the Indians. That he has even armed them and drilled
them to fight—perhaps against us? At any rate, I do not
think he fears the Indians, Señor Beck."

"You're wrong, General. He does have the trust of

most of the Indians in the valley, but not all of them. And others come to make trouble."

"Like who?"

"Just last fall, a band of San Jose Indians under Chief Acacio raided the Yalecumnes Indian village. They kidnapped the young women and took the children as slaves. They dashed the brains out of the old men and women."

"I did not hear of this!"

"I only heard about it later, after I returned from trapping. Captain Sutter went after them with a large force. He was able to overtake the Indians and free their poor captives."

"And what punishment did these Indians receive?"

"Fourteen of them were executed by firing squad."

Vallejo sat down in a big leather chair and steepled his thick fingers to rest his chin. "Perhaps I have underestimated Captain Sutter. And nothing would please me more than to believe he is loyal to Mexico."

"He is," Morgan assured him, "but he is very unhappy about all the trappers who are coming down from the north, many of whom are employed by the Hudson's Bay Company."

"He believes the Mexican government should do more?"

Morgan saw the trap that had been laid and therefore chose his next words very carefully. "He simply wishes to uphold the responsibilities given to him by the governor to protect the rights of Mexico in the interior lands of Alta California."

Vallejo's lips formed a thin smile. "Well said. Perhaps I have also underestimated you. Maybe I could help you in some way, perhaps have a word with the governor about another land grant on the Sacramento River—smaller, of course, but located wherever you choose."

Morgan did not trust Vallejo. "In return for what? Spying on Captain Sutter?"

"Spying?" Vallejo chuckled. "I know what Captain Sutter is doing almost as soon as it is done. What I want, Señor, is for you to be certain your captain remembers that what is Mexico's to give is also Mexico's to take. It is a very small thing I ask, no?"

"And for doing this . . . this 'small thing,' you would speak to the governor on my behalf?"

"It is possible that you and I could work something out to our mutual benefit."

"What about Rosalinda?"

Vallejo's brow furrowed. "What you need and deserve, Señor Beck, is a handsome peasant girl, or maybe an Indian maiden like Señor Rostov once traded for his Russian officer's commission. Such a woman of the land would make you very happy."

The general filled two glasses with brandy and came around the table to give one to Morgan. Vallejo smiled benevolently and held the glass up to the candlelight. "Señor Beck, a peasant Mexican or Indian girl would honor you with strong children. She would not complain because you had no china or crystal, no imported wine or fancy lace or silk dresses."

Vallejo made a sweeping gesture around the room at the walls covered with oil portraits of his family and vibrant tapestries, at the heavy furniture carved by European craftsmen. "Señor, again, it is not your fault. Find a peasant girl and marry her. I will speak to the governor. With our help, you could prosper."

"Go to hell!" Morgan smashed his glass on the tile floor.

Vallejo's voice became a lash. "As I said, stubborn and foolish! Such qualities will earn you only scorn and failure. Good night, Señor Beck!"

Morgan's stomach was as tight as a closed fist and he was shaking with fury when he threw open the door to his room and saw Rosalinda standing beside his window, clutching a beautifully tooled leather traveling case.

"What are you doing here at this hour?" he demanded.

She had started toward him, but the hardness in his voice froze her in her tracks. "Morgan, my darling, I am coming with you to New Helvetia. I am leaving all this because it means nothing to me without you."

The anger and frustration drained out of Morgan.

And more than anything before in his life, he wanted to jump forward and crush this woman in his arms, but the harsh truth of the general's words were booming over and over in his ears.

"You must stay here," he heard himself telling her. "This is no good."

"What?"

She started forward, but he threw up his hands. "No, listen to me! I have nothing to offer someone like you."

"But I love you!" She began to sob, throwing herself across the room into his arms, arms which lifted despite his efforts to keep them locked at his sides.

"Rosalinda, can't you see that this is no good?" he whispered. "You don't know—"

But she was half crying, half making love talk that was driving him wild with desire. Morgan could not resist, much less reason with this woman he so loved. And the very fact that she was willing to defy her uncle and give up so much to be at his side filled him with amazement. "Rosalinda," he said tenderly, "you can't go with me."

"Of course I can! I am not a slave or a captive. I am free to do whatever I wish."

"This just wouldn't be right. I have nothing to offer you. Perhaps someday, but not yet."

Rosalinda threw her arms around his neck and kissed him hard on the mouth. Morgan felt his heart pounding in his ears, and his fingers tore at the buttons of her dress. She sighed with happiness and pleasure as his hands and then his lips found the softness of her breasts, and she shivered with ecstasy. When his hands slipped under her dress and caressed the smoothness of her thigh, she moaned but then whispered, "Please, my dear, if you love me, wait until we have been married. I will love you forever if you give me this dignity and honor. Please."

Morgan turned away from her, chest heaving as if he had run many miles, or had been drenched with a bucket of ice water.

"Morgan," she said in a throaty voice, "forgive me. If we go away together now and find a priest, we can—"

"No, it's just no good," he said. "Not yet, anyway."

"But why? I love you. I have loved you from the moment I saw you in Monterey."

"The first time you saw me I was drunk and smelled like fish."

Rosalinda knelt beside him on the bed and struggled to put her feelings into words he would understand. The moonlight touched the tears on her cheeks, and Morgan thought her so beautiful that his throat ached. He reached out and cradled her face in his rough hands.

"Rosalinda," he whispered, "can you tell me why you fell in love that night with this drunken fool?"

"I'm not sure," she said, looking deep into his eyes. "For I don't understand it myself, though it is all that I have been thinking about for such a long, long time. Perhaps it's because you were so different from all the others that come to my uncle's casa."

"Oh, I'm sure I was, but not in a way that I would be proud of."

"You did not act so important like the others. You were . . . sweet and gracious. And I even thought you . . . Never mind."

"No, please," he said. "I want to know."

"All right, then, you made me laugh. I thought you were funny."

"Funny?" Morgan scowled. "I'm not at all funny."

"You made me laugh and feel happy inside."

"I don't understand."

She shrugged her shoulders and smiled. "Me neither. I can only tell you that, long ago, I grew weary of self-importance. I have seen little else in the men that come to visit my uncle. You had none of that, and I loved you for it."

"You're crazy."

"Love is crazy." She touched his lips. "I am convinced of this. You can only understand it by what you feel inside. If you love someone, then being with him makes you very happy. You want to sing out loud. To shout his name to the world and say, 'I love you, Morgan Beck!'"

Rosalinda cocked her head a little to one side, and she looked amused. "Did ever want to do that with my name?"

"Yes," he admitted a little sheepishly. "I have shouted your name when I thought I was all alone in the forests. I loved to hear the sound of it echo up and down the steep canyons and soar over the mountaintops."

She shivered with joy. "So I am right, no?"

"Yes, you are right. Once, however, a small hunting party of Maidu Indians heard me shouting at the treetops."

"They did!"

"Yes." Morgan chuckled.

"What did they say?"

"They were very kind. They asked me to go somewhere else, because I was scaring all the game away."

Morgan and Rosalinda laughed easily together, but when their laughter died, Morgan said, "Your uncle wants me to marry a peasant or an Indian girl, one that will be content with very little."

When Rosalinda said nothing in response, Morgan stopped and knelt to take her hands in his own. "Well?"

"As you know, my mother and father were lost at sea when I was very young. The governor and General Vallejo, they think they are both my father. You must understand and forgive them for wanting me to marry a rich man like themselves."

"If I were them, I'd feel the same way."

"But they are wrong, because money doesn't mean you are going to be happy."

"It helps."

"Yes, but I know many rich people, and many of them are very sad. They would give everything for happiness and peace of mind. For a lost child. For health or the health of those they love."

"I know this," he told her, "but look around you now. This house, this room, it is filled with beautiful things."

"Things! That is all they are!"

"But you don't understand, Rosalinda. You've never been poor. It kills the spirit. It takes away human joy. It demeans the soul. And for someone like you, who has always had so much, it would be more than difficult."

Rosalinda clenched her hands in her lap. "Morgan, listen to me. We will *not* be poor! Only at first. We will build our lives together. And if we need help, then my uncles—"

"No help," Morgan said bluntly. "I don't want anything from either of them."

"But—"

"If they helped me, I'd never be free of them. They'd own me, Rosalinda! I must find a way to build my own fortune. Only then could I live as an equal member of your family."

"But how? You told me that you have made a promise to work for Captain Sutter for another year."

Morgan stood up. "As soon as that year is over, I will begin to build something."

"You will not take me with you now?"

"I can't! If I did, it would ruin any chances I'd ever have of earning your family's respect. The governor would never forgive me, and neither would Don Mariano."

Her tears glistened in the moonlight. "And that matters so much?"

"Yes," Morgan heard himself say. "And I don't expect you to understand it. You'd have to have lived these past years in my family and seen what being under Mexican authority has done to my father. How it made him bitter and a...a man not to be trusted in all things."

Morgan had almost confessed to her that his father had been a thief. Shaken, he reached for Rosalinda's hands and pulled her to her feet. "You must go now." He gently pushed her toward the door before his will failed.

"Good-bye," he said. "I'll come back because I love you, now and always."

At these words, a cry escaped from her lips, and she vanished into the dark hallway. Morgan stumbled to his bed, knowing that he would not sleep this night. His heart was still pounding, and his fingertips were still tingling from the touch of Rosalinda.

"What have I done?" he asked the darkness all around. "What have I done?"

Silence was his answer. Had he been the fool that Vallejo accused him of being? Had he allowed pride and stubbornness to rob him of the greatest joy he might ever know? Had he lost Rosalinda forever and made vows he was not man enough to keep?

Doubts and fears filled his questioning mind until at last he called out to his God and prayed, though he had never considered himself a strongly religious man. He prayed for the strength, wisdom, and courage to follow his dreams and prevail over all the forces that seemed to be stacked up against him—Sutter, Vallejo, Governor Alvarado—none of whom could be trusted to further his ambitions.

"Only you, God, and Rosalinda and Mama can I completely trust."

Morgan turned his face toward the open window and wished he might see a shooting star, for Eli had always told him they were a sign of good fortune. When at last it came, the night was almost gone, but feeling strangely reassured, Morgan dressed and prepared to leave.

As the first glimmer of daybreak peaked over the eastern hills, he gathered his belongings and his Hawken rifle and departed from Casa Vallejo. The general had promised Morgan the loan of a horse to carry him down to San Pablo Bay, but Morgan was determined that he should never again accept a favor from Vallejo. By starting now, he would be able to reach the captain's supply schooner with perhaps an hour to spare.

He was just outside the Vallejo casa when a voice said, "May I walk with you, Morgan Beck?"

Morgan spun around, Hawken automatically slamming to his shoulder. When he saw the tall shadowy form of the Russian, Morgan expelled a sigh of relief and lowered his rifle.

"Of course."

As they started across the plaza, Morgan's eyes were drawn to Rosalinda's bedroom window. Her presence, so near and so powerful this long night, gripped him

like a magnet, and it was all he could do to keep
walking.

For perhaps a mile, they trudged along in silence.
Morgan set a fast pace, but Rostov did not appear to
notice. The Russian's long, powerful legs did not have
the spring of youth, but he was solid and hard-muscled.

"How far will you walk with me?" Morgan said as the
sun detached itself like a burning ember from the
black, rolling hills.

"Maybe not so far if we begin to talk."

"I have said too much already at this place," Morgan
told the Russian. "I have said too many wrong things."

"Why didn't you take her with you?"

Morgan's step faltered. "How did you know?"

"Rosalinda had to tell someone. It was our job to
calm the general down so that he did not send vaqueros
to rope and drag you to death."

"Oh." Morgan's lips formed a hard line. "Some of
them would have died if they had come after me."

Rostov said nothing, but he did not appear impressed.
When they had walked a second mile, Morgan said, "So
what do you want to talk about?"

"I want to say that General Vallejo is a good man. He
is not your enemy."

"And neither will he ever be my friend."

"He distrusts your captain. This fort that Sutter
builds, with high walls, bastions, and cannon, it con-
cerns all the Mexican officials. Vallejo believes that
General Alvarado has made a bad mistake with your
captain."

"Captain Sutter will remain loyal to Alvarado and the
Mexican government."

"Morgan, understand that the reason General Vallejo
asked me to deal with the Russian American Company
is that he wants their cannon."

Morgan halted in his tracks. "For what purpose? To
be used against some imagined attack by Captain Sutter?"

When Rostov's chin dipped in assent, Morgan scoffed.
"That is ridiculous."

"I am glad to hear you say this with passion, my

young friend. But even saying this, it seems to me that you are walking a very dangerous path."

"Come with me to New Helvetia and talk to Captain Sutter yourself if you do not believe that he has no intention of biting the Mexican hand that feeds him."

"We will, and soon. But what of the señorita?"

"I'll come back someday."

"You should listen to your heart and not your head," Rostov said, voice faintly scolding.

"Like you did with the Pomo Indian girl?"

The muscles in the Russian's jaw corded. "I could not know that she and my child would be killed by a grizzly."

"I'm sorry. I didn't know that you had also lost a child."

Rostov twisted around to gaze back at Sonoma before he turned again to Morgan. "Good-bye. María and I think you have made a mistake by not taking the señorita to wife."

"If I have, it wouldn't be my first mistake, or my last. But I'll be back for her someday."

"Don't wait too long," the Russian advised him solemnly. "Love is not a game to be played like chess. Think too much, and the passion dies and you have already lost."

They shook hands, and Morgan left the big Russian and did not look back, though in mind and body and spirit the pull of Casa Vallejo and Rosalinda was so strong that it took all of his strength and will to keep moving toward the bay.

"I will return," he repeated over and over to himself. "I will return as an equal to Alvarado, to Vallejo, and even to Captain Sutter."

That summer, Morgan joined Captain Sutter and a pair of his most trusted vaqueros and rode to Livermore Pass, then to the old Mission San Jose, where they bought fresh horses before continuing on to Monterey. It was good to be on horseback, and Morgan was as fine a horseman as the vaqueros, though he knew he would never be able to duplicate their magic with a reata.

In Monterey, Governor Alvarado kept his promise

and awarded Captain Sutter eleven square leagues,
over fifty thousand acres, the largest grant permissible
by Mexican law. The captain also hired six good men,
including one Negro who was expected to cause quite a
stir among the captain's Sacramento Valley Indians, who
had never before seen a black man.

They sold their horses and returned to New Helvetia
on a sailing vessel. Sutter's great success was tempered
somewhat by Alvarado's refusal to dispatch Mexican
soldiers northward to halt the increasing numbers of
American trappers.

"If he can't or won't oppose the Americans," Sutter
told Morgan as they left the old presidio of Monterey,
"that tells me I'd better make friends with them."

"But why?"

"Because the land grant that I've just been awarded
will be worthless if the Americans become numerous
enough to overthrow Alvarado and the Mexican government."

Morgan nodded, well remembering his unfortunate
toast to the Americans while in the company of Vallejo
and Anton and María Rostov. But he, like most Americans, had been talking for years about the corruption of
the Mexican officials. It seemed somehow natural that
Spain, Russia, and Mexico each would enjoy a brief
stage appearance in California, only to be finally escorted
into the wings by the expansionist Americans.

As if echoing Morgan's thoughts, Sutter said, "Mr.
Beck, I'm sure you are as aware as I am that the United
States government is looking westward with a pale and
hungry eye. And there is a popular doctrine called
Manifest Destiny that is gaining support in Washington,
D.C."

"What does that mean?"

"It's a feeling by Americans that they should one day
own this continent from coast to coast, that it's inevita-
ble, an American destiny."

Morgan nodded. "Very convenient, wouldn't you say?"

Sutter was amused by his comment. "Convenient is
one way to put it, but the fact is that Mexico was
soundly whipped and driven out of of Texas when the

territory won its independence at the Battle of San Jacinto. I think California is the next American battleground and conquest. And if it is, it's imperative that I be ready."

"But you have been so outspoken against the American fur trappers."

"Of course I have! They're stealing money out of my pockets! But you'll notice I've shown them every hospitality."

It was true.

Sutter paused and then continued. "No, Mr. Beck, I am riding the fence, waiting to see which way the wind is about to blow. I intend to be considered a friend by whichever government is in power."

"Which would you prefer?"

"I would prefer to be left alone to my own designs. What you must always remember is that life is a long, long race. How we finish the race is all that matters."

"I can't do much now except pay off my debt to you."

"Which you are well on the way toward achieving," Sutter cheerfully reminded him. "Before the winter is over, you will again be earning a handsome income. What then?"

Morgan thought of his promise to Rosalinda and even of General Vallejo's hint of a land grant of his own along the banks of the great Sacramento. He decided that this time his hopes and dreams would remain unspoken.

"I am not sure."

"I have been considering your future and thinking that I can use you to better advantage in ways other than as my hunter and trapper. I can find and employ other trappers. Pablo Gutierrez is one, but he is also too valuable to me at New Helvetia."

"Then who?"

Sutter frowned. "What was the name of that Russian you met at Casa Vallejo?"

"Anton Rostov."

"And you say he knows all the rivers and Indian tribes of northern California?"

"Yes."

"And that you invited him and his wife to visit my settlement?"

Morgan nodded.

"Good! I could very well use a trapper like him. And as for you and your father, perhaps you could operate a cargo ship to generate an income on short but lucrative trips to Yerba Buena, Monterey, and Fort Ross. I am talking about a partnership, Mr. Beck."

Morgan tried to appear interested, but the truth of the matter was that he had no desire to return to the coast of California. More and more, he was thinking about establishing a rancho and building a herd of livestock along the Sacramento, either north or south. He could even do this without Governor Alvarado's knowledge or blessing. If the Mexican officials lacked the will or courage to stop the American intruders, then why would they treat him any differently?

Yes, he thought, with hard work, determination and some of the knowledge he'd gained from watching Captain Sutter, Morgan felt confident of success. He could speak all the Indian languages, and he could generate badly needed income in the beginning by trapping the icy Sierra streams during wintertime when his Sacramento Valley land lay fallow. Morgan could see himself and Rosalinda working side by side to build a great rancho. He would become Sutter's equal instead of his hired hand.

"When we return to New Helvetia," Sutter was saying, "there is much work to be done. I want the stockade walls to be finished before wintertime and the new tannery and blanket factory to be in full operation."

"Yes, sir," Morgan said, his mind filled with visions of his own flourishing enterprise.

Sutter was in a generous and expansive mood. And why not? He had just been given more land than most men would ever dream of owning.

"I'm glad that all enmity between us has ended," the captain said, "and I think it is working out very well to have your mother and father at New Helvetia, don't you?"

"Yes. Father's health already seems much improved."

"Of course it is! The Sacramento Valley is for growing things and for healing the mind and the body." Sutter affectionately pounded Morgan on the back. "When your father's debt is paid, I hope you are smart enough to remain my loyal and trusted servant. I will reward you handsomely!"

Morgan knew that some response was expected, so he forced a smile and nodded his head, thinking about the day when he would bring Rosalinda Navarro up this river to his own casa and prosperous rancho.

≈ 8 ≈

Eli Beck was restless and irritable because the temperature was well over one hundred degrees in the shade. Just outside the new stockade walls, the captain was drilling his elite "home guard" of handpicked Indians, young men proud of their blue drill pantaloons, white cotton shirts, and bright red bandannas tied closely about their heads. In their fists they held the scarred old French muskets once carried by Napoléon Bonaparte's invading forces but lost under the deep, deadly Russian snows. The old weapons had found their way to Fort Ross, and Sutter had purchased them from the commander there.

"This here heat is about to be the death of me," Eli complained. "Damned if it ain't more than a man can endure. I don't know how your mama can cook for the captain in this kind of weather. It just plain frazzles me down to a nub."

"It's plenty hot, all right," Morgan agreed, "but your lungs are clear and your color is good. You look ten years younger than when you and Mama first arrived."

"Well, I sure don't feel younger. And marchin' them poor Digger Indians around and around in this hot weather is gonna kill 'em for certain. This heat is awful!"

Morgan nodded. There had been a drought, and Sutter's corn and wheat crops were withered and disappointing. However, his herds were expanding, and water hauled up from the American River was keeping

his young orchards and vineyards green and growing.
Sutter even had his own distillery and delighted in
serving his special visitors a brain-busting grape pisco.

The weather had to cool down before long. Morgan
had just finished trapping high up the middle fork of
the American River the week before, and it had been
twenty degrees cooler in the pines. The trapping was
good, and he'd humped down a backbreaking load of
furs. He was going to have to talk Sutter into lending
him the use of a horse or mule next time. Either that or
Pablo Gutierrez was going to have to come along and
help.

"It was hot like this the first time me, Jim Bridger,
and Kit Carson ever seen the Great Salt Lake," Eli
said. "I believe the year was 1825. Old Jim, Kit, and
me could see that water, and it was a-shinin' like the
sun fallen to earth. Just the sight made us thirstier than
dogs in a desert. So we hurried across the sands to that
desert lake and threw ourselves down and drank deep."
Eli's eyes crinkled at the corners, and he chuckled.
"And you know what?"

Morgan did, for he had heard the story many, many
times over the years, but now he shook his head,
knowing how much his father liked to recount the tale.

"Well, we all came up a-spittin' and chokin'! Old Jim,
he beat on his chest, threw back his head, and hollered,
'It's *salt*water, boys! We've just discovered the whole
damned Pacific Ocean!'" Eli guffawed and slapped his
knees with his big gnarled hands. "Thing of it was, Kit
Carson and me believed him!"

Morgan jointed his father's laughter, for he could well
imagine that picture. "You helped Bridger and Carson
make history."

"Yeah, but nobody will ever remember my name. Or
that of most of the boys. Just a few, like Jim, Kit, Hugh
Glass, Colter, and Jed Smith. Don't matter, though. I
didn't take up the life to be in the history books. I did it
for the adventure. Besides that, a good mountain man
trapping virgin rivers could make ten times what he
could make any other way. And when we had ourselves
a rendezvous, there was enough ready Indian women

and good whiskey to kill the weak and make the strong
howl like starvin' timber wolves."

Morgan had heard all about the famed rendezvous.
They had been annual get-togethers, with men con-
verging from hundreds of miles around, intent on trading their furs for goods, gold, and pleasure. Wild trappers—
mostly drunk—wrestled, footraced, and swapped lies,
horses, and women as they struggled to best each other
in whatever contest was proposed. They played card
games, seven-up, euchre, and poker, and if they won,
they were expected to treat the losers. It was considered mean-spirited to leave with more wealth than you
brought, yet some men departed a rendezvous without
even the dignity of their buckskin breeches.

"Seemed like," Eli had once confessed, "the object
was always to lose our fur and our minds, then go off for
another year of trappin' and livin' off the land the way
God intended."

"Look!" someone called. "A ship!"

All eyes turned in the direction of the American
River to see a sailing ship tacking upriver against the
current. The arrival of Sutter's weekly supply schooner
was reason enough for excitement, but the arrival of a
foreign vessel was cause for a celebration. Everyone
stopped whatever work he was doing and hurried on
down the road toward Sutter's new embarcadero.

"It's a Russian schooner!" Eli shouted, noting the flag
she bore.

Sutter soon arrived, resplendent in his Swiss military
uniform and obviously delighted to play the role of a
gracious host to the visiting Russian officers. When the
schooner docked, crisp salutes were exchanged and
then Sutter marched on board to exchange handshakes
all around. Their captain looked every inch the proud
and decorated military leader.

"Wonder what them Russians are after," Eli grumbled, disappointed like everyone else when it became
apparent that there were no fresh supplies or interesting trade goods to admire.

"I don't know," Morgan said. "The way General
Vallejo talked the last time I visited Sonoma, I would

have thought he'd bought the Russians out by now and sent them back to Sitka."

Later, Morgan accompanied his father back up the hill, following Sutter and the heavily perspiring Russian officials. "Damned heat is about to fry my brains," Eli muttered. "What we need to do is go trappin' up in the high country. You should talk to Captain Sutter about that first thing. I'm ready."

"Sure you are," Morgan said, knowing his father still had a long way to go before he would be strong enough to be of any help trapping.

Eli plunked himself down on a rough wooden chair in front of his little cabin outside the fort's new stockade walls. Because of the fortress walls, everyone was starting to call the settlement Sutter's Fort instead of New Helvetia, just as Morgan had predicted. This rankled the captain, but he probably understood that there was little he could do to change this more popular name. Besides, as far as Morgan was concerned, this *was* a fort.

"I guess we'll find out soon enough what the Russians want from the captain. Your mama will be cookin' and servin' late tonight. The captain won't let her go till it's all finished."

Morgan's eyes tightened at the corners. "Someday," he vowed, "Mama will sit in a fine rocking chair and I'll have an Indian girl doing all the cooking."

Eli looked at him and scoffed. "Hell, son, you're going to wind up just like me, old and crotchety and busted, without no money and damn few friends."

In the past, Morgan had agreed with that assessment, but things had changed since he'd made up his mind to earn the right to marry Rosalinda. Not a day passed that Morgan did not dream of riding to Casa Vallejo on a fine horse with silver trim on his saddle and bridle. Upon his arrival, one of Vallejo's house servants would bow and take his horse, while another escorted him in to meet the general. Vallejo would acknowledge him as an equal and would address him, not as Señor but as Don Morgan. Then they would drink a toast and Morgan

would ask for Rosalinda's hand in marriage, knowing in
his heart that he deserved such a woman.

"Son?"

Morgan snapped out of his reverie. "Yes, sir?"

"Your mind is a-wanderin' again. Seems to be doing
that a lot lately."

Morgan squinted up at his father's pinched and leath-
ery face mirrored by the afternoon sun. "Must be the
heat."

The answer satisfied Eli. "It's a sonofabitch, all right.
Seems to hardboil my brains like duck eggs throwed in
a Yellowstone geyser. Let me tell you, when John
Colter first saw one o' them geysers, he told me he
thought it must be Satan pissin' up from the bowels of
hell. That boilin' water stinks, but in the winter, when
it's forty below zero, it feels better than a squaw under
a buffalo robe."

Morgan nodded, but his mind was already slipping
back to the last night he had held Rosalinda and kissed
her breasts. He could have made love to her. She would
not have stopped him if he'd been insistent. Morgan
swallowed hard. He'd wanted to, all right, but he was
glad he hadn't. Better to earn the right to be her man.

That night Mama Estella was not excused from Sutter's
headquarters until very late. Morgan and Eli were both
waiting. When Mama exited the stockade gates, they
hurried up to meet her. It upset Morgan to note the
weariness in her step and the heavy, stooped way she
moved toward them.

"We can't let him work her so hard," Morgan said.
"She's just too old and tired."

"I don't know why the captain don't make that worthless Kanaka girl help Mama," Eli said angrily. "All she
does is sit around and giggle and look pretty. She must
be something in bed, although I hear the captain is
about to toss her out."

"Why?" Morgan masked his concern.

"I guess he caught her with one of his men. Like to
killed 'em both, he was so mad. Wasn't the first one
that's pleasured himself with Manuiki on the sly. That
girl ain't nothing but a little whore."

"She's . . . all right," Morgan said.

Eli started to say something, but Mama called a weary greeting and they hurried forward, each taking her by an arm and helping her up to the cabin. Morgan eased her down at the table and removed her moccasins, while Eli brought a pail of warm water from the stove.

"Mama, your feet are pretty swollen up," Eli said. "Good thing you're wearin' moccasins. Never get them big feet out of regular shoes."

Morgan began to massage his mother's feet, easing them in and out of the warm water, vowing silently that as soon as the Russians departed he would speak to the captain about his mother being overworked.

Eli brought Mama a bowl of rick elk stew, but she shook her head wearily. "When I cook all day, I'm not hungry at night. Just tired."

"What's going on inside the fort?" Eli asked. "We could hear all sorts of laughing."

Mama propped her chin up with her hand. "Commander Rotchev wants our captain to buy his Russian fort."

Morgan looked up. "General Vallejo told me that he intended to buy Fort Ross. He sounded like the deal was already made."

Mama shrugged her round shoulders. "I only know what I hear. The Russian, he say that Don Vallejo and the Hudson's Bay Company want to buy, but he rather sell to Captain Sutter."

"That means the others backed out of the deal," Eli said. "What did our Captain Sutter tell them?"

"He said maybe he'd buy Fort Ross."

Morgan resumed massaging his mother's feet. "Doesn't make any sense to me. Besides, due to this year's drought, the captain doesn't have any extra grain to sell for cash."

"Ain't nothin' new in that," Eli said. "He just buys on credit."

Morgan had to agree. "Mama, I'll be speaking to the captain about these poor feet and your legs tomorrow. The next day, I've got to go trapping again."

"I'm ready this time," Eli said. "Be cool up in the mountains."

"You'd better wait, this trip. Mama's feet and legs are pretty bad. Might be she'll need you here."

Eli didn't like that, didn't like it at all, but he cared enough for his wife to nod his head in grudging acceptance.

Noting Eli's keen disappointment, Morgan said, "We'll go this winter. That's when the fur is best in this country."

"Sure."

Morgan noted his mother's eyes drooping with the need for sleep. "Now you better help Mama off to bed."

"She ain't gonna be able to get up early and cook the captain and all them Russians a big breakfast. I just won't have it."

"If I have to, I'll cook Sutter's breakfast myself."

"Rouse that worthless whore, Manuiki, and tell *her* to make breakfast!"

Morgan figured that would be a mistake, because Manuiki was probably sleeping in Sutter's bed right now.

He dried his mother's feet, then went outside to sleep under the stars. The night was sultry. Morgan heard laughter, punctuated every half hour by Sutter's home guard sentry crying, "All is well!"

Shortly before daybreak, Morgan rolled out of his blankets, stretched, and them ambled over to a crock of water, splashing several handfuls over his face before shaving. Minutes later, he tiptoed into the cabin and found a clean shirt before heading off to the fort.

A guard opened the stockade gates, and Morgan went directly to a big kitchen, where large hooks attached to the ceiling held slabs of beef, mutton, and smoked ham in anticipation of the feasts ahead. Morgan started a cooking fire and decided that today breakfast for Sutter and his guests would be fried beef, sliced potatoes, and cornmeal mush. Not fifty feet away, in a much larger outdoor kitchen, several sleepy-eyed Indians were already sweating over big iron kettles of acorn mush and beans for the army of Indian laborers.

The sun detached itself from the rim of the earth before Sutter made an appearance. He looked groggy, and his face was bloated from the night's drinking and feasting.

"Coffee," he growled.

'Coffee' often was made from crushed acorn nuts, but in honor of the Russian guests real coffee would be expected, and Morgan had it ready.

"Thanks," Sutter said thickly. "Mr. Beck, do you want to journey over to Fort Ross? We're leaving this morning."

Morgan would have enjoyed visiting the Russian fort but realized that he would never get his debt to Sutter repaid if he didn't go trapping. "Better not, Captain."

"The Russians want to sell it to me for thirty thousand dollars. What do you think of that price?"

"It's the same they asked of General Vallejo."

"Yeah, but they expected immediate payment from Vallejo. They're offering me terms I can't very well refuse. Just two thousand dollars down and the rest to be paid eventually in wheat, tallow, and other goods."

Sutter gulped his coffee and made a grimace because it was very hot and strong. "Mr. Beck, they aren't even requiring any time payments on the remainder of the debt! That means I can string 'em along for years. Now, what the devil kind of fool could turn down such an offer?"

"I don't know."

"Well, I'll tell you something I do know. Commander Rotchev gave me an inventory, and it's longer than your arm. Lumber, workshops, plows, rakes, hoes, and enough flat and angle iron to keep our blacksmith busy for years. There are harnesses, forges, carts and wagons, cooperage equipment for barrel-making, and that twenty-ton schooner down there resting at my embarcadero."

"She's a beauty."

"Damn right she is!" Sutter took a deep breath. Excitement burned through his bloodshot eyes. "And that fine Russian schooner is exactly what I had in mind

when I told you that I had other plans for you and your
father. We can use it to pay off all my debts."

"Yes, sir."

"And livestock." Sutter blew steam across his coffee.
"Mr. Beck, the Russian inventory lists seventeen hundred cattle, a thousand horses and mules, and twice
that many sheep. Got a few pigs and chickens, too, if
we can catch them up. Mark my word, buying out the
Russians would—in one bold stroke—make me the
most important landholder in all of California!" Sutter
licked his lips in anticipation. "And I haven't even
mentioned all the muskets and cannon that will afford
me total independence. I'll be more heavily fortified
than the Monterey presidio! No one will dare to oppose
my authority. It's like a gift from heaven, the answer to
all my prayers!"

Sutter lowered his excited voice. He took Morgan by
the shoulder and leaned in close. "You go trap some
beaver—all that you can. When you finish, we'll talk
about a new arrangement, one that will begin to put big
money in your pocket as well as my own."

"I wanted to talk to you about my mother."

"Your mother?" Sutter was caught off balance. "What's
she got to do with any of this?"

"It's her legs and feet. They're all swollen up. She's
old and she can't work so many hours."

Sutter waved his hand with irritation, spilling his
coffee. "Fine! She can rest while I'm off to Fort Ross.
We can talk about your mother's feet and legs after my
return."

Sutter held out his cup for a refill. "Get Manuiki to
help this morning. She doesn't do anything anyway.
And after breakfast, get packed up and be on your way.
But return before all the leaves have fallen and we've
finished the harvest. I'm going to need you, Pablo, and
a few vaqueros to drive the livestock from Fort Ross
over here. My Indian herdsmen would scatter them all
to hell."

Morgan nodded and poured himself a cup of coffee.

"I'll get Manuiki," Sutter announced. "She'll do whatever you want; she's always been fond of you."

Morgan blushed. "Sir, I'd like to take Pablo Gutierrez with me into the mountains tomorrow."

"I can't spare him. Take a couple of horses, or better yet, pack mules. Is your father fit enough to work yet?"

"No, sir."

Sutter did not look pleased. "We've all got to carry our own weight at New Helvetia. I can't tolerate any slackers."

Morgan blushed with anger and was about to say something, but Sutter disappeared into his adobe and Morgan heard him ordering Manuiki to help cook breakfast.

When she stumbled outside, the Kanaka girl was half asleep, her eyes thick-lidded and her hair tousled. She looked even more dissipated than Sutter. Morgan was sure she had drunk as much liquor.

"Morgan," she said with a yawn as she stood with hands on hips and watched him slice beef, "look at you. Look at me! Cooking like Digger Indians. We should have run away last year when we made love, eh?"

"Maybe so," he told her with a grin. "But right now I need you to slice potatoes."

"Coffee first," she said, brushing her hand across his back as she passed so that he would remember her touch.

Morgan needed no reminders. He had not had a woman since that time with Manuiki, and he seriously doubted that any other could match her skill at lovemaking. No wonder Sutter put up with her.

It was late autumn and the forest was splashed with gold, yellow, and crimson before Morgan returned to Sutter's Fort. He led his weary mules across the stubble of the freshly harvested wheat and corn fields. Despite the drought and the poor harvest, tons of grain and corn had been gathered, and now Morgan watched as Indians waved blankets and shouted to stampede horses around and around a small pen. The pen was filled with wheat, and the horses' hooves were breaking the wheat from the stalks. That accomplished, Indians would gather the stalks and toss them into the wind,

separating even more wheat from chaff. The resulting
grain would be sacked and either traded in Yerba Buena
or delivered to Sutter's new gristmill, where it would
be ground into flour.

Recognizing him, many of the Indians stopped their
work long enough to wave and call a greeting, Morgan
returning their welcome. He felt good, and his mules
staggered under the weight of beaver pelts.

Eli hurried out to greet him. "Damn fine pelts!" he
announced as soon as they were unloaded and stacked
inside a storage room. "The captain is going to be
mighty pleased. He put me in charge of 'em, you know.
I'm also working a little in the carpentry shop."

"Good for you. How is Mama?"

Eli's smile slipped. "I'm afraid she's under the weather right now. Sleepin', I expect."

"Is she seriously ill?"

"Naw, you know Mama. She works herself like a slave
and then gives out for a few days. She'll be fine."

"Is the captain around?"

"He's over to Fort Ross again. Bought the Russians
out lock, stock, and barrel." Eli ran his hands lovingly
across the new beaver pelts, and a faraway look crossed
his eyes.

"Well, I'll be damned," Morgan said. "So who's
running the show while he's away?"

"A new fella named John Bidwell. He straggled in
with an overland party from Missouri. Half starved,
they'd et all their livestock trying to get across the
deserts and the Sierras. Captain Sutter appointed Bidwell
his chief clerk."

Morgan gave the mules over to the care of a Maidu
Indian in charge of Sutter's stables. "In that case, why
don't you make the introductions? I sure don't want to
get off on the wrong foot with this fella."

"He's all right," Eli said. "Seems a little stuffy at first,
but he's fair and hard-working."

His father's assessment proved accurate. John Bidwell
was Morgan's age, but having been a schoolteacher in
Ohio, was much better educated. Morgan liked the
man immediately. Bidwell was modest, unassuming,

and far more capable than Sutter at handling the tedious bookkeeping and letter-writing that the captain detested—especially those communications imploring patience from his many creditors.

"The captain wants you, Pablo, and some of the vaqueros to deliver the Russian livestock," Bidwell told Morgan after the introductions. "In a few weeks I expect to be sent to Fort Ross to oversee the transfer of Mr. Sutter's new property. But the captain would prefer his livestock be delivered before winter."

"Then we should leave as soon as possible. We'll have to swim the herd across the Sacramento River. It'll never be lower than it is now."

Bidwell's jaw dropped. "I hadn't even thought of that! Can it be done?"

"We'll soon find out."

Bidwell, who had been seated at a desk, came to his feet. "You and the others should not be asked to risk your lives."

"I'll keep that in mind."

Morgan prepared to leave, but Bidwell cleared his throat. "By the way, the captain has spoken to me about you and your father operating the Russian schooner that came with the purchase of Fort Ross. Of course, we will need the vessel for the next six or seven months while we move everything on over from the coast."

"Of course."

"In the spring, after a winter of profitable trapping, I'm sure that some kind of working partnership can be created between you, Eli, and the captain. Captain Sutter is the most generous man I have ever met. I can't tell you how much time he's personally devoted to teaching me Spanish and helping me get back on my feet."

"I'm glad to hear that." Listening to this man, Morgan was reminded of the time when he was just as effusive in his praise of Sutter. Bidwell was still in the honeymoon stage with the captain, but that would change soon enough.

"Yes. He's become both a father and a brother to me.

Have you noticed that there are many new American families living here now?"

"I have."

"More come each week," Bidwell said with pride. "Sutter takes them all in, offering them work and a chance to own their own property one day. Mark my words, Mr. Beck, this is becoming a very strong American colony, and we'll both do very well in Captain Sutter's employ. We are blessed to stand high in his esteem."

Morgan saw no point in confessing that, come spring, he wanted to found a rancho of his own, with or without Sutter or the Mexican government's approval.

"Wish us luck crossing the Sacramento River, Mr. Bidwell."

"Are you and Pablo good swimmers?"

"We swim like stones," Morgan deadpanned.

Bidwell did not see the humor. "You take care of yourselves. In a way, I wish . . ."

"Wish what?"

"I almost wish that the captain had not assumed so much indebtedness by purchasing Fort Ross. Oh, I realize it's a great opportunity, but it's a crushing burden, and if we have another year of drought, I just don't know how we're going to meet next year's payment."

"The captain told me that there were no payment dates."

"Oh, but there are. I've seen the contracts." Bidwell began to count off the terms of payment on his fingers. "Next spring the captain must pay sixteen hundred bushels of wheat, a hundred and sixty bushels of peas, forty bushels of beans, fifty quinatles of soap, five thousand pounds of suet, and six thousand two hundred and fifty pounds of tallow. An equal payment is due in the following spring and twice that amount the next year. It's a heavy liability, and one we'll meet only if we have a succession of good harvest years."

"If not, the captain will simply add the Russians to the long list of his other creditors. He knows full well that, once departed, they're not going to be in a strong position to collect payment from Sitka, Alaska."

"They could legally attach this entire settlement for that debt," Bidwell warned. "It's written in the contract."

"Captain Sutter would open up on them with his cannon if they tried, legal or otherwise."

Bidwell expelled a deep sigh. "Let's all just do our best to see that that isn't necessary."

Morgan turned and left without a reply. Once the Russian herd was delivered, he was declaring himself a free man. The furs he'd just brought in were more than enough to repay his debt. It was time that he began to build something for himself and Rosalinda.

It was nearly one month later, and the branches of the cottonwoods along the western banks of the Sacramento River were bare as Morgan, Pablo Gutierrez and a handful of vaqueros drove more than three thousand head of horses, mules, and cattle toward the river. The day was cold, and a thick, dirty blanket of clouds stretched out to hide the loftiest peaks of the Sierra Nevadas. A stiff wind from the west rippled the Sacramento's broad surface.

"What do you think?" Morgan asked his Mexican friend.

Pablo shook his head, worry lines etched deeply in his face. "I think we ought to slaughter these damn cattle right here and ship their hides across that river."

Morgan had to chuckle in spite of the grim circumstances they now faced. "That's probably not a bad idea. It's the hides that are worth all the money. Still, Sutter needs the beef now that he's got an army of workers to feed."

Pablo started to reply, but the heavens growled with thunder and a burst of wind sent whitecaps racing across the water.

"Down there," Pablo said, pointing a little to the south. "That is where we should cross, where that sandbar fingers out near the trees."

Morgan knew that Pablo had already swum a horse across the river in several places, testing the depth, the current, and the footing. Morgan had also heard that the big Mexican had nearly drowned.

"Damn, but I don't like this!" Morgan swore, twisting around in his saddle and studying the solemn vaqueros who had helped him drive the herd more than a hundred miles from Fort Ross.

"Let's get it over with, amigo. We can only drown once, eh?"

Morgan watched a bolt of lightning shiver down from the heavens and he knew that it was about to rain. If he could get the herd across before a storm caused the river to rise farther, their chances were that much better.

"All right! Let's drive them in!" Morgan wheeled his horse around and spurred hard. "Hi-yaw!" he shouted, slashing his fifty-foot leather reata against his leather chaps. The other vaqueros followed suit. All had proven themselves expert horsemen, brave and skilled at trail driving. Now they would have to be, if they were to cross this great river.

The cattle, horses, and mules did not want to go out into the river, but they had little choice. Those in the front were shoved deeper and deeper into the dark, roiling current until they were lifted from their feet.

"Don't let them turn back once they've started across!" Morgan shouted into the wind.

The vaqueros savagely attacked the bellowing cattle with their reatas, whipping them into the water before plunging in themselves.

Horses squealed in terror and mules brayed as the current whirled them around like a slow-moving top. Cattle bawled, pawed water, and drove each other down toward the river's bottom. Halfway across, Morgan's worst fears were realized when Sergio Rodriguez cried out as his horse was rolled under the thrashing herd.

Swearing and spurring uselessly, Morgan formed a loop with his reata and, when Rodriguez's horse reappeared and began to churn directly downriver, Morgan cast his loop. The reata settled neatly over the vaquero's crazed mount and jerked its head around.

The vaquero's spur was hooked in his cinch. When the rawhide reata snapped taut between them, Morgan threw himself from his saddle and used the reata as a lifeline to bring himself to Rodriguez's side.

The vaquero was drowning, kicking and wild with panic. Morgan fought the man, his horse, and the current, trying to free Rodriguez. Suddenly the Mexican's free spur ripped through Morgan's cheek, filling his mouth with river water and blood.

He gagged and somehow cleared his throat. "Hold still!" Morgan shouted, as a bawling cow swept in toward them. Even as he watched, the cow's legs turned straight up in the air. Morgan grabbed Rodriguez, and they were driven under as the cow flipped over them and was swept downriver with dozens of others. One of the animal's flaying hooves smashed Morgan in the lower leg, and he felt it snap like a brittle twig. He screamed underwater, and when his head broke the surface, Morgan summoned the presence of mind to tear his hunting knife free. He slashed at Rodriguez's spur strap until the spur came loose. Before the vaquero was spun away by the current, Morgan looped his arm around Rodriguez's neck and pinned him to his saddle.

"Hang on!"

Rodriguez, more dead than alive, hooked an elbow around his saddlehorn and pried his fingers into his cinch ring. Morgan did the same, but as they clung to the swimming horse, trying to avoid the drowning cattle that hurtled by, Morgan did not believe he would live to reach the west bank of the Sacramento.

But he did. The herd, led by mules, followed by the horses and then the cows, dragged itself up onto the far bank to collapse as rain began to pour down in great drenching sobs.

The people of New Helvetia rushed down from the settlement to help, and when Morgan coughed up blood and water, it was Manuiki who cradled his head in her lap and wept.

"Get away from my son!" Eli yelled, pushing the Kanaka girl aside. "Mama, it's all right, it'll heal clean!"

Mama ripped part of her dress into bandages. Not far away, Rodriguez could be heard retching violently.

"We did not lose any men," Pablo said, kneeling at Morgan's side as the heavens opened with rain and the earth shook with thunder and lightning.

"How many cattle?" Morgan choked.

"Maybe two hundred. That is all."

Morgan gazed up at the crowd of anxious faces. "Sutter can stand that kind of loss. We can fish out the carcasses tomorrow."

"Don't talk like a fool," Pablo scolded.

Morgan stuck his tongue out at his good friend through the hole in his cheek, and Manuiki fainted in the mud.

≈ 9 ≈

Morgan did not leave Sutter that winter after all, because if the captain had not sent the *Constantine* to Yerba Buena for a doctor he would have lost his leg to infection. Because of that, Morgan felt duty-bound to stand by the captain for at least a few more years.

The next spring, Mama Estella caught a fever and nearly died, and this time Sutter himself, with the aid of his medical books, was instrumental in her recovery. After that, Mama could not seem to regain her strength but found contentment and purpose in teaching the Indians about Jesus and pressing Captain Sutter to build a school and a chapel.

Eli also seemed at peace for the first time in memory. He oversaw the collection and storage of the furs that Morgan and several newly hired men were able to trap. Sutter's Fort continued to grow and prosper. Each week seemed to bring a few more Americans, many of them ex-sailors and tradesmen of every description, seeking new opportunity.

In the spring of 1844, Morgan returned to the fort to be greeted by a very excited Pablo Gutierrez, who exclaimed, "You'll never guess who arrived week before last!"

"I'm not any good at guessing games," Morgan said, leading his thin, tired mules with their heavy pelts up the rise toward the fort.

"It's Lieutenant John C. Frémont and Kit Carson!"

"Really!"

151

"Yes," Pablo said, "but you should have seen them when they rode in here—more dead than alive."

Morgan's heart quickened its beat. He'd heard plenty about Frémont, who was being called the Pathfinder after his exciting exploration of the northern territory between the upper Missouri and Mississippi rivers. Always restless and eager for attention, Frémont next had gone west to survey the unmapped regions of the Platte River, then South Pass and the Wind River country. His expeditionary parties included skilled topographers, artists, and scientists, whose reports and maps were of such high quality that they were printed by Congress and widely distributed, earning Frémont national praise and recognition. Many of Frémont's successes were due to his friend and extraordinary guide, Kit Carson.

"Frémont is important," Morgan said, "but it's Kit Carson I want to meet. I'll bet my father and Kit are swapping old mountain man yarns right now."

Pablo's smile faded. "I'm afraid, amigo, that your father is gone."

"What?"

The Mexican raised his hands and then dropped them helplessly to his sides. "He left for Yerba Buena on Sutter's schooner the very day that Frémont and Carson arrived." Pablo toed the earth. "Amigo, he . . . he was pretty drunk."

Had anyone but Pablo said this, Morgan would not have believed him. Why, his father and Kit Carson were the best of friends! Again and again, they'd saved each other from Indians, grizzly, blizzards, and desert thirst.

"Here," Morgan said, shoving the lead ropes into Pablo's hands, "you take these furs into the stockade. Is my mother still in her cabin?"

Pablo nodded solemnly. "She is very sad."

A few minutes later Morgan found Mama sitting at her table reading the Bible, but there was no joy or peace in her eyes.

"Mama," he asked, "what is wrong?"

Tears rolled down her cheeks, and she pushed herself

to her feet and hugged him tightly. "Your father is gone."

"But, why? I don't understand any of this."

"Sit down. You look tired and thirsty."

Morgan sat while his mother found a tin cup and a bottle of Sutter's grape brandy.

"I have something to tell you," she began. "It is about your father. You know the story about the Great Salt Lake?"

"Sure, the one when he and Jim Bridger and Kit—" Morgan's voice fell away as he suddenly understood why his father had run off rather than face Kit Carson. "Mama, were *all* his stories lies?"

"No," she whispered. "But some. I am not sure. Didn't you ever wonder why the stories sometimes sounded different?"

"No... well, I just thought..." Morgan shook his head. First the lie with Sutter's fur money, now this. His father, it seemed, was nothing but a puffed-up old windbag.

"He is a good man!" Mama Estella cried loudly. "And all the stories, what harm did they do?"

Morgan came to his feet. "What good did they do, Mama? He didn't need to tell them."

"He thought so. Besides, your father was always poor. He had to bend his knee many times, first to the Spanish officials, then to the Mexican. But in your eyes, because he was a mountain man, he stood tall."

"Did he do *anything*?"

"Of course! Your father did trap beaver, and I am sure that he knew great men like Kit Carson."

"I doubt it. I really doubt it. All those stories of the rendezvous, of Bridger and Colter and the rest... I doubt that any of them were true."

Mama placed her hands on his shoulders and shook him hard. "Your father married me. He gave us love and a home. Yes, he always wanted money and importance—but for us as much as for himself. Especially for you, his son. Have you grown wise enough to understand these things that a man or woman feels for their children?"

Morgan suddenly felt very ashamed. "Where did he go?"

"I think back to San Pablo Bay."

"I'll bring him back here. I'll leave on the next supply run to Yerba Buena."

"And what will you tell your father when he asks about Kit Carson?"

"I don't know."

"Tell him that none of the stories matter! Tell him my heart aches."

"All right," Morgan promised, "but first I've got to see the captain. He'll know how soon I can leave. If there's not a supply ship leaving here soon, then I'll row down the Sacramento."

That afternoon Morgan met John C. Frémont and Kit Carson. Frémont was of average height with strong features and cool, penetrating eyes. He wore a full beard and mustache and was dressed in the uniform of the army except that he wore a bright yellow sash around his waist through which were shoved two revolvers.

To Morgan's way of thinking, the Pathfinder was aloof. Upon their introduction, his handshake was quick and perfunctory. Without preamble, he said, "Mr. Beck, what do you think of this Mexican government of California?"

Surprised by the directness of the question, Morgan replied, "It does what it can, considering how little support it receives from Mexico City."

"It is weak and corrupt," Frémont pronounced, as if he had lived in California many years. "Mr. Beck, you should begin to think about Manifest Destiny. That's our call."

Frémont turned away, dismissing Morgan and leaving him angry and thinking of the words he should have said to this imperious lieutenant. Frémont might already be famous, but Morgan decided he was also a pompous ass.

Kit Carson, however, was of a different stripe. Eli had always claimed—and Morgan gladly believed him then—that Kit Carson was one of the finest and bravest men ever to explore the West and trap its swift, pure rivers.

"Carson wasn't afraid of hell or high water," Eli had bragged. "His word is gospel, as sure as the sun comin' up."

"Mr. Carson," Morgan said, studying the famous mountain man with more than a casual interest as he curried his horse.

Carson slowly turned and looked up at Morgan. He was not a remarkable physical specimen. Unlike Frémont, Carson would never catch a man's eye or stand out in a western crowd. Short and powerfully constructed, he possessed an unusually mild, pleasant expression. His blue eyes were warm and inquiring rather than bold or penetrating, as one might expect of such a renowned explorer. Morgan guessed him to be in his mid-thirties.

"Sir?"

Carson looked directly into Morgan's eyes and smiled. "Yes?"

"My name is Morgan Beck. I . . . I heard a lot about you, Mr. Carson. It's an honor to meet you."

"Beck? Are you by any chance related to Eli Beck?"

Morgan blinked. "Why . . . yes!"

"I'm sorry that I missed seeing your father after so many years. He was very helpful to me when I first entered the beaver trade."

"He was?"

"Sure. Eli and Jim Bridger were the two men I most admired."

"Were you . . . I mean . . . was he—"

"Is something wrong?

"No, but I was wondering if you were with my father when he and Jim Bridger first saw the Great Salt Lake."

"Did he say I was?"

Morgan nodded.

Kit Carson's mouth split into a wide grin. "Well, I'll be damned! The truth of it is, I wasn't there at all. But I heard about it later. I guess your father's reputation as a storyteller is almost as great as Bridger's. Both men could spin a yarn that'd make you think they discovered everything in the West."

Morgan blushed. "But he really was Jim Bridger's friend?"

Carson nodded. "They cut a lot of trail between them. Is your father coming back before we leave? I'd sure like to see him again."

Morgan didn't remember much of their conversation after that. He didn't need to. It came to him straight that, while Eli Beck was an inveterate liar, he wasn't a fake. He'd been a mountain man, a friend of the great Jim Bridger, and a man that even Kit Carson had admired.

"Lord," Morgan whispered to himself as he walked away feeling as if he'd won some great fortune, "I thank Thee for that. I surely do!"

Morgan was still at New Helvetia when Frémont and his men headed south.

"I do not like Lieutenant Frémont," Sutter confessed as he waved good-bye to the departing expedition. "He acts as if he owns this settlement."

From Pablo Gutierrez, Morgan learned that friction had surfaced between Sutter and Frémont when the lieutenant himself had accused three Americans of stealing sugar. Captain Sutter, authorized by the Mexicans to be the supreme authority in the Sacramento Valley, listened to the accusations and then rendered the three innocent of all charges. Sutter's action had infuriated Frémont, who seemed to feel that his authority had been compromised.

Morgan understood, especially considering Sutter's extremely generous treatment of the American expedition. Frémont and his half-starved men had received food and new clothing when they arrived in rags. Their horses had been shod by Sutter's blacksmith and heavily grained so that they had the strength to carry the Americans back across the hundreds of miles of western mountains and deserts to safety.

"In the innocence of my heart," Sutter confessed to Morgan as the Americans disappeared, "I thought I would do the United States government a favor by not taking advantage of Frémont's distress, but I only cheated myself."

The next day, the supply schooner arrived, unloaded, and prepared to return to Yerba Buena. "Captain," Morgan announced, "I'm leaving to find my father."

"I understand. I wish you luck and Godspeed. And I'll be departing soon myself. I have urgent business in Monterey with Governor Micheltorena."

Governor Alvarado's successor, Comandante-General Manuel Micheltorena, was an appointee of Mexico's new president, Antonio López de Santa Anna. Immediately after Micheltorena's arrival, Sutter had rushed to Monterey to welcome the new governor and had won an extremely generous additional land grant that increased his already sizable land holdings to more than 225 square miles of the richest farmland in all of Alta California. Because of this huge addition to his already immense holdings, Sutter was very impressed with the handsome new governor.

"And so," the captain explained, "it will be good to see him again and I am sure that my services will be most valuable."

"Is he having political problems?"

Sutter nodded. "The governor is a gentleman, but he was forced by Mexico to bring too much army rabble into Monterey. The populace is already calling his troops *cholos*. I have it on good authority that almost all of Micheltorena's soldiers were exiled to California after being released from jails in Mexico City."

"I suppose it's most unfortunate that your friend Governor Alvarado was replaced."

"On the contrary, Alvarado never had the courage to order troops against the Hudson's Bay Company's trappers. That cost me a lot of money."

"I know, but—"

"Besides, my sources inform me that Alvarado and General José Castro are plotting to overthrow Governor Micheltorena."

"Is that possible?"

"More than possible. Both are ambitious and powerful men. I am told that they are ready to blockade the governor in Monterey, forcing him to resign before they decide which of them is to be governor."

Morgan had heard none of this, but of course he had been in the mountains trapping. "I had no idea that there might be a revolution, and yet Alvarado has seized the governorship by force once, so why not again?"

"Why not, indeed? And so, Mr. Beck, I had to decide whom to support. Because of Micheltorena's generosity to me, I chose to warn him of his enemies' plot. I also assured him of my complete loyalty and assistance in any matters related to the security of his person or office."

Sutter looked at Morgan. "I can easily read your troubled thoughts. Yes, I have stuck my neck into the noose, but there was no choice. I had to back the governor or plot to depose him. I chose the former."

"That's quite a gamble."

"The stakes are high," Sutter conceded, "but I have more cannon now than the Mexicans. I have more than thirty loyal Indians trained to use musket and hundreds more to fight at my command. Additionally, I have no less than fifty white men like you and John Bidwell on whom I can count. And finally, these past six months, I have been welcoming all the American trappers, even those from the Hudson's Bay Company. They know that they would receive more favorable treatment from me than from General Castro, who is suspicious of all foreigners—myself being at the top of his list."

"Has Alvarado remained in Monterey?"

"Yes, but I will take pains to avoid him." Sutter frowned. "Why did your father leave so suddenly without informing me?"

"He . . . he had urgent business."

Sutter didn't appear satisfied, but he didn't press Morgan for more information. "By the way," he continued, "I also heard Señorita Rosalinda Navarro is engaged to be married to Don Francisco Cabral, a man of some means who owns a big rancho near Sonoma. Perhaps when you retrieve your father, you might also want to pay her our respects."

Morgan felt as if he had been sledged between the

eyes. A chill passed down his spine and his insides went numb. "When is the wedding?"

Sutter was studying him very closely. After a long moment he said, "No date has been announced. But I'm sure that I'll receive an invitation. Mr. Beck, is there something you would like to confide to me? Perhaps I can be of service."

"No, thank you." Morgan abruptly excused himself and walked in a daze across the compound. Several people spoke to him, but he felt as if he were drifting in a fog and he did not acknowledge their questions. He did not stop walking until he reached the American River, where he sat down, drew his knees up, and rested his chin on his arms.

What else could he have expected of Rosalinda? She had written to him many times during the first year. But Morgan was not a writer, and each time he had tried to pen a letter, General Mariano Vallejo's prophecy had resounded in his ears: *You will never have anything. You are stubborn and too proud. You will always be poor like your father.*

Morgan recalled his nearly forgotten dream of riding a fine horse into Sonoma with a silver-mounted saddle and bridle. Now the dream was shattered, and it mocked him so cruelly that an involuntary sob was torn from his throat.

"Mr. Beck? Are you all right?"

Morgan started and twisted around to see Captain Sutter behind him, wearing an expression of deep concern.

"Captain," he stammered with embarrassment.

Sutter took a seat on the riverbank beside Morgan. "I read your expression of shock at the mention of Señorita Navarro's engagement. I have no wish to intrude upon your private thoughts, my trusted friend, but neither can I allow you to lose something more precious than land or gold. Do you love that girl?"

After a long moment, Morgan said, "Yes, sir, and I have thrown away my only chance at happiness."

"Thrown it away?" Sutter shook his head in disagreement. "Come, come, now, Morgan! You are a young

man in a young country. Opportunity for wealth and
happiness are everywhere."

"Well, I didn't seize it at all," Morgan said bitterly.
"Once, Señorita Navarro almost *begged* me to elope
with her. You have the authority to marry us. We could
have been man and wife. Perhaps even had children by
now."

Sutter picked up a flat rock and skipped it across the
water. "And why didn't you bring that lovely girl to New
Helvetia? I find her totally charming."

"So do I." Morgan stared out at the water. "The first
time we were in Monterey and you were meeting with
Governor Alvarado, she kept me from making a drunk-
en entrance."

"I rather remember that. You caused quite a commotion at the door. The governor questioned Rosalinda
rather sternly, but she never revealed that you were the
cause of our interruption."

"I should have married her, and now she is lost,"
Morgan said, feeling utterly devastated.

"Then why didn't you?"

"I was under a debt to you, sir. And the next year,
when the debt was satisfied, I broke my leg in the river
and you sent your schooner all the way to Yerba Buena
for a doctor, saving my life."

Morgan absently fingered the puckered scar on his
cheek. "After that, it was Mama being sick, and I kept
inventing excuses not to write or pay her a visit. I
wouldn't have been welcomed by General Vallejo, and I
felt unworthy to call upon Rosalinda."

"Take heart, Morgan. It is my observation that a
sense of unworthiness can draw out the best in men."

"How so?"

Sutter cleared his throat. "Once, I confessed to you
that I left my wife and five children in Switzerland and
barely escaped before being thrown in debtor's prison."

"Yes. I remember."

"And you never once told anyone, did you?"

"No. It was a confidence."

"Correct. And because you never told anyone, I was
in your debt. I felt unworthy, and my confession to you

reminded me of my parting vow to send for my dear family when I became a financial success." Sutter clenched his fists together. "But I haven't done that, have I?"

"No, sir."

"I've let it slide, so to speak. But because of a growing sense of unworthiness, I no longer consort with Manuiki. Now I think it is time that we both ought to get down to the business of keeping our promises."

"That is much easier for you, having already achieved your wealth. But I've only my name to offer Rosalinda."

"Nonsense! You've great promise. I will help you obtain a land grant, and I'll extend to you the assistance and credit that others extended to me when I had nothing but my dream of a Swiss empire."

Morgan's heart began to pound with excitement. "Do you really mean that?"

"I most certainly do!" Sutter skipped another rock across the surface of the American River. It bounced seven times. "So let's both stop disappointing our hearts and do what is right and honorable—you with Señorita Navarro, me with my wife and children waiting in Europe."

Morgan looked deeply into his captain's eyes and said, "John Bidwell told me he rather thought of you as a brother and a father. I have a father, but no brother. I will think of you that way."

Sutter blushed warmly before he climbed to his feet. "Mr. Beck, I've just decided it would be best for you not to take the supply schooner downriver."

"Why not?"

"You cannot arrive in Sonoma walking or riding in a damned *carreta!* You should make a dramatic entrance on a fine horse, one with a silver saddle, preferably, because General Vallejo is easily impressed by fancy trappings. Wear a new suit. Our tailor will supply that. And new boots, from my cobbler. Have you saved any money?"

"Almost two thousand dollars."

"Excellent! But beware! General Vallejo might have you shot or hanged for eloping with his niece."

"I'll be very careful."

"See that you do. Bring the girl back here at once. I will order Bidwell and the others that you and Rosalinda are to be protected at all costs until I can return from Monterey and perform an official marriage ceremony."

Morgan's chest swelled with hope. He was certain that he could abduct Rosalinda, but what if—

"While in Monterey," Sutter declared, slapping Morgan on the shoulder hard enough to grab his attention, "I'll petition Governor Micheltorena to give you title to a land grant. I will insist that it be on the Sacramento, either north or south of my own land."

Morgan couldn't believe his good fortune. "That would be . . . wonderful!"

"Come along," Sutter ordered, moving briskly toward his fort. "Also, Mr. Beck, I will extend to you a line of credit for cattle, lumber, and seed. You will, of course, promise not to draw away my best Indian workers."

"Of course not, but—"

Sutter was energized and fairly bouncing with plans for their future. He was in a mood to talk expansively, not to listen. "And we should, working diligently, manage to get our crops planted in time. With good weather and plenty of rain—"

"Captain!"

Sutter glanced up suddenly, again realizing that Morgan was at his side.

"Yes, Mr. Beck?"

"What if Rosalinda chooses to marry Don Francisco Cabral?"

"That's no problem." Sutter shrugged. "I won't marry them."

Morgan almost laughed out loud. The captain's mind was on other things. "But, sir, they could find a priest."

"Then . . . then you'd just have to find another wife, Mr. Beck!" Sutter exclaimed, spinning away and continuing up the hill.

Morgan shook his head in amazement and went to catch the man before his entire life was mapped out, including how many children he would father.

≈ 10 ≈

Morgan rode down from the steep western hills
overlooking his father's shack beside San Pablo Bay.
The familiar chilling fog, the wheeling, bickering seagulls
and the dark, blue-green water all combined to remind
him of the long years he and his family had struggled to
earn a hard existence under California's Spanish and
Mexican officials.

The shack below had been Morgan's home for more
than a decade; he had hiked these lonely, windswept
hills a thousand times. And on spring days such as this,
he had often picked bright blue, yellow, and gold
flowers for his mother's table and dreamed of someday
picking them for his future wife.

Between Morgan's long, muscular legs now pranced a
fine sorrel gelding with a flaxen mane and tail. The
black, tooled saddle he rode was adorned with silver, as
were the bridle and the Spanish bit and spurs that
helped him control his mount. They glittered in the
morning sunlight.

Morgan wore a Spanish nobleman's short coat and
trousers, with gold piping and embroidery. The pants
legs flared over his polished boots, and upon his head
rested a fine new felt hat, ivory-colored and flat-brimmed.
The hat was decorated with a colorfully beaded and
feathered headband, a gift from Chief Anashe of the
Miwok.

Tied to Morgan's saddlehorn was a rope that tethered

two more trailing horses and a pack mule. One horse was for Rosalinda, the other for Eli.

"Hello!" Morgan shouted when he was yet a quarter mile above his father's tired old shack. "Father, it's Morgan!"

As always, there was a stiff cold wind blowing off the huge bay, and it pushed Morgan's words back into his face, carrying with them the taste of salt and rotting seaweed. There was no answer from the shack, nor was there smoke drifting out of the rusted stovepipe. When Morgan rode around in front, however, the door was ajar. It was dim inside, and although Morgan was certain that his old home was deserted, he called once again. "Father?"

His answer was a thin, rattling cough.

Morgan jumped down from his horse and barged inside to see Eli stretched on the old bedframe they'd left behind when they'd moved to Sutter's Fort.

"Dear God!" Morgan cried, dropping to his knees beside the bed and cupping his father's ice-cold hands between his own. Any thoughts he might have had about confronting Eli on Sutter's stolen money vanished. His father had already suffered enough. "What have you done to yourself?"

Eli barely roused. He coughed again, and his breath was fouled with rum. That, coupled with the stench of human waste and sickness, was so overpowering that Morgan scooped his father up and carried him outdoors. Eli weighed nothing, and Morgan propped him up against the windward side of the cabin.

"Father," he said, cradling the man and gently shaking his head back and forth. "Father, wake up!"

Eli's bloodshot eyes snapped open but did not seem to focus. He blinked, scrubbed the back of his hand across his face, then recognized Morgan and muttered, "Son, go away!"

"Not very damn likely," Morgan growled, striding over to his pack mule. "First, I'm going to clean up inside, then I'm going to heat water enough to wash you while we drink plenty of strong hot coffee and fry up a big meal."

True to his word, Morgan had his father and their old shack clean by sundown and Eli well on his way to being sober. "Eat all you can; it'll make you feel a whole lot better. Manuiki packed all this food for me, and she sure wasn't stingy."

Eli, his face drawn and gray, stared at him through liquor-tortured eyes, burped, then climbed up from the table to go stand in the open doorway and watch the sunset over the bay. "So why didn't you leave me alone?"

"Mama wants you back. So do I."

Eli began to cough so hard that tears ran down his sunken cheeks.

Morgan looked away because it hurt him to see his once strong and straight father bent and quaking with his sickness. "This wet climate is filling up your lungs again."

"I don't give a damn!" The outburst pushed his father into another fit of violent coughing. Eli had to reach out and grab both sides of the doorframe to support himself, and he hung as if crucified against the rectangle of brilliant sunset.

Morgan squeezed his eyes shut and said, "You may not give a damn, but the captain wants you back. And if you want to die so bad, why didn't you just shoot yourself in the head and make a clean job of it? Why would anyone want to die the way I found you today?"

Eli finally got his coughing under control. He twisted around, falling back against the wall as he shouted, "I would have shot myself, damn you! I tried, but my powder got wet!"

Morgan blinked. "You can't do anything right anymore, can you?"

"No! And that's why life ain't worth livin'. Not like this it ain't!"

"Mama will die without you," Morgan heard himself say, and saying it, he knew it to be true. "And you're going back to her."

"And I say to hell with you. I'm old and sick enough that I'll do whatever I want with the time I have left."

Morgan went to stand beside his father, a man he was

beginning to realize he did not know well at all. Turning to watch the dying sunset, Morgan's eyes chanced to light on their old, sagging dock. Without constant repair, it would not last through a single winter, and yet somehow, keeping it patched up and standing had been their ritual. That, and sitting on it while building boats and rigging fishing tackle. That dock had been theirs; this shack had been Mama's.

Suddenly he recalled how Eli had always jokingly threatened to pitch him into the bay for the sharks whenever he did not behave.

"If you won't come back to Mama," Morgan said, turning to look deeply into his father's angry eyes, "I'll just have to throw you to the sharks."

Eli's eyes widened, and then he snorted with laughter. "You'd better be ready for a fight, son. I ain't as frail as I may appear."

"I know that; I just wanted you to know it, too."

"The captain, he sure sent you in style." Eli looked his son up and down. "I never seen a Beck look so fine nor ride a fancy horse and silver-mounted saddle. You look good, son, as good or better than any man I ever seen."

"Captain Sutter wanted us to look good when we ride into Sonoma."

"What are you talking about?"

"We're going to see Señorita Rosalinda."

"You don't need me—"

"There may be trouble," Morgan interrupted. "She's supposed to be engaged to Don Francisco Cabral."

"Cabral? I've met him," Eli said. "He's a toady bastard with too much land and money. Another relative of Vallejo's. Them people are thicker'n fleas on a fat dog."

Morgan saw no point in reminding his father that Mama Estella also was part of Vallejo's privileged family. "I need help in Sonoma. Mama sent along your best clothes. I've also brought you a new hat and boots."

Eli scowled. "Clean clothes and new boots won't impress Don Mariano. He's always disliked me for marrying Mama. Tried to talk her into leaving me more than once. Son, I'd only cause you more harm than good in Sonoma. Vallejo will have his men run me off like a cur."

"Not in my presence," Morgan vowed. "Besides, what I have to say is for Rosalinda's ears, not his. If she really loves Cabral, then she can have him with my blessing. But if not, we'll take her away, no matter what the general says or does."

Eli liked that. He brightened a little, but then his shoulders sank and he said, "What makes you think a girl with any sense is going to marry you instead of a rich man?"

"Because I'm going to have land and cattle before much longer. And I know you don't believe that, but Captain Sutter has promised to ask Governor Micheltorena to give me a big land grant on the Sacramento River. It's the finest land in the world for raising cattle or crops."

"And why would Micheltorena favor a Beck with land?"

"Because the governor needs Captain Sutter's help if he is to survive an insurrection in Monterey."

"How do you know this?"

"The captain has good sources. There is a plot against Micheltorena, and the governor won't survive another month in office without Sutter. Naturally, the captain's help won't come cheap. He'll want something in return, for himself—and for us. I've asked for land; I expect the captain will ask for more of the same."

The earlier skepticism vanished from Eli's drawn face. He could not hide the excitement he felt inside. "If this is all true, it could change everything for us, son!"

"Not could, *will* change everything," Morgan said. "And together we'll build a herd and a rancho that will be the envy of everyone in California."

"Yes," Eli breathed. "You'll never know how I've chafed all these years under the rich, ruling class of Spaniards and Mexicans! I hate them lazy, corrupt bastards! Not one of them ever worked in their lives, but they drive the poor Indians and folks like me like

cattle." Eli's voice shook with passion, and he clenched
his bony fists. "I dream of seeing them broken and
humbled! To see men like Vallejo stooping to work in
the fields or covered with blood, fat, and flies as he
hides a beef."

Eli's face, ravaged by sickness, age, and alcohol, now
crawled with hatred, causing Morgan to say quickly,
"Father, this is not a personal vendetta! We're going to
Sonoma to win the hand of the woman I love. I won't
let you destroy everything because of your hatred."

"Not everything. Just a part of Vallejo, when he sees
another Beck steal away a Vallejo woman. It will cut
him to the bone."

Morgan looked away, realizing that he may have
made a terrible mistake by coming here first. His
father's hatred ran deeper than he had suspected. It
was a cancer devouring his soul. He had to change the
subject before anything more of this was said between
them.

"I saw Kit Carson. He said he was sorry you weren't
at the fort."

Eli was visibly jolted by this news and managed to
whisper, "What . . . what else did he say?"

They had gone too far now to deal in lies and even
half-truths, so Morgan replied, "Carson told me that he
wasn't there like you said he was on the day that you
and Jim Bridger discovered the Great Salt Lake."

"I wasn't there, either," Eli said in a small voice. He
sighed and added, "But I expect Carson told you that as
well. And I wasn't with John Colter up in the Yellowstone,
nor—"

"Shut up," Morgan said quietly. "Kit Carson told me
that you and Jim Bridger were his idols when he first
got started in the beaver trade. He said that you were
one of the best trappers—and biggest liars—in the
West."

Eli blinked with surprise. "Christopher Houston Carson
said that?"

"I swear it. Carson said he hoped that he would see
you on the next visit he and Frémont made to California."

A smile tugged at the corners of Eli's mouth, and he

took a quick sip of coffee, then said, "Carson ain't like me, son. He tells the truth."

"I know," Morgan said. "Now eat some more. We'll be riding over to Sonoma to pay General Vallejo a visit tomorrow. There might be trouble, and I'm going to need a good man."

Eli sat up straighter. Even cleaned up, sober, and fed, he looked old, thin, and vulnerable. But now, instead of only defeat and self-loathing, Morgan detected a quiet air of hope and determination in his father. He figured that Eli was going to be all right, and no matter what happened tomorrow, Morgan knew that his father would stand straight, strong, and sober by his side.

It was late afternoon the following day when Morgan and Eli circled the immense vineyards surrounding Mission San Francisco Salano. They tied their horses and the pack mule under an oak tree in the plaza beside the general's impressive two-story adobe.

"You ever wonder why some folks live so damned well and the rest of us live so near to the bone?" Eli asked.

"Yeah," Morgan said, tying the animals. "Luck, guts, hard work, and good timing."

"And family. If you're born rich, you'll live and die rich."

"Captain Sutter wasn't born rich."

"Yeah, but he's got a golden tongue. He could sell snake oil to a rattler and then talk the viper into donating his skin for a fancy hatband." Eli untied a battered old rifle from his saddle. "And he's got more brass than a Spanish bell."

"Leave the rifle," Morgan said, not bothering to touch his own Hawken.

"What?"

"You heard me."

"But what if there's a fight?"

"There won't be. It's Rosalinda's choice to come or stay. Her uncle will abide with that."

Eli wasn't pleased, but Morgan's gaze did not waver, so Eli grumbled and left his rifle behind. "I got my

Green River knife under my coat," he said. "And that's where it's stayin', unless these people try to lay a hand on us."

Morgan knew that he wasn't going to talk his father into leaving his knife. He also realized that the success or failure of this unannounced visit depended on everyone staying calm and reasonable. It was Rosalinda who would decide matters—not himself or Eli or Vallejo. If her love now belonged to Cabral, then so be it; but Morgan had to hear it from Rosalinda's lips alone. And if she denied him, it was no more than he deserved, because Morgan had come to think of love as a flower which could die from neglect, and he'd neglected Rosalinda for a long, long time.

"I wish to see Señorita Rosalinda," he said to the housemaid who answered his knock on Vallejo's massive oak door.

The housemaid bowed and disappeared, leaving them to wait in the tiled entryway, where they admired an oil painting that depicted a bull and bear fight.

"Haven't seen one of those in more'n ten years," Eli grumped. "Them bloody Spaniards killed off most of the grizzly along the coast. Only time you see any now is when the carcass of a whale or seal washes up on the beach."

Morgan nodded, not really listening, because his thoughts were intensely focused on Rosalinda. His palms were sweaty, he felt a shortness of breath, and his knees seemed in imminent danger of buckling, dropping him like a fool at her feet. Taking a deep breath to calm himself, Morgan removed his new hat and motioned his father to do the same.

A few minutes later Rosalinda appeared, flushed and even more beautiful than Morgan remembered. Her eyes were round with surprise, and she was pale as she nodded to Eli and then extended her hand to Morgan.

"Why have you come?" she asked in a voice that trembled in spite of her best efforts. "Why now, Morgan, after so long?"

He was not even sure that he could speak, but somehow he managed. "I've come to ask you to marry me," Morgan told her straight out. "I want you to come away now to Sutter's Fort."

Her lovely face hardened in anger. "Three years—almost four—since I begged you to take me away, and *now* you ask? I thought you dead! It is too late, Morgan. I am engaged to be married. You must go quickly before my uncle hears of this!"

"But Señorita," Eli cried, "the man you're to marry is a toad! A pompous—"

"Father!" Morgan snapped. "Enough!"

Eli's mouth clamped shut, and his lower jaw worked with agitation. "I better wait outside."

Morgan nodded in agreement, and when he and Rosalinda were alone he stepped closer and said, "I know that I have no right to be here, but when I learned that you were engaged to someone else, I felt as if my heart had been ripped from my body. Without you, I am as hollow inside as a rat-sucked egg, and—"

"A 'rat-sucked egg'?" she asked, her eyebrows lifting in question.

"Yes, that empty," he assured her, concentrating hard so as not to lose the thread of his carefully rehearsed speech. "And I have no spirit. Nothing brings me joy now. The world has lost all color, like a day in San Pablo Bay's soupy fog. Rosalinda, I am winter without your love, winter without hope of spring. Darkness, without the promise of even one more sunrise. I am like a flower, untended, that withers without affection, and I need the . . . the water of your sweet love."

There! He'd done it, and he could see that her eyes were brimming with tears and her voice shook with emotion when she whispered, "But you did not even answer my letters!"

"I had an accident during a river crossing. I was hurt for a long time. Then Mama almost died, and . . ." His words trailed off because she was staring at him in a most peculiar way, and then she raised her hand to his face.

"What?" he asked.

The gentle touch of her fingertips against the scar on

his cheek caused Morgan to shiver. "It looks pretty ugly, huh?"

"Beloved, what happened?"

He told her about attempting to swim the Russian herds across the Sacramento River and how he had almost drowned. "We lost about two hundred cattle, but they were fished out of the Sacramento and Sutter sold their hides."

"Morgan, if you were hurt, I would have crawled a hundred miles to be at your side."

Morgan arched to hold her once more in his arms. "I couldn't bring myself to come here again with nothing to offer. But at this very moment Captain Sutter is in Monterey to ask Governor Micheltorena to give us a land grant."

"And if it is refused, will you leave me again?"

"Rosalinda, I don't think you understand. You've always had everything. You don't know what it's like being poor, having to grovel and—"

"Shh!" Her brown eyes flashed with anger. "Maybe I haven't been poor like you. But I understand love. Love doesn't wait for money! It can't be bought, and it has no price. You just feel it inside, not think it in your head."

"I feel it inside," he said, knowing how lame the words sounded.

"Then don't talk to me again about land and money! Tell me—Don Francisco!" Rosalinda exclaimed.

Morgan felt her body tense and when he looked past her face, he saw a man glowering at him with pure hatred. The wealthy rancher was thick, short, brutishly handsome, and so well dressed that Morgan's own clothes appeared shabby in comparison. His coat was wine-colored over a white silk shirt. Cabral wore a black, lacy tie bound loosely at his muscular throat. His pants clung to his powerful thighs and then flared over soft calfskin boots.

"What is the meaning of this!" he roared.

"Don Francisco," Rosalinda said in a hushed voice, "I apologize, but—"

"There's no apology necessary," Morgan interrupted.

"The señorita and I are in love and will be married. I am sorry, but that's the way it will be."

"Señor Beck," Cabral hissed, using Morgan's name like an oath, "you have shamed me, and I demand satisfaction!"

"No!" Rosalinda cried, breaking away from Morgan and rushing over to plead with the man. "This is my fault. But I do love Señor Beck, and—"

The back of Cabral's hand smashed Rosalinda across the cheek, bouncing her against the adobe wall. Morgan rushed to aid the girl. Before he could get her outside to safety, the outraged Mexican yanked a six-shot pepperbox pistol from inside his jacket.

"Move away from her, Señor Beck!"

Morgan tried to push Rosalinda away but she clung to him. "If you shoot, you could be hanged. I am not armed."

"What a pity," Cabral said with scorn.

"If you shoot him, you will also have to shoot me!" Rosalinda cried, her chin rising proudly as she stepped in front of Morgan.

"Maybe that would be best for all," Cabral said with a shrug of indifference.

"My uncle would never allow you to get away with murder."

"General Vallejo is away. By the time he could return, you'd both be buried. I would tell him that Señor Beck shot you and then turned the gun on himself."

A chill passed down Morgan's spine. "Why not let us go?"

Cabral shook his head. "It is a matter of honor. Imagine how humiliating it would be for me if I were jilted for a . . . a nothing of a gringo!"

When the Mexican thumbed back the hammer of his pistol, Morgan shoved Rosalinda toward the door and made a desperate lunge for Cabral. Gunsmoke and fire seared his flesh and thunder roared in his ears, but his momentum carried him into Cabral and they both struck the wall. Cursing, the Mexican bashed the heavy pistol against the side of Morgan's head, knocking him to the floor.

"It is time for you to die, Señor Beck!" Cabral shouted, recocking his pistol.

"No!" Eli screamed, hurling himself through the door with the Green River knife clenched in his fist.

Morgan saw his father's blade disappear into Cabral's belly, the Mexican's eyes bulging as he pulled the trigger of his pistol. The pepperbox exploded between them, and Morgan watched in horror as his father's body was lifted completely off the tile floor. But it was Cabral whose scream blended with the explosion as Eli's blade twisted and ripped upward through his soft belly.

Morgan tried to stand even as he watched Francisco Cabral dance on the blade of the wicked hunting knife and then reflexively pull the trigger once more in death. Eli was hurled against the wall and then slid down to the floor, eyes already vacant of pain. Cabral took three mincing little steps toward Morgan, one hand trying to contain his innards and the other struggling to raise the pistol and fire. The man failed at both and pitched face first to the tile floor.

"Father!" Morgan cried, rushing to Eli, though he knew already that his father was dead.

"Julio!" Rosalinda shouted. "Help us!"

Julio was the head of General Vallejo's household staff, and when he appeared, Rosalinda had enough composure to explain exactly what had happened, how Don Cabral had gone crazy and had intended to kill her along with Morgan.

"Señor Beck must go!" Julio exclaimed. "Don Francisco's men will come, and they will finish this work of death!"

"He's right," Rosalinda said, noting for the first time that Morgan was wounded in the side, though it did not appear to be serious.

"I won't leave my father's body here. I've got three horses and a mule outside, and I'm leaving nothing behind."

Rosalinda ordered Julio to harness the general's finest team to a light carriage and tie Morgan's horses and mule behind.

"Say nothing to anyone. Our lives depend on your silence."

Julio hurried away, but other servants appeared and Rosalinda ordered them to bring water and bandages as she examined the wound.

"It is not deep. God was with you, Morgan; but now we must go at once. If Don Francisco's men heard the shot and come to investigate, we are lost."

"But surely if we explain to Don Francisco's men and the other people of the pueblo what happened, they cannot blame anyone."

"They would never believe us! And because I was betrothed to Don Francisco, his death must be avenged. This you must believe or you are doomed!"

Morgan believed Rosalinda. He didn't want to run away, but Eli had died to save his life and he wasn't about to throw that gift away.

"All right," he agreed, feeling dead inside, "we can drive through the back streets, and when we're clear of town we can circle around the vineyards and race east."

It seemed a lifetime before his horses and the mule arrived. Julio had General Vallejo's carriage ready a few minutes later. Morgan grunted involuntarily as he climbed up to the driver's seat and grasped the lines. The pair of carriage horses were palominos, beautiful and as well matched as bookends. *If their speed and endurance match their looks,* Morgan thought, *then I will have to cut loose Sutter's mule*.

Eli's body was loaded onto the carriage floor, and Rosalinda used a few more precious moments to tell her uncle's weeping house servants once again what had transpired in the bloody hallway. "Tell General Vallejo that I am sorry to bring bloodshed and shame upon this house. But tell him the blood and shame is on Don Francisco's head!"

"*Vaya con Dios!*" many called out, making the sign of the cross.

When the carriage door slammed shut, Morgan drove away. The horses, no doubt feeling his nervousness through the lines, wanted to run, but Morgan held them to a quick, ground-eating trot that carried them out of Sonoma and along a dirt road north of the general's vineyards.

"It's all clear now," he called.

"Then stop! I must come to sit beside you, Morgan!"

Morgan heard the urgency in Rosalinda's voice. The matched pair of palominos danced with impatience, and it was all Morgan could do to bring them to a standstill. Rosalinda was out of the carriage and up beside him in an instant.

"Are you all right?"

Ashen-faced, she whispered, "Hurry, Morgan! They'll come after us!"

But he jumped down and cut the mule free, keeping Sutter's fine horses tethered to the back of the carriage. When he climbed back into the driver's seat and took the reins, he said, "Hold on tight!"

Rosalinda clung to him as the carriage jolted forward, and Morgan let the palominos run until darkness blanketed the flat Sacramento Valley and the horses seemed gilded in the cold moonlight.

At a meadow stream, they drew the palominos to a weary halt and Morgan helped Rosalinda down from the carriage. "We have to let the horses rest for a little while," he said, his eyes straining to pick out a feather of dust or the dark silhouettes of Mexican avengers. Finding neither, he relaxed for a moment.

"How much farther to Sutter's Fort?"

"Fifty miles, at least. Do you think Cabral's men are still coming?"

"Yes. Nothing but death will stop them."

Morgan's face hardened. "Then that is exactly what they will get."

He left her side to retrieve the Hawken and Eli's rifle. His father looked at peace, but that gave Morgan no satisfaction. He checked both rifles and placed them under the driver's seat. He did not allow the overheated animals to drink their fill, and as soon as they had cooled and grazed for a quarter of an hour, Morgan knew that they must push on.

"We'd better go now."

"Morgan, please, hold me first. Just for a moment."

He opened his arms, and Rosalinda filled them, laying her head on his chest and crying softly.

"It's going to be all right," he said gently.

"But your father!"

Morgan swallowed painfully. He had not had a moment to grieve; he knew that would come later. Everything had happened so fast that he was still too numb to feel anything yet.

"My father died to save our lives. He expected to die sick and alone. I think... if he were still alive... he'd be proud again. Does that make any sense?"

"Yes."

"I'm going to miss my father, but right now we just have to try to reach the fort."

"Will this cause great trouble for Captain Sutter?"

Morgan shrugged. "I don't know. That kind of depends on whether or not General Vallejo believes Julio and the others."

"He *must* believe!" she said passionately. "My uncle knows that I would not lie about such a thing, not even to protect the man I love."

Morgan hoped she was right. He helped Rosalinda up to the driver's seat, and they hurried on into the night. She kept looking back, and around midnight he said, "Maybe they've given up."

"No. They are coming," she told him with certainty. "I can *feel* them drawing closer."

A brilliant sunrise burst over the distant Sierra Nevada Mountains and flowed toward them like honey across the valley, but Morgan was in no mood to appreciate the beauty of it. The Mexicans were now in sight and closing fast. He was sure that he and Rosalinda were very close to the Sacramento River and Sutter's Fort, but they might as well have been a thousand miles away, for all the good that Sutter could do to protect them from Cabral's riders.

"Here," he said, pulling up the weary team, "take these lines."

Morgan jumped down with his loaded rifles and said, "There are at least six, maybe seven."

"How far?"

"Less than a mile and coming up fast." He looked up at her. "I'm going to try to turn them back."

He leaned his father's old Kentucky rifle against the carriage and raised the more powerful Hawken. Taking a deep breath to calm himself, Morgan waited, sure that he could feel the ground shake underfoot as the Mexican riders drew closer. When he was certain they were in range, he lifted the heavy rifle, took aim at the lead rider, and squeezed the trigger.

The Hawken's angry roar filled the air. The palominos jumped forward, but Rosalinda was able to hold them in check because they were too played out to bolt and run. Morgan scarcely noticed, for he saw his target rise up in his stirrups and then flip completely over the rump of his mount to roll brokenly across the dewy valley grass.

But the riders did not stop. Morgan snatched up his father's Kentucky rifle. He waited another ten seconds and fired again. The Kentucky let out a bark instead of a roar, but it belched flame, and a Mexican grabbed his shoulder and slumped in the saddle. His horse veered sharply, and the rider clung to the animal's neck as it raced off to the east, while Morgan furiously began to reload the Hawken.

The Mexican charge broke. Several of Cabral's men cursed and fired pistols, a useless and futile gesture that displayed their sudden fear and confusion. Morgan finished reloading the Hawken and even had the luxury of enough time to reload the Kentucky. If the Mexicans resumed their charge, at least two more would die. He watched the horsemen go after their wounded compadre.

"Let's go!" he said, jumping back into the carriage and taking the reins.

"What happened?"

"They're having second thoughts," Morgan said, whipping the exhausted horses into a run.

He had hoped, even allowed himself to expect, that Cabral's men would give up, but he was wrong. A few minutes later he looked back to see that the surviving riders had split into two groups and were racing hard to outflank the carriage. And Morgan knew that if the

Mexicans succeeded, he and Rosalinda would be cut off and shot.

"It's no good!" he shouted, pulling up the team. "We'll never make it, and once we're outflanked, we're lost."

"Then—"

"We've got to ride the captain's saddle horses."

"What about your father?"

In answer, Morgan jumped down and extended his hand to Rosalinda. "He'd want it this way."

Rosalinda understood. Sutter's horses were drenched with sweat, but they were fresher than those being driven so hard by Cabral's avenging Mexicans. Rosalinda was accustomed to a sidesaddle and had to hitch her dress and petticoats up around her thighs, but Morgan was betting their lives that she was an expert horsewoman.

Unwilling to leave his rifles, Morgan struggled for a moment to mount the sorrel with them. When he had both feet in the stirrups, he said, "Let's ride!"

Rosalinda didn't need any urging, with the sound of gunfire in their ears as they galloped away. Black hair streaming out behind her, she rode like a vaquero, and Morgan's heart swelled with pride as their horses left death farther and farther behind.

"Hiiyah!" he bellowed at the top of his voice. "We're going to make it!"

Far back, Cabral's men shouted muffled curses and fired their weapons in reply, and then, before they ran their horses to death, they gave up the chase.

At midmorning, Morgan and Rosalinda trotted up to the bank of the Sacramento River. It had never looked wider or more dangerous, and Rosalinda chose to focus her attention on the distant settlement. "Is that the fort?"

"Yes. Can you swim?"

Rosalinda tried to look brave, and she nodded, unwilling to look at the powerful river.

"Well," Morgan said, "we won't have to."

"But how—"

"Watch," Morgan said, pointing the Hawken to the sky and squeezing the trigger.

The sound of his powerful rifle jumped across the river, and Morgan thought he could hear it echo all the way to the distant Sierras. Even before the echo died away, they saw the gates of Sutter's Fort swing open. Just for the hell of it and as a farewell tribute to Eli, he raised the flintlock and fired again.

"Come on," he said, dismounting and leading his horse toward the river where he knew a flatboat would soon cross. "Come see your new home, my love."

Rosalinda walked by his side down to the water. "If Cabral's men hadn't quit, we'd have had to swim this or be shot," she said, studying the huge body of rolling water.

"We'd have made it. We'd have made it because we had no choice."

His eyes tightened at the corners when he picked out their little cabin. How he wished that they had found the time to build Mama her chapel!

"Are you thinking about your father?"

"Yes, and about my mother. She's going to take this news pretty hard."

"You have told me many times that she is a strong woman."

"That's true." Morgan kissed Rosalinda's cheek. "She's very strong, and I think it will help a little if we promise to give her a grandchild before too long. She's always wanted a bunch of 'em."

Rosalinda hugged his neck, and her breath was warm in his ear. "How soon can we be wed?"

"If Captain Sutter is back from Monterey, we can be married today."

"Then we can start making a child tonight."

"Yes," he said, looking forward to the night but dreading to tell Mama that Eli was really gone.

They were married by Sutter that day, and Mama insisted on giving them her cabin. She had taken the news of Eli's death very calmly and spent that day praying for his soul before going to live inside the fort, where she could be around people all the time, especially Sutter's Indians.

When they had a few minutes alone together after the marriage ceremony, Sutter took Morgan aside. "I have a wedding present for you," he said, trying to hide his own excitement. "I was successful in getting Micheltorena to agree that you should receive a big land grant—two square leagues of river bottom land."

"Two leagues!" Morgan could scarcely believe it.

"Yes, and it's located on the Sacramento River practically on my northern doorstep."

Morgan almost jumped and shouted. He knew that section of the river well—it was where he'd met the Russian and his wife. It was a paradise: rich soil, plenty of wild game, many streams and tributaries; it was prize land.

"It's perfect for you," Sutter was saying. "I'll lend you seed and plows—everything. And I think you can do a splendid business with the American trappers coming down from the Oregon Territory." Sutter beamed. "But not too splendid. If they have money to spend, you can't take it all for yourself."

"Of course not!" Morgan took a deep breath and expelled it slowly. "There are still thousands of beaver in the northern Sierra tributaries."

"Yes, and I'll expect you to continue trapping them for me until your land grant is official."

Morgan's heart dropped. "You mean it isn't official?"

"Don't worry. The formalities always take time. The documents must be sent to Mexico City."

"How much time?"

"A year, at most."

Morgan tried to mask his great disappointment. "It will seem like an eternity."

"Take heart, my impatient friend. Remember that it took me *two* years to obtain full title to all my lands."

Morgan nodded. "I know, but—"

"You can still begin work on your rancho, just as we did here from the moment we landed. I'll help you build an adobe, and I'll sell you cattle, sheep, and horses on credit."

"I can't begin to thank you for this."

Sutter brushed that aside with a wave of his hand.

"Just remember one thing. Everything we both have now depends on keeping Governor Micheltorena in office. If he is overthrown, General Castro and Alvarado will do everything in their power to make sure that we become paupers."

"What about General Vallejo?"

"I've learned that he has refused to take part in any of this. He's too smart for that. He will remain neutral and watch to see which side wins."

"Micheltorena must win," Morgan said. "And I'll fight for my land grant."

"We'll both fight. That's why we must be ready to act. Micheltorena's fate is our fate."

"I understand perfectly." Morgan turned to see Rosalinda watching them. "I had better get back to my bride. Would you object if I took a week or two in order to visit our new land grant?"

"But why? You've seen it many times before."

"I know, but . . . but this time would be very different."

Sutter frowned. "Your bride is not accustomed to the hardships of the wilderness. I think that it would be wiser to remain at New Helvetia. However, that is your choice."

Morgan had made the choice already. If Rosalinda agreed, they would leave tomorrow for their new home.

"She's going to have to get accustomed to it sooner or later. And besides, I want to walk our land and pick a building site."

"Of course you do! The happiest moment of my entire life was the day we landed here and, in what was considered an untamable wilderness, I established a foothold in this wild country."

"I will never forget that day, either," Morgan said, remembering the picture with great clarity. It felt like such a long time ago, although it really wasn't. Much had happened in a few short years.

Morgan pulled his attention back to the captain, who was saying, "Pick your building site close to the Sacramento but on a rise, as I did for New Helvetia."

"I will."

"It pleases me greatly to have you as my northern

neighbor, Mr. Beck. And I think that, barring revolution or some unforeseen catastrophe, we are both destined to be wealthy and powerful men."

"You already are, Captain Sutter," Morgan said, knowing how much the captain loved flattery. "Until my marriage and this wonderful news, I was the one who had nothing."

"Things can change very fast—for the better, or for the worse."

Morgan understood, but with Rosalinda and this big Mexican land grant he was sure that nothing could stop him now.

"Would you like a wedding dinner prepared in celebration?"

"No, thanks, Captain."

"Considering the news of your father, I didn't expect that you would. I'm sorry to hear of his death."

"He did what he had to do," Morgan said. "I know he approved of my wife, and he would have been very proud to know that the Beck name would be attached to a rich land grant. Land that I swear will someday be his final resting place."

Sutter went to his cabinet and brought out a bottle of brandy and two glasses. He poured. "To peace without revolution. I confess that I'm half expecting bad news from Pablo Gutierrez, whom I left with Governor Micheltorena in Monterey. If things worsen, he's to return at once, and I've promised the governor that I'll form a company of men and fight on his side."

"If that happens, I'll go with you."

Sutter looked haggard and worried. "To peace," he said again, raising his glass, "and to your beautiful young bride."

Sutter drained his glass, and Morgan did the same.

"If you go to see your land, do it soon," the captain advised.

"We might leave as early as tomorrow."

"Not tomorrow. Give Mrs. Beck at least a day of rest and . . ." Sutter blushed. "Well, the land will always be there. It is not the same with love and passion."

Morgan's cheeks warmed, and he left the captain a

few minutes later. As Morgan was crossing the compound with a million thoughts swirling around in his head, Manuiki appeared.

"I wish you love and happiness," she said, giving Morgan a beautiful shell necklace. "This is for your new wife."

Morgan was deeply touched. He looked down at the Kanaka girl and saw that her eyes were red and swollen from crying. He didn't know what to say, because he was sure that, in spite of her promiscuity, she had loved him in her own innocent way.

"I thank you," he stammered.

Manuiki rose up on her toes and kissed his mouth, then stepped back. "That is all I have for you, Morgan Beck."

"No, you've given me much more."

Fresh tears welled up in her eyes. "I think I am going back to live with my family in the islands. I am very unhappy."

"Then you should go soon, for you are too beautiful to be unhappy."

She smiled, and for a moment Morgan saw her as he had the first time, a radiant woman-child, and it struck him very forcibly that Manuiki ought to return to her lovely Sandwich Islands. Somehow it had been all wrong for her to come to this place. She would find happiness again only among her own kind, people who would not condemn her for her childlike ways.

"Thank you . . . and good-bye," she said before she turned and ran away.

That night Morgan took Rosalinda to bed. He made love to her very gently, perhaps too gently, for his passion was great, but so was his sadness. She clung to him and, much later, whispered, "Is it always that way?"

"What?"

"You know," she said shyly.

He pushed himself up on his elbows and stared down at her lovely face. "No," he said. "Sometimes it's like a raging storm, wild and rough. Sometimes it is gentle, like tonight, and sometimes in-between."

"I want it all those ways. Will it . . . will it make a difference in the child?"

"How do you mean?"

"If it is strong, will the child be more spirited? Or if it is gentle like this, will our child also be gentle?"

"I don't think it matters very much," he told her, trying to hide his amusement.

Rosalinda said, "I want children with great spirit, Morgan."

He laughed way down deep in his chest. "I will keep that in mind."

≈ **11** ≈

Morgan helped Rosalinda dismount, and they let their horses graze. The day was fair, and a steady breeze from the west made the gray-green leaves of the big valley oaks shiver. Billowy clouds floated toward the Sierra Nevadas like a fleet of Spanish galleons bound for home port. Along the banks of the Sacramento River, trees were just starting to blaze with autumn colors, a jagged rainbow of ocher mixed with brilliant splashes of red and orange fire among the green.

"What do you think about building our casa right here?" Morgan said, stamping his boot down on the top of the rise of land overlooking the river.

"It is magnificent!"

"I think so, too." Morgan began to pace off the imaginary boundaries of the new home he could hardly wait to build. "If you agree, this will be the entry, this the kitchen, and here the—"

"Bedroom," Rosalinda said, greatly enjoying her husband's excitement.

"The bedroom? All right. How many more do you want?"

"At least six—for all the children."

He chuckled and then pirouetted on his heel, saying, "The view from any room will be spectacular. And look!"

Morgan bent and scooped up a handful of rich, dark earth. "Children, crops—everything we want will flourish here. And that lagoon down below will be ideal for loading and unloading supplies. The clear stream feeding it will provide fresh water year round. It's all here, Rosalinda. It's as if, of all the places in the world, God made this exact spot for us alone."

Rosalinda was suddenly filled with a rush of love for this man. She loved him for his boyish delight in simple dreams. No grand political schemes churned in the deep recesses of his mind. Her strong young mate had no illusions of power, no complex designs to enhance himself in the eyes of rich or important people. Morgan just wanted to build a rancho and work with his hands from one day to the next, tending his fields and herds. He was as honest and as natural as this vast landscape.

"Rosalinda, there is only one thing that is missing."

"And that is?"

"My father. He was too proud to bend his knee to Mexico or Spain, too proud to ask any man for help. But I know he always dreamed of owning a piece of land like this."

Morgan tore a clump of grass from the earth and inspected its roots. Captain Sutter had shown him how to inspect roots to see if they were healthy. These were. "The captain says that the thicker the roots, the better the crops."

"Then this earth is rich indeed."

Morgan dropped the grass and earth, wiped his hands on his pants, and stood. "We're going to build something to be proud of, Rosalinda, a home for generations of our children and their children."

Rosalinda threw her arms around his neck and kissed him passionately. "Why don't we initiate our new bedroom right now?" she whispered in his ear.

"In broad daylight, on the top of this hill?"

"Yes. After we come and build a rancho, it will never again be possible. So why not now?"

Morgan's hands caressed her firm buttocks. "Yes, why not?" he said, easing her to the grass. A flock of geese winged over the river below, honking as they swooped down to the lagoon.

"If we hurry," he said, "we can have goose for supper."

"I'd rather eat beans and salt pork and not hurry."

"So would I," Morgan said, losing himself in pleasure with Rosalinda.

They did not return to Sutter's Fort for over a month, and then only because Morgan was concerned about the political intrigue that centered around Monterey. Before they did rein their horses south, they visited both the Miwok and a northern valley tribe of Indians called Wintun. Morgan had often visited these people, bearing gifts for their chiefs and fresh venison downed by his Hawken rifle. This time, however, it was they who presented him and his new wife with many beautifully woven baskets and several exquisite bone figurines carved in the shapes of animals. Rosalinda, who had at first been a little skeptical about sleeping in an Indian village, was sad to say good-bye to her many new friends.

"These are fine people," Morgan assured her, "and once we start building our rancho, we'll be needing their help."

"I hope you don't intend to feed them in troughs like Captain Sutter."

"No, and like the captain, I'll pay them fairly. He has a gift for dealing with Indians, and I'd do well to apply his lessons."

On their return to Sutter's Fort, he and Rosalinda were walking and leading their horses because of all the wonderful Indian baskets placed on the horses' backs.

"Just wait until the captain sees all this loot," Morgan said as they approached the fort. "I think he was hoping I'd take along some beaver traps and return with pelts for his storehouse."

"Trapping can wait," Rosalinda told him.

A few minutes later, they entered the fort to see the captain marching both Indians and Americans around and around in military formation.

"This doesn't look good," Morgan said, leading the horses over to a tie rail.

Rosalinda stayed close to Morgan's side as they hurried to visit Mama, who was surrounded by the Indian children whom she so loved to teach about the Lord. When Mama saw the couple, her smile could not hide her worries.

"What is going on, Mama?"

"There is big trouble. Our captain is going to fight."

"Who? Castro and Alvarado?"

She nodded. "This is very bad."

"Here," Rosalinda said, offering their finest basket to her. "A present for you."

Mama was genuinely pleased, and properly so. The Wintun and their coastal neighbors, the Pomo, were considered the finest basket makers in all of California.

"Mr. Beck!"

Morgan looked up to see the captain march past in his Mexican uniform. "Present yourself tomorrow morning at eight o'clock in my quarters."

"Yes, sir!"

Sutter barked a command, and his men wheeled to the right. In the instant their eyes had met, Morgan had seen enough to know that Sutter was grim yet confident.

This assessment was borne out the next morning when the captain said, "I expect that very soon we will march to defend Governor Micheltorena against Castro and Alvarado."

"Then the rumors were true."

"Yes, and I don't have to tell you that Micheltorena is the key to keeping our land grants without great bloodshed."

Sutter splashed brandy in a glass in spite of the earliness of the hour. "After you left, Micheltorena summoned me to Monterey and gave me a commission as a captain. At a banquet in my honor, I was treated to the highest civilian and military honors. After the banquet, as captain of the Mexican militia, I was asked to review the garrison's soldiers. It was a splendid tribute, and I was deeply honored!"

"An honor well deserved," Morgan said, wishing his captain would get to the point and explain the trouble they now faced.

"Yes, but no sooner had I returned than a message

arrived from the governor ordering me to be prepared to march to his aid. To that end, I have
dispatched our trusted friend, Pablo Gutierrez, to
Monterey with a secret message to the governor. In
it I advised him that I have over fifty white men and
more than one hundred Indians fully trained and
outfitted for battle."

"I'm sure that such news will be greatly appreciat
ed," Morgan said.

Sutter clasped his hands behind his back, and his
expression was animated as he began to pace the length
of his office. It occurred to Morgan that the anticipation
of a victorious military campaign acted as a tonic on this
man.

"My only embarrassment is that in this very place
there is dissension," Sutter admitted, glancing aside at
Morgan each time he passed. "A few cowards are questioning whether we should even become involved in
this fight. They say it is between a corrupt Mexican
government and the old and wealthy Californio families."

"And you told them . . . ?"

Sutter stopped and spun on his heel. "Mr. Beck, I
told them that if Governor Micheltorena should be
defeated and driven from Monterey, the Americans are
next."

Sutter found a Mexican saber, which he strapped
around his ample waist. "It's time to call everyone to
drill, yourself included, Mr. Beck."

Morgan had never drilled in his life. Drilling was
against his very nature. He was tired and footsore, but
he owed Captain Sutter far too much to refuse. "Yes,
sir."

The drill was serio-comic, with men marching back
and forth inside the compound shouldering old French
and Mexican muskets. Most of the captain's trusted
Kanaka were already proficient at drill, but the local
Indians were completely befuddled and bounced around
in the ranks, accidentally clubbing each other with rifle
butts and often tripping. It was a good thing, Morgan
thought, that their weapons were unloaded. Tempers

flared, and after a general brawl, Sutter called a noon rest.

But in the afternoon the grumbling and near mutinous soldiers went at it again until four o'clock when they were mercifully interrupted by Alfredo Escobar, one of Sutter's best vaqueros, who came whipping his exhausted horse into the stockade. Everyone broke ranks and encircled the young rider. The man was so excited that he could not at first be understood.

"Alfredo, get a grip on yourself!" Sutter ordered. "What is the matter?"

Alfredo's knuckles were white as he squeezed the horn of his saddle, and he appeared to be breathing as hard as his winded mount. It was clear to everyone that the vaquero had some terrible news.

"It is Pablo Gutierrez," he gasped. "Pablo is dead!"

Morgan grabbed Alfredo's arm and almost tore him from the saddle. "Are you sure?"

"Sí, Señor Beck! He was caught by one of General Castro's patrols. They found a secret message sewn into the lining of Pablo's boot. It was from you, Captain Sutter, and addressed to the governor. They said Pablo was a spy!"

Morgan's eyes whipped to Sutter, who cried, "Damn! I knew I should have made Pablo memorize it!"

Morgan was stunned by the news of his best friend's death. "So they shot him?"

"No, Señor Beck," Alfredo said in a trembling voice, "they hanged him as a spy."

That evening Morgan was still in shock as he gazed into the fire and opened his heart to Rosalinda. "I loved Pablo like a brother. He was honest enough to tell me when I was wrong. He could be serious or wise, but most often he was just happy and funny. We were always laughing, even when things went wrong. Without saying so out loud, each of us knew he could trust the other with his life."

Morgan sipped his coffee and stared into the flames, remembering campfires he had shared with Pablo while trapping beaver for Sutter. He could almost see big Pablo's grinning face in the dancing flames.

"Pablo wanted to come work for us someday, Rosalinda, but he was too loyal to the captain to come right out and say so. But we both knew that it would have happened. I always figured we'd raise families together—see our children grow up proud and strong."

"You have always told me that Pablo vowed never to settle down with one woman."

"He did like the ladies," Morgan admitted, "but also loved children enough to want to marry and become a father."

Rosalinda took Morgan's hand. "I'm so sorry. First your father, now your best friend."

Morgan swallowed painfully and drew his wife close to his side. "In a way, my father's death was much easier to bear. He was old, sick, and tired, and he died saving our lives. But Pablo . . ." Morgan shook his head. "Pablo was young and full of happiness. And he wasn't a spy! He was just doing Sutter's bidding. He had no more ambition than one of the captain's Indians and was just as eager to please."

Morgan's voice cracked with emotion. "I can almost see how it must have been in his final moments. Some officer screaming at him to confess things that Pablo didn't even know. Pablo would have been frightened, but also proud and stubborn. He would have spit in their faces and refused to answer any of their damned questions. And then—"

"Please!" Rosalinda begged. "Don't do this to yourself! It can't help anything now."

Morgan choked and angrily wiped tears from his cheeks. "Yeah," he managed to say, "you're right. What good does remembering do for poor Pablo now?"

"My darling, I am sorry that I did not know your friend Pablo. And all this talk of fighting scares me. Maybe you should tell Captain Sutter that it is better to stay out of this thing between the governor and his enemies."

"It's too late. The captain has chosen sides, and I will march with him."

Rosalinda stiffened. "So," she said finally, "when are you leaving?"

"I don't think even Sutter knows, but because of Pablo's murder, I am sure it will be very soon."

Rosalinda laid her head on his shoulder. "Your mama and I will pray for you and all the others."

"That'd be much appreciated," Morgan said. "And pray for the soul of Pablo Gutierrez."

"I will."

It was the first day of January before Sutter's little army marched out through the gates of his stockade to the stirring sound of fife and drum. There were eighty-five riflemen, a company of over one hundred infantry composed almost entirely of Indians, about thirty cavalry who were mostly vaqueros, and a small detachment of artillery in charge of Captain Sutter's cannon.

Morgan's job was to scout ahead in search of food or the enemy, and as he left the fort behind, he felt his stomach churn with excitement and fear, along with more than a little pride to be riding beside his captain. Sutter looked magnificent and invincible, wearing his Mexican officer's dress uniform with its epaulets, gold piping, and brass buttons, riding at the front on a prancing horse. About a half mile from the fort, he wheeled his horse around and doffed his hat with a dramatic sweep and flourish to the women, children, and roughly thirty Indian sharpshooters and fifteen white men left behind to guard his beloved New Helvetia. They were to continue on with the work, especially the critical spring planting, if this military campaign took longer than anticipated.

Sutter was in his glory, and as Morgan rode along the flank beside his friend John Bidwell, he thought of all the times the captain had told him about his personal hero, Napoléon Bonaparte. Morgan had never even seen a picture of the great French conquerer, but he thought perhaps Captain Sutter was an American Napoléon. Looking at his captain, he had the feeling that Sutter could rule all of California if that were his desire. He seemed more alive now than at any time since the day of their arrival in this fertile valley. His confidence was total and contagious; even the Indians,

who understood nothing of the politics behind this
military campaign, were grinning and happy as they
marched along, proud of their simple uniforms and the
ancient muskets balanced on their thin shoulders.

Sutter kept the fife and drums playing all afternoon,
and across the long miles the soldiers marched without
a trace of weariness. But several days later the air of
excitement was wearing thin, and during their over-
night rest at the Mission of San Jose, the American
soldiers discovered barrels of wine and became drunk
and disorderly. Early the next morning Morgan was
sent ahead to the nearby pueblo to warn the merchants
to close all places where liquor was sold.

"Captain!" Morgan shouted, galloping his horse back
to their army, which had marched to within sight of the
pueblo.

Sutter rode out to meet him. "What is it, Mr. Beck?
Are we to have a fight?"

"No! San Jose's mayor has fled the pueblo with
almost every able-bodied man he could find."

Sutter could not hide his keen disappointment. "All
right, then we'll march right through the pueblo without stopping. I cannot trust our undisciplined American
soldiers in a pueblo of deserted women."

Morgan had reached the same conclusion, and so, to
the disappointment of their little hungover army, they
marched through the pueblo and continued south along
El Camino Real to join Governor Micheltorena's forces.

That evening they arrived at the ruins of old Mission
San Juan Bautista. Once, the church and its grounds
had been one of the most successful of all the Spanish
missions, with a granary, barracks for the mission Indians, a
monastery, and many other small adobe buildings. Now,
however, the mission was reduced to an arcade fronting
a row of empty, windowless rooms. The mission's thick
adobe walls were crumbling, red tiles were slipping
down the rooftop, and the orchards and fine vineyards
were laid waste by wild horses, cattle, and ragged
vagabonds. In the center of what Morgan supposed had
been the plaza huddled an old well, cracked and broken
like a bowl filled with tumbleweeds instead of fresh

water. But miraculously, the chapel remained unviolated by weather, man, or beast, and when Morgan entered, an old Indian scurried off into the dim recesses of the sacristy, leaving behind a row of smoking votive candles and incense.

Morgan slipped in-between the pews and gazed upward. Behind the altar soared a gold-colored partition called a reredos, with six bell-shaped niches inset with statues of saints and backdropped by scarlet tapestries. Outside the chapel he could hear shouts and curses from Sutter's army, but in this place the silent saints gazed calmly downward and seemed to be asking Morgan to give up all his worldly cares and ambitions.

The six saints drove Morgan to his knees, and he bent his head to pray for the soul of his father and that of Pablo Gutierrez, and for the courage and strength to see this campaign to victory. Quite unexpectedly, time lost all meaning and Morgan felt an inner peace fill his heart. His weariness slipped away, and he might have lost himself for hours in prayer had not an insistent voice drawn him roughly back to the present.

"Mr. Beck?"

Sutter was standing beside him in the aisle, one hand resting on the hilt of his sword, the other on the worn pew.

"Mr. Beck!"

"Sir?"

The captain looked irritated and uncomfortable, but he managed to smile. "I am sorry to interrupt, but I was searching everywhere for you."

Morgan started to rise, but Sutter's hand pushed firmly down on his shoulder. "Never mind. What I needed will already have been done by now. But you could . . ."

"What?"

"You could offer prayers for me and the success of our just cause."

"Oh, yes, sir!"

"Thank you," Sutter said before he turned on his heel and marched back outside, his boots sounding very loud on the cold stone floor.

At the front door he turned and called back, "Oh, yes, and light a few of those candles for us, will you? It can't hurt."

Morgan nodded. For him, the meditation and peace he'd felt were gone and the six saints no longer communed directly to his heart as they had moments ago. Rising to his feet, he found a few old candles and lit them for Sutter's petition, then went outside to hear raucous laughter from the Indians. The source of their mirth quickly became apparent. Sutter's cavalry, galloping ahead of the Indian foot soldiers, had claimed the mission storerooms under the arcade, leaving the Indians to sleep outdoors. However, the cavalry had just been driven outside by armies of fleas and were now hopping about, wildly scratching and cursing.

"Goddamn buggers will eat you alive in there!" an American cursed, dropping his pants around his ankles as his fingernails clawed at his violated flesh.

The Indians, always accorded the worst and the last, found the scene hilarious, and Morgan could not help but agree. Soon all, including the Americans, were roaring with laughter, and that broke the tension that had been building for days.

That night everyone slept outdoors, and late the next morning they were cheered to greet Governor Micheltorena and about two hundred of his soldiers on the banks of the Salinas River.

Actually, the two small armies had nothing in common. Micheltorena's forces consisted of either aristocratic officers or the hated cholos, who had been the prime source of so much dissatisfaction among the Californios, leading to unrest and now revolution. The cholos were universally reviled, and there was an immediate hostility between them and Sutter's troops—especially with the proud and independent American contingent. Soon the two armies had to be separated.

Watching everything with an air of detachment, Morgan was struck by the disparity among so many men, all joined to fight for very different reasons. This army, to his way of thinking, lacked any semblance of cohesion or a single purpose. Whites, Mexican aristocrats, Kanaka from the Sandwich Islands, ex-convicts from Mexico City, and California Indians, they shared no binding spirit, and this greatly concerned Morgan. He wondered what Micheltorena and Sutter could do to weld some kind of bond that would carry this army to victory.

The next morning, Sutter informed his army that Castro and Alvarado had fled south toward the pueblo of Los Angeles. This news was greeted with howls of derision and shouts of victory until Sutter added that their plan was to pursue the enemy and decisively vanquish them.

This information was not as well received. The soldiers were weary of travel, especially the infantry and artillery. Furthermore, they were not well provisioned, and it would be bad for morale to wage a distant campaign in the rainy season.

"Any chance we can overtake them in the next few days, sir?" asked Morgan hopefully.

"I'm afraid not, Mr. Beck. They've too big a lead."

"Hellfire, Captain!" an American groused. "We might end up chasing them all the way down to Mexico!"

"No," Sutter argued, "Governor Micheltorena and I believe that they'll put up a stiff fight at Santa Barbara, or if not there, then at San Buenaventura, or at least at the pueblo of Los Angeles, where they have a large number of sympathizers."

Sutter paused and studied each of them as if measuring their will. "Men, I cannot say with certainty how long this campaign will last. But I *can* assure you that the governor is a respected military leader and former general in the Mexican Army. We'll catch the insurgents under Castro and Alvarado, and when we do, we'll thrash them soundly. Our friend Governor Micheltorena will see to that and will see that we are all generously rewarded!"

Before anyone could think to ask exactly how they would be rewarded, Sutter turned on his heel and retired to his tent, posting orders that he was not to be disturbed. This infuriated nearly everyone except the

Indians and Kanaka, who had never expected any material rewards.

That night the Americans talked openly of how much land they'd demand from Micheltorena in return for their loyalty. Morgan heard some vow to seek huge ranchos the equal of Sutter's grant. Such talk troubled Morgan, so he went off by himself thinking of Rosalinda and his own new rancho, but also of avenging Pablo's unjust execution. *At least,* he thought, *we have superb military leaders in Captain Sutter and Governor Micheltorena.*

But in the wet, difficult weeks that followed, even that small comfort was dispelled as Morgan came to realize that Governor Micheltorena possessed only the appearances of a leader. It became evident that the handsome Mexican governor was all show and no action. He was indolent and indecisive, steadfastly refusing to hurry after the retreating enemy. The winter rains began to pour in torrents, and they averaged less than ten miles a day as they slowly worked their way down past Monterey to the Mission San Luis Obispo and then on to the mission at Santa Ynez. Their progress was slowed even more when, taking to the beach because of a high mountain range, they had to lay planks on the sand in order to reach the mission at Santa Barbara. Desertions became a nightly event, and morale plummeted.

"Captain," Morgan said with exasperation one night, "we've been a month just getting to Santa Barbara. Every day that passes sees us losing soldiers. At muster this morning, ten more were gone!"

"Then we'll catch and discipline every last one of them!" Sutter snapped in anger. "Dammit, I can't see and do everything! You're my scout. Track a few deserters down and hang them! *That* will take care of the problem."

Morgan held his tongue. He wasn't going to capture or hang anyone. He was spending every waking hour either hunting or scouting ahead to ensure that they did not stumble blindly into an ambush. Furthermore, he was feverish and always cold. His rain-soaked blankets were rotting, and he wasn't getting more than four hours of sleep each night. His lungs were drowning in phlegm, and he had a cough as racking as Eli had contracted in the fog of San Pablo Bay. Sutter was healthy, but the man had slipped in other ways. Gone was his confidence and excitement. Gone, too, the swagger and the encouraging word to his struggling troops. Now the captain was drinking again, and his mood was sour, especially after having been forced to buy nearly eight hundred dollars worth of clothes, blankets, and food for his famished men and horses.

"Captain," Morgan said in his most reasonable voice, "the rumor is that General Castro is preparing to fight us just north of Mission San Buenaventura and that his forces are getting stronger while ours are deserting. I say we *must* catch and defeat the enemy before we are hopelessly outnumbered."

Sutter anxiously ran his fingers through his thick mane of hair. "All right," he exploded in anger, hurling the flap of his tent aside and marching out into another evening of cold, driving rain. "Come with me. We're going to see Micheltorena and press him to advance south at first light. No more damned excuses!"

The governor had commandeered a fine adobe villa overlooking the ocean, and when they interrupted his evening of entertaining, Micheltorena was visibly annoyed. "Can't this wait until tomorrow, Captain Sutter?"

"No, it cannot. Mr. Beck, tell the governor what you have just told me."

Morgan repeated what he had heard, but Micheltorena dismissed it with a wave of his hand. "Idle canteen rumors," he scoffed. "They are worthless. You are both sopping wet. Why don't you come inside and meet my friends and warm yourselves by the fire?"

"But Governor," Sutter protested, "we should be on the march early tomorrow morning!"

"What is the hurry, Captain? My own informants tell me that General Castro and Alvarado are in Los Angeles trying to drum up support. No doubt they will fail. Besides, we can't fight in this weather! How could we possibly keep our powder dry?" Micheltorena called out to a waiter for three brandies, which were brought immediately. "Here," the governor said, taking Sutter's arm, "come meet my guests."

Sutter tossed his liquor down and so did Morgan, but while the captain followed the governor like a puppy on a leash, Morgan spun on his heel, feeling the heat of the brandy mix with that of his anger.

"Damn this army!" he said again and again as he stomped back toward camp.

The weather cleared several days later, but there were more storm clouds out over the ocean. Their army marched out of Santa Barbara but not before Micheltorena had enjoyed a final leisurely breakfast and hour-long benediction given at the mission by the bishop himself. As they moved south, the saturated ground made it nearly impossible to drag their heavy cannon and caissons along the shoreline. By late afternoon they arrived at a narrow strip of beach called El Rincon, where a steep ridge of mountains dropped to the shoreline, preventing further advance until the lowest possible tide.

"What are we going to do now?" Morgan asked his captain as their eyes measured the towering coastal mountains, seeking a way up and around the beach.

"The governor and I will discuss the matter at some length," Sutter replied coldly. "And you, Mr. Beck, would do well to act as a scout instead of an inquisitor!"

Morgan spurred his horse away to ride into the hills. Hours later he found a trail along the mountain crest and wondered if it had been used by the Spanish explorers and later by Father Junípero Serra and his devout padres as they journeyed up and down this wild coast along their chain of nine California missions. The trail was so slippery with mud and dangerous that Morgan had to dismount and lead his weary horse. It began to rain again, and Morgan was chilled and miserable by the time he finally breached the range of mountains and gazed out toward the pueblo of San Buenaventura to see what he had almost begun to doubt even existed—Castro's rebellious army.

Morgan's pulse quickened, and he no longer felt wet or cold. The visibility was too poor to see the main enemy encampments, but he could see a few sagging tents beyond the mission grounds. His fatigued mind struggled to consider the dangers that awaited him below, and yet Morgan knew that he could not simply leave without gaining more information. But to enter San Buenaventura would be very dangerous. His face was familiar to Alvarado and Castro, and Morgan had friends among the Californios. They would all recognize him and be aware of his loyalty to Sutter and the governor.

As he tightened his wet cinch, Morgan was torn by conflicting thoughts of what to do. He had already accomplished enough this miserable day. While Micheltorena, Sutter, and the others had remained dry and comfortable inside their tents on the Rincon, drinking good brandy and endlessly debating military strategy, he had braved the treacherous mountainsides to find the old missionary trail to San Buenaventura. But despite these rationalizations, Morgan knew that if Sutter and Micheltorena would at last act decisively and stage a surprise attack, they could, in one long-overdue and bold stroke, achieve total victory right here in San Buenaventura. In a few more days this campaign would be history and he could race home to hold Rosalinda and, next spring, with a grateful Governor Micheltorena's official land grant documents in his possession, journey up the Sacramento River to build his long-hoped-for rancho.

That wish was so overpowering that Morgan knew he *had* to sneak into the pueblo and find out the size of the enemy forces. Otherwise nothing would happen, and the enemy would retreat on down the coast to Los Angeles.

Checking his Hawken rifle to make sure the powder was dry under the oilskin cover, Morgan remounted. He yanked his sopping hat low over his brow, then carefully guided his horse down from the slick green hills into San Buenaventura. He rode past the old mission, hearing loud fandango music coming from one of the large buildings.

"Eh, Señor?"

Morgan's heart froze with fear. He reined in and peered through the falling rain to see a pair of drunken men standing under a dripping olive tree.

"You talking to me?"

"Who else? To be out in such weather, you must be looking for the fandango, eh?"

"Yeah," Morgan said, easing his grip on the Hawken.

"Tie your horse up and join us!"

"Thanks. I've got something to do," Morgan said, prodding his tired horse forward, "but I'll be back soon."

"Don't wait too long," one of them called, "or all the women and whiskey will be gone! But there is always tomorrow night."

"Another one tomorrow night?"

"*Every* night, Señor!"

Both men laughed and staggered back toward the music. Morgan continued down the gutter of mud that was the main street of San Buenaventura until he found a cantina, where he dismounted and tied his horse. He yanked his oilskin-wrapped Hawken out his saddle boot, tugged his dripping slouch hat even lower on his forehead, and entered the noisy room.

His entrance attracted no attention. One glance told him that the cantina was packed with a mixture of hard Californios, as well as whites and a few Indians. The interior was dim and hot, the air fouled with sweat and tobacco.

On top of the bar danced a classically beautiful Mexican girl who could not have been more than fifteen but already had the jaded expression of a prostitute. Grimy hands reached out to caress her slim, bare legs. In the background two Mexicans played guitars in no way accompanied by an Indian on drums. The beat was loud and primitive. The girl danced and bumped to it, heavily lidded black eyes fixed on some imaginary spot where the wall joined the ceiling. Her pouting lips were a smear of crimson, and her legs were smooth and oiled to glisten in the smoky lamplight. Her neckline was enticingly low, though her breasts were small, probably not fully developed. Only when someone managed to grab her flashing legs did the Mexican girl momentarily react, kicking and hissing like a cornered cat, to the great delight of the rough and irreverent crowd.

Morgan edged up to the bar, which was nothing but a series of doors nailed across tall sawhorses. He ordered rum, hoping it would calm his nerves and silence the chattering of his teeth. When the drink came, Morgan tossed it down; it tasted awful, but he ordered another, showing a dollar on the bar between his fingers.

Despite the laughter and drunkenness, Morgan quickly discerned an undercurrent of conversation, all of it boastful in the sentiment that General Castro and the Californios would nail both Micheltorena and Sutter to a cross after their army was defeated.

"Listen to me," a huge, bearded man shouted over the throbbing beat of the Indian's drum. "Sutter and Micheltorena are too chicken to fight!"

One of the listeners put his hands to his armpits and made clucking sounds, dancing around like a chicken. The crowd howled with laughter, and it incited the big man to jump on a table and bellow, "Mark my words, Sutter and Micheltorena will spend this rainy season at the mission in Santa Barbara. By spring, the padre up there will have 'em both chantin' and prayin' the rosary. They'll make a pilgrimage north, and that'll be the end of them crooked bastards!"

Everyone roared again, and the chicken man repeated his ridiculous dance so that the cantina rocked with laughter. When the noise finally abated a little, one of the few sober men present shouted, "Oh yeah, what about Micheltorena's cholos? They're not about to do no prayin'. Fact is, they're supposed to be the devil's own helpers."

"If they're stupid enough to come down this far south," the big man proclaimed, "we'll send them all straight to hell!"

This sentiment was roundly echoed in the cantina. Morgan leaned low over the bar and said to the fellow on his left, "How many soldiers and volunteers would you guess we have to fight Micheltorena?"

The man was staring openmouthed at the dancer's oiled legs. The desire in his eyes was so naked that Morgan actually felt embarrassed.

"Hey," he said to get the man's attention, and repeated his question louder.

The man turned to belch in Morgan's face, roll his eyes, and in a slurred voice drawl, "About ten thousand or so."

Morgan turned away in disgust to repeat his question to the fellow pressed up against his right elbow.

"Three hundred," the man barked with assurance. "But don't worry, there are at least two hundred more coming up from San Diego and Los Angeles."

"For a fact?"

"Yeah. I ought to know. I brought some horses up from Los Angeles and sold them to Castro only yesterday. He told me we'd have even more reinforcements next week."

"Then we'll whip Sutter and Micheltorena for certain," Morgan said eagerly, masking his awareness that those reinforcements would give General Castro's forces an overwhelming numerical superiority.

"Damn right, we will! Why I hear it, Alvarado has managed to convince everyone in Los Angeles and San Diego that Micheltorena's cholos will rape all their women and brain their children if they win the battle. Them people are convinced that they've got to fight or they'll die—and you know they'll fight when they believe they have no other choice."

Morgan had heard enough. "Thanks," he said, turning to leave as he held his big rifle close and unobtrusively at his side.

"Say, what's your name?" the man asked, catching his arm.

"Uhh . . . Pete," he mumbled, pulling away and shoving men aside as he hurried to reach the door.

In his haste to escape, he jostled some rough men, and that was a big mistake because one bellowed, "Hey you! Hold up there!"

Morgan did not know if the command was directed at him or not, but he kept moving toward the door, suddenly very anxious for the safety of the dark, rainy night. He reached the door and was pushing outside when a hand clamped onto his shoulder. It was Ben Dunn, and the seaman's fingers were like steel talons as they dug into Morgan's coat. As powerful as ever, he yanked Morgan back into the cantina and yelled, "This man is Sutter's spy!"

Instead of trying to bat Dunn's hand free, Morgan gripped his big Hawken rifle in both hands and drove it straight up. The Hawken caught Dunn at the junction of his jaw and throat and violently snapped his head backward. Morgan heard a loud crack of bone. Dunn's bloodshot eyes rolled up into his skull, and he collapsed in a twitching heap.

Morgan whirled and raced outside to his horse. Tearing his reins loose from the hitch rail, he threw himself into the saddle as men burst from the packed cantina, clawing for their pistols and knives as they slipped and tried to keep their balance in the sloppy street. Morgan dropped the Hawken across his lap in their general direction and pulled the trigger. The entire front window of the cantina exploded inward, and men threw themselves headlong into the mud.

Morgan whipped his horse across the rump with his empty rifle and went flying north, his mount slinging mud in every direction as it struggled to keep from losing its footing.

"Hey, goddamn you!" one of the men who'd earlier invited him to a fandango yelled as Morgan galloped by, pelting both men with mud. "That goddamn fandango ain't over yet!"

"The hell with you, mister!" the other man cried, wiping gobs of mud from his face. "I hope you drown out there, you stupid, ungrateful sonofabitch!"

Morgan rode like the devil to the east. Then, when he was far enough out beyond the pueblo, he reined north, confident that rain would wash away his hoofprints. Two hours later he looped onto the narrow mountain trail and his heartbeat finally returned to normal, only to race again as he wondered if he could get over the mountain range without tumbling into some rain-gorged ravine in the dark.

It was long after midnight when he finally reached camp. The rain had stopped, but a cold wind off the Pacific froze the marrow in his bones. Morgan unsaddled his horse. There was no grain, so he hobbled the poor animal, hoping that it would find enough graze to quickly regain its strength.

"Captain Sutter," he called, shoving the captain's tent flap aside and groping into the darkness. "Captain Sutter!"

Sutter groaned. He smelled of brandy, and Morgan had a difficult time awakening him.

"What? What!"

Morgan struck a match, saw a candle resting on a trunk, and managed to get it lit. Sutter looked awful.

"Captain, I found them!"

"Who? What . . . what the hell time of the night is it?"

"I don't know. Captain, I was in San Buenaventura! Castro is there with his army! If we left now, we could attack at dawn and—"

"Attack what?" Sutter asked groggily.

"Attack Castro's army! They're having a fandango. Most of them are drunk, and we could take them by surprise."

Sutter blinked and stared at him with dull incomprehension. "Go to sleep, Mr. Beck."

"But—"

"Go to bed! We can't attack tonight! We'll discuss this all in the morning."

"But—"

"Good night!" Sutter was conscious enough to blow out the candle, plunging the interior of his tent into darkness once again.

Morgan doubled up his cold fists and inwardly used every cuss word he knew, which was plenty. As he stomped outside, he asked himself if this was the way great leaders like Napoléon Bonaparte acted. Was there any hope of a victory?

Morgan headed for his own leaking tent and soggy blankets. All right, he would wait until tomorrow morning when his leaders were sober and fully awake. But then, if they still chose not to act, he was going to desert this pathetic excuse for a military campaign and go home to his Rosalinda.

Sutter and Micheltorena did act the next day by breaking camp late in the afternoon. Sutter offered to lead an early morning attack, and Micheltorena, after enough protests to assuage his sense of duty, gladly agreed. He would wait until low tide and then push the artillery south along the beach; the two forces would launch a two-pronged attack soon after daylight.

At sundown Morgan led his captain and most of his men, plus a dozen or so Mexican dragoons and two companies of infantry, up the slippery trail leading over the coastal mountains. That night the storm intensified and both men and horses slipped and fell. Two men tumbled to their deaths, lost in the deep barrancas far below.

Bitter curses were on every man's lips as they struggled along, and at dawn Sutter raged to see that his command was strung out for nearly a mile. Men and animals alike were so covered with mud that it seemed impossible they could even see, much less use their weapons.

A grim council of war was held. Several of the men advised the captain to retreat. "Our rifles are useless covered with mud," they argued. "Not half of them will fire."

"No! We should attack at once," John Bidwell urged. "If we can't fire our rifles, we can use our bayonets and knives!"

To Sutter's credit, he agreed. "I will wait one more hour for the rest of our soldiers to catch up, and then we will attack from those trees on the hillsides just below."

The next hour was an eternity as soldiers desperately attempted to clean and dry their rifles. The vaqueros banded together and prayed, then each vowed to use only his knife and rawhide reata. Very soon the captain ordered his shivering men to form a battle line just inside the forest. Morgan was relieved to see the men square their shoulders with pride and determination.

"They won't be expecting an attack in this foul weather!" Sutter repeated twice as he rode up and down in front of his miserable soldiers and cavalrymen. "And besides, last night they had a fandango and will probably be still asleep or half drunk."

"Lucky bastards," a man beside Morgan grumbled.

"Prepare arms!" Sutter cried, spurring his horse out of the forest. "Charge!"

"Charge what?" the same man swore. "I don't see anything but a few skinny horses."

But that didn't matter to Captain Sutter, and as he swept down the hillside toward the unsuspecting town, they could all hear his wild shouts and see him waving his saber overhead.

"Let's go!" Morgan yelled at the top of his voice.

It was almost a mile to the pueblo, and when someone at last managed to discharge his musket, a few of the Californios down in San Buenaventura staggered off the mission grounds, saw the attack, and promptly disappeared. Moments later, Morgan saw a bunch of them running for their lives down the main street in the direction of Los Angeles. A few shots were fired, but when Sutter's horse slipped and half buried him in the muddy streets, the attack dissolved and half his men surged toward the suddenly vacated cantinas.

Sutter was dragged to his feet, cursing because his uniform was ruined, when they heard cannon shots. "That will be our governor firing from the Rincon!" Sutter cried, dashing forward, sliding to a halt, then reversing direction as he gathered his wits and bearings.

Three or four more cannon shots were fired, and the Battle of San Buenaventura became a complete and bloodless rout. When word arrived from Governor Micheltorena ordering Captain Sutter not to pursue the Californios, everyone cheered except Sutter and Morgan.

"Dammit!" Sutter complained, wiping muck from his uniform and heading toward the same cantina where Morgan had killed Ben Dunn. "Dammit, we could have captured the lot of them and ended this thing so we could go back to New Helvetia and get ready for planting!"

"I know," Morgan said, realizing, as Sutter did, that they had accomplished nothing, and in fact had squandered what should have been a crushing victory over Castro and his forces.

Sutter halted right in the center of a huge mud puddle, and a grin suddenly transformed his weary expression. "But I'll tell you," he said, looking around as if he were standing on some great battlefield, "we were sure something charging down from that mountain! We put the fear of God into them!"

Morgan managed a tired grin and watched John Bidwell save a drunken American thought to be one of Castro's men from a severe beating. "That we did, Captain. That we did! You reminded me of an avenging angel with that sword in your hand."

Captain John Augustus Sutter liked that, liked it so much that he threw his mud-caked arm around Morgan's shoulders and hugged him with a big laugh. "Let's get drunk and celebrate! It isn't every day a man charges into the face of death and emerges victorious."

Morgan wished he felt like celebrating—but he didn't. And there would be no going home soon, either. Instead they'd have to march down to Los Angeles, and Morgan recalled the man in the cantina who'd bragged that every able-bodied adult in that pueblo would fight to the death before submitting to Micheltorena's feared and hated cholos.

Up and down the muddy street, men were shouting and looting. *Enjoy yourselves,* Morgan thought darkly as he followed Sutter into a cantina, *because the real fighting is yet to come.*

≈ 12 ≈

Stretched, gauzy clouds were streaming across the face of a chill, three-quarter moon, and the wind was blowing so hard that flying grit and sand was making sleep impossible.

Across the huge valley to his right, Morgan could see the stark outline of Mission San Fernando Rey de España located only a few miles north of the pueblo of Los Angeles. Farther to the south he could also see the campfires of Castro's opposing army. There were so many enemy campfires that he was sure that Sutter's company was badly outnumbered.

Micheltorena had taken sick the day before, and the euphoria of their nearly bloodless San Buenaventura victory had already been washed away. Now, camped among the ruins of the old Cahuenga adobe, those soldiers who had not deserted were very somber after having heard new rumors that Castro's army was receiving American reinforcements from San Diego daily.

John Bidwell leaned closer to Morgan and said, "Tomorrow will be the fight that decides all our fates."

"We'll win," Morgan vowed.

"I wish I shared your confidence. But you remember that Mexican spy our captain sent into Los Angeles?"

"Sure, I was there when he left last night."

"He joined the enemy."

"Are you certain?"

"Yep. He saw the size of Castro's army and decided the odds were better against us tomorrow morning."

Morgan wished he hadn't heard this piece of news, and he hoped that the others hadn't heard it. Morale was already bad, and Micheltorena's hated cholos were deserting faster than fleas off a dying dog.

Morgan looked sideways at Bidwell. "So now what happens?"

"You won't believe this," Bidwell whispered, rolling over and staring up at the heavens, "but a Mexican from Castro's army came over tonight and offered to be an informer for twenty-five dollars and a bottle of tequila."

Morgan snorted. "I hope the captain shoots him!"

"He didn't. In fact, he paid the man."

"What the hell for?"

"Because we need to know what we're up against. And we're up against every able-bodied man in the pueblo of Los Angeles."

"So I've heard," Morgan said, remembering what he heard at the cantina.

"According to the spy, there's at least five hundred men from the pueblo, in addition to a company of men that has marched up from San Diego."

Morgan said nothing, and in the strained silence that followed, Bidwell removed a pipe and some tobacco from his vest. He carefully packed the pipe, lit it, and puffed rapidly until flickering sparks haloed the bowl. "I'll tell you something else. Come morning, when we can see what's facing us across this valley, we might just want to consider a retreat."

"Not me. If Micheltorena falls, I lose my Sacramento land grant."

Bidwell frowned and puffed faster. "Maybe whoever replaces him—and that'll probably be Pio Pico—will honor it."

But Morgan shook his head. "John, I've grown up in California, and you've been here only a few years. I'll tell you something. If we've backed the wrong side of this thing, Captain Sutter might as well head for the Oregon Territory. Same goes for us."

"I disagree," Bidwell said. "I met Pio Pico in Monterey a year ago, and he doesn't strike me as a vindictive man. Furthermore, Castro and Alvarado are after the governor's hide, not Captain Sutter's."

"But we're *backing* the governor."

"Yes. Unfortunately."

Morgan frowned. "Why?"

"Think about it. What has Micheltorena done for us?"

"Plenty! He's given me two square leagues of prime land along the Sacramento River."

"No, he hasn't. He's *said* he'd give it to you, but that doesn't make it a legal title, and it won't be for some time to come. Plenty can happen before then. Micheltorena might be assassinated. California might become part of the United States of America. Think about it, Morgan. The governor gave you an empty promise which cost him nothing—but it may cost you your life."

Morgan didn't like what he was hearing, especially from John Bidwell, whose opinion he respected. "John, do you know what they say about switching horses in midstream?"

"Yeah, it's supposed to be bad luck."

"Exactly. And right or wrong, we're in this up to our eyeballs. Come tomorrow morning, we better figure to fight—or die."

Bidwell was silent for a long time, and Morgan's depression deepened. *Good Lord,* he thought, *if a man like Bidwell is starting to question loyalties, no wonder desertions are so high.* Come daybreak, he, Bidwell, and Captain Sutter might be the only ones willing to stand and fight. And if it were true that so many Americans had joined Castro's army, then it was really going to be a battle.

Bidwell rose to a crouch. "I'm going to find the captain and see if he's heard anything more. I'll see you in the morning."

"I hope so," Morgan said without turning his head away from the twinkling stars.

Alone with his own fears, Morgan realized that he had never thought much about death until he'd lost Eli and fled Sonoma with Rosalinda. Morgan was sure he'd shot and killed at least one of Cabral's men the following morning, perhaps even two. And just a few nights ago he'd killed Ben Dunn in San Buenaventura. He hadn't really meant to break the man's neck, but he had, and that's what counted.

So, Morgan thought, two and perhaps even three men were dead on his account, men who'd wanted to live every bit as much as he did, who might have had wives or lovers, even children.

Morgan sighed deeply. He believed in God, and until these killings he'd felt that he could stand at the gates of heaven and have a fair chance of talking his way inside. But now the souls of those three dead men might be standing between himself and eternal salvation.

His more immediate worry, however, was the possibility of never seeing Rosalinda again, never making love to her and fathering sons or daughters and then watching them grow. For one brief moment the enormity of what he would lose by dying was so great that it was all Morgan could do not to jump up and run away. He'd get Rosalinda and they'd flee north into the Oregon Territory.

He'd have to do it on foot, though. His own horse had gone lame, and at least half the other mounts Sutter had brought from New Helvetia had been stolen by the deserters. Still, Rosalinda was a good walker, and they could do it. In the Oregon Territory, he'd be more than qualified to sign on with the Hudson's Bay Company as a trapper. . . .

"Stop it!" he scolded himself under his breath. "Your father didn't die to save a coward."

Morgan realized that his heart was pounding. He was glad that Bidwell had left him, because he probably smelled like fear. He turned his head from side to side, eyes anxiously probing the darkness to see the reassuring forms of Sutter's troops. His hand tightened on his rifle, and its cold solidity gave him a measure of comfort.

Among the stars overhead Morgan saw Rosalinda's beautiful face, and he squeezed his eyes shut because loving and being loved was a curse to someone facing death. The more to lose, the more to fear. At least, Morgan decided, that was how it seemed as he waited anxiously into the darkest morning of his life. He must have dozed off shortly before sunrise, because Bidwell shook him awake as the sun was just rising above the eastern horizon.

"Wake up, Morgan! We're getting ready to attack."

His mind, drugged by worry and lack of sleep, rebelled. Morgan had an overpowering urge to just close his eyes and let other men kill other men. He did not hate anyone enough to kill him except in self-defense, and it seemed totally logical that if he refused to fight, others might follow his example and do the same.

"Come on," Bidwell snapped. "You're the best marksman the captain has. Don't go back to sleep!"

Morgan pushed himself to his knees and shook his head, trying to clear it of the night's dark fears. The rain had stopped, and this morning's sunrise was quite spectacular, with salmon-colored fingers stretching across a sweeping azure sky. The air was still, and the earth seemed hushed up to the moment that Captain Sutter ordered his fife and drum players to sound a battle song. He crawled to his feet, shouldered his Hawken, and hurried after Bidwell. The light quickly intensified until the orb of the rising sun coppered everything.

Now Morgan could see the enemy troops hugging the banks of a big river and more dug in along its smaller tributaries. He saw three small cannon being pulled forward, not by mules but by enemy soldiers, and Morgan wondered if those men were as frightened as he was and if their bowels were also cramping like spastic fists.

"It doesn't look too good," Bidwell said, gazing through a spyglass.

Before Morgan could reply, the enemy's cannon boomed and Sutter's men threw themselves to the dirt, covering their heads and whispering prayers.

But the enemy cannonballs dropped far short, and Sutter drew his sword and rode out in front of his men. "Company, advance!" he cried, wheeling his horse around and starting forward.

The fife began to play, and a big bass drum drowned

out the three smaller ones as their army jolted forward, cannon and infantry in the center, calvary on the flanks. To his credit, Micheltorena had finally found the courage to join the battle and was loudly exhorting his damned cholos and young gentlemen officers to fight.

Suddenly the governor ordered the cannon to halt. The fife and drum died and the great valley seemed to hold its breath as the cannon were elevated. A single order split the cold dawn: "Fire!"

The cannon rocked backward, blasting fire, drooling smoke and cinders as all eyes strained to watch a ball lob across the valley. A cheer was torn from their throats as the cannonball struck one of Castro's artillery caissons and reduced its wheel to smoking tinder. The caisson lurched sideways, then collapsed in a pathetic heap. Its artillerymen scattered like frightened mice.

"They're breaking ranks!" someone cried, surging ahead. "They're retreating!"

It was true! Just like at San Buenaventura! Morgan's heart soared, and legs that had felt rubbery moments ago now responded as powerfully as steel springs. He yelled and sprinted across the land, watching the Californios disintegrate into headlong retreat.

Micheltorena galloped forward, and when they reached the river, he threw himself from his horse and ordered his riflemen to dig in.

"No!" Sutter could be heard shouting in angry protest. "Damn you, not again! Charge while they are in retreat!"

But Sutter's protest was ignored, and when Morgan and a soldier named Ike found themselves out in front and practically alone, they were forced to dive into a low depression for cover as a hail of musket balls split the air all around. Every time they raised their heads to fire, they were almost decapitated. They heard more artillery fire and shouts and supposed that legions of brave soldiers were dying while they lay quaking in fear.

"We can't stay here!" Morgan cried. "We've got to *do something*!"

"Like being heroes and getting our heads shot off?"

Morgan knew the older man was right, but he exposed his head anyway and made the Hawken roar. Then, dropping back, he began to reload. Once again he raised his head, and two musket balls kicked dirt into his face.

"Keep your fool head down!" Ike shouted in anger.

Morgan cursed in helpless fury. What was going on out there? He couldn't hear Sutter any longer and wondered if the captain was dead. A quarter of a mile away there was the muffled patter of shots, then silence, and finally the sound of loud arguing interspaced with sporadic firing.

"I can't stand it any longer!" Morgan shouted, pulling his knees up under him and preparing to jump up and race forward.

"You crazy fool!" Ike yelled after him.

Morgan didn't listen. He wasn't about to remain in hiding if Bidwell and Sutter were hurt or dead. Something had to be done.

Taking a deep breath, he gathered himself, but at that moment a tremendous flash of light erupted behind his eyes and a splinter of pain lanced his skull. Morgan cried out and tumbled into a downward spiraling abyss.

"Hey!" a voice called to him. "Wake up, young fella!"

Morgan opened his eyes to stare up at a whiskered, wrinkled face with skin the color of saddle leather and eyes as pale and blue as aquamarine. He gazed at an old mountain man dressed in buckskin right down to his worn moccasins. For a confused, wonderful moment, Morgan thought the man was his father.

"Pa!"

The man had been smiling, but now he frowned and said, "I ain't your pa, young feller."

Morgan's fingers groped for and located a huge knot on the back of his head. "Ouch!"

"Let me see that," the old man said, kneeling at Morgan's side. "Umm-humm! Yep. He sure enough nailed you a good'un."

Morgan was totally confused. "What hit me? A musket ball?"

"Hell, no! That feller that was hidin' in this waller with you did it. Said you was bound and determined to get yourself shot, so he laid the butt of his musket across your skull."

"Ike did this to me?"

"Probably saved your bacon."

Morgan squeezed his eyes closed tightly. "Who are you?"

"Name is Joe Chewy—I'm part Cherokee, part Osage, and the rest stud horse."

Chewy guffawed, and the sound of his laughter sent a needle of pain through Morgan's cracked skull. It was then that he realized he heard no artillery or musket fire, not even the shouts of angry men.

"Is it over?"

"What?"

"The battle!"

"Wasn't what I'd call a battle," Chewy said, pulling at his scraggly gray beard. "Me and the squaws generally battle more'n that before I bed 'em down."

The man guffawed again, but Morgan was in no mood for laughter. He tried to get to his feet, but a violent, stabbing pain felled him again.

"Best be still for a day or two, young feller. You got a real goose egg, and you might even have a broken skull."

Morgan cradled his head in his hands and ground his teeth in pain. He tried his best to put his thoughts in order, but nothing fit. "What happened to Captain Sutter and Governor Micheltorena?"

"Oh, them and that other fella, Bidworth or—"

"Bidwell? John Bidwell?"

"Yep, that's the one. Anyway, they were captured and took away to the pueblo."

"To be shot!"

Chewy's face twisted. "Well, what for?"

"For. . . for being the enemy leaders, for chrissakes! Ohhh!" Morgan groaned, squeezing pain through his eyes.

"Hey, young feller, what you need is a big swaller of aguardiente. Here," Chewy said, unslinging a skin bag from around his neck and then uncorking it before shoving it at Morgan. "Ain't no doubt that this'll make you feel better."

Morgan didn't see how he could feel any worse, so he upended the bag and drank until tears rolled down his cheeks and fire hotter than lava filled his belly. He handed the bag back and croaked, "Thanks."

"That's all right."

Morgan sleeved his cheeks dry. "Mr. Chewy, I'd sure appreciate it if you'd tell me exactly what happened. How many of our men died, and what happened to Micheltorena and Sutter? Tell me everything from the start."

Chewy satisfied his own thirst, then wiped his arm across his mouth as Eli used to do before saying, "The truth of it was, nobody really wanted to fight. I could see that right away. I've fought Indians, and *they* fight. But not these folks."

"Of course it was a fight," Morgan snapped. "Those were sure real musket balls flying my way."

"Oh, sure, there was a lot of lead flyin' at first, but mostly we were just shootin' over your heads."

"You were?"

"You're an American, ain't you? I sure as hell ain't goin' to kill my own kind." Chewy raised an eyebrow in question, then grunted. "You mean you was *tryin'* to kill us?"

"Well, I only fired once or twice," Morgan hedged. "How many died on each side?"

"Lemme see, now." Chewy considered the matter carefully. "All right, we did lose a mule. Got its fool head blowed off by a cannonball." Chewy took another pull on his skin bag and indicated that it was all right for Morgan to do the same. "Lucky shot for somebody, unlucky shot for the mule. Big, good-lookin' sonofabitch, too."

"Are you saying no one was killed?" Morgan asked in disbelief.

"Oh, a couple got winged, and of course you got brained pretty hard, but that's it."

Morgan was astounded. It seemed incomprehensible, and yet . . . and yet, no one had died at San Buenaventura, either, except for Bill Dunn.

"So what will happen to Captain Sutter and John Bidwell?"

"I don't know. I suppose they'll have a pretty good dinner and be turned loose sooner or later."

Morgan didn't believe it. "And Governor Micheltorena?"

"Well, sir, he and Castro's family are old friends down in Mexico, from what I could tell by listening to them. I got a hunch they'll both return to Mexico City. The Americans and Californios both insisted that them damned cholos will have to go south, too."

"Then . . . then that's it?" Morgan raised his hands, then let them fall. "The war is over?"

"I keep trying to tell you that this weren't no war, young feller. Just a little disagreement."

Morgan had a sudden, overpowering urge to get drunk. "Mr. Chewy, can you get more aguardiente?"

"Why sure, but—"

Morgan fished a dollar out of his pocket and slapped it into Joe Chewy's wrinkled old hand. "I haven't been drunk since a day on the beach at Monterey six years ago. But I think I'm going to get drunk now."

"Well, you ought to come on into the pueblo of Los Angeles first. There's gonna be a hell of a fandango there tonight and lots of celebratin' by both sides." Chewy winked. "There's some pretty señoritas that'd take a real shine to you. Probably make you feel like wigglin' in the dark."

"Nope," Morgan said. "I'm going to stay right here and get drunk. Come tomorrow, I'll go to Los Angeles and see my captain. But today . . . well, nothing has gone right or makes the least bit of sense."

Joe Chewy took the dollar. "I got a blanket and some jerked beef I'll leave, then I'll be back soon enough—if I don't get attacked by a señorita."

"Then by all means be careful, Mr. Chewy," Morgan

said, lying down again and gazing up at the sky, only
to realize that it was almost sundown.

A minute later the old man returned with a blanket
and a chunk of black beef. "See ya tomorrow, young
fella."

"Mr. Chewy?"

He turned.

"You a mountain man?"

The row of rotten teeth appeared. "Sure am!"

"You ever hear of Eli Beck?"

"'Course I have! I wrestled him for a Shoshone
squaw at the first rendezvous we had at Henry's Fork of
the Green River in the year of 1825. It was a hell of a
fight, but she was a hell of a good-lookin' woman."

"Who won?"

"I did," Chewy said proudly. "'Course, Eli was drunker
than me, but I beat him fair and square. Two years later
he outshot all of us at Bear Lake and won a Ute girl and
six Appaloosa ponies."

"Yeah, he told me." Morgan drank a little aguardiente
and scrubbed his face before he drank again.

"Why do you ask?"

"I'm Eli Beck's son."

Joe Chewy cocked his head, first one way and then
the other, like a crow peeking down from a tree.
"Humph! I'd a thought he'd have taught you better
than to allow yourself to get brained thataway."

"I'm a slow learner," Morgan confessed. "If you see
Captain Sutter, tell him—"

But the old man was already walking away. "I ain't
going to see him. I'm goin' to find a pretty señorita to
play with after the fandango. So you can lay out here in
the dirt and get drunk all by yourself if you want, but it
don't make no sense to Joe Chewy."

Morgan watched the lean, bowlegged man disappear
over a hill, moving toward the south. Chewy even
walked like Eli Beck. Morgan gazed back up at the sky.

"It doesn't make any sense at all to me, Father," he
said. "I heard of all the battles you were in, all the hard
fights. But it wasn't a fight at San Buenaventura a
couple of days ago, and I've just been told it wasn't a

fight here, either. I don't understand it, but I'm glad to be alive."

Morgan chewed some jerked beef and washed it down with aguardiente, feeling the raw liquor ease the pain in his skull. One thing for certain, he wasn't leaving until Captain Sutter and John Bidwell were free. After that he was running north to be with Rosalinda.

"But my land grant is gone," he told the sky.

Morgan sighed and drank more aguardiente. *The hell with it*, he thought. *Rosalinda and I will claim that land anyway, and the authorities be damned*. If this was the way the victorious Californios handled things, they probably wouldn't bother a poor Sacramento Valley squatter.

By the time Morgan had reached the pueblo of Los Angeles the next day, with a splitting hangover, a peace treaty already had been signed. Only later, as the remnants of Sutter's once proud little army rode north on horses bought on credit, did Morgan learn that Micheltorena had agreed to return to Mexico along with whatever cholos could be rounded up.

"I had only to promise that I would not take up arms again," Sutter conceded. "But the cost was very great and will set me back for years. I lost more than one hundred good saddle horses and thousands of dollars out of my own pocket for equipping my soldiers. I had better have an abundant harvest this fall, or I am ruined. The promissory notes on Fort Ross due the Russians are heavy this year."

Morgan thought about offering to remain in the captain's employ as a trapper, but when he also thought about his own dream and the beautiful rise of land where he and Rosalinda had made love and planned their future, he kept his lips sealed. Old Joe Chewy had decided to go to New Helvetia after Sutter offered him an attractive deal if he'd organize a trapping party and take more beaver.

"We can recoup," John Bidwell said to Sutter, trying hard to sound optimistic. "If we have good spring rains but no flooding, our harvest should bring in enough cash to pay the Russians this year's amount and even settle a few of your other outstanding debts."

But Sutter was nearly inconsolable because of the humiliating defeat. "I deserved better. Do you know that I was thrown in a cell at the Cahuenga adobe and they asked for my sword?"

Neither Bidwell nor Morgan said anything, knowing that Sutter wasn't expecting an answer.

"Fortunately, I recognized an officer by the name of Eugenio Montenegro, a captain of their cavalry, and I told him that he should inform his superiors that they knew nothing of the civilities of war, since they put an officer of my rank under a common guard. This had the desired effect. My sword was returned, and I was invited to another room where Castro's officers were drinking and was asked to join them."

"Alvarado and Castro know how important it is to remain your friends," Bidwell said. "You are too powerful to topple."

"Yes," Sutter agreed. "Besides, I was able to convince my captors and Governor Pico that I was simply acting as a loyal Mexican citizen in obeying Micheltorena's orders to march in his support. Governor Pico, Castro, and the rest, they understood. In fact, they have assured me a continuation of full authority over my inland domain."

Morgan said nothing, but he was amazed that any of them were still alive—especially Sutter, whom he had expected to be executed, ensuring that New Helvetia became a victory prize. It seemed to Morgan that Sutter and the governor owed their lives to an old-fashioned sense of honor among the Californios which prevented them from executing their enemy leaders. And while honor was admirable, Morgan thought that it would be ignored when the Californios were inevitably challenged by U.S. army officers like John C. Frémont.

In the long, difficult weeks that followed their defeat, Sutter did not order what remained of his army to retrace its path along the Pacific Coast from mission to mission. The captain judged it very unlikely that the coastal settlements of California would assist a defeated army which had backed an unpopular ex-governor. So they rode up the hot, dry central valley, following the San Joaquin River. The trip was a severe hardship on everyone. They had little food except what Morgan could bring down with his sharp eye and powerful Hawken rifle, and their poor horses suffered badly. Many had to be left behind after going lame, and several more drowned trying to ford the mighty torrents of the snow-fed King, Merced, and Stanislaus rivers.

But at last they came upon the American River and saw Sutter's Fort with its flag proudly flying. Many soldiers cheered with joy, Indians wept like children, and Morgan's throat ached with the thought of finally returning to Rosalinda's arms and holding his dear mother once again.

But Sutter, after a long pause, bent his head and tears flowed down his cheeks.

"What's wrong!" Bidwell exclaimed.

"My fields . . . they were not planted!"

Morgan and Bidwell stared, and their hearts sank. The captain was right. For some reason, the vast fields lay fallow, even though it was well past normal planting time. Without some miracle, there would be no harvest, no money to pay Sutter's crushing debts.

"I'm ruined," Sutter moaned. "I have lost everything."

Morgan turned away. He would wait another year to leave his captain. If absolutely necessary, he'd trap more beaver than ever before, and he'd teach Sutter's Indians to do the same.

Somehow, some way, Sutter and his California empire must survive.

≈ 13 ≈

The moment Captain Sutter and his exhausted troops were seen from the fort, a shout went up and everyone came racing headlong out to greet them. Morgan spotted Rosalinda and galloped ahead to dismount and swing her around in his arms.

"You can't imagine how much I've missed you," he said, burying his face in her rose-scented hair.

Her kiss told him that he'd been missed, too, but then she pulled back and took his hands in her own, her face suddenly very grave.

"What's wrong?" he asked in alarm.

"It's Mama," she told him. "She died two weeks ago."

Morgan groaned, and she held him tightly. "Your mother died peacefully in her sleep. God took her very gently."

"Show me where she's buried," Morgan managed to say.

Hand in hand and oblivious of the joyous shouting of dozens of reunions, Rosalinda led her husband back up the hill to Sutter's little cemetery and a fresh mound of dirt marked by a small white cross and decorated with wildflowers.

"Here."

Morgan knelt down next to the grave and touched it gently. "She never got her chapel."

"Her chapel was inside of her heart."

"Yeah."

"And look," Rosalinda said, "this grave belongs to your father."

He followed her gaze to the mound beside that of his mother. "I . . . I don't understand."

"General Vallejo had your father's body delivered in a wagon soon after you left. My uncle did not come personally, but he wrote a letter wishing us love and happiness. He believed Julio and the other servants and does not blame you for the death of Don Francisco."

Morgan knelt between the graves. The earth was warm to his touch as he smoothed his hand over the mounds. "They never had much of anything," he said. "That troubled my father very much, but Mama didn't care. She had a good husband and faith enough to move mountains."

"And a good son," Rosalinda said. "To her last day, she talked about you and our new rancho on the Sacramento River."

Morgan looked up, and his expression was bleak. "Micheltorena is being exiled from California. His promise to give us a rancho has become meaningless. Castro, Pico or whoever takes over as governor will never give us land."

"It means nothing to me."

"Doesn't it?"

"Well," she conceded, "a little. But—"

"Listen," he said quickly, "I believe we should just say to hell with the Mexican government and homestead a claim anyway."

"But that would be illegal."

"There are millions of acres of empty land up and down this valley that are just waiting to be claimed by someone bold enough to make a stand. Besides, Captain Sutter hasn't changed his mind, and he'll still help us."

"He said this?"

"Yes. Only, well, right now he's in big financial trouble." Morgan gestured out toward the fallow fields. "Why weren't they planted early this spring?"

"The Indians refused to work for anyone but Captain Sutter. And then about two months ago a Mexican official arrived with the terrible news that you had all been defeated at San Buenaventura and taken as prisoners."

Tears sprang to her eyes. "Morgan, I almost died imagining what you might have to endure. I went to my uncle in Sonoma to beg him to intercede, and that's when he told me that the news was untrue, that you had routed the enemy and were marching for Los Angeles."

"Yes," Morgan said, the spur of humiliation still tearing at his flesh. "We should have come home instead. It was all such a fiasco. I'm just grateful to be back."

"There is great trouble here, too. Just a few days ago we heard that there was an attack on one of the ranchos nearby. Indians from the south along the San Joaquin River killed Señor Lindsay and ran off his cattle. We have been expecting an attack as well."

Lindsay had been a good friend of Sutter's, and Morgan had known him well. "There won't be an attack now, and the captain will want to go after the murderers and bring them to justice."

"But you have just returned! And you are all so thin and weary." He put his hands on Rosalinda's shoulders and stared down at the graves. "Sometimes bad news comes in bunches."

"Come inside and I will cook for you."

Rosalinda reached for Morgan's hand, but he shook his head. "You go inside and start cooking. I need to be alone for a moment. I'll be along soon."

"You promise?"

"I promise."

Rosalinda went inside, and Morgan contemplated the silent graves. He wished that he had been present when his mother died, and he would have given anything to have his parents alive again to tell them how much he loved and respected them. Mama had lived a hard life, but she'd never lost hope or her dignity. Eli had shared stirring adventures among the famed mountain men, and in the end he'd died very bravely.

"Morgan?"

He looked up to see Joe Chewy, who removed his hat and said, "I'm sorry about your ma. Sutter wanted me to tell you he was sorry, too. He said she was a damned fine old gal."

"That she was."

"I guess you haven't heard yet, but there's Indian trouble hereabouts."

"I heard."

"Captain says he'll understand if you don't want to go with us."

"I'm going."

Chewy nodded. "Figured you probably would," he said, and turned and started to walk away. "Oh yeah, there's something else the captain wanted you to know. The Russian is here. The captain seems to set quite a store by him."

"He's one of the best."

"Seems to me that the Russian might want to be Sutter's main trapper."

"Be fine with me. There's room for you, or you might even want to homestead some land for yourself. That's what I mean to do before long."

"Me? Homestead?" Chewy barked a rough laugh. "Hell, I got way too much Indian in me for that. You see, the way I figure it, the land has a claim on *me*—not the other way around. Nobody really owns the land; they just use it awhile before dyin' or movin' on."

Morgan managed a thin smile. "You do think like an Indian, Joe."

There was an awkward silence before Chewy motioned toward Eli's grave. "So that's where he rests, huh?"

"Yeah."

Chewy cocked back his head and gazed into the sweeping distance of the great, warm valley, which was flattered by the soft glow of the setting sun. "Nice view of the river and the trees comin' into bud. The Eli Beck I knew would have liked it fine here near the captain's fort and overlooking them big rivers."

Morgan stood up. He was a little taller than Joe Chewy, but only because the older man had bent to his many hard years. "When does the captain want to go after the Indians?"

"Tomorrow. First light."

"Get me a fresh horse and bring it around at daybreak. I'll be ready."

The old man's eyes dropped to the graves, then lifted to meet those of Morgan. "Life is hard out West. Harder on a woman than a man. Could be you'd do your missus a favor by stayin' where she's got friends and protection."

"I've thought on it," Morgan said. "We've talked. She wants her own home the same as me."

"Then I guess we'd better catch them murderin' Indians so they don't kill folks like you," Joe Chewy said, turning and walking away.

As Morgan watched the mountain man, he realized he admired Joe Chewy for the same reasons he'd admired his father. That breed of man was noble, uncompromising. They had no bend to them when it came to their code or to rules and authorities. But you knew exactly where they stood on any issue, and their word was their bond.

"Daybreak!" he called.

Joe Chewy didn't break stride, holler back, or show any sign that he'd heard Morgan's call. But he'd heard, all right.

They galloped out of the fort to a drum roll and raced south on fresh horses. Captain Sutter, wearing his dirty Mexican campaign uniform, was in the lead, flanked by Morgan and Joe Chewy with their long Hawken rifles. Sutter had picked a corps of twenty-two men—whites, Kanaka, and his best of the local Indians. Every one of them was a proven fighter, and the mood was grim. Most of them had been on the ill-fated expedition to Los Angeles; lean and bitter, they were in an avenging mood.

Morgan was an excellent tracker, but so was Chewy and all of the Indians. As it turned out, a blind man could have followed the murdering Indians and the three hundred cattle they were driving south along the

San Joaquin River. In just three days of hard riding, they overtook the renegades.

"They've seen us, Captain!" one of the advance scouts reported as he hurried back to join them.

Sutter raised his Mexican saber and yelled, "No quarter! No quarter!"

Sutter spurred forward, and Morgan had to whip his horse hard to catch up with the man. The Indians outnumbered them by a large margin, and they did not appear inclined to abandon their stolen cattle. New Helvetia's Indians, some with bows and arrows but most with old muskets probably supplied by Sutter's little armory, prepared to fight. Glancing across at Chewy, who was also trying to overtake the captain, Morgan yelled, "Is *this* going to be a fight?"

"Hell, yes! Watch your scalp, Mr. Beck! Yeee—yiipp-yip-yeeee!"

It was an old Ute Indian battle cry and one that Morgan had heard Eli demonstrate long, long ago. Not to be outdone, Sutter bellowed something in Swiss that sounded like a cat screeching with its tail caught in a slamming door.

Morgan did not fire until he was almost on top of the Indians, and when he did, the massive Hawken's blast struck an Indian in the chest, igniting his shirt as the impact lifted him from his mount. Morgan heard a bloodcurdling scream and saw Joe Chewy almost behead an Indian with the heavy barrel of his rifle. Since there was no time to reload, Morgan figured he'd best do the same if he were to whittle down the odds. The next few minutes were flushed with extreme exhilaration and absolute terror. Morgan took a bullet through the fleshy part of his upper left arm, and his horse was shot out from under him. He kicked free of his stirrups, and his Hawken went flying. He rolled, came to his feet, and tore an Indian from his horse. With a demonic cry, Morgan ripped his Green River knife from its sheath and buried it in the man's belly, gutting him like a buck.

It was a swift but terrible battle. One of the Kanaka was trampled by a dying steer and several others were badly wounded before the Indians broke and ran for the woods. Chewy shot one between the shoulder blades just before he disappeared into the trees. A few of Sutter's Indians were gripped by a blood frenzy and mutilated their dead enemies.

"Enough!" the captain shouted until he was hoarse and the frenzy ended.

"You all right?" Joe Chewy asked, gripping Morgan's arm and cutting away his sleeve.

"You tell me," Morgan groaned, feeling the pain of his wound now that the battle was over.

Chewy studied the wound for a moment. Then he actually stuck his own knife blade into it and fished around for one excruciating moment.

"Ball went clear through."

"You could have figured that out by seeing holes on both sides!" Morgan swore through gritted teeth.

Chewy used Morgan's torn sleeve to bind the wound. "Your woman might baby you real tender, but not Joe Chewy. No, sir! Your pa was tough—you be the same."

Morgan felt lightheaded. He sat down on a rock and breathed deeply as he surveyed the carnage.

"Juan Vaca is dead," someone said.

Morgan twisted around to see the captain kneeling beside Vaca's lifeless body; he had been one of Sutter's most loyal workers, and when Sutter raised his head, his expression was stricken. "Anyone else killed?"

"Nope," Chewy said, looking around, "but we got a few wounded."

"Then let's round up the stolen cattle and get them back to their home ground."

"What about these dead Indians?" a man asked.

Sutter's expression was hard and unforgiving. "We'll leave them where they lie."

No one argued with the captain. The next few days were an agony to Morgan and the other wounded as they drove the cattle back up the San Joaquin. When Morgan finally arrived at his cabin, he practically toppled from his saddle.

"He's got a fever, Señora," Joe Chewy said, dismounting and helping Rosalinda get Morgan inside.

"Better boil some water and make some bandages. We need to clean out that festering wound."

Rosalinda wasted no tears as she ripped the dirty bandage from Morgan's arm and studied the dark, suppurating wound and the black lines radiating outward just under her husband's pale skin.

"I'll be back with help," Chewy promised, also staring at the arm. "He's going to live, Señora. And he ain't goin' to lose that arm. I'll give you my word on it."

Rosalinda said nothing. Morgan was on fire, and the arm be damned. It seemed the best she could hope for was to save her husband's life.

Anton Rostov and his wife María arrived less than ten minutes later, and the Russian immediately took command. He unslung an Indian medicine bag from around his neck and gave it to his wife. "María will prepare a poultice."

"Have you used it before?" Rosalinda asked anxiously.

"Many times," Rostov said without looking up. He carefully examined the wound. His blunt fingernail traced a big poisoned vein down Morgan's forearm. He studied the hand and the fingers, finding their nails to be purplish with the first signs of infection.

"We must hurry," María said, adding more wood to the fire as they waited for water to boil.

Rostov's fingers brushed across Morgan's cheeks. "Can you hear me?"

"Yes," Morgan whispered.

"I'm going to have to cut open your arm," the Russian said in his soothing voice. "It will be a deep wound, and it will smell of decay. But I don't want you to worry. Everything will be fine."

Morgan was bathed in sweat. The room was smoky and stiflingly hot. He felt as if he could not breathe. The idea that he might lose an arm filled him with mindless terror. "Don't cut it off! Please don't cut my arm off! I would rather die. A one-armed man can't take care of a woman. He'd never—"

"Lie still and be silent!" the Russian commanded. "Do you think I would kill a man because he might lose his arm?"

"No, but—"

Rostov shook his head. "You are not talking good sense, Morgan Beck. Do not say anything more that is stupid."

Rostov turned to the women. "We need to wash the arm now before I cut."

María forked a steaming rag out of the kettle of near-boiling water. She quickly washed the arm and then—before Rosalinda or Morgan were expecting it— Rostov jabbed the point of his knife into Morgan's arm and cut.

"Aiee!"

Joe Chewy appeared as if from nowhere and threw himself on Morgan's chest, pinning him down with the help of María and Rosalinda while the Russian excised the dark, rotting flesh. Morgan lost consciousness, and Rostov did not stop cutting and squeezing until the black, poisoned blood turned bright red.

"Wash it again, please," Rostov ordered. "Then we will apply the hot poultices."

Rosalinda's hands were shaking badly, but she managed to fish a poultice out of the now boiling water. "Drop it here," Rostov said, pointing to the open cavity in Morgan's violated flesh. Rosalinda did as he ordered, then turned away quickly as Morgan's entire body convulsed and a deep groan was torn from his lips. Rosalinda paled, and her hand brushed across her eyes as she struggled against a fainting spell.

Rostov's dark eyes sent a message to his wife, and María acknowledged it with a nod, then took Rosalinda's arm.

"Señora Beck," she said gently, "you need a little fresh air, perhaps. We can do the rest."

"Are you sure?"

"Yes. Señor Chewy, will you help her, please?"

"Sure," he said, taking Rosalinda's arm and leading her outside, where they collapsed on the grass. Rosalinda buried her head in her hands.

"He's going to be all right," Chewy said, patting her shoulder clumsily. "That Russian and his wife act like they been doctorin' every day of their lives."

Rosalinda took a deep breath to clear her senses. "María told me she once assisted the padres at the old Mission San Rafael with sick and dying Indians. Years later, she and Anton lost their infant boy to the fever. Together, they have seen much sickness and death."

Inside, Rostov and his wife worked expertly together. "We'll let it bleed a little more," Anton said, his face tight with concentration.

"Here," María said, easing another hot poultice onto the wound before looking up at her husband and asking in a hushed voice, "Do you think he will lose the arm?"

"No," Rostov said as Morgan stiffened again at the searing heat penetrating his flesh and drawing out the poison.

The Russian placed his bare hand over the poultice and compressed it tightly. He studied Morgan's bloodless face and saw himself as a young man, back when he was an eager young officer working for the famed Russian American Company and receiving his orders from no less a legend than Governor Alexander Baranov. The crusty old Russian empire builder had picked Rostov to help found and build Russia's first settlement on the rugged coast of Alta California. And they had done it, only to lose it for a handful of Captain Sutter's promises that might never be kept.

"Anton?"

He snapped back to the present. "Another poultice, please."

María laid it on Morgan's arm after Rostov removed the cooling one. "It is a good thing that we brought the Pomo Indian medicine," she said.

"Yes." Rostov studied Morgan's face. "This is a good man, and he has a good wife."

María nodded.

"And this is a very good cabin," Rostov said, looking around as he placed his hand over the steaming poultice and pressed it hard to the arm. "Would you like a cabin like this, María?"

"Would you?"

He smiled. "Don't answer my question with a question. You would like a cabin here, wouldn't you?"

"All right," she admitted. "I would want to teach the children God's word. And have a chapel—and a school for the Indian children."

"I am told that is what this man's mother also wanted."

"I would build it myself if necessary."

"I am sure that you would. But it will not be necessary. As part of the condition of working as Sutter's chief trapper, I will ask for the things you desire."

"The captain has many problems."

"Everyone has problems. The fields can still be planted if he gets the help. There can still be a fall harvest. Captain Sutter is not the kind of man to quit."

"Would you build me a cabin?" she asked. "One like this?"

"If you asked, I would build you a palace," he told her. "But first, another poultice."

Morgan awoke the next morning and his fever was gone. Gone, too, were the ominous black lines radiating out from his wound.

"How do you feel?" Rosalinda asked.

"Good, but very tired."

"Your fever broke last night. Pomo Indian medicine and prayer saved you."

"And you," he said, taking her hand.

"And the Rostovs, as well as Señor Chewy."

Morgan rolled his head sideways and stared at his heavily bandaged arm. "Thank God you didn't let Joe take care of it. He'd probably have cut it off at the shoulder."

Rosalinda smiled with happiness. "We are going to have new neighbors, Morgan."

"Who?"

"The Russian and his wife. Captain Sutter ordered his carpenters to work this very morning. The captain forbids us to leave until you are completely healed and strong again."

"I'm strong right now," Morgan argued with a grin as he encircled her slender waist.

"Oh?" Her eyebrows rose in question. "Exactly *how* strong?"

"Strong enough," he said, feeling a surge of intense desire for her.

Rosalinda stood and quickly undressed. Morgan saw from the blush in her cheeks that she shared his own desire.

"We must be very careful not to bump your poor arm," she breathed into his ear as she crawled into bed next to him.

Morgan groaned with satisfaction. Right now, one arm was as good as two.

During what remained of the spring, Sutter worked day and night exhorting the Indian laborers to get his fields planted. Because it was so late in the season for planting, there was the risk of an early frost killing the plants before they were ready to be harvested, but the captain's back was to the wall and there was little choice.

That summer there was another Indian uprising, this time caused by the Mokelumnes, led by their chief Raphero, who openly boasted that he would kill all the whites in the Sacramento Valley and set a torch to their grain fields. Sutter picked Joe Chewy to track down the Mokelumnes. Soon Raphero was captured, returned in irons to Sutter's Fort, and court-martialed. The captain himself sentenced the unrepentant Indian chief to death. After his execution, Raphero's head was severed and jammed onto a pike for display above the main gate.

"It's anti-Christian," Rosalinda stormed in anger, glaring up at the grisly head, its long black hair blowing eerily in the wind.

"That it may be," Morgan said, "but it's also a very effective warning to the Indians that rebellions, killings, and theft will not be tolerated in the Sacramento Valley."

María Rostov, her husband off trapping, happened to be with them. "It will bring Captain Sutter nothing but ill fortune," she prophesied. "He should take it down and bury it with poor Raphero's body. Even then it will be a curse on this place and on the captain himself."

"What value does superstition have in God's world?"

Morgan questioned, disturbed by the dire predictions of these very religious women.

Neither woman said anything for a full minute as they stared at the decaying face, and then María turned away and said, "That is wrong, Señor. You should tell the captain that he must take it down at once."

"He wouldn't listen to me. But from your expressions, I wish he'd take it down just to be on the safe side."

A week later, Rostov and María moved into their new cabin and a few days later, Sutter hired a tall, withdrawn carpenter named James Marshall. Marshall found time to make both María and Rosalinda some very nice furniture, along with working on the construction that never seemed to slacken at New Helvetia.

Morgan's wound healed, but not as quickly or as cleanly as he had hoped. The infection had moved up into his shoulder joint, causing it to become a little stiff, and the wound drained, necessitating that it be constantly bandaged. In August, Rostov lanced it and applied more Indian poultices. By the end of August the arm felt much better and the residual stiffness caused Morgan only slight discomfort.

That fall, Rostov, Joe Chewy, and a number of the Indians began in earnest to trap beaver along all the major Sierra rivers, and very quickly the pelts began to fill Sutter's large fur storeroom.

By October, the fields were harvested again, and thanks to good rains, Sutter had a bumper crop of wheat, oats, barley, and corn. His orchards and vineyards finally had matured, and whatever was not consumed by his army of workers was easily sold in Yerba Buena at very high prices.

"We did it," Sutter boasted one crisp November day as Morgan counted out five hundred beaver and two hundred prime river otter pelts to be shipped to Monterey. "We brought New Helvetia back from the very edge of financial ruin. As soon as these furs are sold and the money deposited to my account, I'll be able to make most of my payments."

Morgan watched as the Indians whipped the horses

around and around in the threshing pens, just as they had done for the past five years. "It's taken time, but nothing can stop you now, sir."

"Of course not!" Sutter placed his hands on his hips and surveyed his vast holdings. As far as the eye could see in all directions, except toward the river, his harvested fields, herds, and orchards lay before him, all showing a profit that could only grow, year by year.

"I will soon send for my family," he told Morgan. "The other day, while watching you with your wife, I was struck by a great feeling of loneliness. I suddenly understood that New Helvetia has cost me the pleasure of watching my children grow into adulthood. Mr. Beck, my oldest son is a man now, and I would not know him if he arrived and walked up to shake my hand."

Morgan said nothing; this was familiar talk. Whenever Sutter was seized by a sense of melancholy, he would decide to send for his family. Maybe he would, someday, but Morgan wasn't going to hold his breath.

"Next spring," Sutter announced, his restless mind pushing on to other business, "I definitely want you to go up the Sacramento and establish a rancho of your own. I'll extend you all the credit you need, along with cattle, horses, tools, farm equipment—everything. You'll have ten times the opportunity I had when we first arrived here."

Sutter pointed down toward the American River. "Right there, Mr. Beck. Do you remember how afraid we all were when those Indians began yelling and waving their weapons?"

"You were the only one who went out to meet them," Morgan said, recalling that dramatic moment as if it were yesterday. "I had my old Hawken rifle trained on a warrior that I was sure was going to try and split your skull."

"Thank God for the old mission padres who taught a few of those Indians Spanish."

"That was one of the bravest acts I ever saw," Morgan said, meaning it.

"Brave? Not really. You see, in my wake was a string

of creditors stretching from Europe to Yerba Buena. I had no place left to run. I *had* to found this colony. And now..." Sutter's eyes grew distant as he stared at the river.

"And now, what?" Morgan asked.

"And now, it seems as if my dream of New Helvetia has somehow been lost."

"Why?"

Sutter removed a silver flask from inside his coat pocket and drank deeply. "This isn't going to be a New Switzerland. Instead, it'll be the New America. Look around and you'll see growing numbers of ambitious young men from Boston and Santa Fe, from St. Louis and New York. Americans, Mr. Beck! They'll begin to arrive in waves next year, thousands of them, each demanding land and freedom. Hell, they won't learn Spanish or convert to the Catholic Church! They'll thumb their noses at Mexico City and Monterey. They'll grab what they want and be strong enough to keep it. That's why you need to stake out your own claim—now— before the Americans take it first."

"I will," Morgan vowed, suddenly anxious for the place he and Rosalinda had claimed on a hill overlooking the Sacramento.

"Next spring at the latest," Sutter continued. "And I need to send Mr. Bidwell up to my new land holdings at Hock Farm before some bold pioneers realize that California's wealth isn't in furs but in its rich soil, perfect climate, and abundant water."

Morgan had not realized there was such urgency. Like the captain and many others at New Helvetia, he was aware that the growing anti-Mexican sentiment was in direct proportion to the number of new immigrants. However, he had not even considered that the American unrest might culminate in a revolt for at least another decade.

"Then you believe that Mexico's days are numbered in California?"

"Of course! Just as they were in Texas. And even though my Mexican authority in this valley is still supreme, I'll not exercise it against Americans. I backed

the wrong horse once in Micheltorena; I can ill afford to
do it a second time."

"We are right on the path of the immigrant trail,"
Morgan said. "Nearly all the American immigrants
entering California will come through here."

"That's right, and the same goes for those journeying
down from the Oregon Territory. That's why I welcome
them, one and all. I give them provisions, jobs, and
expect their loyalty in return." Sutter winked. "And I'll
have it, too, if Mexico ever attempts to overthrow us."

Morgan remembered those words very clearly a few
weeks later when a large party of Mexicans rode up to
the fort. He recognized General José Castro and soon
learned that one of the other officials was Andres
Castillero, *comisionado* from Mexico City with orders
to make an offer to buy Sutter's Fort for one hundred
thousand American dollars.

"I am stunned," Sutter admitted, taking aside his
closest confidants. "I simply have never thought of
selling out. What do you think, gentlemen?"

John Bidwell said, "Accept their generous offer! You
can use a fraction of that money to improve Hock Farm
and live the rest of your days as rich as a lord."

But Anton Rostov had a different view. "The Mexicans
are not to be trusted. They will entice you with a great
sum of money; then, when you have departed, they will
find reasons not to pay." Rostov paused for a moment,
his dark eyes boring into Sutter. "As a gifted military
officer, Captain, you most certainly cannot fail to understand that whoever commands this fort with cannon
commands both the Sacramento and American rivers.
They could easily cut off your supplies from the coast as
well as your shipments down to Yerba Buena. You
would, sir, be entirely at their mercy."

Sutter blinked, and Morgan knew the man well
enough to realize that Sutter had missed this funda-
mental but critical point made by the Russian.

There was a long silence before Sutter scrubbed a
hand across his eyes, cleared his throat, and said,

"Why, yes, Mr. Rostov. Of course, I understood that
and I fully agree. Mr. Beck, your thoughts, please."

"I was thinking about the people here. They all
depend on you. Many of them have come to think of
this as home. The Miwok Indians under Chief Anashe
would not leave and go to work for you up north in
Maidu territory. I would worry that they would be at
the mercy of the Mexicans. They might be treated like
slaves, made to work against their will and paid nothing."

Sutter had been sitting down, but now he came to his
feet and began to pace back and forth.

"A hundred thousand dollars," he said, shaking his
head. "Why, I could buy the entire Oregon Territory for
that amount of money! I could buy a fleet of ships and
harbors in every coastal settlement from San Diego to
Yerba Buena. I would be rich!"

Morgan met Rostov's eyes and read nothing from the
Russian. Bidwell, who had just advised Sutter to take
the Mexican offer, was bent over with a frown, silent
and looking troubled, probably having grave second
thoughts because of the comments he'd heard from
Morgan and the big Russian.

Sutter paused beside his window and gazed out at his
bustling settlement. He could see his many storerooms
bulging with the wealth of furs, tallow, hides, blankets
from his looms, wool, and tons of grain from his newly
harvested fields. He could see that his compound was
crowded with Americans, all anxious to know what was
transpiring between their leader and the Mexican officials. They were agitated by wild rumors and specula-
tions. The thought also may have crossed Sutter's mind
that he might be lynched if he betrayed their trust. The
Americans were hot-blooded, hard fighters and not
very forgiving when it came to lapses of loyalty.

Sutter turned about dramatically and announced,
"Gentlemen, this land has finally opened her arms, and
I am richly rewarded. The harvest is bountiful, and it is
only the beginning. So . . . I will decline the offer. Not
so much for the wealth, but because I am duty-bound
to protect my people."

"I think you should reconsider," Bidwell said, raising his head quickly.

"No." Sutter expelled a deep breath. "History may prove that today I made a great error. But I did so because of loyalty and honor. So be it!"

Sutter left the room to inform the Mexican officials of his decision. Morgan smiled, and Rostov looked as pleased as he was capable of appearing.

Only Bidwell looked morose and said, "He has made a grievous error, my friends. Grievous, indeed."

Morgan and Rostov said nothing. A hundred thousand dollars was a fortune, and Morgan wondered if he would have had enough character to decline the Mexican offer.

As they walked outside, Morgan said to the Russian, "I pray with all my heart that Mr. Bidwell is wrong."

He glanced up and saw the parchmentlike skin splitting across the skull of Raphero, and the dire prophecy of Sutter's destruction hit him quite forcibly.

Rostov followed his eyes and muttered, "I am going to take that damn thing down and bury it with the body. It will bring us all bad luck."

Morgan agreed. "I'll help you," he offered, hoping that their belated act might still protect his captain from death or destruction.

≈ 14 ≈

In March 1846, Morgan, Rostov, and Joe Chewy returned from a long winter foray up into the Sierras with mules heavily laden with pelts. It had been a very profitable trip. All three of them would be amply rewarded by Sutter for their efforts, and as they descended along the middle fork of the American River, they could see the warm central valley blanketed with vibrant spring flowers.

"Captain Sutter is going to be mighty pleased with these furs," old Chewy said. "What are you boys going to do with your earnin's?"

Anton Rostov said, "I'm going to buy María a new dress and myself a new rifle. I'll stash the rest of it away."

They looked at Morgan, who had given the matter a good deal of thought. "I'm going to use mine to buy seed, tools, a plow, and other farming implements. It's high time that Rosalinda and I went up the Sacramento and claimed that land for ourselves before someone else takes a notion to do it. What about you, Joe?"

Chewy scratched his whiskered jowls. "Well, sir, I reckon I might just take a boat ride down to Yerba Buena and see if I can find me some pretty girls. Either that or buy some of Sutter's baubles and head back into the mountains in search of a squaw."

Rostov shook his head. "Why don't you look for a good woman and settle down? We're trapping beaver now, but you know that can't last forever."

242

"Yeah," Chewy said, "I know that, but I ain't the settlin' kind."

Morgan and the Russian exchanged amused glances, and they rode across Sutter's fields, smelling the birth of another beautiful California spring. At the fort they were welcomed by everyone, and the long, cold weeks of trapping in the mountains were instantly forgotten. But within the hour their spirits were dampened, because Captain Sutter was in a high state of anxiety.

"It's that damned Frémont!" he raged, with the smell of liquor heavy on his breath. "Do you know what that arrogant fool has done now?"

The three trappers indicated that they did not.

"Well, he's started a revolution! He's built a fortification and raised the American flag over Gabilan Peak, just northeast of Monterey. He's defying General Castro and the whole lot of them!"

"Wooo-weee!" Chewy shouted. "Goddamn! I knew old Frémont and his boys were gonna bust loose and raise hell!"

Sutter was clearly appalled by Chewy's reaction. "My Lord, man! Don't you see that this could be a catastrophe? Frémont has only about sixty men—Micheltorena and I had over four hundred, and look what happened."

"'Scuse me for sayin' this, Captain, but you didn't have Kit Carson and Frémont's mountain boys. They're as tough a bunch as ever crossed the Sierras. One of them is worth five of your trained Diggers."

Sutter's cheeks flamed. "Mr. Chewy, I won't hear that kind of seditious talk. I'll remind you that I am still a captain of the Mexican Army of California, with a responsibility to protect Mexico's interests."

Chewy's grin died, and his eyes sparked. "Captain, that there fancy title and that fancy uniform you parade around in ain't going to be worth spit when Captain Frémont and them mountain men of his whip Castro and that whole corrupt bunch. Even as slick a jasper as you can't straddle the fence much longer."

Sutter's cheeks blew out in anger, and he went white around the eyes. "Mr. Chewy, I won't have a disloyal man staying at my fort!"

Chewy pounded the buttplate of his hunting rifle down so hard that the floorboards shook. "I'm for the Americans, and I thought you were, too, Captain. I'm backin' John C. Frémont and Kit Carson all the way down to Mexico City, if that's what it takes to whip them bastards!"

"Get off this post at once."

Morgan stepped forward to place himself between the two men, who were both ready to fight. He searched for words that would calm them down.

"Captain," he said, "I'm sure that we agree that California's future is with the United States of America. You've told me yourself that—"

"That will be enough, Mr. Beck! I am still an officer of the Mexican Army, and I won't hear talk of revolution!"

"You'll hear it whether you want to or not, I reckon!" Chewy said angrily. "And I'll be takin' my pay right now!"

Sutter grinned with satisfaction, and his voice was heavy with sarcasm when he said, "How unfortunate, Mr. Chewy, that I haven't the cash to pay you just now."

Chewy started to lift his rifle, but Morgan grabbed it by the barrel. "Don't," he ordered.

Joe Chewy was so mad he was shaking. "Then I'll take my pay in fur. That's only fair, and I sure hope that neither you nor Anton will try to stop me."

Morgan nodded in agreement. He was loyal to Sutter, but a man had a right to take what he had honestly earned. Joe Chewy, though at least thirty years Morgan's senior, had done his fair share in the Sierras, and he was entitled to payment.

"Take what belongs to you and go," Rostov said. "No one will oppose you."

"Are you both backing him, too?" Sutter cried furiously. "Because if you are, you can all leave."

Rostov's dark eyes tightened. "Captain, tomorrow, when you are sober, you can tell us to leave and we will go. But not now."

Morgan thought Sutter was going to explode. Instead he cried, "Get out of here! All of you!"

Morgan spun on his heel and headed for the door;

ten minutes later he and Rostov watched as Chewy angrily gathered a pile of prime beaver pelts and lashed them into a heavy bundle, which he slung over his shoulder.

"You boys are makin' a big mistake not comin' with me. The captain is bound for a hard fall."

"He's not thinking clearly," Rostov said. "Too much drink. You should stay. Tomorrow he'll be better."

"Nope," Chew said, shaking his head, "tomorrow he'll probably just get drunk again."

"But we were a good team," Morgan said, motioning toward the storeroom full of pelts. "We can still make a lot of quick money."

"The hell with money!" Chewy lowered his voice. "Money just gets me into trouble. Don't you boys see that we got a chance to really *do something* important for once by joinin' up with Carson and Frémont? Hell, we're fixin' to win California just like General Sam Houston and his boys won Texas!" Chewy looked off to the west. "I thought Captain Sutter was the kind of man I could follow—but he ain't. So I'll join up with Frémont. You should, too."

Before Morgan or Anton could reply, the old man raised his head and sniffed the air like a dog on a scent. "Smell something?" he asked, wrinkling his long, hooked nose. "You boys smell it, too?"

"Smell what?" Morgan asked.

Chewy sniffed again. "Why, I do believe it's rot! This hull damned fort smells of rot."

Morgan and Rostov exchanged grim looks. "You'd best ride on out," Morgan said, knowing the old man had made up his mind to leave.

Chewy shook hands with them both. Now that his decision was made, he looked almost happy. "So," he declared loudly enough for everyone inside the fort to hear, "I'm bound for Gabilan Peak and glory! Yes, sir! Me and old Kit Carson are going to lead the Pathfinder and his boys to victory over the Mexicans! We're going to chase them brown bastards all the way down to the Eeee-quator!"

Morgan could not help but smile a little because

Chewy was raising such a ruckus and causing everyone
to stop what they were doing and watch him.

"We're goin' to war again, only this time it's for the
Uuuu-nited States!"

Chewy stuck out his hand. He was grinning with
mischief and obviously quite pleased with himself, but
now the show was over and it was time to leave. "You
boys take care of yourselves. If things go to hell, my
advice would be to cut loose of King Sutter and head
south."

"South?" Morgan asked.

"That's right. The country up the Sacramento and
along the northern Sierra rivers has been pretty well
trapped out already by the Hudson's Bay Company
men. But down south, that country is virgin. You can
just bet them big rivers leadin' up into the Sierras are
crawlin' with beaver."

"Why don't you go there instead of joining Frémont?"
Rostov asked.

"Hell, twenty years ago I would have. But I'm tired
of trappin'. I purely am. With a couple of young bucks
like you, it's not so bad. But to go into virgin territory
alone, worryin' about Indians and freezin' to death by
yourself, that's mighty poor." He grinned. "Besides, I'd
rather whip the Mexicans!"

"Good luck," Morgan said as the man turned to lead
his pack animal away.

Chewy looked back. "I got a hunch I'll be seein' you
again. If we ain't killed at Gabilan Peak, you can bet
that Frémont will come runnin' here to lick his wounds
and pull King Sutter into the fray—even if it's kickin'
and screamin'."

When Joy Chewy was gone, Morgan and Rostov
headed back toward their cabins. When they were
outside the fort, Rostov said, "Much of what Joe says is
right. Frémont's action is going to force Captain Sutter
to choose sides."

"I know," Morgan said, "and he'll go with Frémont
and the Americans. But the pressure seems to be
getting the best of him right now."

"Is that why he's drinking so much?"

"Probably. That and the fact that he has an intense dislike for Frémont. I think he's afraid the man will actually take command of this fort if the Americans stage a revolution."

"Frémont would do that?"

"He would do most anything to further his reputation and his career," Morgan said.

"But the captain has cannon and too many soldiers."

"I know," Morgan said, trying to explain. "But if there is a revolution and the United States seizes California, Sutter would be in serious trouble if he opposed Frémont. It would be another disastrous miscalculation on his part—even worse than backing Micheltorena."

Rostov nodded his head with sudden understanding, and the two men parted company, each wrapped in his own dark thoughts.

Rosalinda was waiting for Morgan, and when she saw his troubled expression, she wanted to know at once what was wrong.

"It's the captain," Morgan confessed. "He's drinking again, and he fired Joe."

"Oh, well, tomorrow, when he is sober, he will apologize. You know him."

"Yes," Morgan admitted, "but Joe is gone."

"I'm sorry," she said. "I know you thought a great deal of him."

"I do, but I also think a great deal of the captain. You'd think that he wouldn't have a care in the world, given all his wealth. I know he's still got some big debts, but he's much better off than a year ago, and the future is promising." Morgan shook his head. "I don't understand why he's drinking so hard and why he isn't happy."

"Having money, herds, and orchards isn't what makes us happy," Rosalinda said. "Only God, family, and friends bring us inner peace. You know that."

Morgan sighed. "I do. It's just that being poor is one curse that I mean to avoid, if possible. But it seems to me that the captain ought to be dancing. Why, think what he's done in just seven years since arriving here!"

"The captain," Rosalinda said, "will never be happy until he sends for his wife and five children, whom he hasn't seen in twelve years. Captain Sutter has sent Manuiki away, but he's consorting with young Indian girls he keeps under the pretense of cleaning his office and quarters."

"So you know about that, too."

"Of course. Everyone knows. He's trying to drown his guilt in liquor."

"Should I tell him that?"

Rosalinda shook her head. "It would do no good. The captain does not want to hear you or anyone else tell him what is right—he knows, and the truth is eating him from the inside out. María and I pray for him every day."

"I'm going to miss Joe very much."

Rosalinda kissed Morgan. "Do not be so sad. You will see your friend again, and this darkness on the captain one day will pass."

"Maybe, but I can't help being reminded of how both you and María prophesied that Raphero's head would bring destruction upon the captain."

"It was a stupid, superstitious thing to say, and I am sorry. Please forget it."

"In a day or two, if the captain is better," Morgan added quickly, "I'm going to tell him that I want to leave and go claim our land."

"Tell him even if he is *not* better, Morgan. Because if you don't, then sooner or later you will say something just like Señor Chewy, and then we will also be banished."

"Captain Sutter would never do that to us!"

Rosalinda did not argue, but neither did she recant her words.

Two days later, one of Sutter's Mexican spies returned from Monterey at a hard gallop and went straight into Sutter's office, refusing to answer any questions on the way. Soon after, Anton came looking for Morgan at the blacksmith shop. "Captain wants to see you."

"Trouble?"

"Looks like."

Morgan nodded and went to see Sutter, who appeared very upset. Sutter closed the door behind them and said, "Did you kill Ben Dunn in San Buenaventura?"

Ice filled Morgan's spine. He took a deep breath. "I think I did, sir."

Sutter groaned. "Why didn't you say anything?"

Morgan curbed an angry response. "I . . . I didn't want to upset you any more than you already were. We were fighting a war. I killed Ben Dunn in self-defense and to help you to victory."

Sutter collapsed in his chair and found a flask of liquor. He poured himself a tall drink. "You want some?"

"No, sir."

"Well, you've really done it, Mr. Beck. The Mexican authorities want your hide. They know that you work for me, and that messenger just came from General Castro. He says that either I hand you over or be considered a traitor."

"Sir, I would never knowingly put you in this fix."

Sutter tossed down his liquor and refilled his glass. "I know. I know. This is all just smoke to hide the general's real intention, which is to humiliate me and this fort. It's an excuse, if you will, to strip me of my official title and attach my assets."

"Maybe I will have a drink," Morgan said dejectedly.

The captain poured Morgan a big glass of his potent aguardiente. "The messenger also told me that Captain Frémont has abandoned Gabilan Peak after being warned that General Castro was preparing to march upon him with two hundred soldiers and artillery."

Sutter raised his glass in salute, and Morgan did the same. They drank, and then the captain said, "Guess where the great and famous Pathfinder is going?"

"Here."

"Exactly." Sutter doubled up his pudgy fist and banged his desk hard. "Dammit, I do not like the man, and I resent his interference in California's affairs! If there is to be a revolution, then I, John Augustus Sutter, will lead it, not some egotistical fool like Frémont!"

"I have become a liability to you," Morgan said after a moment of deliberation. "I will leave at once."

"No, no. What is done is done. Wait until we discuss these matters with Captain Frémont. Perhaps by then we will see better what must become of you."

"Would Mexican troops be dispatched here to arrest me?"

"Quite possibly. Castro will use this to put me in the worst possible light. Of course, I would oppose any such action to remove you to Monterey for trial."

"Either way, you'd lose."

Sutter waved his hand as if it did not matter. "I am resigned to the fact that if I oppose your arrest I will have, as your mountain man friend put it, gotten off the middle of the fence."

"He didn't mean anything against you, Captain. Joe is the kind of man who says exactly what he thinks."

"Like your father?"

"Yes."

Sutter peered over his glass at Morgan. "I think that when Frémont arrives I will suggest to him that he and his men leave California at once."

"Will he listen?"

"What choice will he have?"

Morgan wasn't sure, but he remembered Chewy's statement that sixty mountain men were worth three hundred Mexican or Indian soldiers. Morgan wasn't ready to admit that Frémont and his troops could forcibly take control of Sutter's Fort, but he knew that they could sure play hell if there was a fight.

"I'm sorry about this," Morgan said. "It's one more problem you don't need."

"Forget it," Sutter replied wearily. "General Castro has long been searching for a reason to crush me and relieve me of all authority. If it wasn't this, it would be something else. Now go along, Mr. Beck. I'll keep you abreast of things."

"Yes, sir," Morgan replied as he left the man to his drink and his troubles.

*   *   *

During the next few weeks Morgan was anxious and inclined to be short-tempered, not with Rosalinda or the Rostovs, but with the animals and the Indians and mostly with himself. Not a waking hour passed in which he did not glance up at the sentry positioned above the gates, half expecting to hear him shout that Frémont and his command had arrived, or perhaps even the anticipated Mexican troops dispatched from Monterey to arrest him for the death of Ben Dunn.

The Mexican soldiers did not arrive—but Frémont did, and Sutter greeted the man with respect but an obvious lack of warmth. Morgan waited anxiously for a summons, and when it came, he was ready.

"I believe you have met before," the captain said, indicating that Morgan should take a seat.

"We have," Frémont snapped, looking ready to fight.

Sutter clasped his hands behind his back and started to pace back and forth, revealing his hidden agitation. Most revealing was the fact that he had chosen to wear his Mexican officer's uniform, an obvious goad to Frémont.

"I've informed Captain Frémont of my position in this valley, Mr. Beck. He already knows that I am sworn to uphold Mexican law and will do so faithfully."

"But sir," Frémont exclaimed, "how could you turn against your own kind?"

"Against any and all aggressors," Sutter said, showing amazing restraint. "And furthermore, I have informed the captain that you, Mr. Beck, are wanted for the death of Ben Dunn, an act committed on my behalf and in self-defense."

Frémont scowled and popped to his feet. "Mr. Sutter," he said impatiently, "we can dispense with all this and get right to the point."

Sutter blushed with anger and clenched his teeth.

"Which is," Frémont continued, "that you, Mr. Beck, should join my forces, at least for the time being while you are being actively sought by the Mexican authorities."

"What?"

Frémont's eyes chilled. "You heard me!"

Morgan turned to stare at Sutter. "Captain! I have a wife, and if war is to come, my place is here at the fort."

"Mr. Beck, you are a free man—free to come and go, whenever and wherever you choose. However, I think that you should accept Captain Frémont's offer. He is on his way north to the Oregon Territory. This will have the desired effect of calming the Mexican authorities. It will also give me valuable time to supervise the rest of my planting and prepare a defense for you."

Morgan was anything but happy, and it must have shown, because Sutter excused him. But the next morning the captain elaborated. "I need someone I can trust to watch Captain Frémont."

"You mean spy on him."

"I must have a man who will keep me informed of Frémont's movements and intentions. And while you are absent, I will do everything possible to persuade the Mexican officials that you killed Mr. Dunn in self-defense."

"They'll never believe that. There was a cantina full of witnesses."

"We can also find witnesses to swear under oath that you were attacked by Mr. Dunn."

"For a price."

"Yes," Sutter admitted, "for a price."

"Rosalinda is going to be very upset."

"Not as upset as she'll be if the Mexican officials come and arrest you."

Morgan had to agree. "How soon is Frémont leaving?"

"As soon as I can replace a few of his saddles and horses." Sutter's voice took on a brittle edge. "The man comes here and *demands* replacement stock and supplies, with never more than a vague promise of future government compensation."

Sutter clenched his fists. "Watch him very closely. If it begins to look as though he is going to do something crazy, as he did at Gabilan Peak, come to me immediately."

"Yes, sir." Morgan turned to leave.

"Mr. Beck? I am sorry about all this. I know that you killed Ben Dunn while trying to gain information for our army, but . . . well, I just wish you had not done it. The act may cause you great difficulties."

"I know."

"By such mistakes are our lives ruined," Sutter said quietly as his eyes drifted out across his compound. He stood lost in a reverie for a moment, then turned to Morgan and forced a tired smile. "Good luck, Mr. Beck."

"Thank you. And sir, if anything should happen to me, well, I know that you'll see that Rosalinda is well cared for."

"Of course. And she has a wealthy family if she were to choose to return to Sonoma or Monterey."

"*We* are her family now," Morgan said before he closed the door and went to tell his wife what was sure to be very disturbing news.

≈ **15** ≈

Frémont's true motives were unclear to Morgan. They had hurried all the way up to the Oregon Territory, only to be overtaken by a secret government courier rumored to have orders directly from President Polk himself. Upon receipt of these orders, Frémont had abruptly changed his plans and rushed back to Sutter's Fort.

Upon their return, Morgan found Captain Sutter drunk and extremely agitated because of the unruliness and insubordination of the Americans, who were arriving in droves. They were a rough sort, always quarreling, drinking, and fighting. Even worse, they had practically taken over the fort and stolen everything in sight.

"I think they would gladly kill me for my holdings," Sutter fretted aloud. "I'd throw a lot of them out if only I could. But if I failed, they'd slaughter not only me but also any of my loyal friends."

Morgan was reluctantly inclined to agree. The new American emigrants were spoiling for a fight against Mexico or anyone else they perceived as representing an obstacle to their avaricious desire to grab all the wealth they could in California.

"Just stay out of their sight," Morgan advised, knowing how his words would grate his captain.

"And be a prisoner in my own fort!" Sutter wailed. "God, what have I done to deserve this plague of thieves and murderers?"

Morgan shrugged his shoulders without answer. Each day, he risked his life in a futile attempt to protect

Sutter's herds, orchards, and fields, but it was like trying to hold back a rising tide. Even the Indians, sensing Sutter's despair and disintegration, had begun to steal from their longtime master. And since their misdeeds were petty compared to those of the rapacious Americans, Morgan made no attempt to punish them severely, as Sutter would have done in prior years when he was in command and sure of his authority.

It was a terrible time, and Anton had to leave to go trapping, so Morgan had few trusted assistants. Bidwell was renovating Sutter's Hock Farm, and Sutter himself was lost in a haze, fed as much by Frémont's arrogance and disdain as by his own liquor. More and more frequently Sutter because intoxicated early in the day, and by noon he would summon Morgan to his office and spend hours lamenting his earlier decision not to sell the settlement to Mexico. He also talked constantly of abandoning everything to flee north to the sanctuary of Hock Farm, where Bidwell was making rapid progress on his home and outbuildings.

"If I could sell this accursed fort along with my adjoining lands," he said, desperation in his voice, "I would go north to Hock Farm and never return. I'd let the rabble fight over the waste of my dreams like dogs over scraps of bone."

Many a time, Morgan was awakened in the night and summoned to Sutter's office to find his captain drunk and lost in the pits of his alcoholic hell. Morgan spent uncounted hours trying to keep the man from throwing it all away and fleeing north.

"Hang on," was Morgan's advice. "At least hang on to Sutterville."

The captain would nod his head sadly and say, "Yes, this fort will go to ruin, but Sutterville, now, *that* will one day be my legacy."

And then they would get out the drawings and sketches of Sutter's dream settlement just west of them, on the banks of the Sacramento River. Sutter would brighten, and his spirits would take flight as he spent hours telling Morgan of the grand city that he would found. It would begin modestly, of course, just two hundred city lots, but it would have the finest gravel roads, a plaza, and a modern sewage system.

"Sutterville will become a model city," the captain boasted, "a city that even Europe will envy. It will be a lasting tribute to my name, even if this fort falls into ruin."

"This will all be over soon," Morgan promised. "Frémont will stage his revolution, and the Americans will seize California and scatter like leaves in the autumn wind."

"But will they?" Sutter shook his head. "I fear they will return drunk with victory to pillage whatever remains here."

"No," Morgan said angrily. "While they are gone to fight, we can reestablish order, recruit and retrain the Indians so that when the Americans return it will be to find your fortress gates locked and your cannon manned by resolute soldiers."

Sutter smiled sadly. "I've thought of that and try to believe it, really I do. But . . . but once discipline is lost, respect gone, then it is impossible to regain."

"No!" Morgan slammed his fist down on the table between them. "You welcomed Frémont and the Americans, and now look what's happened. Next time, things can be different."

Sutter's chin bobbed up and down. "Yes!" he said in a voice husky with emotion. "We'll do better next time! We won't make the same mistake again of being so charitable! We'll be constantly on guard."

Morgan grinned to see the old spark of determination flash in his captain's eyes. But that night Captain Sutter drowned the spark in liquor, and the fires of hope again were doused colder than wet ashes. Morgan himself struggled to keep up his own spirits. He would have been lost without his Rosalinda, and he desperately wished for the additional wise council of Anton Rostov, who was still trapping somewhere in the towering Sierra Nevada Mountains.

The day came when Captain Frémont nearly destroyed an already fragile Sutter by placing one of his own officers in command of the fort.

"I'm leaving Lieutenant Kern in command here, and he will be assisted by ten of my best recruits," Frémont said coldly. "Your authority will extend only to matters unrelated to the defense of this fort while I am on campaign."

"I won't stand for this outrage!" Sutter exploded.

"You have no choice. You are incapable of making a rational decision about anything," Frémont said with a sneer.

After Frémont left the room, Morgan struggled to control his captain. "We'll have some coffee and talk; then we'll have it out with Frémont."

But within an hour, Morgan could see that there was little fight left in his captain. "No, Mr. Beck. The cards are stacked entirely against us now. I want you to march with Frémont's army. I *must* understand his intentions."

It was the last thing that Morgan wanted to do, yet he hadn't the heart to deny Sutter. "Where do you think he is taking his little army?"

"To the coast, I should imagine. To Yerba Buena, then on to Monterey, unless I am mistaken. There are even rumors that he intends to capture General Vallejo and use the old man as some kind of pawn in this game."

"But the general poses no threat! He's old and wants nothing but to be left alone. Besides, he's more sympathetic now to the Americans."

"That may be, but he is still in some danger. But please, do what you can to see that no harm comes to Vallejo and that I am honestly informed. Joe Chewy arrived back late last night. We've settled our differences, and now I've asked him to go with you."

"Thanks," Morgan said, because not only did he want to help the captain, but he also owed Vallejo a favor for returning his father's body for burial. "At least with Joe riding at my side, I'll know there's one man among them that I can trust."

"Be careful," Sutter pleaded.

Morgan joined Frémont at his encampment the following morning. After that, events transpired very rapidly. Before the Americans had marched two days westward, Frémont dispatched a crusty old frontiersman named Zeke Merritt to Sonoma, and Morgan made sure he was present when the night-raiding Americans captured the Mexican general asleep in his bed.

Dawn was just breaking when Vallejo was hauled outside in his nightshirt. Morgan stayed apart, but when a big man threatened Vallejo's life, Morgan intervened with drawn pistol. "This man is an officer and will be treated as one."

"You *are* a goddamn Mex traitor!" the big man hissed.

Morgan swung the barrel of his pistol in a mean arc that connected with the side of the man's jaw, and then he cocked his weapon and turned it on the others, halting them in their tracks. It was no small relief to find that Joe Chewy was right at his side with drawn pistol.

"Stay out of this, Joe!" one of the onlookers snarled.

"You come at him, then you come at me, too," the old mountain man said, teeth drawn back from his lips in a chilling grin.

Morgan pulled the badly shaken General Vallejo closer. "I'm no traitor!" he told the hostile Americans. "And I'll pledge my word of honor that the general won't try to escape."

"Your word of honor?" Merritt scoffed, pushing through the ring of angry men. "How about your *life*?"

"Very well," Morgan said grimly. "That, too."

Vallejo, badly shaken, managed to whisper, "*Gracias, Señor Beck.*"

"*Por nada,*" he said, "a favor for a favor."

The Americans didn't like it, but when one of them called out from the casa that he had discovered Vallejo's liquor cabinet, they quickly turned their thoughts to more pleasant things.

"We could loot and burn this pueblo," Merritt said, throwing his head back and drinking from the bottle. He wiped his lips. "And we could have the household women for our pleasure."

Morgan was about to say something, but Joe Chewy did it for him. "Merritt, if you quit this pueblo now— like a man of honor—you'll be well remembered."

Merritt drank again. "Hell, Joe, the truth of the fact is that I don't give a damn *what* folks remember."

"Then remember this: If you let things get out of control here, I'll feed your guts to Vallejo's pigs."

Merritt choked on his next swallow of whiskey and forgot the women long enough to order his men to lower the Mexican flag.

"Put up ours."

"How you going to do that?" Chewy demanded. "We ain't got the full blessin' from the United States, and we ain't got a flag of our own."

"Yeah, we do," Merritt said. "Made one last night. You'll see."

A few minutes later everyone did see a soiled, crudely made flag rise on Vallejo's flagpole.

"What the hell is it?" Chewy demanded.

Merritt was outraged. "It's a *bear*, you half-blind fool!"

Someone had found a red flannel shirt, torn a strip out of it, sewn it along the bottom of the flag, then printed the words CALIFORNIA REPUBLIC.

"That's one beautiful sonofabitch, ain't it?" Merritt crowed, gawking like a kid through a candy store window. "We're callin' this the goddamn Bear Flag Revolt!"

Morgan said nothing, but when the flag caught the breeze and snapped to attention over the plaza, he was surprised to feel a shiver of excitement. He realized that despite the pathetic flag and the looting, the profane and boisterous soldiers gathered about, this was indeed a historic moment, one that Eli would have given anything to witness after so many years under the heel of Spain and then Mexico. And when the rowdy Americans cheered, loudly and lustily, Morgan took a deep breath and nodded his head with approval, thinking, *Like it or not, I am now an American*.

When the cheers died, Merritt snapped, "Vallejo, we're taking you and your friends back to Sutter's Fort."

Vallejo looked in alarm to Morgan, who said with more assurance than he felt, "Better do as he says. I'll guarantee your safety."

"Then I will get dressed," Vallejo said, tearing his

eyes from the new California flag and starting back toward his casa.

"Now, wait a minute!" Merritt protested. "If we leave you unguarded, what's to prevent you from trying to shinny through a window out back and escaping?"

"Señor, I am too old, too fat, and too slow. And also," he added, "too big a target. No, Señor, I will not try to escape. You have my word of honor. All I ask is that you and your men also behave with honor."

"A'course we will!" Merritt snapped, glancing at Morgan. "And besides, you heard the deal—if you or any of our other prisoners try to escape, we'll shoot your Mex-lovin' friends."

Vallejo addressed Morgan. "You also have my word—no one will attempt to escape."

"Thank you," Morgan said, meaning it.

When they arrived back at the fort, Rosalinda was among the first to greet them. After hugging Morgan, she turned to see Vallejo under obvious guard, and she paled.

"It's going to be all right," Morgan said quickly. "He'll be safer here than in Sonoma during the next few months."

Rosalinda went up to stand beside Vallejo's horse. "I am sorry you are being treated this way."

Vallejo reached down and touched her cheek. "It is not so bad," he told her, studying the fort closely. "Sometimes bad things turn out to be good."

Rosalinda nodded. "I will see that you are well fed."

Vallejo patted his protruding belly and laughed. He had seemed, right from the start, to be in amazingly good spirits, and his cheerfulness had already won over many of the Americans.

That same day, Frémont made it very clear that Captain Sutter would be responsible for the security and guarding of Vallejo and his friends.

"We've got other more important things to do," Frémont announced. "Just don't fail me with these prisoners."

Sutter bristled. "You seem to forget just whose property this is."

"And *you*," Frémont said with unconcealed contempt, "seem to forget that we are involved in a revolution! Vallejo is our enemy. He and his friends are prisoners of war, and they will be treated accordingly."

But Captain Sutter disagreed and treated Vallejo and his friends so well that Frémont returned a few days later in an awful temper. Storming into Sutter's office and catching the captain and old Vallejo laughing, playing a game of chess, and sipping brandy, he ordered the Mexican outside.

"Dammit, this is no officers' club! I understand that you're not posting a guard on your prisoners and you're treating them like houseguests!"

Sutter was sober, because it was still early but also because Vallejo's companionship was proving to be a tonic. Both men were well read, and Vallejo was wealthy, gracious, a man of taste and culture—the kind of man that Sutter admired.

"Answer me, damn you!" Frémont swore. "Don't you even know how to treat *prisoners of war*?"

"Indeed I do, Captain Frémont," Sutter replied coldly. "I have been a prisoner myself."

"Well, then?"

"Captain Frémont," Sutter said patiently, "what you completely fail to understand is that these are all propertied and wealthy gentlemen. There is no danger of them attempting escape."

"I'll be the judge of that!"

"If you're not satisfied, then take charge of them yourself."

Frémont had not been expecting this response and was caught off guard. "But . . . but who the devil could I place over them?"

Sutter shrugged. "Perhaps my clerk, Mr. Locker. He is a gentleman and absolutely dependable."

"All right," Frémont snapped. "I don't have time to worry about this. But I don't want them eating at your table, and I think it weakens the will to fight when my men see you treating our prisoners like royalty."

"That is their problem, not mine."

"Sir, do not push me too far. You are but a very small obstruction."

"And *you*, sir, are a very big pain in the ass."

Frémont blanched and even choked before he wheeled about and stomped outside past Morgan, who had heard everything.

Frémont and his swelling American force left the very next day, and on July 1, 1846, word reached Sutter's Fort that the man had seized the abandoned garrison at Yerba Buena and made a big, public display of spiking Spanish cannons already hopelessly rusted from nearly a half century of disuse. Proclaiming his victory to anyone who would listen, Frémont vowed to march south and capture Monterey.

On July 7, however, the Commodore of the U.S. Navy, John D. Sloat, captured Monterey without firing a shot. When news of this reached Sutter's Fort, Captain Sutter had everyone arise before dawn on July 11 to greet the historic occasion.

Morgan, Anton, and the others watched dawn peek over the Sierra Nevadas and fire the valley as Sutter's cannon exploded in celebration, the blasts so loud and sustained that most of the glass windows were shattered. With the echo of cannon receding into the foothills and the sound of fife and drum, the American flag was raised overhead.

A huge flock of ducks, frightened by the cannon and commotion, circled noisily overhead, and out in the fields cattle, sheep, and horses snorted and danced nervously as the music played.

Sutter, looking more alive than he had in months, jumped up on a low platform and raised his hands for attention and to silence the music. This morning, unlike others of great occasion, he wore neither his Mexican nor Swiss uniform, but instead a fine suit of clothing made in his own tailor shop. He raised his hands overhead, and when the festive crowd fell silent he smiled, then bowed slightly to the ladies present.

"Ladies and gentlemen, a new day is upon us, and it is rich with promise. Change has come over this land,

and it will be—I believe with all my heart—for our betterment. So lift your eyes gladly to the Stars and Stripes and rejoice! Pledge your loyal allegiance and all your will and power to help imbue in your new country a fresh, generous spirit toward all men, red, brown, or white!"

Sutter glanced at Vallejo and his wealthy Mexican friends. "Too long, we have been divided. Too long, we have viewed each other with suspicion. From this moment forth, we are all *Americans*.

The deep, ominous silence that followed was broken by General Vallejo, who shouted a cheer. Then everyone was yelling and clapping, tossing their caps high and pounding each other on the back and shaking hands.

Morgan hugged Rosalinda and kissed her, and then he turned and gripped Anton's thick paw. "A new day!" he yelled to his friend.

The Russian threw back his head and laughed, then began to dance with his wife, reminding Morgan of a graceful bear. Vallejo and his captured friends clapped their hands, and music began to play; the Mexican gentry appeared surprisingly gay, considering that the new American government would undoubtedly strip them of their great land grants. Captain Sutter ordered another round of cannon salute proclaiming that California was wed, now and forever, to America.

After that they all had a great breakfast and talked of war, for even though Monterey had fallen, there were still Mexican soldiers and presidios farther to the south, as Morgan, Sutter, and the other veterans of the earlier expedition could ruefully attest.

And it did not surprise Morgan when, much later that day, Anton sadly remarked that, had it possessed the will and the vision, Russia could have captured Yerba Buena and Monterey many years earlier and laid claim to all of California. Thirty years ago the Spanish military outposts had been even weaker than they were under Mexico's rule. Back then the unpaid Spanish soldiers had been more concerned with their efforts to eke out a living than with protecting California. And, back then, it had been Fort Ross that had commanded the respect of everyone in Alta California, just as Sutter's Fort had before Frémont's arrival. Anton's reminiscence held a note of bitterness, and when Morgan thought about it, he realized how quickly wealth and power could change hands.

"What are you thinking?" Anton asked.

"I'm thinking that when this trouble is over I'll finally be leaving with Rosalinda, claiming my land and fighting to hold it."

"Good!"

"And you?"

"I don't know." Anton managed a smile. "Once, I also dreamed of a rancho of my own. Now María is happy teaching the Indian children about the Lord. But if our captain does not find his soul, well, I don't know. Maybe we will become your neighbors."

"Nothing would give Rosalinda or me greater pleasure," Morgan said.

It was a hot, anxious autumn without any rainfall to settle the delta dust. The rivers shrank from their banks, and in the fields the grain stood brittle, parched, and stunted. Word reached Sutter's Fort that Commodore Robert F. Stockton had succeeded Sloat as commander of the American forces in California and had bestowed upon Frémont the rank of major and officially placed him in charge of the California Battalion. Soon afterward Stockton's naval force occupied the pueblo of Los Angeles, but the small company he left behind was overthrown, and more American reinforcements were advancing to retake that pueblo.

The Bear Flag Revolt was already beginning to seem unrelated to Morgan, and Anton, who could not forget Russia, was indifferent to the struggle.

"The captain is not drinking so hard now," Anton remarked one evening. "He has changed. I think he even likes Lieutenant Kern."

"I know he does," Morgan said. "But there is something else."

"What?"

"He is finally sending for his family."

Anton stopped, and his lips formed a big smile. "No! Could this be true?"

"It is. Did you notice that Manuiki is gone?"

Anton winked. "How could one fail to notice the absence of her beauty?"

"She has returned to the Sandwich Islands. Sutter is preparing for his family."

"Good!" Anton said with genuine feeling. "Perhaps the prayers of our wives have not been entirely in vain."

Near the end of September, two weary travelers arrived at Sutter's Fort announcing that an emigrant party numbering close to one hundred men, women, and children was struggling across the Nevada wilderness, desperately hoping to cross the Sierras into California before winter. The party was described as near starvation and already being forced to devour many of its oxen.

Alarmed by the pair's skeletal appearance, Sutter ordered five pack mules to be loaded with food and supplies. He dispatched two of his best Indians, along with one of the emigrants, to help the struggling pioneers.

"What is the name of the group?" Morgan asked as the rescuers disappeared into the Sierra foothills.

"The Donner Party," Sutter replied. "I just hope that they can get through the Humbolt Basin and over these mountains before the first deep snow falls."

"There's plenty of time," Anton said. "A man could almost crawl that far before the first big winter storms."

"I know," Sutter said, "but from what one of them, Mr. Stanton, told me about the Donner Party, there's a lot of bickering and dissension. My advice was to bury their differences and hurry forward. They sound like good family people, the kind we could really use to farm this valley."

Almost a month later, another visitor from the party appeared. His name was James Reed, and he had been expelled from the Donner Party for getting into a fight and killing one of the other members.

"It was self-defense," he explained. "I swear it! If it hadn't been, they'd have executed me. My God! I've a wife and four children on that wagon train!"

Both Morgan and Sutter believed Reed, and his account of the Donner Party's extremely slow progress to Truckee Meadows at the eastern base of the Sierras was very worrisome.

"When are they coming over?" Sutter asked.

"I don't know. Maybe next month. Who can say? Right now they're resting and fattening up their stock."

"They're what?"

"Their animals are too thin to pull wagons over those mountains. They've got to wait until they regain strength."

Morgan, Sutter, and Anton exchanged anxious glances, fully aware how deep the snows could get up in the high mountain passes.

"This George Donner must be a fool," Morgan blurted.

Reed looked away, not willing to argue the point, and in the weeks that followed they heard no more of the Donner Party.

"I assume they've decided to wait and cross the Sierras next spring," Sutter said one day when they awoke to see the mountains dusted with their first mantle of snow.

"I'm sure that they have," Morgan agreed.

The wagon train was temporarily forgotten when the fort received the shocking news that an overland American force led by General Stephen Kearny had been met and defeated outside San Diego at the Battle of San Pasqual.

"It won't change matters," Sutter said confidently, "any more than the Alamo changed the outcome of Texas independence."

Sutter's prediction proved to be correct. By the end of the month, word reached them that Kearny's defeated column had joined with Commodore Stockton's forces to defeat the Californios at San Diego, then at Los Angeles.

"It is finished," Sutter announced, breaking open a case of champagne.

That night they had a little party in celebration.

Fiddles and guitars were joined by lusty voices, and everyone danced until long after midnight. Morgan and Rosalinda were awakened at dawn by shouts echoing down from the foothill country.

"Who the devil could that be coming here at this hour?" Morgan said with a groan. "The captain will kill them for waking everyone up after last night."

"Then maybe you should go see what is wrong," Rosalinda suggested.

Morgan nuzzled his wife's soft breasts, ran his hands over her sleek body, and whispered, "I would rather make love to you and sleep until noon."

Rosalinda giggled, but then they both heard more cries.

"I *had* better investigate," Morgan said, jumping out of bed and reaching for his clothes.

Anton was several yards ahead of him when Morgan rushed outside and saw a party of half-dead emigrants staggering down from the Sierra foothills.

"Good Lord!" Morgan cried, appalled to see that at least half of them resembled walking skeletons. "Who can they be?"

"I think," Anton said as he ran forward, "it is all that is left of the Donner Party."

≈ 16 ≈

Neither Morgan nor any of the others who listened in stunned silence would ever forget the tale of horror that was revealed to them. There were five women and two men, just seven survivors of the original fifteen who'd dared to assault the highest Sierra passes and reach help.

"Our party was cursed from the minute we took the Hasting's Cutoff out of Fort Bridger," a young woman explained. "We got lost in the Nevada deserts with little food and even less water."

"That's where we left Mr. Hardkoop," another woman mumbled. "That poor old man couldn't keep up on foot, and no one would take him in his wagon."

"You just left him in the desert?" Anton asked in disbelief.

The woman's sunken eyes pierced the Russian. "You can't possibly imagine what it was like," she whispered in a dead voice. "None of you can. Mr. Hardkoop couldn't keep up, and there wasn't even enough food or water for the little children. I believe the poor man wanted to die."

"No, he didn't!" the first woman cried, wagging her head back and forth. "He was beggin' us for water. We could hear him cryin' out for it as we moved on! I could still hear him cryin' out for it when we was freezin' to death up in the pines! I could hear his voice just a-cryin' in the wind and blowin' snow—only then he was cursin' us for leavin' him to die."

Morgan's chest constricted. He glanced sideways toward Captain Sutter, whose face was ashen. Yet what else could they have expected to hear but wild rantings? These Donner Party survivors had been trapped in the high mountain passes until they were half crazed with starvation. Given what they'd endured, the wonder was that any of them were sane. They'd already admitted that many of their numbers had died of cold, hunger, and deprivations that were too horrible to describe.

"I'll send another party right away," Sutter vowed. "We'll get everyone out who's still alive. I swear we will! Your party just started too late across the passes."

A man with a frostbitten nose and inflamed eyes croaked, "Mr. Sutter, you don't rightly understand. We wanted to come sooner, but by the time we crossed the Humbolt Basin and reached Truckee Meadows, most of the stock were either dead or too weak to pull our wagons over the mountains."

"Damn the wagons!" Anton growled. "You should have left them behind. Better to lose your wagons and save your lives!"

The man's snow-blinded eyes brimmed with tears, and he roughly scrubbed them dry with the back of his ragged sleeve. "That's easy enough for you to say. But we had nothin' 'cept what was in 'em. Nothin'! And we didn't know the storms would come so early. Whosoever we spoke to said we had plenty of time for a crossin'. Plenty of time!"

Anton looked suddenly ashamed. "I'm sorry. You did what you thought was right. We've never had such early storms in the mountains as there are this year."

The skeletal man dipped his pointed chin. "Maybe it is God's will that most of the Donner Party are going to die up in those mountains, Captain Sutter."

"No!" Sutter cried, voice reaching up from the very depths of his soul. "What happened to all those provisions and the five pack mules I already sent over with my Indians?"

"We ate everything, Sir, even your mules."

"And the Indians, too," a short, sun-blistered woman

giggled, her eyes merry with lunacy. "We ate them along with Mr. Dolan and Mr. Postdick and—."

"Shut up!" the man shrieked.

The woman blinked and looked away to sob brokenly, "Mr. Sutter, I—I musta forgot. We didn't eat your Indians, not *really*. Honest!"

Sutter reeled and Morgan heard his captain cry, "My poor Indians. Dear God, they're *eaten* Lewis and Salvadore!"

One of the women, a frail thing with matted red hair and sunken green eyes, touched Sutter's arm. "We're sorry. They were brave Indians. They did everything they could to trap food. They wouldn't touch human flesh, not like the rest of us. Mr. Foster was merciful when he shot them. They got too weak to go on. They seemed to understand. You got to believe me, Mr. Sutter. They were *ready* to die. I swear it!"

Another woman nodded. "They knew it was their time to die, Mr. Sutter. Like Mr. Stanton did. On the fifth day out of Truckee Lake, he couldn't go on anymore. He said we should go on. That he'd catch up. I remember. It was snowin' hard. Wind cutting us like a knife, but he'd stopped shivering. He said his last words real slow, with a soft smile. He said, 'I am coming along soon.' So we left him sittin' by the fire." The woman's eyes took on a faraway look, and she said to no one in particular, "Mr. Sutter, you'll find his body whole, unless the wolves ate it already. But *we* never ate him. I swear it!"

Everyone avoided looking at the woman and Morgan was filled with the memory of Stanton. He'd been the one who had gone with Sutter's Indians and pack mules to the Nevada Territory to help rescue the party from starvation. In his mid-thirties and a bachelor, Stanton had been small but wiry and tough, the kind of man who would endure an immense amount of hardship without complaint.

Morgan forced himself to hear the rest of the story. These few had left their frozen death camp at Truckee Lake with only six days' rations. By the time they'd finally reached a friendly Indian camp at the western base of the Sierras thirty-two horror-filled days later, they'd been reduced to cannibalism. They'd stripped away flesh, roasted it, and then choked it down. And, God help them, what they didn't immediately devour they'd labeled by name so that none ate members of their own families.

At night wolves had howled, ravenous at the scent of roasting human flesh, while the party had shivered under wet, frozen blankets and endured a cold so intense that they'd yearned for an endless sleep. Those who did not succumb in the night arose each morning to claw their way out from under fresh snow and spend another hellish day breaking trail through canyons buried more than fifty feet deep.

During a blizzard, they survived by digging snow caves. When the days were overcast, they staggered around in circles, having lost all sense of direction without the benefit of a guiding sun. On good days they measured their progress in a few precious miles.

Sutter took Morgan, Anton, and a few others aside. "I will organize and provision a rescue party at once. It will take the best and strongest men we can find, and even then it may be hopeless."

"I'm volunteering," Morgan said, and Anton, along with several of the others, quickly volunteered as well.

"I'll find others to join you," Sutter promised. "Unfortunately, I'm in no condition to go. I'm forty-three years old and my health isn't good."

Morgan could see that his captain was ashamed, but realistic. Sutter could not have climbed the Sierras in the best of weather. "Captain, you're needed right here."

"I'm going back with you!" James Reed announced with passion as he joined them. "It's my wife and four children starving to death up in those mountains."

"No," Anton said gently, "you're still too weak."

Before Reed could protest, Anton said, "You would only slow us down. You'd not travel twenty miles in deep snow before you collapsed. Then one of us would have to bring you back, and that would mean less food for your family."

The Russian's logic was irrefutable, and Reed dipped his chin in sad acceptance. "All right. But in a few more days, I'll be ready."

Anton turned back to the captain. "When can we leave?"

"The moment I can get everything together. Soon. Very soon."

Two days later they set out from the fort and rode hard on horseback to the Bear River, and when the snow became deep they continued on foot. Each man carried between fifty and seventy-five pounds of food, and by hiking night and day with only short rests, they managed to reach the pass after two brutal weeks. By the time they struggled through the last deep snowdrift to overlook the camp, they were all shaking with cold, fatigue, and self-imposed hunger.

Morgan could not believe his eyes when he saw the stranded emigrants' camp. Their log cabins were almost completely buried under the snow. Most of the rude structures were covered by frozen ox hides, others just by branches. Piles of burned logs dotted the landscape. All the trees near the camp had been hacked down, and farther out others stood with amputated limbs against a cold, gray sky.

"I wonder how many are still alive," Anton said, raising the question they all feared to ask.

Morgan cupped his hands to his mouth and shouted, "Hello!"

His voice echoed across the frozen white wilderness. Morgan, Anton, and the others exchanged anxious glances, and for the next few moments time ceased to exist.

"Hello the camp!" a man named Tucker finally bellowed.

And then, like prairie dogs scurrying up to daylight, the survivors emerged from their white prisons. They were mostly women and children, gray creatures wrapped in stiff, dirty rags. One pointed up to the rescue party, and all stared in confusion as their poor minds grappled to comprehend that someone had actually arrived to help them after so many unanswered prayers and so much dying.

Suddenly and without any warning, one of the gray creatures threw her head back and unleashed a high, keening sound that floated upslope, causing Morgan to shiver uncontrollably.

"Dear God!" another woman cried, breaking from the others, throwing herself forward into the snow. "Dear God, we *are* saved!"

Morgan jolted forward through the deep snow along with the other rescuers. Whooping and tumbling, fighting back to their feet to buck their way forward, they rolled, sledded, and clawed their way through chest-high drifts, spiraling down the mountainside in an avalanche of joy. Hoarse, unintelligible cries filled their throats until they were buried by the starving, wailing survivors below.

When they met, they hugged and shrieked with joy as packs were ripped open and cold meat, bread, and apples were devoured. One of the laughing women hugged Anton and cried, "Are you from California, or heaven?"

The Russian's mouth worked silently. He could not speak. A few minutes later he regained enough reason to pull away the food, crying, "It has to be rationed! Please! It *has* to be rationed!"

Morgan and the other rescuers realized Anton was correct. They pushed the people away. It was hard, but terribly necessary. And after a few moments, when sanity again prevailed, the people fell silent. They understood—even the gaunt children. And then a million questions poured forth—mostly about the fifteen who'd gone for help. When they learned the names of those who had made it to Sutter's Fort, they wept with happiness. When they hard about Stanton and the others who'd died, they wept with grief. It tore Morgan's heart to shreds to see them try to comfort one another.

So many questions. Were more rescuers coming? Any more food? Was it warm in the Sacramento Valley, and could they eat all they wanted for just a little while? Any milk for the children? Doctors? Doctors to amputate frozen toes and men of God to excise the demons of madness earned from the things they had done in the name of survival.

It all seemed unreal to Morgan as he patiently answered questions that day. He had never imagined that human beings could endure such suffering, and there were instances when he had to bolt away from these people to stand apart, dragging in deep chestsful of air to clear the numbness of his mind.

Morgan did not know how many of the Donner Party had already perished, but he said, "Let's leave food for the weakest, take those who think they can make it out, and leave as soon as we possibly can."

Anton and the others agreed. All of them glanced at the sky, anxious about the next blizzard.

"If the weather is good, my vote would be to leave tomorrow," Anton said. "Each day here costs us food."

The remainder of that day and late into the night, they attended to the sick. George Donner, his hand rotted with gangrene and his eyes hot and crazed with fever, was among the dying. Morgan and the others felt helpless to save the worst cases; they had brought little in the way of medicines, and many were so far gone that they could not even swallow food.

What struck Morgan was that none of the party could stop talking. Over and over they asked the same questions, as if to reassure themselves that this was not a dream, that help really had arrived, and that there was, after all, hope. Mostly they kept asking about California. It seemed incomprehensible to them that the sun could shine so warmly that men could work in shirtsleeves even during the winter, that a fabled Swiss named John Augustus Sutter really awaited them with beef, corn, milk for their babies, and clean, warm woolen blankets. Their minds, warped into unreality, failed to comprehend any world other than one filled with pain, ice, and hunger. Over and over Morgan and the men from California described a place where it never snowed, where even now there was grass in the valleys and birds sang in the trees and nothing died of the cold or of starvation.

Of their cannibalism, nothing was said. Instead they talked of boiling the ox hides that they'd first used as roofs for their cabins. When the hides were almost gone, they'd consumed the leather of their shoes. One girl about twelve years of age broke down and sobbed uncontrollably while admitting that her little dog Cash had fed her family for an entire week.

"Honey," Morgan said, his voice quaking with emotion, "Cash is in heaven, and he's glad that you're still alive here on earth."

That night Morgan awoke more than once bathed in icy sweat, grappling with hideous nightmares of ghouls devouring human limbs while gnashing crimson teeth around campfires. The second time this happened, he bolted up a stair of ice to reel under a blanket of stars. Heart pounding, fear-sweat freezing on his flesh, he clasped his hands to the sides of his head and collapsed to his knees as his mind tilted toward madness. To save himself, he found an ax and chopped firewood until dawn.

That cold, clear morning, twenty-one judged themselves strong enough to leave. Fifteen of them were children. Never in his life had Morgan felt a greater responsibility, and he was sure that Anton and the other rescuers also felt the same staggering burden.

They left as much food as they dared, and as the morning struggled over the snow-clad pines, Morgan witnessed heart-wrenching scenes of families being divided.

Tamsen Donner, strong and determined, chose to remain with her dying husband, but Mrs. Reed elected to leave her youngest pair of children behind with friends.

"Darling Patty," she said, "you stay and watch your little brother. Your father will come soon. More help will be along in just a few days."

The girl, cheeks hollow with hunger, nodded and tried to smile. "If I do not see you again, Mother, do the best that you can."

Morgan turned away, face hard, eyes stinging. "Let's go!" he managed to say, almost choking on the words.

No one needed any urging. Emigrants and rescuers alike knew how suddenly the capricious mountain storms could sweep in on them with the deadly force of a high plains blizzard. All that first day the weather held as they hurried up and over the high passes, then descended, following their earlier trail. But the next afternoon a blizzard struck. The Donner survivors, already starved and weak, began to fail.

"We need to find cover!" Anton shouted, bulling through the driving snow, hunting shelter.

A refuge was found under a ledge of rock, and for a day and a night they clung to life around a small fire, nursing the last morsels of their food supply and listening to the wind howl like the hounds of hell. When the storm passed, they dug their way back to the sun and pushed onward, strong helping weak.

Anton and Morgan broke trail until they were too exhausted, and then others took their places so that the emigrants could pass more easily down the steep mountainsides. Even so, it was heartbreaking to watch the procession. Children were carried, the wind seemed always in their faces, the skies were dark and threatening.

Two children died on a bitterly cold night. By morning they were frozen solid, buried deep in the snow. The party went on, and when their food ran out, Morgan raged in helpless fury for a rifle to shoot a very thin doe he spotted a quarter of a mile away.

"Maybe we can kill her without a rifle," Anton said. "We could if we drive her into that canyon. She'll flounder in deep snow."

Morgan nodded grimly. If they did not get meat into the weakest among them, more would die this night. "Let's give it a try."

It seemed hopeless, a costly waste of precious energy. The doe saw them and began to buck and lunge through the heavy drifts. Long before they drew close, Morgan thought he could smell the animal's fear. He surged ahead of Anton, broke trail for almost thirty yards until his lungs were burning, then stopped, fell in behind the Russian, and went thrashing onward. By alternating every twenty or thirty yards after that, they managed to narrow the distance.

The doe was weak. Morgan could see her ribs, even hear her small, terrified cries of distress. Her thin legs and little hooves were nearly useless in deep snow, but somehow she found enough strength to keep lunging forward.

"She . . . she won't go over the side and into that canyon!" Morgan gasped.

"Don't . . . don't need her to!" Anton panted.

Just then the doe fell into a deep drift. Her head began to thrash at the thick crust of ice, smashing it away. Morgan's hand found his knife, and when he threw himself on the steaming, terror-stricken animal, his blade found her jugular and she died in a single merciful instant. The warm blood flowed brightly, crimson on pure white. Morgan, chest burning, stared into the doe's large brown eyes and watched them glaze as her life seeped out into the snow. She quivered and seemed to stare up at him until Morgan's hand brushed her eyes shut.

"What is the matter?" Anton breathed when he could speak.

"Nothing."

"What is it?"

"I don't like killing helpless things," Morgan said, feeling angry and stupid. "And I never really looked into an animal's eyes like that before."

Anton's breath steamed through his nostrils; his salt-and-pepper mustache was ridged with ice. He reached out and patted Morgan on the arm.

"Look into the eyes of the starving children when they eat this animal, and you will feel much better. Eh?"

Morgan nodded, pushed to his feet, and brushed the snow from himself. They lifted the doe so that everyone could see her and understand that, for at least the next day, they would be sustained with meat.

Within the hour they lit a twenty-foot pine tree afire and crowded close as quarters of the doe were seared, then gorged upon. If anyone thought to save venison for tomorrow, those thoughts remained unspoken as even bones were cracked and sucked for their hot, thick marrow.

Anton scraped the hide and fashioned a crude travois

for the weakest children. Starting early the next morning and feeling much stronger, Morgan and Anton each gripped a pole and dragged the travois on down the mountainside, and before the day was over their prayers were answered when they met James Reed and a second rescue party dispatched from Sutter's Fort.

When Reed saw his wife and two oldest children, he began to run forward, shouting like a madman. The couple embraced, and Morgan offered up a silent prayer that little Patty Reed and her younger brother were still alive.

James Reed and the new rescue party stayed only an hour before pushing on up the mountain. His last words before leaving were a solemn vow. "I'll get them down alive. I swear I will!"

The next day, their ordeal ended at Sutter's Fort, and by the time it was over, a third rescue party was dispatched. By spring, the last survivors which included the Reed children were brought down from the mountains, but not without a great deal of controversy. Lewis Keseberg had been found stirring a kettle of boiling human liver and lungs, and it was speculated they belonged to poor Tamsen Donner and her husband, who had disappeared along with their life's savings. The rescuers were appalled and revolted by Keseberg. They threatened to hang the man on the spot, but suddenly he "found" the money and they spared his life but refused to give him comfort or assist him on the way back down to Sutter's Fort.

It wasn't until May of that year that a final, grim tally of the dead and the living was completed. Of the eighty-one members of the ill-starred Donner Party, only forty-seven survived. Everyone knew about the cannibalism. The papers were filled with it from coast to coast, and the grisly account was printed as far away as London and Paris. But mercifully only Keseberg seemed to be held to blame, because in a moment of appalling lunacy or stupidity he had publicly declared that human flesh was tastier than ox meat because it was not so tough and dry to swallow.

"Do you blame him, too?" Rosalinda asked Morgan one hot July afternoon when Sutter's fields were golden with wheat.

"I don't know," Morgan admitted.

"His mind is addled." Rosalinda argued. "Morgan, they say... they say that wherever he goes, children cry in fear and men shout, 'Stone him! Stone him!'"

Morgan shuddered a little. "Keseberg made my flesh crawl whenever I saw his face. He ate and robbed the Donners. He was possessed by the devil."

"He should be judged by God alone, not by men. He has suffered enough."

Morgan nodded. "I'm going to tell the captain that we are leaving. It's time to build a ranch of our own."

"When?"

"If you agree, within the week."

"Have you told the Rostovs?"

"Yes. They will come with us."

Rosalinda smiled. She had grown very close to María. "Whenever you are ready," she said.

Morgan took his young wife into his arms and held her tight. He did not want to admit that he had fears about leaving the womb of Sutter's Fort. But it was time to go; the captain was prospering again and more sober now since Frémont's departure. Captain Sutter could hire plenty of trappers. Yes, it was time to strike out on their own and make a future for himself and Rosalinda.

≈ 17 ≈

It was a warm, blustery day in October, and a rainbow armada of colorful leaves raced down the Sacramento River as Morgan and Anton prepared to depart on the captain's schooner. Sutter was in an expansive mood, even though he had drunk too much wine the night before, toasting this departure.

"Well, my friends, I think that I've provisioned you and your lovely wives with everything that you will require to establish a rancho and trading post up north."

"Everything," Morgan said, "and more. You've been very generous."

Sutter allowed himself a smile. "Generosity may be my principal failing, but you and Anton have long served me well, and I am prospering. Besides, I treasure your friendships; through my severe trials with Frémont, you both stood me well."

"We'll be visiting often," Morgan said. "We won't be very far away, and once I get things going, I hope we'll conduct a lot of profitable business together."

"Of that you can be sure. More and more settlers are arriving from the Oregon Territory, and you'll be the first real trading post they'll find. But please leave a little money in their pockets for me!"

Morgan laughed. They all knew that Captain Sutter would get his share.

The captain turned to Anton Rostov. "Are you sure that I can't persuade you to remain here as my chief trapper?"

"I'm sure. Morgan will need my help. After that . . . well, I have been thinking a lot about showing María my homeland."

Both Morgan and Sutter blinked with surprise.

"Yes," Anton confessed, "and perhaps also revisit the old fort and trading post at Sitka before it, too, is abandoned."

"I can understand that." Sutter expelled a deep breath of longing. "I often think back fondly to Switzerland. But California . . ." he said, pointing to the earth between their feet, "make no mistake, *this* is where our future lies."

"I know," Anton said, "but María also wants to meet my family before they are gone."

"Of course she does! I also hope to see my own family before much longer." Sutter pumped their hands. "So, then. I bid you all farewell. Start by building your cabins and fur sheds. You've plenty of food, beaver traps, and trading supplies to last the winter. Early next spring I'll send seed, plows, and oxen to pull them. Hurry on, now, while this northwesterly wind is strong enough to buck the river's current."

"I can't thank you enough," Morgan said. On impulse, he hugged the captain.

Sutter was a little embarrassed. Morgan didn't care. The man was like a second father. And despite his pronounced and destructive weakness for Indian maidens and strong spirits, he was good, kind, and generous to a fault.

"Good-bye," Sutter told them when the lines were cast. "Godspeed. I shall miss you all dearly."

"As we shall miss you," Morgan shouted, hoping and praying that their departure would not send his captain into one of his deep depressions and prolonged bouts of drinking.

Their journey upriver proved uneventful. Two days later they rounded a bend and Morgan's anticipation died when he saw at least a dozen American trappers camped on the land he and Rosalinda had already chosen to homestead. Worse yet, they'd raised a couple of crude log cabins, probably to protect their furs and supplies.

The Russian at his side frowned. "It's a big party."

"Who are they? Hudson's Bay Company trappers?"

"No, or I'd recognize at least a few of them. They are free trappers."

Morgan was bitterly disappointed and expected trouble. Even from a distance the trappers appeared to be a rough bunch, unlikely to inconvenience themselves unless rewarded handsomely.

"I will pay them for their cabins," Morgan decided out loud. "After all, they are worth something."

"A good idea," Anton said, hoping it would be enough to prevent trouble.

When the trappers saw the big schooner, they hurried over to the muddy riverbank and sized up the heavily laden vessel with more than a little interest. Lines were cast and secured to the water-loving cottonwoods. When María and Rosalinda appeared on deck, the trappers stared and then began to snicker among themselves and grin boldly.

"Go below deck and stay there," Anton said to the women. "Captain Tucker?" he said to the schooner's captain.

"Yes?"

"I do not like the look of these men. Pass the word to your crew to stand ready for trouble."

Tucker nodded grimly. "They have a hard and hungry look about them, all right. I'll arm my crew but warn them to hold steady."

"Good."

Morgan and Anton checked their rifles before they climbed down a rope ladder and waded onto the shore.

A short, powerful man with long, greasy black hair and a wicked knife scar across his face stepped aggressively forward. "My name is Ed Hauser. Who are you?"

Morgan introduced himself and then Anton before turning to the schooner. "Our vessel is operating under the orders of Captain John Augustus Sutter. Are you with the Hudson's Bay Company?"

"We answer to none but ourselves." The man turned around to his companions. "Ain't that right, boys!"

They shouted a defiant assent, then one said, "Why don't you ask them Mexican women if they'd like to meet us and have something to drink? Both of 'em are real pretty. Not young, but seasoned prime and—"

Anton's fist silenced the man, dropping him quivering to the ground.

"Goddammit!" Hauser swore. "You had no call for that!"

"If he speaks of my wife that way again, I'll thumb his eyes out," Anton growled.

Hauser backed up a step and balled his fists. He was built like the trunk of an oak tree, perhaps five-ten but weighing over two hundred pounds, with thick, sloping shoulders.

"Old man," he sneered, "you're a little long in the tooth for that game. If one of them is your wife, maybe she needs a young man."

Anton swung again, but Hauser was ready. He ducked and slammed a thundering blow to Anton's ribs. The Russian doubled over, and Morgan was just about to jump in when the Russian lashed out with his leg and kicked Hauser alongside his knee.

The man grunted in pain and staggered but did not go down.

"Goddamn you!" Hauser cried, drawing a wicked Arkansas toothpick. "I'll cut your heart out!"

"Hold it!" Morgan ordered, snapping up the barrel of his rifle. "There will be no killing this day."

But the trappers lifted and cocked their own rifles.

"Anton!" María cried.

When the Russian turned his head for an instant, Hauser saw his chance. He leapt forward, knife streaking toward Anton's belly.

Age betrayed the Russian, and Morgan heard his friend grunt with pain as Hauser's knife split his buckskin shirt. Blood stained leather.

Morgan took a step forward, but Anton pulled his knife and bellowed, "Stay out of this!" as he went into a crouch. Knife blades up, he and Hauser began to circle each other warily. Hauser feinted a thrust which Anton ignored. The younger man began to slash and advance. Anton kept backing up, and when one of the trappers stuck out his leg and almost tripped him, Hauser lunged for the kill.

Morgan's heart filled his throat, and just when he thought that Anton was a dead man, the Russian somehow regained his balance, spun sideways so that Hauser's knife missed his body, then grabbed the younger man. The pair locked, each gripping the other's wrist and trying to wrestle his knife away. Hauser sank his teeth into Anton's forearm. The Russian slammed his forehead into Hauser's right ear. Once, twice, and then Hauser bellowed in pain.

They matched power against power, shuffling and straining, faces white and tendons distended from their thick necks like wires. Anton was much the taller, but Hauser was the young bull, quick and deadly. Grunting and cursing, eyes bulging with their herculean efforts, they suddenly began to whip their legs, attempting to trip the other down.

Hauser tried to sink his teeth into Anton's collarbone, but the Russian butted him again, this time breaking the man's nose as they crashed to the earth, gouging, punching, and rolling into the Sacramento River. Somehow Anton ended up on Hauser's back. He laced his fingers into the man's greasy hair, then yanked his head back as he put his knife to Hauser's exposed throat.

"Order your men to drop their weapons!"

Hauser made a strangled sound.

"Drop them or he's a dead man!" Anton shouted to the circle of trappers.

They dropped their rifles.

"Now step back!"

They could not take their eyes off the two fighters, but they backed up and Morgan's rifle waved across their chests like a probing finger of death.

Anton climbed off Hauser, who gagged and clutched his throat, now slippery with blood.

"You'll live," Anton gasped, "but you'll have a little scar to remember this day."

"You sonofabitch!"

Anton grabbed the man by his collar and hauled him to his feet. "Get out of here before I cut you from ear to ear."

Hauser clawed up the muddy bank to join his men.

"We're claiming this land!" Morgan said.

"Mister, you'll make your claim in hell," a tall, gaunt trapper warned.

Morgan raised his Hawken and pointed it at the man's broad chest. "You'd better go now. I'm not as merciful as my friend."

"What about our rifles, furs, traps, and supplies?"

"You'll get them back," Morgan promised. "But later."

The sullen trappers turned and made their way to a nearby grove of cottonwoods just beyond their log cabins.

Anton said, "I should have cut his throat while I had the chance. He'll lead those men against us as soon as it's dark."

"I know."

Morgan looked up at the deck of the schooner, thinking of his wife and of how, if he were ambushed, she would be at the mercy of these lusty trappers. He pivoted to study the low, grassy hillock where he and Rosalinda had planned to build their new home and where they'd playfully made love. But against his will his eyes were pulled to the ill-made log cabins, the litter of charred bones and empty whiskey bottles and the greasy, stinking pelts stretched to the sun.

The magic of the place was gone. He'd never bring it back, even if he could somehow drive the Americans away or buy them off. As the Indians would say, this place was now bad medicine.

"Anton, this is no good anymore. Let's get out of here."

"Are you sure?"

"Yes," Morgan said, committing the faces of these men to memory so that if he ever met them again he would be on guard. "Even if we could drive them back to wherever they came from, they'd return for venge-

ance one day. They'd ambush us both and use our
wives."

The Russian had arrived at the same sad conclusion.
He picked up his rifle and waded into the river.
Morgan waited until he knew Anton was back on board,
and then he also climbed the ladder to the deck of the
ship.

The schooner's lines were cut, and the Sacramento's
powerful current swung the vessel around to allow the
captain to guide it downriver.

A few weeks later as the Rostovs finished packing and
readied themselves to leave California and journey to
Russia, Morgan found it impossible to say how much he
would miss his Russian friend.

"Maybe you don't realize it yet, Anton, but in your
heart, you are an American now."

Anton chuckled. "This I will find out."

"Come back," Morgan said, "and we will build our
ranchos together."

"We will see," Anton said quietly as he took his wife's
arm.

There were tears in María's eyes, but Morgan knew
that she wanted to see her husband's homeland. And
when they rode out of sight, he put his arm around his
wife's shoulders and said, "They'll return. I believe that
with all my heart."

Rosalinda nodded. "It's time we started to get on
with our own lives."

Morgan agreed, but it was hard to think of leaving
Sutter and his fort. This had been his home for many
years, and he knew he'd be leaving a part of himself
when he and Rosalinda departed. This thought was still
very much on his mind when Sutter approached to wish
them farewell.

"So," the captain said, "this is good-bye."

Morgan finished inspecting his horses and string of
pack mules loaded with gifts from his old friend. "I'm
afraid so, Captain."

"Do you know where you'll settle?"

"Somewhere to the south. Joe Chewy told me the southern Sierra rivers were teeming with beaver."

"He was long on talk, but that part is probably true," Sutter conceded. "Last I heard, Mr. Chewy had left Monterey. It wouldn't surprise me if he showed up here looking for work. Despite our falling out, I'd hire him again as my lead trapper."

"He was a good man."

"So are you." Sutter grinned. "I'm glad that you've agreed sell me whatever furs you get down south. You know I'll give you top dollar."

"Yeah," Morgan said. "I know that."

Sutter stepped forward to make a quick adjustment on Rosalinda's bridle. "There's something else you could do, if it suited you better."

"What?"

"I need a sawmill built. I've found an ideal place up on the south fork of the American River. It's about thirty miles west of us, with plenty of good timber."

"But I heard that you've already offered James Marshall a partnership."

"Yes, we have talked. There's big money to be made in lumber."

James Marshall had quickly proven to be one of Sutter's best carpenters. A tall, eccentric man who fancied wearing buckskins and bright Mexican serapes, Marshall was a hard worker, although many thought him half crazy because of his habit of constantly talking to himself. He was also quarrelsome and extremely opinionated on almost any subject. But he was an artist with wood.

"Marshall is a better man for the job than I'd be," Morgan said.

"Then trap plenty of beaver for me in those big southern Sierra rivers."

"I will," Morgan promised, shaking hands again with his captain. Then he mounted his horse alongside Rosalinda, and without another word of farewell they both reined south, because no good ever came out of long good-byes.

At the top of a ridge they turned to have a last look at their little cabin beside Sutter's Fort. It was quite a remarkable picture from their high vantage point, one that only someone who'd been with the captain right from the start could fully appreciate because of the changes that had occurred in just nine years. Out of the wilderness, they had hewn a settlement that was something to envy. No western military post could compare to Sutter's Fort, and even the great farms of Pennsylvania and the Carolinas couldn't match the thousands of acres under cultivation.

By Sutter's own account, there were nearly three hundred white people now living and working there, more and more of them families trying to build a stake before settling their own rich farmland. And rich it was, beyond anything! This fall alone nearly forty thousand bushels of wheat would be harvested by the captain's five hundred California Indians.

Cattle, sheep, and horses belonging to the settlement grazed the hills and valley as far as the eye could see. Within the fort itself was a flourishing society, where Sutter's Indians operated looms to make hats, coats, and woolen blankets. In the tannery, thousands of hides were processed each year, and their tanned leather made fine belts, boots, gloves, saddles, and harnesses, much of which was shipped around Cape Horn and sold to eager buyers in New England. Sutter's empire was so immense that five oxen or cattle were slaughtered each day just to feed his workers.

"What are you thinking?" Rosalinda asked.

"Ahh," Morgan said with a shrug of his shoulders, "I was thinking that I'm proud to have been a part of building all this."

"Yes, but now it's time for us to build together."

"I'll never match him. Nobody will."

"It doesn't matter. Come along," she said, reining her horse about. "Sutter has created his life; now it's time to start ours."

He nodded and followed, knowing she was right, as they rode south toward the valley and the river of San Joaquin.

* * *

They wintered with the friendly Yokuts Indians near the junction of the San Joaquin and the Merced rivers. When Morgan wasn't trapping beaver and buying Indian ponies to carry his growing number of beaver pelts, he and Rosalinda spent their time exploring up and down the San Joaquin Valley looking for a site for their rancho. But the following summer of '48, plagued by the searing low valley heat coupled with clouds of mosquitoes, they decided to look up higher in the Sierra foothills.

"High enough to be out of valley heat and fog, but low enough so that the snow doesn't get very deep," Morgan repeated often.

"You are expecting a paradise."

"And we'll find it before winter."

In October they did find the place. It was big-shouldered foothill country butted right up to glistening pine forests overlooking the Merced River. The view from any direction was breathtaking, and there was a gushing spring as sweet as hard-rock candy.

"What do you think?" Morgan asked, cocking a knee around his saddlehorn and tipping back his hat. "Do you think you'd go crazy up here with me?"

Rosalinda swallowed. To the east were towering, already snowcapped mountains. To the south paraded one misty purple ridge of Sierra foothills after the next. Just to the north, shining like a necklace of pure silver, tumbled the swift Merced River. To the west lay the soft, heat-hazy valley of the San Joaquin.

"This is the most beautiful country I have ever seen," Rosalinda declared.

"I think it was meant for us to call home. But I am worried that you might get lonely."

"I'm a little worried about that, too," she admitted. "Are there any Indian villages around here?"

"Bound to be. We'll find them. Give them gifts and make friends. But it wouldn't be the same as the company we had at the fort."

"With you and our children, I can be happy here."

Morgan slid down from his saddle and reached up for

his wife. "Do you remember how much fun we had laying out our first plans for a home?"

"Yes."

His eyes twinkled with mischief... and something else. "Well, I've been thinking this is exactly where I want to build our cabin. And you know what?"

"I think I can guess. We just happen to be standing right in the middle of our bedroom."

He chuckled. "You're right!"

Rosalinda kissed his mouth as they sank to the earth and his hand moved down over her new buckskin dress, pushing it up and up.

"I want to stay right here—on this very spot—and have your children," she whispered. "And grow old, and when I die, I want us to be buried here."

"Under the bedroom floor?"

She laughed and pretended to struggle against him. But not much.

≈ 18 ≈

It was a cool morning in October. The air was still, and down in the meadows that bordered the Merced River, a peregrine falcon plummeted out of the sky to sink its talons into a rabbit. The falcon labored for altitude, screeching in hoarse victory as it carried its kicking prey into the boughs of a huge oak tree.

"Dinner is ready!" Rosalinda called.

Morgan buried the blade of his ax into a block of wood and straightened with weariness. His muscles ached from the unremitting hard labor of building a snug log cabin and a sturdy fur barn. Now he took a moment to gaze all around, and he smiled. This was beautiful country! Morgan praised every blessed inch of it, and even though he was worn down physically, he had never been happier. Rosalinda seemed happy, too, especially since realizing she was pregnant. It had been one of the friendly Yokuts Indian women who'd first sensed that she was with child. After that the Indian women had paid almost daily visits to their log cabin, bringing corn, soft tanned deerskin, and pretty beads for Rosalinda and her expected child.

Wrinkled brown face wreathed in a toothless smile, the old medicine woman named Walks to the River had conducted a daily ritual using smoke and chants to ward off evil spirits. She'd also been reluctant to inform Rosalinda that her firstborn was to be a girl. To the old squaw's amazement, Rosalinda had clapped her hands with happiness. She'd wanted a daughter first, one that

291

could keep her company when Morgan was out trapping for beaver.

And this was incredibly good beaver country. There were dozens of little streams feeding both the Tuolumne and the Merced rivers, every one teeming with beaver. Morgan's fur shed was already nearly full, and he would either have to build a second one to store his winter's catch or buy additional Indian horses in order to transport his furs up to Sutter's Fort.

"Your dinner is getting cold!" Rosalinda called again.

Morgan washed his hands and face, dried them on his sleeve, and hurried inside the cabin, which was furnished with an ax-hewn table, two benches, and a bed covered by a lumpy grass mattress.

"You're working too hard," Morgan warned Rosalinda as he eased down on a hard wooden bench.

"So are you," Rosalinda replied, brushing back a damp tendril of hair as she set two bowls on the table. "But we can rest a little this winter."

"I'll be doing even more trapping," he said. "Winter fur is of higher quality and will bring a better price."

She filled the bowls with a thick venison stew seasoned with wild onions and garlic she'd collected with the Yokuts women earlier in the summer. There was also fresh Indian bread and squaw tea, bitter and stimulating.

"If you like," he said, watching her closely, "we could go to Monterey. Might be easier to have the baby there."

She shook her head with a soft smile on her lips. "No. I've already made plans. My friends will help me. I'll be just fine."

"Are you going to bear our child the Indian way?"

"Yes. And the women will help."

Morgan had great confidence in squaws. Over the years, he'd concluded that they were extremely capable in whatever they undertook, often far more capable than their men.

Morgan ate slowly. "I need to decide about our fur," he said. "Either I build another shed or we take them north to the fort."

"I know you miss Captain Sutter. Let's go visit him

now, while I can still mount a horse and ride any distance."

"All right," Morgan said. "We'll trade the captain beaver pelts for plows, oxen, tools, and harness. Maybe he has some iron and an anvil he could spare so that I could forge my own nails and horseshoes."

"You're no blacksmith."

"True, but I've dabbled in blacksmithing. It's not that hard. We're going to need wagons, and that means that I'm going to have to start making chains, wheels, and other hardware."

A distant shout interrupted Rosalinda's response. "Hello the house!"

Morgan was sure he recognized the voice, and he hurried to their cabin door. When he looked outside, he saw a familiar buckskin-clad figure, slight, bent, and even a little pigeon-toed as he led a couple of pack mules forward.

"It's Joe Chewy!"

Rosalinda clapped her hands with delight, and they were both waiting outside the cabin when Joe Chewy dismounted, his pale blue eyes gauging the new cabin and shed with approval before settling on Rosalinda's bulging waistline.

"Well, well! I do believe you've swallowed a melon!"

Rosalinda blushed. "I think you know better than that, Mr. Chewy."

"Well, I do, I do! Good gracious, sweet child, I knew that you'd get yourself in a fix if you married this big galoot!"

Morgan beamed, and Rosalinda said, "The Yokuts women believe I will have a daughter."

"Ahhh!" the old mountain man scoffed. "They don't know about such things! What did they do to come up with that idea? Roll bones in the dust?"

"I *want* a daughter!"

"Oh. Well, more often than not," he amended quickly, "them old squaws seem to be right about such things. In fact," he said with a sly wink, "regardin' this kind of prophesy, I'd say that they're almost always right."

"They are?"

"Yep!"

Rosalinda was delighted. "Come and have dinner with us. Morgan was just about to finish my stew, but there's enough left to take the edge off even your hunger."

A short while later, as Chewy mopped up the last of his meal with a big hunk of Indian bread, he reached into his leather jacket and pulled out his smoking pipe. "You mind, Rosalinda, honey?"

"Of course not."

Chewy packed his pipe, and when he got it smoking to his satisfaction, he frowned, cocked one of his thick brows, and said, "I'm afraid I've got some bad news."

Morgan glanced at Rosalinda, and she came over to sit at his side on the rough wooden bench.

"What is it?"

"You remember James Marshall and that sawmill he went up to build on the south fork of the American River for the captain?"

"Sure."

"Well, he built it just fine, but then he went and discovered gold."

Morgan blinked. He didn't understand. "Why is that bad news?"

"That's a right natural question to ask," Chewy said, "and I'll do my best to explain. They tried to keep it a secret, but old Sam Brannan—that big Mormon fella that had the general store—well, he took a glassful of gold over to San Francisco and ran up and down the street yellin' his head off that gold had been discovered at Sutter's Mill."

"And that caused a stampede," Rosalinda said, a look of understanding now filling her dark eyes.

"Yes, it did, sweet child. The rush started this past spring, and by now I'd guess you could shoot cannon-balls through the streets of San Francisco and not hit anyone. Whole town is emptied. Monterey, too. Every-one came runnin' for the diggin's."

Morgan still didn't understand. "But if the captain owns the mill and—"

"But he *don't* own it," Chewy said. "Oh, he gave the Indians a few trinkets and got 'em to sign away the rights to that strip along the American. Then he sent a man to Monterey to petition the new military governor of California to honor the treaty, but that failed. So other than the land that the mill stands on, Sutter doesn't have any legal rights along the American."

Morgan scowled. "But I'd think the captain could reap a fortune selling grain, cattle, and all manner of supplies to the hordes of gold seekers."

"You'd have figured that, wouldn't you?" Chewy shook his head. "And he tried. The truth of the matter is that all his own people upped and ran off to pan gold. They pretty much left him unprotected. Folks just started pouring across his fields, slaughtering his livestock, stealing anything that they could get their hands on, even including the apples from his orchards and the grapes from his vines."

"And there was nothing he could do?" Morgan was appalled.

"He tried. The captain yelled and threatened. He posted signs saying that trespassers would be shot. He did everything possible. I even ran some cattle rustlers off myself, but a bunch of 'em came looking to hang me, so I had to light out for the hills in order to save my own hide!"

"What about John Bidwell and the Kanaka?"

"Bidwell is still trying to help, and there are a few Kanaka left, but not many. You and Anton Rostov were the only ones that might have made a difference. But you both left."

Chewy shrugged his narrow shoulders. "I tried to talk to the captain, but he don't listen to me or anyone else. Not even his son."

"His son is there?"

"Yeah, but that ain't helpin' matters, either. They're fightin' all the time. He's always tellin' the captain to stop drinkin' so much, and that just makes him madder than hell and bound to get drunker."

Morgan shook his head. It sounded like a nightmare. He'd hoped that when the first of Sutter's family finally arrived it would greatly change the captain's outlook for the better. Apparently it had not.

Chewy continued. "Everyone that the captain used to count on-is off pannin' gold and hopin' to strike it rich. I'd go myself, only the cold river water makes my bones ache."

"So you came down here."

"That's right. Sutter asked me to send word that he needs your help. Things have gone crazy along the American River. Them people are loco over that gold. Sutter, he don't know what to do, and it's gotten so that he's drunk more often than sober."

"He was doing better, except for the day we left."

"Sutter's worse now, and he isn't thinking clear. Left his settlement and joined the gold rush is what he done this spring."

"Really?"

"Yep. He took a couple of wagon loads of supplies and a bunch of them Kanaka Indians up to Coloma. He found some gold, too."

"But then—"

Chewy winked. "My friend, findin' and keepin' gold are two entirely different things. I hear tell the grog shops moved in among the prospectors, and before long the captain and his Indians were drunk and broke. Sutter came draggin' back to his fort lookin' more dead than alive."

Morgan climbed to his feet and began to pace back and forth. "It will destroy the captain if he loses his fort and everything he worked so hard to build."

"What are we going to do?" Rosalinda asked.

"We'll pack up all the furs we can take and go to Sutter's Fort. After we get there, we can decide if there's anything we can do to help."

"It'd be like trying to dam the American River itself," Chewy warned. "The gold stampede is already too damn big. The people will keep comin' in waves as long as the strike lasts. It's gonna ruin some men like the captain and make others richer than kings. Like to see you be one of the latter, Morgan."

"Not me," he said. "My gold is right here on this

piece of land. I've got a shed full of prime beaver pelts and—"

"Beaver prices are down some. Beef is what sells now. Them that got beef can sell it for gold. Hides are worth more than ever."

"I've got no beef," Morgan said, "but maybe the captain will trade me a few cattle for the pelts. He can protect the pelts in his fur storage rooms."

"That's a fact," Chewy said. "And he might as well trade, because people are stealing his cattle faster than he can swill down his liquor—and you know that's damn fast."

Morgan had to agree. Seeing old Joe Chewy riding up had sent his spirits soaring, but now they were lower than a snake's belly. "I want to leave tomorrow. Will you stay here and take care of things until we get back?"

"Sure. We'll unload my traps and supplies, and you can use my pack mules to help tote your furs. But compadre?"

"Yeah?"

"There ain't a thing anyone can do for the captain now."

"I don't believe that," Morgan snapped, "because the captain still owns a huge amount of land."

"Maybe so, but it's all Mexican grants. Ain't nobody I know of willin' to pay good money or gold for Mexican land titles. Your captain, well sir, I think there's a fair chance he'll end up with little more than what his fort is sitting on and maybe that Hock Farm of his up on the Feather River."

Morgan was filled with desolation at this news. "I sure hope you're wrong," he said, unable to accept that anyone's fortunes could take such a dramatic and sudden downturn.

"So do I. But the Russians are threatening to attach every blessed thing Sutter owns in repayment for the debt he owes on Fort Ross."

"What a tragedy that would be!" Rosalinda exclaimed. "Why, if it hadn't been for Captain Sutter, this valley might not have been settled for years! He bravely fought for ex-Governor Micheltorena, and—"

"That was the beginning of his problems. Because of that mistake, there's still lots of folks that would like to see the captain fall hard."

"I'll bet the men, women, and children he saved from the Donner Party don't feel that way," Morgan said, remembering how unselfishly Captain Sutter had acted in saving as many emigrants as possible.

"Probably not," Chewy admitted. "But then again, I don't seem to recollect any of them standing by his side or guarding his fields or herds when the gold rush started this past spring."

Morgan's expression was bleak. "I should have stayed with the captain," he said in a tired voice.

"Neither you nor the Russian could have stopped what happened," Chewy said. "It was like a horde of locusts comin' through a ripe field of grain."

"I'll start packing right now," Rosalinda said after a long, heavy silence.

When Morgan and Rosalinda topped the rise of land from which they'd last gazed down upon Sutter's flourishing empire, the blood drained from Morgan's face. "Look at what they've done!"

Rosalinda nodded, mute with shock to see thousands of gold seekers crawling all over the fort like ants on a decaying corpse. Hundreds of buildings and tents had sprung up like dusty mushrooms, many right in the middle of Sutter's stripped orchards and wheat fields. Along the banks of the American River vessels of every description lay abandoned in the mud, their passengers and crew no doubt digging frantically in the nearby gold fields. Morgan noted, too, the rotting wheat in Sutter's fields and cattle slaughtered in the pastures, some bloated and covered with flocks of crows.

"I have never before seen such devastation!" Morgan whispered. "What could possibly be in the minds of men to do this to Captain Sutter?"

"I don't know."

Morgan heard a deep weariness in Rosalinda's voice.

Their child wasn't due until spring, but this long journey had been much harder on his wife than expected. "Let's go. I'm sure that the captain will be able to find us suitable quarters."

When they rode into the fort, however, Morgan had second thoughts. Every square foot of the compound was blanketed with tents and crawling with rough gold seekers. The former workshops backing to the fort's thick perimeter walls were jammed with merchants hawking every manner of shoddy goods at extraordinarily high prices.

"Hey, trapper!" a big, dirty man wearing a shapeless hat called as he rushed over to Morgan with an outstretched hand. "I'll take care of your animals for just a dollar—each."

"No, thanks," Morgan said, ignoring the hand.

"Well, now," the man said, his smile dissolving and his voice turning nasty, "I guess you might think that you can find someone who'd care for them cheaper. Well, you won't!"

"Go to hell," Morgan said, driving his horse and their pack mules forward, almost trampling the man.

He found a place to tie their animals beside Sutter's office and living quarters. "Let's get inside and find the captain." Morgan helped a frightened-looking Rosalinda down.

The captain was drinking in the company of a half dozen disreputable-looking men. There were two empty bottles of rye whiskey on his table and a third nearly drained. At the sight of Morgan and Rosalinda, Sutter surged to his feet, almost overturning the table.

"Dear friends!" he bellowed, "what a pleasure to see you again!" The captain tripped in his haste to reach their sides.

Morgan steadied him. "Can we talk in private?"

"Well, of course!" Sutter exclaimed expansively before turning to the other men and grandly dismissing them. "Gentlemen, please do me the great kindness of returning for dinner."

The men weren't pleased. One of them grabbed what

remained of the rye and shot Morgan a hard look before marching outside.

Sutter didn't notice. "I can't begin to express to you what a pleasant—"

"What has become of you? Once you entertained dignitaries and gentlemen—now you're getting drunk among panhandlers, swindlers, and the lowest sort of riffraff, the kind of ballast that will pull you down!"

Sutter's lopsided smile froze, then cracked like dried mud until he turned away quickly with an anguished sob tearing from his chest.

"I'm sorry," Morgan apologized quickly as guilt overpowered him. "I didn't mean to lose my temper, but how can you just sit here getting drunk while everything around you is falling into ruin?"

"You can't possibly understand."

Morgan helped his captain into a chair. Sutter was trembling; he looked very unwell. "Captain, Joe Chewy told me about the gold rush. I couldn't imagine it. Where did this hard crowd come from?"

"Everywhere." Sutter paused for a few moments. "My friends, they are arriving daily from all over the world, and every one of them lusting for gold. So . . . so what can I do?"

Morgan glanced at his wife. She shook her head, as lost for an answer as himself.

"Have you hired a lawyer? Someone who could—"

"Never! The honest ones have all fled to the gold fields. And those that remain are vultures eager to pick my bones. I'll not pay them to do that, Mr. Beck." Sutter wagged his head back and forth vigorously. "No, I will not!"

Morgan nodded. *My Lord,* he thought, *the captain has gone mad.*

Sutter's hand shook badly as he reached across the table for his glass of rye. Morgan had not the heart to stop him. He watched as the captain swallowed the liquor, his body convulsing with every gulp.

"Please," Rosalinda begged. "Take it easy!"

Sutter squeezed his eyes shut. "My dear friends, I am lost and very, very tired."

"You need to refresh both mind and body for a while," Morgan said.

Sutter didn't hear him. He held up his hands and stared at them. "Trying to hold back the tide of destruction is like trying to hold water with your fingers. It's impossible." The captain sighed. "You shouldn't have come."

"What about your son?"

Sutter stiffened, and his face grew almost savage. "I rue the day I sent for him! Do you know what he's done to me?"

"I've heard he's sold lots down by your levee and named the place Sacramento."

"Damn him, yes! And not the slightest mention was made of a Sutterville!"

A strange glint appeared in the captain's bloodshot eyes, followed by a low chuckle that caused the hair to rise on the back of Morgan's neck.

"Just you wait, Mr. Beck," Sutter said with a sly wink, "for they will pay dearly. Spring floods will come and destroy Sacramento—if not one year, then the next!"

Morgan tried to hide his alarm, because the captain's talk was crazy. "Sir," he pleaded, "you need rest!"

Sutter's mouth pinched down at the corners, and he shook his head. "You see," he whispered, "they all refuse to go to Sutterville, which is safe on high ground! Instead they despoil everything within the boundaries of my sight and smell."

"Easy," Morgan said, afraid that Sutter was very near the borders of hysteria. "We will reason with them."

"It's too late! You see, my son is a Judas reincarnate!"

A chill raced up and down Morgan's spine when he looked into the captain's bloodshot eyes. "Sir," he said, leading the man to his bed and easing him onto it, "you must sleep now. Later we'll see what can be done to help."

But Sutter's head wagged back and forth on his pillow. "Dear Mr. Beck, I'm afraid you still do not fully understand. There is nothing that can be done. It's all lost."

"Captain Sutter," Rosalinda pleaded, "please, just sleep now."

He closed his eyes and was snoring within a few minutes. While Rosalinda watched over the poor, tortured man, Morgan hauled his furs into the office, then stacked them along the entire length of one wall. "We'll have to sleep in here until we can find something better."

"What about our animals?"

"I'll find a man that can be trusted to care for them."

Rosalinda pulled the curtain aside a little and peeked out at the compound, where a circle of yelling, carousing men were betting furiously on a bloody dog fight. "I can't believe my eyes," she whispered. "Everything here is now insane!"

Morgan was about to agree when a man barged in through the doorway. He was clean-shaven, fair-complected, and well dressed. He was also immediately recognizable as the captain's son.

"Who are you, and what are those furs doing in my father's office?" he demanded.

John Sutter, Jr., appeared to be a man accustomed to privilege. His voice was heavily accented German, just as his father's had been upon his arrival in California.

Morgan introduced himself, then his wife, aware that neither of them made a very good impression dressed in buckskins and coated with dust from their long journey. He ended up saying, "We are both good friends of your father."

The young Swiss nodded, but there was little warmth in his greeting. "Yes, of course. My father wrote often of you and many others."

John, Jr., went over to Sutter's bedroom, glanced inside, and closed the door before motioning toward chairs. "Sit and tell me what brings you to Sacramento."

Morgan ground his teeth but managed to say, "Your father's welfare."

"And why is that any of your concern?"

Morgan's voice took on a hard edge. "Because, as I've already explained, we are his friends."

John, Jr., relaxed. "I'm sorry," he said quickly, "I am not myself these days. Not myself at all. It's his fault, of course. All those years my father wrote of how rich he'd become, and then I arrive here to find . . . chaos."

The young emigrant wrung his smooth, womanish hands. "I am doing everything in my power to prevent a complete dissolution of my father's holdings."

"He's extremely upset that you have promoted Sacramento. You must know that first New Helvetia, then Sutterville, were his dreams."

"Flawed dreams, like all his many others. I don't know about this New Helvetia. Back in Europe, no one in my town or family ever took that pipe dream seriously. And as for the other, well, I tried to promote his Sutterville. People laughed in my face when I offered them city lots. Instead they came on up here and started building along the riverfront, not even bothering to seek legal title, which most don't believe my father can sustain in the United States court system."

The young man made a gesture of resignation. "What else could I do but try to gain some recompense for my father? Mr. Samuel Brannan helped me. Father blames him for going to San Francisco and starting this entire business, but it would have happened with or without Mr. Brannan's promotion."

Morgan found himself nodding his head in agreement. "You can't hide a rich gold strike forever."

"Of course not! And the Russian American Company—naturally assuming my father is flush with newfound wealth—has demanded immediate repayment for its Fort Ross properties. To avoid their rightful claims, my father has given me the power of attorney over all his business dealings."

"He has?" Morgan was astonished. Sutter must have been very drunk or desperate indeed to take such a measure.

"There is more. We are selling this fort and its questionable land grant for whatever it will bring."

"What!" Morgan lowered his voice. "Surely you can't mean it!"

"I do. As you can see, my father's mental state is extremely unstable. I fear for his health. I am convinced that he must be rid of this place at once."

"But what will become of him?" Rosalinda cried. "Where will he go?"

"To Hock Farm," the young man answered, "just as soon as the matter can be arranged. In the meantime, I will try to salvage whatever I can. I'm sure you can see that he is now a complete liability."

Morgan glanced at Rosalinda, who, though shaken, nodded her head in reluctant agreement.

"All right," Morgan conceded, turning back to John, Jr. "What can I do to help?"

"Are you serious?"

"Dead serious."

For the first time, the young Swiss demonstrated the hint of a smile. "You can attempt to salvage what remains of the herds and then organize the few loyal riders left and drive them north to Hock Farm."

"I saw almost no cattle, horses, or sheep."

"There are a few remaining." John, Jr., shook his head. "Perhaps not sheep. They are most easily carried off and slaughtered."

"I'll do what you ask, but in the meantime, my wife is expecting a child. We need living quarters."

"I'll find something. As you can see, we've rented everything to the merchants. Their payments are the only thing that has kept us from bankruptcy."

"I can't believe this." Morgan groaned.

"Oh, really? Mr. Beck, try to imagine my own shock and dismay when I arrived here to discover that my father—instead of being the richest man in California—had become instead a drunken sot sleeping with dirty savages and—"

Morgan's hand streaked out to grip the man's shirt-front. "*Don't* say another word!"

"But it's the truth! Just look at what father had and lost!"

Morgan released his grip. Taking his anger out on

this arrogant fop would do more harm than good. "We'll help do what we can for your father," he managed to say. "We'll take whatever is left of his herds north to Hock Farm. But after that . . . I wash my hands of this entire affair."

John, Jr., stepped out of reach and smoothed the front of his wrinkled shirt. "I don't believe you were ever asked to put yourself *into* this affair, Mr. Beck."

Morgan growled, "I'm finally beginning to see why your father waited so many years to send for you."

The younger man's face blistered with anger, but he was wise enough to hold his tongue.

They didn't find much livestock to drive to Hock Farm—less than a thousand head of cattle and horses. When they left with Captain Sutter, the man was plunged into the depths of depression, seemingly without hope or spirit. To make matters worse, not a single person they passed even bothered to wish Captain Sutter a good journey or the best of luck, let alone thank him for opening up the interior of California. And when the captain looked west toward the abandoned city lots of his fantasy Sutterville, Morgan saw that his face pinched with bitterness and his eyes were cold and wintry.

But several days later, when they rode into view of Hock Farm, Sutter underwent a dramatic transformation. His back straightened and his chin rose because the house and outbuildings looked well constructed, and everything, in contrast to the chaos he'd left behind, appeared to be in fine order. Indians were tending new seedlings, there were young colts and lambs in the pasture, and stalks of corn were growing in the small but well-irrigated fields.

Sutter filled his chest and threw his shoulders back proudly. Lifting his chin, he said, "John Bidwell designed and oversaw the construction of the house, my fields, and the outbuildings. I see that he did his usual fine job."

"No question about that," Morgan said, delighted by the sudden change in his captain.

"But we must not forget that Hock Farm is only six hundred acres," Sutter reminded them solemnly. "Not much land compared to my Mexican grants of more than forty thousand acres."

"But here the title is clear," Morgan said, keenly aware that the squatters were attempting to strip Sutter of all his Mexican land grants. "And no matter what happens in Sacramento, this is your farm and no one can attach it for other debts."

Morgan's reminder had the desired effect on Sutter. "Yes, the vultures cannot feed upon me here. I'll come back," Sutter vowed, his eyes clear and alert. "I'll send for my family, and I'll come back bigger and stronger than ever before."

"Of course you will!"

"And we'll both make huge fortunes." Sutter gestured toward the herd they were driving with the help of a few loyal vaqueros. "I want you to take a hundred of my best cattle back down to your ranch on the Merced. Consider it a wedding gift."

A year ago Morgan would have accepted, because Sutter's cattle had numbered so many thousands. But not now. "I insist on paying for them."

"I won't take your fur money."

"Then I'll pay off one of your creditors."

Sutter waved his hand as if it were of no consequence. A faraway look came into his eyes. "I did do a lot of things wrong," he mused out loud, "but I did a few right. Buying this farm with a clear American title was one. It's something to build on all over again. Isn't it?"

"Absolutely, Captain!"

Sutter nodded as if trying to convince himself. "My biggest regret is that I can't be young again and filled with energy and optimism—like you, Mr. Beck."

"You're still young enough," Morgan said earnestly.

Sutter did not believe that for an instant, but he roused his flagging spirits enough to say, "Of course I am!" And to prove it, he tore off his hat, swatted it across the rump of his horse, and went racing off toward Hock Farm to the delight of everyone.

"Just look at the captain!" Morgan exclaimed. "He's

like the man I saw jump into that crowd of hostile Indians on the bank of the American River!"

"Do you really believe he can start again?" Rosalinda asked.

"I don't know," Morgan admitted, his smile fading. "Right now he's clearheaded and full of optimism. If he can stay that way, I think he could become the first governor of the state of California or anything else he wants."

"So could you."

"Not me. I've seen what power and politics can do to a man, and I want no part of either. All I want is you, a passel of healthy children, and our rancho."

"The captain may need you again," Rosalinda said, watching Sutter gallop into the yard of his fine new home.

"If he does," Morgan said, "I'll have to come."

"I know that. And I'll come too."

A slow smile widened across Morgan's lips as he watched their captain jump from his horse and unleash a whoop of pure exuberation. *So,* Morgan thought, *our captain hasn't really lost his joy for life.*

Sutter turned to wave and beckon them to come and join him. Without a moment's hesitation, Morgan and Rosalinda touched spurs to their horses and galloped forward.

≈ **AUTHOR'S NOTE** ≈

John Augustus Sutter did run for the office of California's first governor but was soundly defeated. His wife and remaining children finally arrived at Hock Farm in 1850, where most of the family resided for the next fifteen years.

For the rest of his life, Sutter waged a hopeless legal battle seeking compensation for the huge losses he had sustained during the California gold rush. In 1864, the state of California finally granted him the paltry compensation of $250.00 a month, not nearly enough to satisfy a man of Sutter's expensive tastes and generous nature. The next year, Hock Farm was torched by an arsonist and burned to the ground. A bitter Sutter and his wife forever turned their backs on California.

Sutter spent his final unhappy years petitioning the U.S. Congress for monetary damages. He also sought restitution for the vast agricultural holdings he had lost because of the discovery of gold, a discovery that had greatly benefited the United States and led directly to the opening of the American West. In 1877, just when it appeared that a stingy Congress was about to award a long-overdue settlement, Captain Sutter died in a hotel bed, nearly penniless.

Sutter's remarkable rise and fall took place in the span of a single decade, 1839–1849. His sad ending convinced many historians that the little dreamer from Switzerland lacked real character. Ultimate failure, coupled with a pronounced weakness for liquor and Indian girls, have caused the man to be judged very harshly. However, it should be remembered that Sutter was incredibly generous, brave, industrious, and resourceful. At the pinnacle of his success, he was arguably the richest man in California.

Regarding his moral and financial collapse, who can say that anyone could have withstood the crazed onslaught of the greatest gold rush in history? Sutter was later to explain, "The country swarmed with lawless men. Talking with them did no good. I was alone and there was no law."

In view of that, perhaps John Augustus Sutter deserves a kinder place in history than he has generally been given.

And what about James Marshall, the taciturn discoverer of gold at Sutter's Mill? If anything, Marshall fared even worse than Captain Sutter. Like Sutter, Marshall attempted to win title over a large portion of the American River. And, like Sutter, he was simply overwhelmed by the gold rush stampede and later thwarted in the courtrooms by popularly elected judges.

Desperate to reap at least a portion of the great discovery he'd made, Marshall joined the rush but was a dismal failure at prospecting. To compound his misery, Marshall was hounded by forty-niners who believed he possessed mystical powers enabling him to discover gold. Unable to satisfy those who relentlessly pursued him from one strike to another, Marshall was often set upon and vilified.

By 1857, when the California gold fields were nearly picked clean, Marshall scratched together enough money to buy fifteen acres of land near Coloma, where he planted grapes and made very good wine, most of which he drank rather than sold. In the ensuing years, whenever sober, Marshall used his considerable skill as a carpenter to make and sell furniture, saddle trees, water wheels, and coffins. Later he tried quartz mining but failed at that, too.

Twenty years after his historic gold discovery, Marshall was a full-blown alcoholic and generally considered an eccentric derelict. For a short while he attempted to earn money on a lecture tour, telling people about how he'd been the first to discover gold in California.

In 1872, Marshall's fortunes at last seemed to take a turn for the better when the California legislature awarded him a monthly pension. However, budgetary reductions caused an outraged and somewhat inebriated Marshall to barge onto the State Assembly House floor waving a bottle of liquor and demanding that his full pension be reinstated. The offended legislators denied the impassioned appeal and eliminated the pension entirely.

Marshall's final years were bitter reminders of the great opportunities he'd squandered. The old man gratefully accepted odd jobs and charity and eventually established himself as something of a local celebrity, equally prized and pitied by the community.

James W. Marshall died penniless in 1885 at the age of seventy-five and is buried on a hill overlooking the site of his famed gold discovery. Five years after his death, thousands attended the unveiling of a great monument depicting James Marshall pointing to the very spot where his and John Sutter's long slide into ruin began on January 24, 1848.

If you enjoyed Gary McCarthy's epic tale, THE AMERICAN RIVER, be sure to look for the next installment of the RIVERS WEST saga at your local bookstore. Each new volume takes you on a voyage of exploration along one of the great rivers of North America with the courageous pioneers who challenged the unknown.

Turn the page for an exciting preview of the next book in Bantam's unique historical series

≈   RIVERS WEST: BOOK 8   ≈

The Snake River

by Win Blevins

On sale in Fall 1992 wherever Bantam Books are sold.

≈ 1 ≈

They called him Weasel, said he hated it.

The name came from his mother's brother, Rockchuck, when Weasel was born. For years he liked it because the weasel, for its size, was the most fierce and most brave of the four-leggeds. And a fine hunter.

But when Weasel was twelve, and getting ready for his first hunt, his grandfather told him that the name was a tease. Rockchuck saw the new baby shortly after birth, shortly after his mother died in childbirth, and the child's hair was brown, not black like a true Shoshone's, because the child was the son of Shoshone woman and a white man, as everyone knew.

"Brown and white," muttered Rockchuck bitterly. "And skinny. Like a weasel." The name stuck.

That was one of the ways these people mocked him, and would always mock him. *Numah-divo* they called him. It was the people's word for half-breed, their word for *Shoshone* spliced onto the word for *white man*. They had similar words that meant Shoshone-black white man and Shoshone-Mexican. All were words of scorn.

After tonight someone would give him another name. After tonight.

In his own mind he kept another name for himself anyway: Sima. When he found out why he was named Weasel, he asked his grandmother (his *un gagau*, his mother's mother) if his mother had spoken before she died of bearing him.

Yes, his grandmother had said. She murmured, "*Sima unduahsie.*" My first son.

His grandmother added, "She loved you."

He liked the Sima part. First. He was something new, a *Numah-divo*. Yes, the first, and something new.

Tonight he would show them.

He was waiting now, frustrated. Waiting for his friend Yahoop, which meant Fatty. It seemed to him a lot of being a young man was waiting—waiting to go on your first pony raid, waiting to get to help steal ponies instead of just holding the horses, waiting to get into a real fight, waiting to get a coup, waiting to marry, waiting to be recognized for what you are, a man.

He was sick of waiting. He would make it end tonight. If Yahoop ever came.

He bent his attention back to the rock. He'd come to this outcrop because the warm lava rock drew the lizards, and he could hear the *shoosh* of the Snake River churning by. He found flowing water soothing. And he liked to catch lizards with his quick hands. While his friends clowned around and missed and acted like they didn't care, he could catch ten, two hands' worth and sometimes more, without having one dart away. Like the sound of the water, catching them eased his mind. When he was watching a lizard he thought of nothing, not his intolerable situation, not his future, nothing at all. He looked, time stopped, and his hand darted. Simple. Clear. Beautiful in a way. It took his mind off the festering within him.

Tonight.

He festered all the time. He raged half the time. He hated his life.

Weasel hated the trapper who fathered him. Back when the Frenchmen first came to hunt beaver on the Snake River, this man had spent a winter with his people, with his mother. When spring came, the trapper simply left, abandoning a people who had adopted him, and abandoning a child in his mother's belly.

The Frenchman didn't give a goddamn. That was what Weasel always called the man out loud. Goddamn Godin. He chuckled whenever he said it. The whites said each white man had two names, not a secret name and a public name but two public names, which they called first and last. No one knew his father's first name, so Weasel gave him one—Goddamn.

It was one of the few white-man words Weasel had learned, and he knew it well. The other trappers who had come, the Americans they called themselves, had told Weasel all about it. It was a word of bad medicine, a curse. They seemed amused at his interest. So Weasel hoped if he called his father Goddamn instead of Godin, whatever that meant, his father's *woah* would burn when he pissed, or the Crows would steal all his horses, or his children would all grow up to hate him. As Weasel did.

The next fall, in the moon when water begins to freeze at the edge of the streams, Weasel's mother died in childbirth. So he was raised by his mother's parents. That was usual enough. Many first children were raised by their maternal grandparents. They were called old people's children, and were often spoiled rotten. But Weasel was raised with half the family anyone was entitled to, among a people to whom family was everything. And they never let him forget it. *Numah-divo.* Half of the people. Not quite one of us.

Well, goddamn them too.

Tonight.

His resentment got a sharp edge when he was getting ready for his first hunt. Then, in the Shoshone way, his father's brother should have become his teacher, to show him the ways of the earth, the ways of the rooted, and winged, the water dwellers, and the four-legged. This man should have taught him how the four-leggeds leave their signs on dirt and sand and mud and snow, and how to follow them, how to know what they will do, how to catch them and take some of their power or, if necessary, their lives. This man should have prepared him to find a dream that would show him his power, his personal, special way to walk the earth.

Instead Rockchuck played this part, his mother's brother, and the man who gave him the mocking name. Weasel's grandfather had died the winter before. No one knew even one man of his father's family.

His grandfather's death hardly mattered. Of all his

family, only his grandmother felt truly like family, and a woman could not teach a boy the ways of men. She always held out the hope that Goddamn Godin would come back and be a father. But Weasel didn't want him back. Weasel would learn carefully the lessons Rockchuck had for him, and despise him every moment. And Goddamn could go to the Ninabee, the devils with tails who eat children. No, the Joahwayo, the big fool with a hairy face and scaly body who ate grown-ups.

≈ **2** ≈

Wh-r-r-r!

Rattlesnake!

Weasel jumped up. He couldn't see it. Which way should he run?

Goddamn!

He jumped off the rock, fell to the ground, scrambled away.

Whomp. Someone landed on him from behind. Held his head down. Grabbed his scalp lock.

Weasel felt the hot prick of the knife. He shook himself, but the man was too heavy, too strong.

"Ha-ha-ha. Ha-ha-ha." A laugh, slow and elaborate.

His captor stood up. Weasel rolled over and looked up at his big friend, Yahoop. His grin was wild, his eyes big as moons. One open palm held the rattlesnake rattle, a big one. He and Weasel had even killed the snake together.

"Cousin," said Weasel weakly. He reached out and put a hand on his cousin's shoulder. "You could have bit me." He was still getting his breath. Weasel was a slight, wiry youth, Yahoop a big one, and fat.

"A Crow would have lifted your curly hair," said Yahoop, putting his knife away. Weasel was always sensitive about his hair, which not only was brown but curly. His hair and his light skin made him look *Numah-divo*.

"So what do you want, cousin, that's such a secret?"

Now Weasel looked at him in the eyes. Here was a real test for Yahoop. The deed would be exciting, but tomorrow some people would shun Fatty. He might have to take the full blast of One Bull's anger, and One Bull was a plenty mean old man.

Weasel felt cold in his gut like a blade. Maybe Yahoop would say no. Maybe Yahoop would say yes and flee when he was needed.

Weasel sat down on the lava rock and motioned Yahoop to join him. He looked at his cousin and best friend nakedly. "Tonight I'm going to steal Lupine." He let it sit.

Finally Yahoop said, "One Bull will kill you. Horn's kinsmen will kill you."

Weasel shook his head and smiled a slow smile.

They both knew. Lupine and Horn had been betrothed when they were infants, in the way of the Shoshone people. Now they were seventeen winters old, and would be married soon.

One of the penalties of being *Numah-divo* was that no girl child had been promised to Weasel. He was only a sort of Shoshone, so unfit. He could feel the bile again.

The great good in Weasel's life was that Lupine thought him marvelously fit. She admired him as a hot-blooded young woman admires a hot-blooded young man. She let him know with looks, glances, even furtive touches. It was risky, but she did it. Her love and Yahoop's friendship were all that made this tribe a home. And his grandmother.

Among these people the great crimes were to kill a kinsman, to steal a kinsman's horse, or to steal his wife. Any could mean blood or banishment.

But there was one way out.

"We will run to Nakok's people," Weasel said. Nakok was a kind of rebellious leader, and his band lived on the Wind River.

Yahoop's eyes locked on him. Excitement? thought Weasel. Fear? Both?

"Then in the moon when water begins to freeze at the edge of the streams, you and I will go against the Crows. Alone." His eyes gleamed. Just two young men against the Crows, a daring stroke. "We will bring Horn so many horses he will forget a mere woman." His lips tossed off the words mockingly.

Yahoop knew Weasel was right. It was a bold plan, but workable. Horn might feel humiliated, rejected by his woman for another man. But neither Horn nor his family could refuse the payment of the horses. That was the custom. Then Weasel and Lupine would come back to the tribe, in their own lodge, a full-fledged family of the people. Their children would be true Shoshones.

And Weasel and Yahoop would be looked on with new eyes. To go alone against the Crow and run off their pony herds!

"Yes-s-s," Yahoop said, hissing his excitement.

Weasel shook his fist in the air. He wanted to fill the sky with shouting, but that would have been dangerous.

"Here's the plan," he began.

≈ 3 ≈

Weasel got ready to take the plunge.

He'd been lying here in the shadow of the lodge for almost enough time to see the Seven Sisters move against the black sky. He had walked quietly through the village, not exciting dogs, which knew his smell, then letting One Bull's war horse, staked by the lodge, snuffle him without getting alarmed.

Weasel was entirely naked, painted red-brown all over his back side and face, white all over his front to his chin. He and Yahoop, aware that he had no vision, no medicine, had chosen this paint from his namesake, the weasel, also wrapping his braids in ermine skins borrowed without permission from Yahoop's mother.

His name was the only pretense of medicine he had.

He had streaked his face with many colors in crazy patterns, angling wildly, many of the streaks bolts of lightning. His eyelids were white, and they made a weird effect when he blinked. Yahoop had greased his hair, twisted it into horns, and tied it high and spiky.

Weasel was a *zo-ahp*, a ghost. If anyone saw his face, not only would they not recognize him, he would scare them half to death.

Since the night was cool, the lodge skirts were down. Now even the last of the fire was out, and everyone asleep, One Bull and his wives at the center rear, their last daughter on the buffalo robes at their feet. Lupine.

He took a deep breath to ease his tension, then another, and another. He wondered how Yahoop was doing in the ravine with the three horses. Yahoop was his only friend, but Yahoop acted dumb sometimes. What if he got scared of the real ghosts and ran off?

Weasel couldn't afford doubts now. It was time. He crawled several steps and sat still in the shadow. He waited. No man or beast had heard. No one raised the alarm.

Weasel lifted his knife and began, ever so slowly and ever so softly, to cut the thongs that held the hide cover of the lodge to the pegs in the ground.

≈ **4** ≈

Black. Black like he had a Frenchman kettle on his head. Black like the heart of One Bull. Weasel couldn't see anything.

So he would go by feel. He knew very well where everyone's buffalo robes were, that Lupine was just to his left, her feet near him, her head at the far end. He would ease around and get next to her ear and whisper to her ever so softly.

He was not sure she would come with him. To ask her directly would have been clumsy. It would have gotten him rejected, then and forever. But once, within her hearing, he'd told the story of Red Forehead, who stole Lance's wife. He had watched Lupine's face. The flicker of eyelashes seemed an answer. Everyone knew Red Forehead and the woman had been happy, had stayed together for years and had lots of children.

A flicker of eyelashes. But it would have been unmanly to ask more.

Weasel lifted himself slightly on his palms and moved to his left. Again. Once more.

"M-m-m-m?"

Goddamn!

His foot touched flesh. Goddamn you, you stupid . . . !

He lay still as stone.

"M-m-m-m."

Stirrings over there. Were they looking around the lodge, trying to see what moved? He thanked *ezhupa*, coyote the trickster, for the blackness.

Rustling of robes and blankets. Scrapings. Maybe Old Bull was sitting up looking around. The first moan had been female, the second male.

Weasel wanted to sink into the dirt like spilled water.

"M-m-m-m."

"M-m-m-m."

More rustlings.

A couple of more moans.

Then other sounds, touchings, stirrings, little sounds of pleasure.

Goddamn.

And then the ancient, rhythmic slurp of human beings obeying the force of life within them. The sound Weasel had heard hundreds of times in his life, though he had never touched a woman in that way. The sound Lupine had heard hundreds of times, and never made herself.

Zond-yogo-sie, he thought amiably—there's some humping going on here.

Weasel lay next to Lupine, close enough to hear her breathe. He thought maybe he could feel her breath on his face. He lay stiller than still. He felt his *woah* fiercely erect. He squeezed the handle of his knife so hard he thought the bone might crack.

He wondered which of his wives One Bull was on top of. One was old and fat, the other not so old and comely. The old fool was so lecherous, so *nia-shup*, he probably liked both of them, and any other woman he could get. Pictures arose in Weasel's mind, the heavy-set old man bouncing around on top of one, then the other, playing lewdly, laughing, mocking Weasel, who would never have a woman.

A fantasy touched him. Lupine's body lay the length of his, warm, soft, luscious. She was still, gentle, not yet beginning to move against him, her long hair on his cheek and chest. He felt the lips caress his neck. That caress was more real than any human touch he'd ever felt.

He shook himself and broke the illusion.

Fortunately, he'd bumped no one when he shook himself.

Lupine was so close. She exhaled deeply, and he felt her warm spirit on his lips.

The two lovers were quiet, except for an occasional stirring, a sigh of satisfaction, a wordless murmur.

Weasel would have to be quiet for a long time before he whispered to Lupine. The lovers would lie awake for a little while, and half awake for a long time. He needed them deep in their dreams.

He could be patient. Rockchuck had taught him patience, as when you wait for an animal. He could put his mind into a kind of stillness, a peaceableness, and wait for hours. He had plenty of time. He was where he wanted to be. He would think of Lupine as he often thought of the animal he was stalking, think of her and bring her those final inches, from enticingly close all the way into his arms. He pictured the parts of her, her slender limbs, her lissome body, her small girl's breasts, her undulating hips...

He never knew he was falling asleep.

≈ 5 ≈

Lupine heard breathing, rhythmic, relaxed breathing, one of the sounds of the earth. She enjoyed it dreamily. It made her imagine running water, the lulling sound of water flowing lightly over rocks.

Then an awareness began to seep into one part of her mind. She could feel breath on her face.

The wind. She lolled pleasantly, her mind shushed by the sound of water, warmed by a soft breeze.

It was warm. It was moist. It was animal.

Lupine, daughter of One Bull, born to the Burning Water clan, opened her eyes and saw a ghost. She flinched, then froze.

The ghost opened its eyes, its mad, white eyelids wagging at her.

Lupine screamed like a woman-child about to die, a shrill, ululating horrific, mind-shattering cry.

≈ 6 ≈

From behind, One Bull saw not a ghost but a man in his virgin daughter's robes. He was on his feet when the intruder was on all fours and slammed one shoulder into the man. He knocked him hard against the lodge skins, rolled on top of him, and pinned him with his left. Then he grabbed the greasy hair, jerked the head back, and turned the face sideways.

He looked hard. Then he snapped in disgust, "*Numah-divo.*"

Lupine screamed and screamed.

One Bull started slapping Weasel's face hard, deliberately, over and over. He held the hair with one hand and made Weasel's face jerk with the other.

"I'll kill you later," he growled.

≈ 7 ≈

But One Bull did not kill Weasel. The two clans, Lupine's and Horn's, sat in a lodge and smoked and talked. There was a good deal of cackling over a boy who came to steal a girl and fell asleep. They had no debate because the punishment was a foregone conclusion. Weasel would be banished.

The accused demanded that he be allowed to speak to the clans in his own defense. Rockchuck brought the message. Why? they asked. Anyone can see he tried to steal Horn's woman. Yahoop, found holding the horses, even confessed.

Rockchuck didn't know why. He simply repeated the request.

≈ 8 ≈

Weasel sat in the place of least honor in the lodge. He sat with his eyes on nothing, seeing nothing, but refusing to cast his eyes down, to act obsequious in front of the circle of men who condemned him. Who mocked him and then condemned him.

He drew on the pipe defiantly, and offered the smoke as a prayer. Without knowing what he was going to say, he began.

"I do not care what you say." He spoke in a controlled voice, so they wouldn't hear his anger, his fear, his outrage.

"I do not care what you think of me."

He nearly shook. He had no idea what to say next.

"You have treated me as a white man. From today I will be a white man."

He was shocked at himself.

Yes, this was it.

"I will go to my father's people. I will get my father's medicine. I will never ever think of the Shoshone people again."

He stood, ready to leave. Then he thought. He walked between his host and the fire, a deliberate insult, and strode out of the tepee.

The men in the circle muttered angrily. When they were calmed down, and decided to ignore the manners of a boy, and a *Numah-divo* at that, they talked a little. Then they banished Weasel for life.

≈ 9 ≈

The old woman found him beside the little creek. The blanket was pulled over his head, and it was shaking. The boy was sobbing.

She was sorry. She loved him. But he was strange—he had always been strange. Finding his own way would be best for him.

She sat down beside him, close, letting him feel her shoulder and her knee as she sat. She waited, and waited, and after a while he stopped crying and looked at her.

"I heard what you said," she told him. "Sometimes even anger is wise. I think maybe your medicine is with the *Hookin-divos*." It was their word for the French trappers.

That was all she said. There was no need for more words. She would give him a horse, a blanket, some moccasins, and a little pemmican. He would take his weapons. After sunset today, anyone who spoke to him or gave him anything would be punished. Even his grandmother.

After a long while she added, "I'll get your things ready." She looked at the boy's wet cheeks. "They've sent Yahoop out hunting with his father so you can't say good-bye."

≈ 10 ≈

The tall, skinny teenager and the shirt, skinny old woman walked side by side away from the pony herd, in the bottom land between the junction of the two rivers. They said nothing. The old woman held the boy's elbow, perhaps for steadiness, perhaps from affection. She turned her face up to his. Her skin was crevassed, almost like the bark of the cottonwood. Her eyes were rheumy, she no longer saw well. She couldn't see her grandson's face clearly unless she held it close.

She had had him a few years, and now she would lose him to his father. She had always felt the strangeness in him anyway, surely from his father's people. Maybe it was something good for him. Even Frenchmen, though they acted the fool, had some sort of power. Every living creature had its power. With Frenchmen it was the clever things they made.

Lucky. The boy had spoken in anger and bitterness, and wisdom had come out of his mouth. Luck came from the powers.

She held him back and eased herself onto a log. She could not walk far these days. This was all the distance she would go with him. He must make the journey alone.

"Well?" she asked.

"It's all right, Grandmother." he said.

She held his face close and looked at it clearly for the last time.

"Tell me about the journey," she instructed.

"I go down this Snake River for about thirty sleeps. There the river goes northeast into a deep canyon, impossible to travel through. The Frenchmen call it the canyon of hell. I leave the river there and follow the old lodge trail north. After a fifteen more sleeps the trail will come back to the river, and it will turn west. Then the river will flow into a huge river coming from the north. There I will find the Frenchman fort."

"Good," said the old woman. "We call this river the Snake. What do the Frenchman call it?"

Weasel laughed sardonically. "Mad, Accursed River."

The old woman made a severe face. "It is mad. Keep your distance."

"And what will I find among the Frenchmen, Grandmother?" Weasel said bitterly.

"Your medicine," the old woman said.

"And maybe my father," said Weasel. "Goddamn Godin, my mad, accursed father."

≈ 11 ≈

She stood and embraced him.

"I will come back, Grandmother. With many horses," She hugged him. She didn't think he'd come back.

"*Sond-bash*," she said. Go well. Implying, this is all I ask of you.

He mounted, looked back once, tried to smile, and set the overloaded pony to walking.

He had a hard way to go, and dangerous, through the country of a lot of blood-thirsty people. He'd have to travel at night. The horse probably wouldn't last, but he could always eat it. She hoped he made it to the Frenchmen. Some people were born to strange medicines.

It was hard to see a grandchild leave, almost unheard of among the people, a loss grievous as death. She had raised him as her own. But he had to go where he belonged.

It was hard to imagine him living among strangers, in some foreign place. Those people ate a lot of fish, or so she heard, and some flattened their heads. The whites stank like fetid feet, left their women at home, and took everybody else's.

There were no people like the people.

She couldn't see him now, not with these eyes. Maybe that dark shape was him. She waved. If you come back, Grandson, she murmured, I will no longer be walking the earth.

The worst part of getting old was losing the people you loved.

SON OF THE PLAINS

Terry C. Johnston

Few names of the American frontier resonate like that of George Armstrong Custer. His fiery temperament and grand vision led him to triumph in one season and tragedy in another. Now bestselling chronicler Terry C. Johnston brings to life the Custer legacy as never before in a masterful new trilogy.

❑ LONG WINTER GONE
28621-8 $4.95/5.95 in Canada

In 1868, George Custer captured a raven-haired firebrand of only seventeen. Though she was his prisoner, it was he who was held hostage by her charms, risking marriage, reputation, and career for her. For in love, as on any other battlefield, Custer would never know retreat.

❑ SEIZE THE SKY
28910-1 $4.95/5.95 in Canada

What should have been Custer's greatest triumph, a march on the Sioux in June, 1876, became an utterly devastating defeat that would ring through the ages and serve as a turning point in the Indian Wars.

❑ WHISPER OF THE WOLF
29179-3 $4.99/5.99 in Canada

Yellow Bird, the son of George Custer, must grow to manhood in the Cheyenne world, bound to his father by their warrior's spirit, preparing to fight for his home, his life, and his own son.